IMMORTAL ASCENDING

AN IMMORTAL PROPHESY SERIES
BOOK 4

J.G. SAUER

OLIVERHEBERBOOKS

Cover art by Dar Albert at Wicked Smart Designs

Published by Oliver-Heber Books

0 9 8 7 6 5 4 3 2 1

 Created with Vellum

ACKNOWLEDGMENTS

I am a great believer that angels come in all shapes and sizes and continually surround us with love and joy. I'm blessed to have so many angels in my life. With regards to this series—and in particular, this episode of the story—I have a few angels that I'd like to thank, so bear with me...

Leading the pack (as always) is agent extraordinaire, GDC—Christine Witthohn. I don't get to talk to you often enough, and hardly ever get to see you face-to-face, but like any good angel, your presence is always felt. And the best part? I know that when needed, you're only a phone call away. You've taught me so much about this weird thing we do with words, whether you know it or not. You are a blessing, my friend.

As always, thank you, Liz Lipperman for being my CP and walking with me on this journey that we share. Like GDC, I don't get to talk to you 'live' as much as I'd like and emails will never satisfy like a long conversation over a glass of wine or a good cup of tea. Having you as my critique partner has been, and continues to be, a delight. I love you, my friend.

Much love and gratitude goes to my long-time friend and sista, Natalie Bellissimo. Nat, after all these years you still make me smile and fill me with joy with your enthusiasm for my stories, no matter what I write. Of course, your editing and grammar skills are the stuff of legend, but you are and always will be...family.

A very special thanks to Melissa Jenck (my fantasy barometer), Val 'Valine' Braun, and Kelli McMellon. You guys really ROCKED the beta-reads, and your insight was amazing.

And finally, a huge shout out to Tanya Anne Crosby and her entire team at Oliver Heber Books. Girl, there are no words to express how grateful I am to be a part of OHB. I can write what I want, in the way that I want, and am celebrated for it. The freedom that brings is truly amazing. Thank you for the support and providing a healthy space for what we do.

Blessings to you all...

1

It was a brutal scene, devastating. It seemed like buildings were in collapse or engulfed in flames everywhere you looked. The very air shimmered with the heat of it, searing the lungs and making it difficult to even draw a breath. Ruined vehicles of all makes and sizes were scattered like children's toys, the stench of death hanging heavy in the air like a malignant cloud, the destruction made almost unbearable by the unnerving silence that accompanied it. It was as if she was watching a disaster movie in a theater with no sound to go with the horror on screen, making the scene that much more terrifying.

"Hello?" the young woman called, but her voice failed to carry, sounding thin and insubstantial. "Is anyone here?"

With this kind of devastation in every direction, how was it possible that there was no one—not one body, no cries, and no evidence of human life?

Or death?

Without the aid of the usual breeze coming in off the water, columns of thick, black smoke rose like inky pillars near and far, practically blotting out the sun as their acrid haze continued to spread. The sparkle of Elliott Bay was scarcely visible through the smoke and ash as the woman hurried past 4th Avenue on Union Street toward the waterfront. For a brief moment, she could just make out a ferry half-submerged and smoldering between piers 57 and 59 before the smoke obscured her vision again.

As she skirted an overturned van at 3rd Avenue, a deafening explosion near Pike Place Market split the silence and sent a plume of fire and debris into the air. A deep, eerie rumbling followed, shaking the ground so violently that it made standing impossible. Falling hard to the pavement, she cried out as she scraped her palms and bloodied her knees right through her thin cotton pants. But seconds later, she had to scramble to the side to keep from being steamrolled as a small sedan engulfed in flames careened past her down the hill.

She scarcely recognized the city of her birth. What was happening here? And where was everyone? A better question might be how to get out of harm's way when she seemed to be smack dab in the center of a disaster of incredible magnitude. It was like the end of the world.

Armageddon in real time.

She knew in her heart of hearts that she was dreaming. She'd endured frequent nightmares since childhood, so knew the captive, suffocating feel of one like a second skin. There had also been visions and prophetic dreams—at seventeen, she'd seen her own parents' deaths in one of those—but mercifully, those dreams had dwindled in her adult years, thanks in part to various medications. But right now, she wished—and not for the first time—that she had the ability to wake, to pull herself out of this frightening, shattered landscape, though she knew that wasn't the way it worked. She'd just have to ride it out and endure the worst of it.

"Child of Light, this is an apocalypse in the making," a disembodied voice whispered. "A future where the world you know is gone—decimated. In this moment, this is the future."

She looked up to find a pair of exquisite amethyst eyes staring down at her out of a stunningly handsome face. His skin was tanned and creamy-smooth, almost ethereal, and his shoulder-length, jet-black hair—pulled back with a leather cord—stood out in stark contrast. Tall and broad of shoulder, the man wore jeans and a long charcoal duster over a snowy-white, button-down shirt...and his feet were bare.

"You're not wearing any shoes," was all she could think to say. It was absurd, ridiculous, as dreams most often were. Sitting on the scorched pavement in the middle of hell on earth, she'd conjured the most beautiful man she'd ever seen, and all she could think about were his remarkable eyes and his bare, impeccably shaped feet.

Looking down, he seemed to realize the error, and before she had a chance to even blink, heavy black boots appeared on his feet like magic. "Is that better?"

"The world is burning," she replied.

"Yes."

For some reason, the flat tone in that one word sent a sliver of fear down her spine. "This is all so confusing."

"It's only confusing if you think of it as a nightmare."

"But it is a nightmare."

"Is it?" The man reached out a hand and pulled her to her feet. "Open your eyes. Look around you, and tell me what you see, what you feel."

With her heart beginning to pound, she did as he asked, but rejected everything she saw, all the destruction and pain. Though there was a strange familiarity about the scene, it couldn't be anything but a nightmare...could it?

"Yes," he said as if reading her thoughts. "It is terrible to think about, is it not?"

"We wouldn't do this to ourselves."

"True. Humanity always seems to need that ever-so-slight push to delve into the darkness. And at just the opportune moment. It has been so for eons." He gave her a pitying look. "I'm afraid that those wheels are already in motion yet again."

"No. No. This can't be."

Though, in her head, she knew this was a nightmare, no matter what he said, she couldn't stop the panic from beginning to spread, from rearing up and threatening to choke her. "I don't want to be here anymore," she said on the edge of that panic. "I want to wake up now."

The man tilted his head and narrowed those lovely amethyst eyes. "You're thinking about this all wrong. You don't need to wake up."

"Don't be stupid. Of course, I need to wake up. It's the only way I can leave the horror of this place."

"In time," he corrected.

"What?"

"The horror of this place...in time."

"You're not making sense." The woman stumbled back several paces, and she shook her head frantically as terror flooded her system. "I don't want to be here a minute longer. Just who the hell are you, anyway? I don't remember seeing you before."

"Ah, but I have been with you for centuries."

"Centuries?" she whispered. That made as much sense as his bare feet or nonsensical answers. "You're talking in circles, and I'm done listening."

The man gave a brief nod, and his leisurely smile showed even, perfect teeth. "All will become clear very soon."

"Stop it. None of this is real," she yelled, trying to get herself under control and failing.

He stepped closer and, reaching out, tenderly brushed a bit of ash from her cheek, then took her by the shoulders. She felt the fire of his touch right through her blouse. "Make no mistake. Evil is coming, Child of Light. You must trust in what I say. There is still time, but you must be vigilant. Aid is on the way from an unlikely source. But for now, sleep, Kinna McComish." He gave her shoulders a gentle shake. "Sleep, Child of Light...and leave this place in time."

Kinna McComish awoke then with a gasp and jack-knifed

into a sitting position. Covered in perspiration and slightly out of breath, she flopped back down amongst her crumpled pillows and rubbed her eyes, concentrating on slowing her galloping heartbeat.

"Jesus. That was grueling."

She hadn't experienced a nightmare like that in ages. The slight tang of smoke still clung to her nostrils and coated the back of her throat, but she knew that really couldn't be. Yet, she could almost *feel* the pain in her knees and the palms of her hands from her fall to the pavement.

And most disturbing of all was the fact that she still had the sensation of the man's fingers on her shoulders, knew exactly where they'd been in those final moments before waking.

Evil is coming...You must be vigilant...Aid is on the way...

She could clearly hear his voice inside her head—still feel the terror his words evoked, yet she had no idea who he was or where he'd come from.

Or what she'd been so terrified of...

"No. Stop it. Stop being so damned melodramatic," she said out loud, if only to hear her own voice. "It was a friggin' nightmare. Nothing more," she muttered, throwing an arm over her face.

Yes, she'd had visions, waking dreams, prophetic nightmares, and voices in her head from a very young age, all of which had frightened her parents. They'd done what parents were supposed to do—they'd tried to make it better. But by taking her to one doctor after another, they'd only succeeded in making it worse.

As an adult, Kinna had tried everything under the sun to block out what only she could see and hear. She'd dabbled with hypnosis and drug therapies, both legal and illegal. She'd self-medicated with alcohol and hallucinogens, and most recently, had tried a magical potion she'd gotten from a friend of a friend who claimed to be a witch. And though she'd been skeptical at the time, she had to admit that the witch's potion had worked, well, like magic, and better than anything she'd previously tried. She hadn't had a vision or prophetic waking dream since taking the potion. She hadn't had any nightmares, either, that she could remember. Until now, that was. She'd have to give the witch she'd gotten the potion from a call to see if she could get something stronger.

Glancing at the digital clock on the nightstand, Kinna heaved a sigh. Nine twenty-five. She'd over-slept...again. Flinging back the covers, she swung her legs over the side and hauled herself out of bed. She had an appointment with her latest therapist at two-thirty, and needed to make an appearance at Java Jive beforehand. Her grandfather would roll in his grave if he knew how she'd recently been neglecting the business she'd started in his honor after his passing four years ago. The coffeehouse had a great staff, and the manager she'd hired —her oldest friend in the world—was terrific, but Kinna, herself, hadn't been in for over two weeks. She could almost hear Brenden McComish's voice in her head. *Feeling sorry for yourself, little girl? Remember, sorry is for suckers. Now get moving!*

"All right, Pops. I'm moving." With a laugh, Kinna shook her head and started for the spacious bathroom attached to what had once been her grandfather's master bedroom and was now her own. Hopefully, a shower would wash away the remnants of the nastiest nightmare she'd had in quite a while.

Stripping off her sweat-dampened pajamas and dumping them in the hamper, she turned and caught her naked reflection in the full-length mirror on the wall. Frowning, she stepped closer...and froze.

"What the—?"

Plainly visible on both shoulders—in the exact spots where

the man in her nightmare had grasped her—were faint golden marks that looked suspiciously like...

"No. No way."

Her breath grew short and her heart started to pound again as she ran her own fingers over the glowing spots on her left shoulder. But even as she did so, the golden marks began to rapidly fade, and within seconds, were completely gone on both shoulders.

She bent over and took several deep breaths, trying to get a grip on her rising panic. After a moment, she checked both shoulders again and found nothing. Staring at her reflection in the mirror, the old terror began to simmer in her belly.

"Why is this happening again? And why now?"

THE ARCHAIC STONE castle that housed the Immortal High Council was the last remaining trace in the modern world of the Avalon of legend. Hidden away from prying mortal eyes with a veiling spell set in place long ago, it alone remained connected to the epicenter of Avalon's all-encompassing power, a touchstone for the Immortal world.

And it was drafty as hades, Morianna, Ancient Elemental Immortal and High Priestess of Avalon, thought to herself. She pulled her fur-lined, burgundy robes close and hurried up the stone steps to the second floor where Merlin's chambers were located.

It was unlike the head of the Immortal High Council to summon her in this way, and on such short notice. Morianna strived to set aside a myriad of anxious thoughts of what his request for this meeting could mean. It had been a handful of years in this mortal realm since she and Merlin had fought together on Glastonbury Tor to put down Deidre's attempt to raise Darius and lay waste to mortals and Immortals alike. Morianna shook her head at the memory. Darius had been her cousin—a sweet child in his youth—who'd taken a turn toward darkness in adulthood. He'd craved power, hungered for more—the ability to rule over all.

Morianna had battled her cousin one fateful night centuries ago on the Tor in the very spot where Avalon, the Isle of Glass, had its origins. That was the night, as the Prophesy foretold, that the Chosen One would rise. Isadora Winthrop indeed died that night and arose reborn an Immortal savior. It had taken three centuries, but Isadora had finally put an end to Morianna's cousin Darius on the very ground where she'd become the Chosen One. Again, as the Prophesy had predicted.

Several years ago, just before a pandemic swept through the mortal world, Deidre, High Priestess of Avalon and fellow Immortal Council Member, had tried to use her unnatural dark magicks to bring her lover, Darius, back from death. The Immortal Council had fought alongside the Chosen One, her Warrior, and a ragtag band to rid their fallen world of an abomination in the making, but it had been up to Isadora and Lucinda, Darius' Halfling child, to strike the final blow. To rid this realm of both Deidre and Darius for good. Though it had been a very long time since she'd fought on a battlefield in this realm, Morianna could freely admit that there had been a ruthless part of herself from a century past that had enjoyed the exercise immensely. However, it had been a hard-won battle and too close for her comfort. In the past few years since that clash, they had all enjoyed a respite from things that go bump in the night, from evil that would seek to destroy. Morianna prayed Merlin's urgent summons would amount to nothing quite so dire as the fate of the world.

Approaching Merlin's outer chamber door, Morianna knocked twice. She heard his deep response moments later.

"Come."

Pushing open the heavy oak door with its elaborately carved runes and hieroglyphs, Morianna entered and found the head of the Immortal High Council, her oldest friend, sitting behind his massive, old desk.

Merlin.

"Ah, Morianna," he began as he rose and came around the desk to greet her. "Thank you for coming with haste. We've much to discuss, and I fear, very little time to do so."

"What is this about, Merlin? Your summons seemed unusually abrupt." She gave him a clever smile. "Nothing too dire, I hope."

Merlin didn't answer her questions but simply gestured to the huge fireplace where comforting flames snapped and crackled. "Let's have a seat here by the fire, and I will tell you what I know."

Morianna studied her friend as she settled in one of the overstuffed chairs pulled close to the warmth. He looked much the same as he had the last time she'd seen him. Though today, his long, silvery hair was pulled back with a leather cord, and his matching beard was braided a bit differently. However, when she looked beneath the superficial, she saw the concern dampening the ever-present sparkle in his icy-blue eyes. His fatigue was plainly obvious, which gave her pause. But there was something else, something...more.

"What's happened, Merlin? I can see that you are troubled."

The Ancient Immortal sat back in his chair, steepling his long fingers over his ample belly, and those crystalline-blue eyes took on a faraway look. His voice was low when he finally spoke. "Do you remember The Global War in this realm?"

Morianna frowned. The Global War. She had not heard those words in a very long time.

She cleared her throat and slowly nodded. "I do."

Oh, there had been centuries of war in this world before it. The Crusades, the Hundred Years' War, the French Revolution, what the history books called World Wars I and II, to name but a few. But The Global War had put them all to shame, had been apocalyptic. What a smudge of true ugliness that had been, now a blip in time—thank the Almighty—that no child would ever read about in a history book.

"And do you remember how it ended?"

Morianna stared into the fire, seeing bits and pieces of the horrors in her mind of a war that had been reversed, expunged. Purged from this fallen world with expert precision. The clock had turned back and the damage to the planet had been erased. Indeed, there were only a handful of Ancients who even remember it had been. But she remembered too much of that dark time, one of a dreadful few over the centuries, when the mortal world almost ceased to be.

"I remember," she murmured.

Merlin sighed. "It was not the first time in history that one such horrific event disappeared without a trace," he said, as if reading her thoughts.

"I am aware." Turning back to him, she narrowed her eyes. "Why do you ask, Merlin? What's wrong? For clearly, something is."

He glanced up then, and she saw resignation in his gaze before he looked away. "There has indeed been a development, Morianna. It began with an extremely unexpected visit two nights past."

"From whom?" Morianna asked. "Whose visit would give you such angst?"

Turning those ice-blue eyes on her, he heaved a sigh. "I was visited by Jerahm."

Merlin's words hung in the air between them, and Morianna

leaned forward with a stunned look. Surely she'd misunderstood him.

"I beg your pardon, did you say Jerahm?" She shook her head. "Are you telling me that *Jerahmeel* was here? In this very room?"

"Now you see why I summoned you." Merlin turned to gaze into the fire. "It's not every day one has a visit from an Archangel."

Morianna sat back, her thoughts racing. "What on earth did he want, Merlin? Why was he here?"

A smile spread across Merlin's face as he continued to stare into the fire. "Oh, nothing much. Just a request for our assistance with perhaps saving the world. Yet again. And, of course, the skills of the Chosen One and her Warrior."

2

The sun was just peeking over the horizon as Dory Winthrop got herself another cup of coffee and headed out onto the back deck to watch the start of another glorious fall morning. Henry, Kaden's big Rottweiler, followed her out and sprinted toward the tree line at the back of the property, presumably to take care of his morning business. Halloween, her favorite holiday, was right around the corner, and the days were getting shorter. There was a snap in the morning air and a touch of frost on the ground, but it would be sunny and in the mid-sixties by noon.

After another grueling night of bizarre dreams, or more like nightmares, Dory had been up for a couple of hours doing research on what she could remember of them, which was mostly just bits and pieces. She'd been having the same kinds of nightmares for the last six weeks but wasn't sure what to make of them. There had been prophetic dreams in her past, but she never knew what was actually foretelling and what was just her mind weirding out on her. But these recent nightmares were beginning to concern her.

Pulling her sweater closer around her shoulders, she sat

down in one of the weathered deck chairs and surveyed the gradual approach of another day. Soon the weather would turn toward winter, but for now, it was perfect. Or at least, what she thought of as perfect. And with over three centuries on the planet under her belt and soon to complete another year in a matter of days, she'd seen her fair share of perfect weather.

Born in 1682 in Sussex, England, Isadora Winthrop had died at the age of twenty-eight caught in the middle of a clash between two warring Ancient Immortals. Upon her death, she'd been reborn as the Chosen One, an Immortal protector of sorts, designated so by an ancient Prophesy. Though she was considered young by Immortal standards, Dory had lived many different lives, seen thousands of sunrises, watched the world evolve in a myriad of ways.

She'd changed locations more times than she could count, staying ahead of the questions of why she didn't age. She'd lost family members to old age or disease while she herself barely aged at all. She'd had to learn to live with the loneliness which had been with her for so long, a constant, living thing, building year after year after year.

Looking back, there were many times that she'd wished for a death that wouldn't come, but Immortals were extremely hard to kill, could only truly die in a few very specific ways. Her Immortality had become a curse, a prison of sorts. After all, becoming the Chosen One had not been her choice at all but a choice made for her.

Then, after decades of a solitary existence, of keeping to herself, not letting anyone get too close, she'd found her soulmate. Well, Dory thought with a smile, she hadn't actually found *him*. No, he'd bullied his way into her life even as she'd tried to push him away. And just as she'd finally let down her guard and accepted his love, she'd watched him die in a battle not of his making. The pain of that loss—still so raw, so fresh in her memories—had been too much for her to bear. She'd been unable to let Kaden go, and though it was forbidden without the High Council's authorization, Dory had brought him back to life, making him immortal as well.

Now, the loneliness that had plagued her for so very long was gone. She was no longer alone.

Yes, Dory had weathered untenable situations, lived through terrifying battles, seen unspeakable things. So, she supposed that these latest nightmares weren't too bad in comparison to some of the horrors she'd endured over the last three-hundred-plus years. But they were definitely escalating and felt more disturbing, more urgent somehow than anything in recent memory. Although, she couldn't put a finger on exactly why.

She was pulled from her thoughts when Henry came racing back to her, tongue lolling, and plopped down next to her chair.

"All finished up with your morning routine, buddy?" She reached down and gave his head a quick rub. "It's cold but a beautiful start to the day, right?"

The slider gliding open at her back caught her attention as Kaden Crenshaw, her Chosen Warrior stepped out onto the deck. An ex-cop in his past life, Kaden was now a building contractor by trade—when he wasn't backing her up as Chosen Warrior in one fray or another. He was sharp with a quick wit and handsome enough to make her mouth water every time she looked at him. Dory loved him beyond reason, had risked her own life to save his not so long ago...

But that was something she didn't want to dwell on. The poisoning. The Dragon's Breath.

"Couldn't sleep?" Kaden asked as he sat down with his own cup of coffee in the chair next to hers and gazed up at the now-pale morning sky. "Again?"

Dory glanced over at him and felt her pulse trip, as it often did, at the sight of him. There would be one more day on the remodel that he and his crew were finishing up in town, and he was dressed for it in jeans and well-worn work boots. The plaid flannel shirt in browns and caramels he'd thrown on over a white tee matched the butterscotch of his eyes, though she knew he'd have no idea of it. She studied him. His rugged, square jaw —that he'd yet to shave—and his normally short, sandy-blond hair that was getting longer, curling, and starting to look slightly beach-shaggy around his ears and face.

Her heart just swelled.

"More nightmares?" he asked nonchalantly before taking a first sip of his coffee.

"Nightmares?" His question may have been posed casual-as-you-please, but she knew it had been asked that way intentionally. "What do you mean?"

Kaden turned to her then with a steady look of his own and murmured, "Really? That's how you want to play this?"

"I...look, it's just...uh..."

He shook his head as she struggled with an answer. "Jesus, Dory. You've been having these nightmares for a month and a half. You do realize that I sleep right next to you, correct? Did you really think I wouldn't notice?"

Dory frowned. "You knew? Why didn't you say something?"

"For the love of..." He ran a hand over the stubble of his jaw before growling, "Woman, you try my very patience. In the beginning, I was trying to give you some time to see if the nightmares were just a fluke. But then they continued to escalate, and you never said a word. I've been waiting for you to talk to me about them for weeks. After this last one, don't you think it's about time?"

"Look, I wanted to do some research first on what I could remember of them."

"Which you've been doing for a while now. So, you want to try again?"

"It's been pretty confusing and jumbled, is all. I didn't want to worry you until I had a better handle on the whole thing."

"Well, now that's just bullshit, and you know it."

"Kaden—"

"No, Dory. What you've been doing is keeping secrets again. We've had this conversation on several occasions, remember? You know how I feel about secrets. Especially these kinds of secrets."

She sighed. "I know, I know. And I'm sorry." She reached over and took his free hand. "I still struggle with the instinct for self-protection, which I had to do for a few centuries, remember? Old habits, I guess. I really am sorry. I should have talked to you about them sooner. I just didn't want to trigger—"

"A visit from Morianna?" he asked with a grin.

At Kaden's mention of the Ancient, Henry whined and lowered his big head to his paws.

"Don't! Don't even say her name. Even Henry knows that's all it usually takes for her to turn up like a bad penny."

Morianna, High Priestess of Avalon was the Ancient who had made Dory immortal over three centuries before on the Glastonbury Tor, and had a terrible habit of materializing out of thin air when you least expected her.

Kaden grinned. "You know she's going to eventually show up here. I mean, sure, with the pandemic and all, we've had a bit of a pass. It's been pretty quiet, paranormal-wise. No crazy Immortals trying to take over the globe, nobody killing Immortals to raise evil from the grave, no demons stirring the pot." He squeezed her hand. "But you had to know that would come to an end at some point, babe. After all, you are the Chosen One. And as we've seen, the Prophesy doesn't lie. There's going to be more work for you and me to do. What we have here is a never-ending gig."

She shook her head. "I've been doing this for over three

centuries and have mostly just been trying to stay one step ahead of any recent doom. You've only been part of this life for a few years and have seemed to take to it like a bird to flight. You just spread your wings and glide. How do you do that?"

Kaden let go of her hand and rubbed the stubble of his chin again with a thoughtful look. "Well, I don't know anything about gliding. I just put one foot in front of the other and take what comes next." He looked over at her and winked. "That's really all we can do, love."

"I guess."

He made a show of looking at his watch. "So, I've got about thirty minutes, and we're wasting time talking about stuff we can't change. You wanna tell me about these nightmares?"

Looking out over the backyard and the dense trees of the hillside beyond, she struggled with where to start. She wasn't even sure how it all connected. Or how much of what she'd seen was real.

"Were they like before?" he asked quietly.

She knew what he meant. The last time she'd had prophetic nightmares, they were bloody, horrific. Someone was killing Immortals, cutting out their hearts. And she'd seen his death along with it in the same way. It was brutal and crystal clear. This was not.

"No. These are nothing like that, love. I would've told you that at the onset. These are different, at least, the snippets that I remember are different. This is more widespread devastation as opposed to individual murders."

"Oh, well, that's a relief," Kaden said with a roll of his eyes.

Dory chuckled. "Yeah, I don't know which is worse. But, again, I've only seen bits and pieces. Like, Seattle in ruin. I mean, serious destruction. The city was nearly leveled and burning, yet there was no one to be seen, no bodies, not anything." She stopped for a moment and frowned as a clip scrolled across her memory.

Kaden sat forward. "Dory? What is it?"

"That's not exactly true," she murmured. "I just remembered something. I did see a young woman, maybe mid-to-late twenties. She was standing in the midst of the devastation without a scrape. Just staring at the waste and ruin, dazed and horrified. Then she turned and looked right at me. Her mouth was moving but I couldn't hear her words. There was a blinding flash...and I woke up gasping for air."

"You didn't recognize her?"

"I'd never seen her before. I'm sure of it."

"What about the other nightmares. Were they all the same as this one?"

"Generally, yes, the destruction, whole swaths of cities burning. Though last night was the first time I've seen another living human being." She shook her head. "You were right. These nightmares are escalating. In the last week or so, they've clearly gotten worse."

"Or maybe you're just remembering more details now."

"I suppose that could be." She frowned. "Either way, I think something's coming, Kaden. I don't know what it is, but it's bad."

"Whatever it is, we'll get through it, babe."

Dory closed her eyes for a moment and took a deep breath before telling him the rest of it, the part that had been eating at her. "So, there's been something else. I have been putting off telling you this part."

"Okay," he said slowly. "Is this something new? Or recurring?"

She turned to look at him. "It's been recurring and has been part of it right from the start. It's one of the things I can always remember when I wake up. And it terrifies me."

"I can see that. What is it, Dory?"

She took another deep breath, let it out slowly. "Black veining covering my arms, climbing up my neck."

Kaden went very still. "Dragon's Breath," he whispered.

She could only nod.

Dragon's Breath was a potent combination of demon venoms that had no cure and was designed to kill an Immortal in the most heinous of ways—incinerating the victim from the inside out. She'd saved Kaden's life a few years ago after he'd been poisoned with it. She'd used her healing powers to pull it out of his system and into her own. No Immortal had ever survived a poisoning with Dragon's Breath.

Only the Chosen One had.

"Babe, after the battle on the Tor where you spewed out that black nastiness to destroy Deidre and Darius, you were cleared of the poison. Even Morianna said so. The veining, the infernal heat, there's been no indication that the venom is still present inside you."

Dory nodded. "You're right. However, I'm the only Immortal to ever survive a poisoning with Dragon's Breath, and Morianna also said that as Chosen One, I'm an anomaly. That somehow the combination of venoms bonded with my system. It's how I was able to live with it for so long, how I was able to use it to destroy the two Ancients and survive, remember?"

"Okay, fair enough, but I haven't seen any signs of it. Have you?"

"No. But what if it did bond with my DNA or something? What if it's just been dormant inside me over the past few years since the Tor?"

"Then I'd say you've been living with it quite well, wouldn't you?" He shrugged when she just stared at him. "Look, if that's the case, then we'll deal with it. But let's not borrow trouble just yet. What we need is more information. We should start tracking these nightmares and work the case."

"Work the case?" She smiled then. "Spoken like an ex-cop."

He chuckled. "Yeah, speaking of old habits." Holding out his hand, he grinned back at her when she took it. "Together, right?"

She laughed along with him and felt a bit of the weight lift from her shoulders. "Together. Absolutely."

The words were no more out of her mouth when she was scared out of her wits by a voice directly behind them.

"It is so comforting to see the Chosen One and her Warrior in such good spirits on this fine morning."

They turned to find Morianna, High Priestess of Avalon standing there in all of her Ancient Immortal glory.

Dory looked at Kaden. "See. What did I tell you?"

Kaden's rich laughter rang out in the stillness of the morning. "Well, hello, Morianna. Your name came up just a few minutes ago. How are you?"

"I thought I felt my ears burning, briefly." Morianna came around his chair and grinned at Kaden. "And I am quite well, Warrior. Thank you for asking."

"Don't encourage her," Dory grumbled. "She knows I hate it when she just silently appears without notice."

"I have missed you, too, Infant," Morianna said with a nod. She crossed to Dory and tilted her head, making a show of looking Dory over from head to toe. "You look much the same as I remember, and I see that your unpleasant manner hasn't improved." Bending over and taking Dory's chin in her hand, Morianna narrowed her eyes. "Though it looks as if your grumpy attitude may stem from your poor sleeping habits. And perhaps...bad dreams?"

Dory sputtered and pulled away. "How could you possibly know—"

Kaden laughed again. "Darlin', you have got to work on not telegraphing. Those five little words just told her everything she needed to know. That is, if she hadn't known already."

There was a gleam in Morianna's gaze, and she winked at Kaden. "Very perceptive, Kaden Crenshaw. Although, it is easy enough to see the turmoil in Isadora's eyes."

"Okay, I'm right here. Don't talk about me like I'm not." Dory frowned. "Why are *you* here, Morianna? What's happened? If you knew about my nightmares, it must all be connected. That's how these things work, right?"

"Very good." Morianna nodded her approval. "I see you have gained some understanding of how, as Chosen One, you are connected to a great many things."

"Whether I like it or not?"

The Ancient ignored her and, turning, walked to the end of the deck and glanced up at the pale blue of the morning sky.

Dory had told Kaden that she thought something bad was coming, but when Morianna turned back to them, she could see that there was definitely something on the way. And it was worse than bad. The Ancient might not be telegraphing, as Kaden had said, but it was written all over Morianna's aura.

Dory wasn't stupid. If whatever it was had the Ancient worried, it scared Dory right down to her bones.

Morianna nodded as if she were reading Dory's thoughts. "Yes, Isadora. It was brought to Merlin's attention that something is indeed coming. The Chosen One and her Warrior are again needed, and this time, the fate of this world hangs in the balance."

Kaden frowned. "Wow. That doesn't sound dire at all," he quipped with sarcasm.

The Ancient walked back to them and skewered him with an impatient look. "Make fun, if you dare, Warrior, but this is a deadly serious situation. I won't tell you that it will be easy to overcome, because it will not be. What's coming will test the both of you. And yes, it could very well end this fallen world, as scripture calls it."

"Morianna, how did Merlin come across this potential threat? What brought it to his attention?" Dory asked, though she wasn't sure she really wanted to know the answer.

"Not what, Isadora, but whom. Merlin had a very important visitor. A visitor that you both will be meeting soon enough."

"I'm assuming the bits and pieces of widespread destruction, the cities burning in my nightmares? Those are all connected to what you're talking about?"

The Ancient nodded. "Yes, everything is connected. But first, there are a few things you both will need to understand."

"Such as?" Kaden asked.

The look in the deep blue of Morianna's eyes conveyed her resignation, her acceptance of what they were facing with the coming threat. She took a deep breath and exhaled slowly, as if preparing herself for what she would need to impart. "There are many events throughout the ages that came close to destroying this world. This is not the first of its kind, although it poses the greatest threat of all."

"Sure." Kaden ran a hand through his hair. "We obviously haven't treated the planet with an abundance of care, and the human race has also just about warred itself and everything else out of existence on several occasions."

The Ancient nodded sagely. "While that is true, the history books do not contain all. Several more dangerous events were expunged."

Kaden sat up in his chair. "Expunged? What the hell does that mean?"

"Just what I said. Purged from history." She tilted her head, and a faraway look came into her eyes. "For instance, there was once a great war, to this day known only to a few as The Global War. It was a terrible thing, the earth burned. Then time was reversed, the trajectory changed, the damage was corrected. The entirety of that war was removed from history's timeline."

"What the—how is that even possible?" Kaden asked in a stunned voice, then quickly put up a hand. "You know what? Never mind. Forget I even asked." He glanced at Dory. "This damn rabbit hole just keeps getting deeper and weirder."

Dory sighed and shook her head. "Okay, say this is all possible, and I'm not buying it all just yet, but who could do that?"

"The Almighty, the Divine Creator, Jehovah, Yahweh, God. Take your pick. All religions have a name for the Supreme Being. And as I said, this alteration of timelines has been done before."

"Yes, but how exactly has it been done, Morianna?" Kaden asked.

"It was done with The Key, the Charge of Angels."

"Uh-huh. The Key." He looked skeptical, but made a 'go on' gesture.

"The Key has been passed from generation to generation, and with it, the ability to go back in time, to change the future. Some generations never need correction." The Ancient waved a hand in the air. "For example, there may be a war, but it doesn't have the teeth to end things, so no modification is required. It's allowed to play out as is. Or a natural disaster takes place with incredible damage and loss of life, but it results in replenishing the earth, it encourages new growth, no correction needed. There have been ages that had no such events at all, but The Key was there and dormant just the same."

"So, why now?" Dory asked. "What's coming?"

Morianna frowned. "That is the problem. The Key has been activated but it's not exactly clear why."

Kaden shook his head. "Okay. Now, I'm confused. If this Charge of Angels, this Key was activated, who did it? And if there isn't anything really terrifying happening, why would it need to be triggered? I mean, has this happened in this way before?"

"All excellent questions, Warrior, which will be answered in time."

"But again, who was Merlin's visitor that brought all this to his attention, Morianna?"

The Ancient's smile was crafty and slightly amused.

"Oh, no. Huh-uh. No way," Kaden said, shaking his head again. "Charge of *Angels*? Are you kidding me with this? Merlin's visitor was a friggin' angel?"

Morianna's laughter rang out then. "His name is Jerahmeel, and he is much more than an angel, I assure you. He is an Archangel. The Archangel of visions...and dreams."

3

"Okay, okay, wait a minute." Kaden scrubbed his hands over his face as if he might clear away a portion of his confusion. "Now, I can't profess to have a great deal of knowledge of the hierarchy of angelic realms, but as I recall from my meager experience growing up with religion, I thought there were only seven Archangels." He paused. "And I really can't believe I just said that out loud." He turned to Dory. "Did you know about any of this?"

"Are you kidding me?" She narrowed her eyes at him. "So, you're thinking what? That I would've kept something like this to myself?"

"Well, after our earlier conversation, do you really want me to answer that question?"

"Oh, for the love of...Listen, I didn't even know about demons until we blundered into the one in Texas, remember?" She glared at him and then shrugged. "But I guess it stands to reason that if there are demons among us, why wouldn't there be angels?"

"I'll say it again for the hundredth time—deeper and weirder. And just when I was getting used to the idea of Immortals, Halflings like Lucy Devereux, and shapeshifters like Tanner Sweetwater." Kaden shook his head and huffed out a breath. "Anyway, getting back to these seven Archangels. I know I'm gonna show my ignorance here, but other than Michael, Gabriel, and maybe Raphael, I couldn't name the rest of them if my life depended on it. However, I don't remember a Jerahmeel being one of them."

Morianna smiled and nodded. "Yes, Warrior. In this fallen world, your Catholic Church reveres seven Archangels. In the Christian Bible, the Archangels are named as the ones you've already mentioned plus, Uriel, Selaphiel, Raguel, and Barachiel. Although, there are variations in some of the names depending on the source which you use. Jerahmeel is sometimes referred to as the eighth Archangel in several texts. However, in others, he is also known as Ramiel or Uriel, which would make him one of the original seven Archangels."

"Pretentious much?" Dory muttered, and Kaden struggled with a grin at the sour look on her face.

The Ancient ignored her and wandered around the deck as if teaching a class of children who were sadly lacking in religious education. "In Jewish tradition, the Archangels are named as Gabriel, Michael, Jeremiel, Raguel, Raphael, Sariel, and Uriel. Although, Jerahmeel is also known as Remiel and is listed that way in various sources. Remiel means Thunder of God, Mercy of God, or Compassion of God." She turned to them with a tiresome look. "Again, depending on your source. In any case, Jerahmeel is the Archangel of hope and faith. And as I said, the Archangel of visions and dreams as well."

"Okay, now you're just showing off and trying to make us feel stupid," Dory groused.

Kaden burst into laughter, but at the blue flame that sparked in Morianna's eyes with her agitation, he sobered. "Alright, alright, so as much as I may think meeting an Archangel would be both amazing and truly terrifying, why in hell would he need our help? I mean, what could we possibly do that an Archangel can't?"

"Seriously," Dory chimed in with a nod and pointed at him. "I'm assuming this Jerahmeel is the keeper of The Key. If he didn't activate it, then who did? And why doesn't he just go get it and use it somehow to find out what's happening?"

"The Key is not an 'it', Isadora," Morianna said in a tone that made it clear she was disappointed with Dory's suggestion. "The Key is a powerful entity that resides within a human host. Indeed, it's an innate part of the host which was born to carry it and use its power should it ever become necessary."

Dory frowned. "Oh, gee, and let me guess. This 'human host' doesn't know that they're The Key, that they're the Charge of Angels, right?"

When the Ancient looked away without answering, Kaden grunted. "Great. This just keeps getting better and better."

Dory got up and walked to the end of the deck, much as Morianna had done earlier. "Does this Archangel know who the host is? Or are we supposed to search for the proverbial needle in a haystack?" she asked over her shoulder.

This time, Morianna gave a heavy sigh. "Don't be an imbecile, Isadora. Of course, he knows the identity of the host who carries the entity, as well as exactly where to find her."

"Her?" Kaden pounced on that tidbit. "Sounds like you know who The Key is as well."

"I do not know her name. Yet. But I have seen her." The Ancient turned toward Dory. "And so has Isadora."

Dory swung around, looking confused. "I don't know what you're talking about. How would I have—"

"Yes. You saw her last night, did you not?" Morianna interrupted with a penetrating stare.

Dory paled and, walking back, dropped down into her chair.

"The woman in my dream? How is it possible that I dreamed about her but have never met her?"

"Jerahmeel," Kaden murmured after a brief moment.

Morianna nodded. "Yes, Warrior. He has many names and responsibilities. One of which, I repeat, is the Archangel of visions and dreams."

"But again, why?" Dory asked. "I mean, I'm with Kaden on this. What on earth would this Archangel need with us in this situation?" She put up a hand when Morianna would have spoken. "And besides that, why now? I mean, we just about lost this world to Darius and Deidre a few short years ago. You know, if Deidre's plan to raise Darius had worked, it would have had civilization-ending consequences for the entire globe. Where was this Key then? Why wasn't it used? Why did we have to defend humanity when The Key could have easily corrected the problem?"

After an uncomfortable moment, the Ancient *tsked* and shook her head. "Are you asking me to explain the plans and choices of a Supreme Being, Isadora? Or are you just questioning said Supreme Being's plans and choices? Either way, do you think that prudent? Are you sure that's where you want to go with this?"

"Well, I...no, I just..."

Kaden put a hand on Dory's arm and stepped into the fray. "Look, Morianna, it's not that either of us would question the Creator, Supreme Being, God, or whatever name you use, and trust me, we'll do anything that's needed. It's just that we need a little more to go on, you know?"

"We do understand that a plan is required, Warrior."

"A plan, yes, but more than that, some idea of what's coming, of how much time we have to get our shit together, of what may be involved. Are we talking about war or some other catastrophe? Hard to put together a solid plan when all you have to go on is burning cities in a recurring nightmare."

"Exactly!" Dory blurted. "I've been trying to research these nightmares for weeks, but there have just been bits and pieces, or at least, that's all I've been able to remember." She sighed. "Just snippets of incredible destruction. This morning was the first time I actually remembered seeing another living soul in all of my dreams."

"Does Jerahmeel know the extent of what's coming or how it will begin? Or has it begun already?" Kaden asked, his mind now racing with possible scenarios.

"Jerahmeel does know what is afoot and will provide answers to your questions very soon to help you in this endeavor. He will explain what he requires of you and give you guidance then. In the meantime, you must begin preparations. Gather help, whomever you think you'll need, but do it quickly. We cannot give you specifics yet, but I can tell you that time is of the essence."

Kaden looked at his watch and grimaced. "Looks like mine is as well. I need to go call my foreman on this job and give him some last-minute instructions. I'm already ten minutes late leaving."

"No, Kaden," Dory said. "Just go on in. Morianna and I will figure something out."

Already heading for the house with his cell phone to his ear, Kaden turned back and shook his head. "Absolutely not. This remodel job is nearly complete. It's basically just last-minute finish work, so I can check on it later. I'll be right back, and we'll get started on getting the band back together."

"But—" Dory began, though Kaden was already laser-focused on speaking with his foreman.

"Hey, Cal, it's Kaden," he said into the phone as he slid open the sliding glass door and stepped into the kitchen. "Yeah, I know. I'm running behind. Something's come up, and I'm not going to make it in right now."

As Kaden closed the slider behind him, the silence on the deck was deafening for several moments, with the occasional chirping of a bird the only sound breaking the quiet of the morning. Dory finally looked up to find Morianna staring at her intently.

"What?" she asked the Ancient.

"How much of your dreams have you shared with Kaden?" Morianna asked quietly.

"I told him everything this morning just before you got here. Why?"

"You had been intentionally keeping this from him for several weeks?"

"No, not intentionally. I..." Dory sighed and relented, "Okay, yes, I suppose I had. It's just that I wasn't sure what was real and what wasn't—I don't know—just something I ate." She tried to laugh it off, but it came out hollow even to her own ears, and the Ancient only continued her steady perusal.

Finally, Morianna shook her head. "I understand that you have never been comfortable with your gifts or the mantle of Chosen One, and I am sorry for it, for the pressure it laid upon you. However, you know in your heart what is and isn't, and have always stepped up to do what was needed. This is no exception. Your weeks of research tell the tale, child."

"Yes. Kaden knew what was happening and had been just waiting for me to come clean. When I didn't...well, he wasn't happy. He accused me of keeping secrets again. That's what his snarky comment regarding our previous conversation was about. I suppose I can't blame him for being angry."

"Of course not. You and your Warrior are a team, Isadora." Morianna leaned in with a slight smile and gave Dory's earlier sarcastic words back to her. "Whether you like it or not."

"Ha-ha. Very funny," Dory replied.

"The truth of the matter is that you diminish that team when you hold back vital information from Kaden. He is meant to fight by your side in every conflict. How can he do so with any degree of success without all the knowledge he requires?"

"I know, I know. I was honest with him in the end. I've just been alone in this for so very long. Running for my life when Darius was released from stasis every century, not knowing, in the beginning, why he was so intent on destroying me. Then, not knowing who to trust or where to turn for help. There were times when I was so exhausted and overwhelmed that I prayed for it to be over, actually hoped Darius would just find me, and I could be done with it all."

"Though you were never alone, child. I was never far away during each of Darius' reprieves."

"Maybe so, but I can count on one hand the number of times you made yourself known."

Morianna gave a curt nod. "It was hard on you, but there were reasons, rules about interference that I was required to follow."

"Whatever." Dory rubbed her forehead where a headache was beginning to brew. "Then I ran across a stubborn ex-cop turned contractor who wouldn't be pushed away no matter how horrid I was to him."

The Old One chuckled. "He is stubborn, your Warrior, and has great...stones."

Dory's mouth dropped open. "Oh, my God," she said, making a disgusted face, but then began to laugh in spite of herself. "Well, I guess you're right. He never seems to give it a second thought about following me into the worst kinds of situations. And the way that he's stepped right into this weird life that we now lead, accepted the most bizarre or frightening realizations almost without batting an eye? Well, that's rare and something I cherish."

"As well you should. He is the other part of you."

"He is. And then I almost lost him after finally finding him. I guess that's why I have a hard time with sharing pertinent information. Deep down, I still feel the need to protect him although I know how stupid that sounds."

"Do you trust Kaden, Isadora?"

"Of course," Dory replied. "With my life. I just have to remember that I am no longer alone in this, that's all."

"Ah, progress. Very good," the Ancient said with a touch of sarcasm. "And you told Kaden everything about these latest dreams?"

"Nightmares, you mean. And if you're referring to the part about Dragon's Breath, yes, I told him about that as well."

Morianna nodded but continued to stare at her.

The intensity of that stare unnerved Dory more than she liked.

"Morianna..." She wasn't exactly sure how to ask or if she really wanted to know the answer, but she couldn't stop herself from trying. "Look, I just need to—"

"You wish to know if it still resides within you. That horrible concoction of demon venom."

Dory took in and then let out a long, slow breath, trying not to let the panic she felt inside bubble up to the surface. "Yes, I suppose that's what I'm asking. Do you know? You told me in London that there was no sign of it in my system when my temperature had returned to normal after the ordeal on the Tor. But..."

"But you have seen it in your dreams? The inky veining of the poison climbing your arms and neckline?"

Dory looked up at her and nodded. "Yes, on several occasions. And you did tell me in Savannah at the height of my infection, that as Chosen One, the venom seemed to have bonded with my system. I haven't seen any sign of it in the years since, but what if it's just been dormant?"

Morianna sat down next to her and gazed out over the backyard. "Unfortunately, I cannot tell you if some portion of the Dragon's Breath remains in your system, or if it may still be at your disposal, for that matter. Is it possible that it changed you on a molecular level? Perhaps. But again, no one, not even the Immortal High Council, knows what you are capable of as Chosen One." The Ancient took in a deep breath, before turning to Dory. "Like it or not, you are an anomaly, Isadora. Unprecedented. The Prophesy alludes to the might of your powers, but it is vague and gives few details of what those may include. The incident with the demon venom was just an example of what's possible, of the power that lies within you."

"I'm aware that no other Immortal has survived a poisoning with Dragon's Breath since it was designed specifically for that purpose," Dory murmured.

"That is true. That you survived the poisoning is a miracle in itself, but that you were able to use the Dragon's Breath as a weapon against those who'd infected you and to destroy the threat to this world only serves as evidence that you are different, special."

Dory got up, feeling the sudden need to pace. Morianna had been right. She'd never been comfortable with being the Chosen One or with the possible powers that came with the title which was one of the reasons she didn't push the boundaries of her abilities as Kaden so happily did as Chosen Warrior. He continued to find new skills and ways to use them as often as he could, while she was leery of what might be hiding away inside her.

"Special," she all but whispered. "That's just it, Morianna. I don't feel special. Actually, it's just the opposite. I often feel like a fraud and think that perhaps the Prophesy has made a horrible mistake. Most of the time, I'm just trying to figure out what to do next." She shook her head and looked over at the Ancient. "I mean, how did you even know that I was to be the one? Did the Prophesy actually mention my name?"

Morianna stood and crossed to Dory and, slipping an arm around her shoulder, pulled her close. And though completely out of character for both of them, Dory closed her eyes and leaned in briefly. The Ancient smelled surprisingly of warm gingerbread and cloves, which Dory found oddly comforting. Although, with her recent nightmares, it may have been just her lack of decent sleep that was bringing on hallucinations. In any event, standing there in the soft morning light, she swore she felt an energy move through her, something she'd not felt in a very long time. She just couldn't put a finger on what it meant.

Morianna gave her a light squeeze. "That the Prophesy is somehow wrong is an impossibility, child. This is not some tattered piece of parchment that was found on the back shelf of a dusty, old library. It is a divine tome set down centuries ago by the Original One, the Creator of the Universe." The Ancient turned then and tenderly took Dory's face in her leathery hands. "You are exactly who and what you need to be. Never doubt that."

The Ancient dropped her hands then and stepped back, pulling her robes closer. "As for how I knew you were the one? You appeared on the Tor and stepped between me and my cousin Darius during our battle at precisely the moment that he hurled a bolt of electrified plasma meant for me. This, again, the Prophesy foretold."

Dory was stunned at that. "Wait—what do you mean I 'appeared'? I've always thought that *you* brought me to the Tor that night."

"I am aware." The look on Morianna's face became shuttered. "However, I did no such thing. I simply completed my part of the Prophesy by sending Darius into stasis and bringing you back from death. You are the Chosen One, Isadora. It is your destiny." She raised an eyebrow. "Now, are you finally going to embrace that destiny and become that which you were meant to be? Or shall you continue to waste your precious time and persist in acting like a petulant child made to do something she doesn't want to do?"

And we're back, Dory thought, crossing her arms and frowning. "You know, you don't always need to be such an insensitive ass, Morianna."

The Ancient gave her a bored look. "Then don't be such a self-indulgent fool, Infant."

"Hey, hey," Kaden interrupted as he stepped out onto the deck. "What's going on out here? I can feel the negative energy from where I'm standing."

Dory shook her head and grinned at him. "Oh, nothing. The Old One and I are just hashing out some family business. Her being condescending, and me, evidently, being whiny and petulant."

Kaden looked back and forth between them. "Okay," he said slowly. "So, are you done? Can we get back to putting a plan together? Or did you two want to keep mucking about?"

Dory laughed out loud. "No, love. I think we're done for now."

"Good deal," he replied. "Then let's go in. Some thoughts have occurred to me on this whole situation, and I want to get started on reaching out to a few people."

"Right behind you." Dory turned to Morianna. "Are you coming?"

The Ancient shook her head. "I have business elsewhere at the moment but will be in touch very soon. Jerahmeel will want to meet with you, so get your team in place and be ready."

With that, Morianna, High Priestess of Avalon, disappeared in a burst of glittery silver swirls.

"Seriously?" Dory hollered. "Silvery glitter? I swear, she embellishes her disappearing act more and more every time. It just annoys me."

Kaden laughed and took her hand, leading her back into the house. "I suspect that's exactly why she does it, my love. Now, come on. We need to make a bunch of phone calls."

4

Kinna was still dealing with the residue of her nightmare when she got to Java Jive an hour and a half later but worked to put the nightmare out of her mind. The last thing she needed right now was the old recurring stress that came with her visions and nightmares. The mid-morning rush—or 'a.m. happy hour' as friend and manager, Kari Burke, liked to call it—was just beginning to clear out as Kinna came through the front door.

"Hey, Kinna!" Deana Graft, a perky little blonde with big baby blues called from the counter. And with just that quick welcome, Kinna felt her mood begin to lighten. Having been with Java Jive from almost the beginning, Deana was a free spirit and had a way of lifting a person's spirits with nothing but a greeting.

With a grin for the woman, Kinna let herself behind the counter via the pass-though. "Hey, lady. Looks like happy hour kept you busy."

The woman chuckled. "Oh, you know. Coffee's still flowing, day in and day out. Where ya been, girl? We've missed you."

Kinna scrunched her face. "Had almost a week chock-full of

quarterly meetings in Seattle. Believe me, I'd have much rather been pouring coffee here at the Jive than sitting through endless meetings there."

"Sounds like a big old drag to me. But that's what you get when your wealthy grandpa leaves you everything in his will, right? Responsibilities, my friend, responsibilities."

"I guess." Kinna paused as if considering. "So, does that mean you don't want to change places with me anytime soon? 'Cause you know, you could go in my stead next quarter."

"*O-o-h*, no." Deana shook her head vehemently and laughed out loud, a robust sound that seemed incongruous for her petite size. "No, ma'am. Not me. No way. I may not have a boatload of money in the bank, but I like my carefree lifestyle just fine— nobody else to worry about but me and my cat."

Kinna heaved a sigh. "Well, can't blame a girl for trying." Looking around, she frowned. "Okay, it's awfully quiet in here. You're not all by yourself, are you?"

Deana gave another blast of laughter. "Oh, hell no. Gigi went to the ladies room just before you walked through the door, and Charlie's doing inventory in the storeroom. Kari, of course, is where Kari always is...in her office doing manager things."

"Good to know. Worried me for a minute. Anyway, I've got a lunch date in less than an hour, so I need to check in with Kari before I go." Giving a wave, Kinna headed for the back. "Keep the customers happy, girl," she called over her shoulder.

"You know it, boss lady."

As Deana went out to clear and wipe down tables, Kinna slipped down the back hallway to Kari Burke's office. There, she found the slender brunette pouring over paperwork, a scowl on her face.

"You know, you keep frowning like that, and your face is gonna stick," Kinna said from the doorway. "At least, that's what my mom always used to tell me when I was little."

"Yeah, yeah. Don't bug me. I'm almost done here," Kari replied without looking up. "I've got a bitch-of-a-boss that'll be showing up anytime now wanting the latest numbers."

"Hey, don't blame me. You took the job." Kinna plopped down in the chair opposite the desk and shook her head. "So, are we gonna make payroll this month or what? Her bitch-of-a-boss asked with a cheesy smile."

Kari finally looked up at that and grinned. "We're running well into the black, thank you very much. How was Seattle?"

"Mind-numbingly boring. You know how much I enjoy board meetings. Prospectuses, stock prices and buy backs, consumer surveys...blah, blah, blah. Financial gobbledygook—most of which I couldn't care less about. Anyway, I'll have another round here at the Portland office next week, and then it's done for another quarter."

"I'll say it again—you should hire someone to attend those meetings for you, like a competent business manager."

Since Kari was one of her oldest friends and knew all about her unhealthy background, as well as her grandfather's will, Kinna laughed out loud. "And *I'll* say it again—you know very well Pops made it a requirement in his will that I personally attend all board meetings unless I'm incapacitated. I think it was his way of making sure that I wouldn't let his companies go to rack and ruin, that I wouldn't fall back into old habits with his money and blow it on drugs and drink." Kinna wiggled her eyebrows for emphasis.

"Please. Don't be stupid. First of all, your grandfather believed in you and saw your abilities as miraculous, which they are." Kari stabbed a finger in her direction. "And don't roll your eyes at me. You have an incredible gift, Kinna, whether you choose to use it or block it. Secondly, as I recall, you were doing just fine monetarily before he passed. And as for the drugs and drink? It's not like you're an addict or anything, and you've gotten a handle on your weird visions. So, there's no need to self-medicate, and definitely no need for a provision like that now."

Kinna sighed. "Oh, don't kid yourself. I still self-medicate. It's just in a different, less-harmful and flamboyant way, that's all."

"Look, all I'm saying is that if he could see you now—if your parents could see you now—and all that you've accomplished, they would all be so proud. So, there must be some legal way to get around that draconian provision your grandfather put in his will."

"Draconian? Really? That's a bit *harsh*, don't you think?"

"Ha. Ha. You're very funny. You should put that freakish knowledge of vocabulary to good use and become an author or something."

Kinna snickered. "I don't have that kind of discipline, and you know it. Anyway, several business managers came with the package, so I really don't need any more. But the good news is that all the Seattle-based McComish enterprises are, as you say, running well into the black and raking in the dough." She frowned slightly and glanced toward the meager window. "Seems like everything my grandfather touched turned to gold," she murmured.

"That's a good thing, right?"

"I guess."

"Uh-huh." Leaning forward on the desk, Kari gave her a hard stare. "So, why do I feel like there's another *but* hovering in that head of yours?"

Kinna shrugged. "I don't know. It's just that...well, sometimes I don't feel all that connected to any of it, you know? Like I'm just the tiniest bit out of step, like I don't belong here...or anywhere, really."

Kari made a rude noise. "What ridiculous bullshit."

"Probably. Maybe I just don't know what I wanna be when I grow up. If I ever grow up, that is." Kinna tried to laugh off the feeling, but it came out sounding flat. Waving a hand in the air, she shook her head and gave Kari a wry smile. "You know what? Don't mind me. I had a long drive back from Seattle yesterday in heinous Thursday afternoon traffic, then slept really poorly last night and got up late. I'm still not feeling myself today."

"Are the nightmares back?" Kari asked, a sympathetic look in her bright green eyes. "Or was it just good old-fashion insomnia?"

Kinna blew out a breath. "Not sure, but I'm hoping last night was an anomaly, for sure." She really didn't want to entertain the idea that it may be anything else, lest she make it so, but it continued to nag at the back of her mind. "Anyway, not worth discussing."

"Or saying it out loud, right? Putting it out there into the universe?" Kari asked as if reading her mind.

"Yeah, there's that." Shaking off the dower mood, Kinna leaned forward. "Besides, I want to hear about what's been happening here. Give me a distraction. Anything take place in the last week that I should know about?"

"Naw, sorry, my friend." Kari leaned back in her chair. "Business as usual: brisk and consistent. Had to call a plumber out for the employee bathroom yesterday—probably about the time you were stuck in that heinous traffic. One of the suppliers sent us a sample box of their new 'green' straws—which completely suck, no pun intended—but not much else to report. Same stuff, different week. Oh, the girls have a new 'coffeehouse hunk' that has them all atwitter, but other than that..."

"Ooo, a new hunk? Do tell. Give me the details, and your verdict?"

"Haven't actually seen him up close but pretty much worth the twitter from what I could tell. Tall and built with long, dark hair. There's a cross between biker and rock star sort of vibe to him. From a distance, he checked several of my own boxes, if you know what I mean. Sissy Paxton says he turns her insides to goo with his smile." Kari finished the statement off with a shake of her head.

"Yeah, well, I don't think it takes all that much to get Texas Sweet Tea's motor running," Kinna said of their front counter Lone Star transplant.

"Agreed. However, I hate to stereotype, but her drawl does seem to get more pronounced when she yammers on about him. '*Oh, Gawwwd, he's just so yummy, y'aaall*'," Kari mimicked with an over-emphasized twang.

"Now, now, don't make fun of the Lone Star State." Kinna chuckled. "How's Charlie dealing with this new hunk?"

Charlie Taylor was assistant manager and the lone male on staff. All the girls seemed to love him, not because he was pretty to look at—he was actually sort of goofy looking in an Ichabod Crane kind of way—but because he was a genuinely nice guy. Most of the female staff thought of him more as a big brother.

Kari tilted her head and considered. "Actually, I think he's found it kind of amusing. They've had their handsome regulars to drool over in the past, but they've all seemed to go a little over the top with this one. Although, Charlie hasn't made fun of any of them this time around and did say that the guy gave him a... *good feeling*, whatever the hell that means."

"Well now, that's an interesting change. Guess I'll have to check this guy out for myself." Glancing at her watch, she sighed. "But for now, I've got a lunch date with Olivia out in Hillsboro in thirty minutes and an appointment with my therapist in Tigard at two-thirty, so I'd better get a move on it."

Kari frowned. "What's Miss Thing doing in Hillsboro? Her office is downtown, and her condo is in the Pearl."

"Evidently, she's doing some lawyer-like work, but I didn't ask. Anyway, I'm not promising, but I'll try to get back in here later."

"Thanks for the warning, but don't feel the need to come back here on our account if you don't have the time. This shit can always wait."

Kinna turned back at the door and grinned. "Well, maybe I'll want to see those numbers then, so get to it."

"Yeah, yeah. Get the hell out of my office."

"Ha! I'm going, I'm going. In any case, I'll see you for dinner Sunday night if I don't get back in today."

THE DRIVE from Java Jive in Tanasbourne to the restaurant in Hillsboro wasn't too bad yet traffic-wise, so Kinna had enough time to stop and fill her gas tank. With her mind on lunch and the few errands she needed to run following her therapy appointment, she pulled out of the station's lot and headed toward the restaurant.

She hadn't gone but two blocks when a bent old man with a cane stepped into the crosswalk directly in her path without benefit of a walk sign or even looking in her direction. She slammed on her brakes so hard with both feet that she just about threw herself through the windshield. Fortunately for them both, she came to a stop with a couple of feet to spare amid the squeal of tires and the pounding of her heart in her ears.

For his part, the old guy didn't seem a bit fazed that he'd just about been creamed but turned to grin at her through the glass. Kinna shook her head and started to smile back, but as she did, the old man's face began to change. As she watched, it continued to distort in a really frightening way until it finally melted into the most demonic visage she'd ever seen.

"What in God's name...?"

The whole thing didn't last long, but for a brief moment it was like watching a horror movie in slow motion. Then the driver in the car behind her honked his horn, making her jump and throw a quick look into her rear view mirror. When she turned back to the old man, he had continued across the street and was on his way as if nothing whatsoever had happened, leaving her to wonder what she'd *thought* she'd just seen.

"Geez, Kinna. You're really losing it. Not only a new round of nightmares, but now hallucinating in broad daylight?" She shook her head again and took a steadying breath. "Not cool. So not cool at all."

This time the guy behind her laid on his horn and then zipped around her, giving her a dirty look as he passed.

"Yeah, yeah. Don't mind me, buddy. Just having a small mental breakdown here." The nervous laughter that bubbled out of her didn't give her much comfort, but she drove on anyway. Better that than lose it completely on a busy street.

"Just breathe, Kinna. That's all you have to do. This will pass...this *will* pass," she whispered to herself although it lacked conviction.

By the time she arrived at the restaurant, she was still shaken up by the incident but working on not showing it. She found Olivia at a table in the bar chatting with the very cute waiter. The Italian spitfire was looking typically stylish as usual in her subtle gray suit with her sable-colored hair pulled up into an elegant French twist.

"Hey, sorry I'm a bit late," Kinna said as she sat down and linked her fingers in her lap to hide the fact that her hands were still trembling. "Had to stop and get gas on the way."

Olivia stared at her for a long moment, dark eyes probing, and then glanced at her watch. "Yeah, you're not late. In fact, you're a few minutes early which is an oddity in itself as you are never early. But we'll table that for now. Terence here was just going over the specials for me, weren't you, darling?"

"Yes, ma'am. Can I get you both something to start?"

"Absolutely. I'll have a very dry, very dirty martini...to start."
Olivia beamed at him before turning to Kinna. "Merlot for you?"

"Yes, thank you." Kinna gave the waiter a quick smile before
watching him walk away to get their drinks. "Unbelievable.
Leave it to you to find a young hottie to flirt with while you
waited for me to arrive. What do you think? Twenty-four-ish?"

"Twenty-five and a half." Olivia wiggled her eyebrows. "I
asked."

"Geez, Liv." Kinna clucked her tongue.

"What? I like younger men. They're so...eager. Besides, I
think anything less than a decade younger is fair game, don't
you?"

"He is adorable. I'll give you that—and in that 'less than a
decade' range, as well." Kinna laughed out loud. "Of course, not
by much."

Olivia narrowed her cool, brown eyes, and then studied the
menu the hottie had left behind. "Don't be mean. At thirty-two,
I'm in my prime."

"Yes. Yes, you are, my friend," Kinna confirmed and perused
her own menu. "So, I say go for it."

Olivia sent her a withering glance over the menu. "And don't
patronize me."

Kinna laughed again and felt better for it. By the time
Terence came back with their drinks, they'd both decided on
lunch options and ordered.

"Okay, now spill it," Olivia demanded as he took their menus
and walked away.

"What do you mean? Spill what?"

Taking a sip of her martini, she gave Kinna a speculative
look. "Don't be coy. Whatever's going on with you today, that's
what."

"I don't know what you're talking about. There's nothing
going on with me."

Olivia leaned back in her chair and took another sip, staring at Kinna over the edge of the glass. "Liar."

She laughed at Kinna's stunned look and went on before she could respond. "Sweetie, I'm sorry to say that it's written all over you. Though there is more color in your face now than when you arrived, your hands are still shaky which tells me there *is* something going on, something you'd rather not talk about. What gives?"

"How did you—"

"Know? I'm an attorney, remember? And a damn good one, darling. It's a very important aspect of my job to observe people, look for tells, know when they're lying or hiding something." She shook her head and gave Kinna a sympathetic look. "Your tells are so out there for all to see. Plus, no offense, but you look like you haven't had a good night's sleep in days."

Kinna's mouth dropped open. "Wow. Thanks a lot."

Olivia smirked. "Please. That part is nothing anyone else would probably pick up on, but besides Kari, I am your oldest friend in the world. And as such, I'm obligated to speak the truth. So, what is it? Tell Livy everything. Is it the visions? Or the nightmares again?"

Kinna started to deny there was a problem, but relented with a sigh. Olivia would know she was lying and hound her until she came clean, anyway. "Alright, alright. It's maybe a little of both. I had a bad night...and a fairly weird scare on the way over here." She proceeded to explain about the old man she'd nearly hit and what she'd thought she'd seen.

"Holy crap!" Olivia took another gulp from her martini. "That's...quite disturbing."

"Which part? That my visions have possibly returned? Or that I may have been just hallucinating in broad daylight? Considering my history, I'd say disturbing is an understatement, wouldn't you?" Kinna ran a still slightly trembling hand through her hair. "Add to this recent incident, there was the nightmare I had last night."

"Uh-oh. I thought Sorcha gave you something for those," Olivia said with a frown. "Normally, that girl's remedies are miraculous—whether you believe in magic or not."

Kinna nodded. "She did, and though I was skeptical at first —yeah, witchcraft and all—the potion she gave me has worked really well. I don't get it. I haven't had a vision or prophetic dream in months, not since I've been taking it. Until now, that is. And the apocalyptic doozy of a nightmare I had last night? Well, let's just say that I woke up in a cold sweat which is probably why I look like I haven't gotten much sleep...because I haven't."

"Oh, Kinna. I'm so sorry." Olivia reached out and took her hand. "So, you'll just call her and have her make you up something a little stronger, that's all. Maybe you've just built up some kind of immunity to it or something."

"I don't think that's how this magic thing works, Liv." Kinna sighed. "At any rate, I'm way ahead of you. We're meeting on Monday. I was hoping to get with her today after my appointment with Dr. Newcomb, but Monday was the soonest she could fit me in."

"Dr. Victoria Newcomb," Olivia sneered and withdrew her hand. "I don't know why you're still seeing that quack."

"Oh, Liv, don't start." Kinna took a sip of her Merlot. "You just don't like her because she snubbed you at that cocktail party that what's-his-name—that smarmy attorney—invited you to last year."

"Please. I couldn't care less what she thinks of me. And as for what's-his-name, Dorian Smyth is a slick one—polished, always says the right thing—but I don't trust him any more than I do her. And no attorney jokes, please. His kind gives us all a bad name."

"Then why did you go to his party?"

"You've heard the phrase 'keep your friends close and your enemies closer'? I only went as a mole of sorts for my firm after he'd offered me a job. As if." She curled her lip. "No, Victoria Newcomb and Dorian Smyth are two of a kind, believe me, which is why I wish you'd dump her. Add to it, another friend of mine told me that he'd dropped her like a hot stone after two sessions, said she gave him the willies."

"She is a little different, I'll give him that. But it's only been a little over four months since Dr. Addison retired—"

"*Retired?*" Olivia blurted with an incredulous look. "That was the most sudden and suspicious retirement in the history of therapy, Kinna."

"Liv—"

"And to announce it to his patient list via email? Are you kidding me? Who does that? Then encourage all those patients to transfer to Slick Vicky—without actual proof that it was him doing the encouraging, I might add. Then just disappear? Literally *overnight*? You do know that no one has seen or heard from him since, right?"

"So, what are you insinuating? That something happened to him?"

"I don't *know* what happened to him, and neither does anyone else. That's the point. It's not only alarming, but as my friend put it, creepy as hell. It seems like something out of a thriller novel or a—"

"Horror movie," Kinna finished under her breath.

"What?"

"Nothing. Never mind. Look, I know it was all very weird, but don't make it out to be some kind of plot, Liv. Dr. Addison is probably sitting on a beach somewhere, drinking margaritas and trying to block out all the crap he's had to listen to over the years from people like me." Kinna rubbed her forehead where the beginning of a headache was starting to brew. "Anyway, I just wanted to give her a chance, you know? I thought she deserved it. But..."

"But?" Olivia pounced. "But what?"

"Well, you know she's been against me doing anything to block my visions and dreams."

"Uh-huh. And?"

"So, I didn't exactly tell her about the potion I got from Sorcha or how well it's worked, but I think she knows I've done something. The last few visits? She's basically been more interested in any voices I've heard or visions I've had than helping me to understand what they mean. It's like that's all she wants to talk about—if I've had any new visions, what were they about, the time frame, those kind of things. I don't know, I thought maybe that's just how she works, but it is getting pretty strange."

"Strange? Oh, for the love of...I repeat, you need to dump her, Kinna. And I mean, like, yesterday. She's not helping you, and you know it. Like I said before, she's a quack, but what's worse, I think she's dangerous. I've only met her face-to-face a couple times, but I've had a bad feeling about her from the get-go."

"I know you have, and you're right. She's not helping."

"Darlin', it's more than that, and again, reading people is one of my superpowers. Look, I've never said anything, but I've done a bit of digging into her background, okay? I didn't find anything specific, but I'm telling you, there's something not right about her. I'm not kidding."

"Well, that's unsettling." Kinna sighed. "But it's a moot point anyway. I'm going to tell her today that this will be my last session. Therapy has never really helped me much. I mean, I know it works for a lot of people, but my issues are..."

"Unique?" Olivia reached out and gave her hand a pat. "I know, sweetie, and I get it. But I have faith in you and am here to support you all the way. If you decide to go it alone, you'll find a way to sort it all out which would be preferable to dealing with someone who's creepy and dangerous. So, it's a win-win."

Kinna laughed at that, which she knew had been Olivia's goal—to lighten the mood. "Thanks, Liv. Now, can we please talk about something else?"

"You bet. Just promise me you'll think about what I said."

"I will." Kinna nodded. "I promise."

It would be just about all she'd be thinking about.

They changed the subject and, as the rest of their lunch conversation went back to more mundane topics, Kinna tried to push it all to the back of her mind, at least for the lunch hour, but without much success. Olivia's words continued to echo her own thoughts even after she'd climbed into the car to head to her last session with Dr. Newcomb.

5

It didn't take long for Ian Casey—the old Scot tracker turned Immortal—to arrive on Dory and Kaden's doorstep, seemingly fully briefed on the situation at hand. As a matter of fact, he'd shown up just a handful of hours after Morianna had pulled her disappearing act. Ian had left England long before Morianna's visit, as he'd taken an early-morning flight non-stop from Heathrow into Seattle. From there, he had rented a car, drove down the Oregon coast highway, and had shown up at the house looking fresh and ready to rock, which Dory found a bit annoying. She didn't understand how it was possible to travel non-stop for better than thirteen hours and arrive looking so refreshed and energized.

However, she was actually grateful for Ian's presence, especially at the beginning of the crucial planning stage of whatever this mission would become. Ian was an integral part of the team, and someone she was only too happy to have with them in any dangerous or sketchy situation, and this new challenge was looking as if it would probably slide in that direction. Plus, in the past, Ian had seemed to have his finger on the pulse of the Immortal Council, and now, all the more so since becoming

Immortal himself. That alone was a significant advantage because the Council was nothing if not secretive. They seemed to feel the need to hold pertinent information close to the vest until the last possible moment. It was another thing Dory found annoying. She wasn't a fan of being kept in the dark in ominous situations, all the while being expected to resolve them.

"So, Ian, what do you think is going on here?" she asked, as she and Kaden sat down at the kitchen table to brainstorm with the tracker. "Morianna didn't give us much in the way of details. Only that an actual Archangel had met with Merlin with a request for assistance in finding someone important called The Key. I mean, have you seen this Archangel?"

"Did you know about all of this beforehand? And if so, how long have you known?" Kaden asked, pointing an accusatory finger at the old tracker. "Morianna was just here this morning. And then you show up four or five hours later? You must have been briefed with more information than we got."

Ian shook his head. "Unfortunately, I didn't get much more than you did, laddie. I was told that there was something coming, something bad, but other than that, I hadn't a clue. And as for the Archangel, no, I've not clapped eyes on him, either." The tracker tilted his head and regarded Kaden with a thoughtful look. "And although it's quite an interesting turn of events, it feels just a tad intimidating, you know?" he murmured with a smile.

Kaden grunted. "Ya think?"

"Well, me being a good Catholic boy, we were taught about angels, for sure, about how they were always with us. So, I guess this revelation shouldn't be the surprise that I found it to be." Ian shrugged. "I suppose, in this day and time, the reality of what we were taught has gotten somewhat diluted."

"I'll say," Dory chimed in. "I was raised in the Church of England. I guess I shouldn't be surprised, either, but I was still pretty stunned when Morianna told us about this Jerahmeel. I actually went online after she left and looked up the name. And there he was. Like you said, in this day and age, it seems so unimaginable. Angels. In our daily life."

Kaden crossed his arms and nodded in her direction. "On the other hand, it was only a handful of years ago that I called you a vampire when I watched you die and come back to life. As I recall, I had a bit of a time coming to grips with the whole immortal thing." He grinned at Dory. "Now, I am one. Go figure."

Dory rolled her eyes, and then turned a suspicious glance to the old tracker.

"What's that look for, lass?" Ian asked when he realized she was studying him.

"I'm just wondering what else you've been told? What other little tidbits you've heard."

"I don't know what you mean."

"Don't give me that innocent look," Dory said with a laugh. "I find it hard to believe that you weren't told or haven't a clue about any of this other than 'something bad' was coming."

Ian frowned. "Now, why would you think that? For the love of mud. You're the Chosen One. You've been immortal for over three centuries. I've only been an Immortal for a handful of years. Why would any of the higher-ups tell me anything that they wouldn't tell you?"

"Please." Dory smirked. "You've had an in with the Council even before you were made immortal. You told me yourself that you've actually attended a High Council meeting on several occasions when you were just a mortal tracker. And now that you're immortal, you hang with Morianna more often than not. Don't deny it."

"Well, that is true. But then, she is the Ancient that made me an Immortal, remember? And yes, I did attend a couple of the

High Council meetings...at their request. The first was a formal-
ity. I had to sign the contract to work with you and Kaden when
you were searching for Winn Mackintosh. But the second time, I
was no longer a mortal. I was there to confirm what had
happened on the Tor the night you'd destroyed that evil bastard,
Darius. I've told you all of this before."

Kaden grinned and poured himself some more iced tea from
the pitcher on the table. "Ah, yes, but what have you been doing
in the last few years?"

"I don't know what ye're yammering about." Ian looked
annoyed. "What is it you think I've been doin'?"

"Come on, Ian. Are you telling us that you haven't even
heard whispers of what's happening?" Dory asked. "You've
always had an ear to the ground, always knew what was
brewing."

The old tracker sighed. "Not this time, Isadora. What I do
know is that there's real concern at the High Council level.
Whatever it is, it's being held under wraps, and tight as can be.
However, there was one other thing that I heard, but I don't
quite know what to make of it."

"And that was?" Dory asked.

"It was made clear that this Key must be found and secured
as soon as possible. That was paramount. I think whatever is
coming, it's coming for the Key. And that has the higher-ups
quite aflutter, I can tell ya. But again, I don't know the whys of it."

Kaden sat back and frowned. "Well, we can probably give
you an idea or two there."

"Oh? Do tell." Ian leaned in.

"When Morianna was here earlier, she did tell us what the
Key is for," Dory said, turning to Ian. "Evidently, it's been used
throughout history to...correct atrocities. Those events that
could have a world-ending conclusion."

"The exact word she used was 'expunged'," Kaden added.

Ian blanched. "Expunged?"

"Yes. She said, 'Time was reversed, the trajectory changed, the damage was corrected.'" Kaden's look was grim. "And if that doesn't get *you* all aflutter, I don't know what will."

The old tracker nodded. "If this Key has the ability to turn back time, so to speak, or maybe reverse events, then in the wrong hands, that could be a devastating thing for this world. So, yes, I can see now why the Council is worried."

"From the little that Morianna told us, it does sound like the Key has been activated somehow, and they don't know how or why. Or they're not willing to say just yet," Dory added. "So, I can definitely see that as a huge problem globally. Just think of all someone could do with the ability to go back in time and change outcomes of all kinds." She gave him a narrowed look. "And I still can't believe Morianna didn't tell you any of this. That's just unacceptable."

"Aye. All she said was something bad was comin', and that I should hightail it over here as soon as I could do it. So, I got on a flight, flew non-stop from the UK to Seattle, and drove down the coast as fast as I could." Ian huffed out a breath. "Anything else she told you that I should know?"

Kaden chuckled. "No, man. That's about all we were told."

"Well, she did tell us about something called the Global War," Dory said. "It was one of the terrible events that took place that was expunged. But her little story was just an example of what the Key was capable of, I guess."

Ian shook his head. "A Global War? Purged from history? 'Tis a frightening thing."

"That it is, my friend," Kaden replied, leaning back in his chair and stretching out his long legs. "So, I'm thinking we'd better prepare ourselves for battle. Because I don't know about you, but I am not okay with someone going back in time and adding this Global War back in."

"I'm with you on that, for sure."

Dory made some notes on the pad she'd brought in from the office. "Okay, then. We need to get organized here and decide who else we're going to bring into the loop. Did you hear back from Ethan yet? Are he and Lucy available to fly up from California to assist?"

Ethan Walker, a Los Angeles detective and Kaden's former partner, had fought beside them on the Tor during the heinous battle against Deidre and her minions a few years back. He, like Kaden, was a very grounded individual and had struggled initially with learning about the Immortal world. But in the end, he'd stepped up to the plate and became part of the team's inner circle.

Of course, it helped to smooth the way that Ethan had been dreaming about Lucinda Devereux, Darius' Halfling daughter, long before he'd known about the bizarre world in which his friend now belonged. And while Lucy wasn't actually immortal, as a Halfling, the offspring of a union between a mortal and an Immortal Ancient, she was pretty close. Halflings enjoyed some of the perks from their Immortal side. Ethan had been a goner for Lucy from the moment their eyes had connected. They'd been together since the battle on the Tor.

Kaden shook his head. "No, I haven't heard back from Ethan, but when I spoke with him earlier, he said he'd get back to me when everything was set. So, he and Lucy will be here. I'm just not sure when. We'll know when we know."

Dory nodded. "Then we need to get down to it. You, me, Ian, Lucy, and Ethan. Do we keep the team tight for now? Or are we calling anyone else in?"

Ian cleared his throat and glanced at Dory but said nothing.

"Ian? Did you have something to say?" she asked with a raised eyebrow.

"Well, though I know how unpopular this may be, I'm gonna suggest we pull Tanner into the mix."

Tanner Sweetwater had been part of the team during the battle on the Tor. He was of Native American descent with an outstanding information network both inside and outside of the Immortal world. A bit of a loner, Tanner was also a shapeshifter, or skinwalker, a pertinent fact which he'd kept to himself. That omission had almost gotten Kaden killed during an ambush by deadly Erinyes on a beach near Hilton Head. It wasn't the only time they'd had trust issues with Tanner during their last association. However, it was a final straw for Kaden and still a sore point, so Dory wasn't all that keen to go there again, especially since they really didn't know what they'd be getting into yet. She was about to say so but Kaden beat her to it.

"I'm not so sure that's such a good idea, Ian." Kaden chose an oatmeal cookie from the tray in the center of the table and then gestured with it. "I mean, Tanner doesn't exactly play well with others. He's secretive and a wild card which is not a good trait going into...well, whatever this is going to be. And the fact that he is prone to keeping relevant information to himself and putting others at risk doesn't make him a ready choice for me. At least, not at the onset."

Ian nodded and then swirled the last of the iced tea in his glass. "Aye, I'll give it to ya, laddie, there is truth in that. We did have some trust issues during our last go round. That's for certain. However, I think that there's a bit more to consider here where Tanner's concerned."

"Such as?" Dory asked.

"Well, we don't know what we're going to be up against, but what we *do* know is that we'll be getting our marching orders from an Archangel, yes?"

"So it seems," Dory agreed.

Kaden nodded. "Weird, but yes."

Ian drank the last of his tea and then set the empty glass on the table before looking back and forth between them. "If we're dealing with an Archangel, what do you think the odds are that there will be more demons in the mix somewhere down the road before it's all said and done?"

Letting that question hang in the air, Ian poured himself another glass of tea and chose a cookie of his own from the tray before grinning at the both of them. "Didn't think about that, now didja?" he asked, and then took a bite of his cookie.

No, Dory hadn't thought of that, and from the look on Kaden's face, neither had he, though it should have been obvious. Hadn't she just said as much to Morianna only hours ago?

"Well, shit." Kaden sat back and shook his head before glancing at Dory. "Unfortunately, he's got a point, babe."

"Yes. He certainly does," Dory murmured. "And Tanner does have a vast knowledge of demonology, but do we take the chance with him again?"

"Well, he did come through in the end. Once we had our little come-to-Jesus moment in Savannah." Kaden frowned. "I hate to say it, but we may just have to accept the fact that he could be a possible asset at some point in this mess. I have a feeling we're gonna need every advantage we can get before, as Ian says, it's all said and done."

Dory took a deep breath and blew it out slowly. "Okay, so how about this? We wait to make this decision until we've had our meeting with Jerahmeel, until we know exactly what we're up against. Morianna said it wouldn't be long, that time was of the essence, right?"

"That she did," Kaden replied.

"I say we get Ethan and Lucy up here and read in. Then,

once we meet with this Archangel, we make the decision." She looked at Ian. "Okay by you?"

"Okay by me."

"Good. Next?" She took in the smug look on Kaden's face. "Suggestions?"

He grinned. "You know what I'm going to say. If we're considering Tanner..."

"Wyatt Macintosh?" she asked quietly.

Kaden nodded.

"He is the only one left to consider from our previous team," Ian murmured. "Wouldn't take long to bring him up to speed, either."

Dory had mixed feelings in that quarter as well. Wyatt was a mercenary and sometime bounty hunter. He was well known in the Immortal world. He'd been part of Deidre's heinous plot to kill Immortals for their energy, energy gathered with the sole purpose of raising a monster from the grave. However, as bad as that was, it was Wyatt's relationship to another monster that still gave Dory pause.

Kaden laid a hand on her arm, and she could see in his eyes that he was thinking the same thing.

"We all have some difficult history with Wyatt's asshole brother," he said. "Winn Mackintosh tried—several times—to kill us both. He was responsible for Ian's mortal death as well. But we all know that Wyatt wasn't part of that. And though he started out on Deidre's payroll, killing Immortals for their energy to raise Darius, which is bad enough, he also stepped up and did what was right in the end."

"I would agree with Kaden here, lassie," Ian added quietly. "I'm obviously harboring no love of Winn Mackintosh, may that evil soul rot in Hell. He got what he deserved at the end of it. However, Wyatt saved us all on that beach in South Carolina, fought beside us and put his own life on the line." The tracker stared into his glass for a moment, then glanced up with a sober look. "Now, maybe it was done to save his own skin. However, if he hadn't given us a heads up of what was comin', and then fought with us? I have me doubts that any of us would be alive to complain about it now even with the Dragon's Breath that you used to wipe out those terrible Erinyes. In fact, even after you finished off those beasties, if it wasn't for Kaden here, Wyatt himself would've died for his trouble on that very beach."

Dory sighed. "I suppose you're right. And besides, after Morianna healed Wyatt's injuries, she did make it clear to him that if he betrayed us, there was no place he could hide."

Kaden chuckled. "I seem to recall something about keeping his organs on the inside of his body where they belong so long as he was a good boy and did as he was told."

Dory grinned. "Morianna can be quite persuasive when she feels strongly about something."

"Ha! I'll say."

Ian smiled. "Wyatt is a capable warrior, one who I think saw the consequences of the bad choice he'd made, and then learned from it. I, for one, wouldn't mind knowing he was there watching our backs with whatever's comin' now."

"Well, if Vee's changed her mind about him, I guess we can as well," Dory said ruefully.

Velma 'Vee' Reed was Dory's long-time Sentinel, as were her ancestors before her. And where the role of the original Sentinels was to watch Immortals and document without inter-fering or aiding, Velma's role was very different. Dory had made a deal with her ancestors to work together as a team before Velma was even born. They gave Dory assistance with whatever she needed, and she protected them and gave them data about Immortals for their archives. Now, Velma lived at Dory's London townhouse. She was not only Dory's Sentinel, managing finances and assets, providing anything Dory required at a moment's notice, but a friend and confidant. Velma was quick, efficient, and sharp as a tack. Dory had no idea what she would do without her.

The Sentinel had been furious when the team had shown up in London with Wyatt in tow. Velma been there and seen all the heinous things his brother had done in pursuit of power and money. She'd watched Wyatt with laser focus the entire time they were preparing for battle. Wyatt, for his part, had taken all of Velma's vitriol in stride, and the two had engaged in a delicate adversarial dance around each other for days. From everything Dory had heard and seen since, the mercenary had finally won her Sentinel over. Last she'd heard, Wyatt was dropping by the townhouse a couple times a month or more, depending on if he was in town. It just made Dory shake her head. *But to each his own*, she thought.

"How about we take the same track with Wyatt that we're taking with Tanner?" Kaden asked, interrupting Dory's thoughts. "We hold off with both of them until we see what's what with this new gig."

"I'm good with that. Ian?"

"That's fine," Ian replied. "We should know PDQ what this is gonna involve, so we won't have to hold off on either for long. Speaking of Vee, have you tagged her yet?"

Dory nodded. "Kaden got on the phone to Ethan right after Morianna left this morning, and I called Vee, filled her in the best I could. Though it was a short conversation with what little we know. Anyway, she's on alert and will be ready to do what's needed as soon as we have a plan."

"Good deal. That girl's a pip."

"She is indeed," Kaden agreed.

Ian smiled. "I try to check in with her whenever I'm in London, which, unfortunately, hasn't been often, of late."

Kaden nodded. "We haven't seen her face-to-face since

before the COVID outbreak. Our communication has been limited to online conferences which just isn't the same. We need to get back to London when this whole thing is over."

"Agreed," Dory said. "Now, if we could get a timeline set up for a meeting with this Archangel, we could get this train moving. I just wish we knew how long this was going to take."

"Oh, it seems that it will be sooner than you think," a deep voice said from the doorway.

They turned in tandem to find a spectacularly handsome stranger leaning against the doorjamb. He was tall and imposing with shoulder-length, jet-black hair that emphasized his tanned skin and incredible amethyst eyes. The stranger was dressed like a biker in jeans and a long charcoal duster over a pristine, white button-down shirt, yet he had an otherworldly feel about him. Then he smiled with perfect, even teeth that were as white as his shirt, and Dory swallowed hard.

It seemed that Jerahmeel, Archangel of hope and faith, visions and dreams, had arrived.

6

By the time Kinna got to Dr. Newcomb's office, she was still debating on how best to explain—without too much excess drama—that this would be her last appointment. After her conversation with Olivia, Kinna realized that she'd had some of the same misgivings since Dr. Addison's strange retirement but had simply been too caught up in her own issues to really think about it. The last two or three sessions with his replacement had gotten progressively more uncomfortable for her, and now those misgivings seemed a bit more glaring. Olivia was right—it was time to do something proactive.

The waiting room was empty when she arrived, and Tess, the doctor's receptionist, looked up as she came through the door. The petite redhead had been Dr. Addison's receptionist before he'd retired and had stayed on during the transition. She was normally friendly with a bubbly personality, always putting Kinna at ease. However, the last few visits she'd seemed to be more and more withdrawn and had been acting increasingly odd. And now, the troubled look in the woman's bright-green eyes gave Kinna pause.

"Hey, Tess," she began uncertainly.

When the woman said nothing but continued to stare at her with the strained look, Kinna felt the first prickle of concern begin to stir. There was something off here, something definitely not right. And with the way her day had started and progressed, adding in the conversation she'd just had with Olivia, Kinna was so not up for any further turmoil today. The 'break-up' conversation with Dr. Newcomb was probably going to be hard enough.

"Tess? Is everything okay?" she asked as she stepped up to the reception desk. "You look...upset."

The woman leaned forward, motioning her closer and speaking in a low voice, as if someone might overhear, though they were the only two in the room. "Kinna, I'm sorry to be so abrupt with this, but I've been waiting for you and hoping you'd get here a little early so I could warn you."

"About what? Is there a problem?"

"You could say that. Look, I don't want to frighten you, but I don't know how else to tell you this, so I'm just going to say it. It's about Dr. Newcomb, and it's going to sound crazy. So, I need you to keep an open mind and listen carefully...because you're in danger here, and we don't have a lot of time."

Kinna slowly grinned. "Is this a joke?"

"Do I look like I'm joking?" Tess asked quietly.

Scanning Tess's face, she realized that the woman was quite serious. Her grin quickly faded, and Kinna put up a hand. "Okay, back up a minute. What are you talking about?"

"I'm talking about Dr. Newcomb not being who you think she is, Kinna."

Sirens began to blare in Kinna's head like a fire alarm gone mad, and Olivia's words came back to her loud and clear.

She's dangerous...bad feeling about her from the get-go...something not right about her.

Tess flicked a glance at the office door, as if someone might be listening. "I've been watching her carefully since she took over—since Dr. Addison's disappearance."

You know that nobody has seen or heard from him since, right?

Olivia's words echoed in Kinna's head.

"Disappearance? That's a bit over the top, isn't it? I mean, granted, his retirement was unexpected and pretty unconventional, but he did retire, right?"

Tess sighed and shook her head. "Unfortunately, that's another aspect of this that we don't have the luxury to discuss right now. Look, I've tried to give you subtle nudges over the last few appointments in hopes that you'd drop Newcomb, that you'd find someone else. You can't deny that you haven't been as happy with her as you were with Dr. Addison."

"Well, no, but that's no reason—"

"I'd tell you to go now but we're literally out of time. She's on her way out, so you're gonna have to suck it up."

Kinna glanced at the office door. "How do you know tha—"

"Please just listen…and trust me. This is for your own good." The receptionist began scribbling on a sticky note. "She's zeroed in on you, Kinna, and will use anything you tell her against you. So, make shit up if you have to but don't tell her anything of consequence. Do you understand?"

"No!" Kinna hissed. "I don't understand any of this." Frantic laughter bubbled up inside her, and Kinna put a hand to her lips. What the hell was happening today? Had the entire world gone mad? "Tess, why would Dr. Newcomb be 'zeroed in on me'? What does that even mean? And how in the world would she use anything I tell her against me? I'm just an average person with normal issues. Trust me, I'm not harboring any state secrets, and it's not like I'm crazy or a risk to anyone."

"This has nothing to do with your mental stability, Kinna, or national security—that I'm aware of, that is. Listen, she's…she's not *from* here. Like I said, I've been watching her. She's part of an incredibly malicious group that's searching for something they consider extremely rare and valuable. I think she's convinced that you may have the answers they're looking for."

"Tess, this is absurd." Kinna gave another incredulous laugh. "And what do you mean, *not from here*? You make it sound like she's some kind of alien." She briefly pressed her fingers to her eyes. "Geez, I can't believe I even said that."

"Kinna—"

"So, answers about what? What is this rare thing they're looking for, and for God's sake, why would they think I'd know anything about it?"

"Listen, I'm not exactly sure, but I'm telling you, we don't have time to discuss it."

"But—"

Tess shook her head again and held out the note to her. "Not here, not now, Kinna. Just get through the next hour, and then call me at this number later. I'll meet you anywhere you like and explain everything I know, but for right now you need to focus. Can you do that?"

Kinna's head was swimming with confusion, and she wanted to question the woman further, but within seconds of taking the sticky note from Tess, the office door opened, and Dr. Victoria Newcomb stepped out. "Oh, Kinna, good, you're here. And early, too. Excellent."

"I was just about to buzz you, Dr. Newcomb," Tess said.

Victoria Newcomb presented an intimidating figure in her cobalt-blue power suit and four-inch stiletto heels. Though not a champagne-colored hair on her head was out of place, the woman smoothed her French roll and smiled. "Thank you, Tess. Well, come on back then, Kinna, and we'll get started. I've been looking forward to our session today."

Kinna looked down at Tess who was smiling at her as if nothing had happened. The thought crossed her mind that perhaps she'd just had another hallucination but for the sticky note crushed inside her fist.

No, you're not hallucinating. Now focus! Blink once if you understand me.

Kinna's eyes went wide. It was Tess's voice inside her head though the woman hadn't said a word out loud and continued to smile at her. What the hell was happening here?

Stunned, Kinna blinked.

Good, now go. And please do what I told you. Your safety may well depend on it. I promise, I'll explain everything later.

"Kinna? Are you coming?" Dr. Newcomb asked from the doorway.

Giving an awkward laugh, Kinna shook her head and, putting on a brilliant smile, turned to the doctor. "Of course, of course. Sorry, it's been a very odd day, and my thoughts are kind of all over the place."

Shoving her hands into her pockets, Kinna deposited the note and followed the doctor into her office, casting a final glance at Tess over her shoulder as Dr. Newcomb closed the door behind her.

"Have a seat, Kinna," the doctor began as she sat down in one of the stylish leather club chairs. Smoothing her skirt and crossing her long legs, she picked up her pad and pen from the side table and gestured to the club chair opposite her. "How have these last few weeks gone for you? Anything of note happen that you'd like to share before we dive right in?"

While her most recent nightmare and the incident with the old man she'd nearly ran over leaped to the front of her mind, Kinna struggled to keep a straight face, to keep the hysterical laughter that threatened at bay. If she'd entertained the thought of coming clean on current events, Tess's words—however outlandish they may have sounded—echoed in her head. The tone of her earlier conversation with Olivia was also fresh in her mind, and something inside said to heed her warnings.

"Well, I spent most of this week in Seattle sitting through really boring quarterly board meetings which is always so much fun."

Dr. Newcomb chuckled. "Yes, I know how much you enjoy those."

"And, oh boy, I have another round here in Portland next week. So, yay, me!" Kinna cried sarcastically. She took a breath and blew it out slowly, trying to settle herself. "Other than that, it's been pretty ordinary. I can't really think of anything else worth mentioning."

"Really?" The way Dr. Newcomb drew out the word gave Kinna the crazy feeling that the doctor knew exactly what had been going on, but of course, that was impossible. Yet, for some reason, the smile on the woman's face sent a chill down Kinna's spine.

Obviously, you're letting your imagination run amok, Kinna thought to herself. But then, this entire day had taken on an ominous feel, like something vile was just out of sight but inching its way closer with each passing moment. *Okay, stop it! For the love of God*, she berated herself.

Clearing her throat and trying to shake off the dark thoughts, Kinna shrugged. "Yeah, you know...the last few weeks have been...more or less uneventful."

Something flickered in the doctor's dark brown eyes, but when Kinna blinked, it was gone.

"So, no nightmares?" she asked. "No visions?"

"Nope. Not a one," Kinna lied with a shake of her head. "I mean, I haven't even had a weird dream—that I can remember —in ages. And, well, that's kind of what I wanted to talk to you about today."

Dr. Newcomb raised a perfectly arched eyebrow. "Oh?"

Might as well get it over with, Kinna thought. "Yes. I've decided to take a break from therapy."

There was absolute silence for a moment or two, and Dr. Newcomb set her pad and pen back down on the table. "I see. And what's brought about this decision, Kinna?"

Kinna leaned forward. "Look, no offense, but I don't think this is working for me anymore. Actually, if I'm being completely honest, I'm not sure it ever has. Therapy was never really my decision in the first place, not something I'd chosen for myself."

"Ah, yes. Your parents began the process, didn't they?"

Kinna nodded. "And I get it. They didn't understand the things I was seeing and hearing when I was young—the voices, the prophetic visions and dreams. It all frightened them. As you're probably aware, therapy wasn't the only thing they tried... to make me normal."

"Yes, it's all documented in your records. Unfortunately, the paths they took were extreme at times. But Kinna, you have to know that normal is very subjective. What may seem ordinary to one person, can likely be abnormal or even abhorrent to another."

"Oh, I know that. I don't blame my parents for anything they did. They...just didn't understand, that's all."

The doctor tilted her head and gave Kinna a considering look. "You've been in therapy for a long time, Kinna. What makes you so sure it's not helping you, that you don't need it anymore?"

"Like I said, I haven't had the nightmares or visions for some time."

"And the voices?" the doctor asked quietly. "What about those?"

Kinna paused for a moment. "Gone," she finally said, then laughed. "Maybe I've just outgrown them."

Or maybe it's because of the witch's potion you've been taking. Did you really think you could hide it from me, you foolish child?

Kinna's breath backed up in her chest so fast that she felt the blood drain from her face.

"I-I'm sorry. What did you say?" Had she really just heard the doctor's voice? Inside her head?

There was that flash of something in the doctor's eyes again before a concerned look crossed her face, and she reached out a hand. "Kinna, are you all right? You've gone white as a sheet."

There was a ringing in her ears for a few seconds, and Kinna made herself take a deep breath and blow it out slowly. The voice she'd heard in her head was Dr. Newcomb's much like she'd heard Tess's voice earlier. What was happening to her? Was she actually hearing their thoughts?

"Kinna?"

Swallowing hard, she pasted a smile on her face. "Yes...yes, I'm fine. I just...I just felt a bit queasy for a second or two."

"Well, that's not good. Shall I get you some water? Or would you like to lie down for a bit?"

"No. No, I'm okay. It's passed now, but thanks. Listen, Dr. Newcomb, I appreciate the time we've had together, I do, but I've made up my mind about this."

The woman narrowed her eyes. "Yes, I can see that. I just want to make certain that you've thought this through carefully."

"Trust me, this isn't a spur of the moment thing, I assure you. Though I made the final decision recently, it's something I've been thinking about for quite a while. I just wanted to tell you face to face."

Dr. Newcomb stood and crossed to her desk at the window. After a moment, she turned back. "All right, Kinna. I will support your decision, but will you do me one last favor?"

Kinna nodded hesitantly. "What is it?"

"Make one more appointment for three weeks from today." She put up a hand when Kinna started to object. "Please, hear me out. If all goes well and you feel the same way in three weeks' time, you can simply cancel the appointment—no harm, no foul."

Dr. Newcomb came to her then and took her hand as she stood to leave. Kinna had to steel herself not to pull away or react to the queasy feeling that enveloped her again the moment the woman touched her.

"Kinna, you know that I only have your well-being at heart, don't you? I just want you to take a few weeks to be sure. After that, if six months or a year from now you decide you'd like to come back, you have only to call and make an appointment at that time. Deal?"

Kinna slowly pulled her hand from the doctor's grip, and the cold, queasy sensation began to subside. It was all she could do not to rub the palm of her hand on her pants in an effort to wipe away the feeling. "Okay. I'll speak to Tess about an appointment on my way out."

"Excellent."

"But I'm afraid it won't make a difference. I won't change my mind."

Dr. Newcomb smiled then but it didn't quite reach her eyes. "If that ends up being the case, then I wish you well, Kinna McComish." Then she looked deep into Kinna's eyes, and Kinna felt that chill chase down her spine again. "But be careful out there, my dear. This world can be a...chaotic place, and you never know what's around the next corner, do you?"

With that disturbing cautionary note, Kinna cleared her throat and tried not to bolt from the room. "Okay, then. Um, thanks again and take care of yourself."

Really, Kinna? Thanks again and take care of yourself? she thought. *What kind of lame shit is that?*

She made herself walk to the door, and the minute she opened it, felt some of her rising panic begin to ebb. As she approached the desk, she could actually *feel* the doctor's eyes on the back of her neck from the doorway, and she gave Tess a brittle smile. "So, looks like I need to make another appointment for three weeks from now, Tess."

"You bet. I can handle that." Tess glanced toward the doctor and gestured to the man reading a magazine in the waiting room. "Your three-thirty appointment is here, Dr. Newcomb. Must be a day for the early crowd, huh?"

Kinna glanced back only to find the doctor watching her closely.

"Well, come on in, Elliot," Dr. Newcomb said without taking her eyes from Kinna. "It's your lucky day. Looks like you get some extra time."

Kinna finally breathed a sigh of relief when the man went into the office, and Dr. Newcomb closed the door behind him.

"Are you all right, Kinna?" Tess asked as she pulled up the doctor's schedule on her computer and made out a reminder card. "You don't look so good."

"Ya think?" Kinna frowned. "I don't feel so good after that short session. What the hell is going on here? And how it is that I heard your voice in my head? It happened in there with Dr. Newcomb as well."

Tess looked up, stunned. "You didn't let on with her that you'd heard it, did you? Because that would be bad, Kinna. I mean, really bad."

"What? Tell her that the voices are back? No! Don't be stupid. Of course, I didn't. But it made me friggin' nauseous for a few minutes, and she sure as hell noticed *that*."

"Uh, that's not good, either. But wait, what do you mean, 'the voices are back'?"

"That's a long story for another time." Kinna waved away the question then hooked a thumb toward the office. "What is the deal with her? I mean, I've never felt any of that before, and I've been seeing her for several months. Just after I told her I wouldn't be coming back after today's session, I could literally feel a sickening panic rising in my chest. It was all I could do to get out of that office and away from her."

Tess leaned forward and held out the appointment card. "Look, like I said before, I can't go into it here," she said quietly. "The office closes at five-thirty, so call me later at the number on the sticky note I gave you, and we can meet. I'll explain everything I know then, okay?"

Kinna took the card she offered and stuck it into her pocket, then nodded. "I guess."

"Listen, I know this seems weird—"

"Seems? *Seems* weird?" Kinna scrubbed her hands over her face. "On a scale of one to ten, I gotta say, this day has just risen to a solid thirty on my weird-shit-o-meter."

Tess put up a hand. "Okay, okay, keep your voice down. I don't know how much she can hear from in there."

"What? Are you serious?" Kinna asked with a laugh. "You think she can hear what we're saying through the walls?"

"Believe me, I'm deadly serious. Now, go home and call me at that number later."

As Kinna turned to leave, Tess called softly. "And Kinna?"

"What?" she asked from the doorway.

"Be careful, okay? Keep your wits about you." Tess shook her head. "I don't know what she'll do next, but don't keep the appointment I just made for you. Don't come back here. Ever."

Kinna stared at the woman for a few moments, feeling like

she was losing her mind before turning to leave the office. As she walked out into the warm, afternoon sunshine, she stopped dead in her tracks, and a chill skittered up her spine when a familiar voice whispered in her head.

You really think it's going to be that easy?

There was stunned silence in the kitchen as Dory, Kaden, and Ian simply stared at the new arrival leaning against the doorframe. Even Henry perked up in his dog bed next to the pellet stove. And Dory couldn't help her wide-eyed amazement. It wasn't every day—or really, any day—that one expected to find that an angel of any kind, and particularly an Archangel, had soundlessly appeared in one's kitchen.

"I do apologize. Am I interrupting?" Jerahmeel said into the silence in a deep baritone voice that rolled over them like dark honey. "I was under the impression that you were expecting me."

"I...uh," Dory began but found she couldn't quite put her words together properly.

"It's fine, Isadora. I get that a lot." Jerahmeel pushed away from the doorjamb, and then paused, tilting his head. "Or should I call you Chosen One?"

Dory let out a breath in a whoosh. "You can call me whatever you like," she blurted before she could stop herself. "I just...don't know how to act. I've never seen, let alone spoken to an Archangel before, or any angel, for that matter."

Jerahmeel sent her a brilliant smile then, and she felt the warmth of it all the way to her toes.

"Ah, but one of us is always nearby," he said as he took a few steps closer, then paused again. "I think I'll call you Isadora. As I like that name immensely." He pursed his lips, as if considering something compelling. "Did you know that the name Isadora is of Greek origin? It means 'gift of Isis'. Isis, of course, was an ancient Egyptian goddess associated with life, rebirth, and healing magic. Incredibly appropriate for the Chosen One, don't you think? After all, you had life in the beginning, you died and were reborn, and now, you possess all sorts of magical gifts. I love the continuity of it all."

He turned and looked around the table with curiosity. "And who else do we have so far? Kaden Crenshaw, the Chosen Warrior, and Ian Casey, freshly minted Immortal."

Ian blinked like a confused rabbit, his Adam's apple bobbing up and down several times. Dory would have found the scene amusing in any other situation, but she could sympathize with Ian as she knew exactly how he felt—completely out of his depth.

"I-I've been immortal for several years now," Ian finally said. "Kaden and I became immortal at almost the same time."

Jerahmeel grinned at the old tracker and nodded. "That's fresh and bright as one of your new pennies where I come from."

Before anyone could respond to that, Henry stood with a soft whimper. The big Rottweiler crossed to the Archangel with head lowered and sat at Jerahmeel's feet.

"Of course, Henry. I would never forget you," Jerahmeel murmured as he bent to rub the dog's ears. "Such a good boy you are. Now, go on back and take a nap. I have things to discuss with your humans."

His tongue lolling to one side of his mouth and what could pass as a dog grin on his face, Henry, the good boy, did exactly as instructed.

A stunned look crossed Kaden's face as he cleared his throat and found his voice. "So, you're Jerahmeel? And you really are an Archangel?"

Dory experienced an odd yet comforting sensation as Jerahmeel pulled out the chair next to her and sat down, giving Kaden a quizzical look. "I am. Why? Did you require some kind of proof?"

The question was posed quite amicably but there was a sudden undercurrent that Dory could literally feel in the air and was certainly wary of, and it seemed that Kaden was aware of it as well.

"Nope. I'm good with it." He put up both hands. "Just checking."

"Excellent. Then we can dispense with the pesky skepticism and move on to more important things." The Archangel leaned back in his chair and crossed one booted foot over his knee. "Now, when is the rest of your team arriving?"

Kaden cleared his throat again. "We don't know for sure. A couple of them will probably be here by the weekend, and if not, by the first of next week."

Jerahmeel nodded. "Ethan Walker and Lucinda Devereux."

"How did you—" Kaden began but wisely let it go. "Never mind. Yes, Ethan and Lucy. We were just debating the other two. We'd decided to wait until we'd had this meeting with you to see if they would be needed."

"They will be." The Archangel gave Kaden a look that brooked no debate. "Tanner Sweetwater will be needed for a few reasons, but one that you three have already discussed."

"His knowledge of demonology," Dory said.

"Yes. That would be one reason." Jerahmeel reached for a cookie from the tray but stopped short of choosing one. He glanced at Dory. "May I?"

A nervous giggle bubbled up and out of her throat before she could get a hold of herself. That an Archangel would ask permission for a cookie struck her as completely hysterical. "Absolutely," she said, finding her voice. "Take two. They're small."

The Archangel chuckled at that and made his choice before taking a bite of the oatmeal raisin cookie he'd chosen.

"I'm assuming that—" Kaden began, but Jerahmeel put up a finger, silencing him.

They all watched in fascination as the Archangel seemed to savor each bite he took, as if trying to pinpoint each ingredient he was tasting.

"Yes, quite delicious," he declared with a nod, and then turned to Dory. "Well done." Brushing the crumbs from his long, elegant fingertips, he licked his perfect lips and smiled. "Now, down to business. Where were we? Oh, yes. You had a question," he said to Kaden.

"Well, you said, '*they* will be' when I wondered if the last two of our previous team would be needed. I'm assuming that means that we'll need to call—"

"The mercenary/bounty hunter?" Jerahmeel nodded. "Indeed. You should contact Wyatt Mackintosh as well. He has some...specific skills and connections that may come in handy."

"Handy for what?" Ian asked hesitantly. "If you don't mind me askin'."

"Not at all, Ian. I am here to give you as much information— and context for that information—as I can." The Archangel tilted his head in a considering fashion. "However, you do understand that there will be some things I cannot share.

Having said that, this may get a tad...messy, as dealing with demons often does. Wyatt, and Tanner for that matter, tend to excel in this area."

"Oh, good. More demons," Kaden muttered. "Ethan will be so pleased."

Jerahmeel laughed out loud at that, a rich sound that made Dory want to laugh along with him. She found herself smiling and wondered, vaguely, if all angels had this kind of effect on humans.

"Yes, Kaden. I am aware that Ethan Walker is not fond of demons, having been thrown into the mix with them several times in your last few skirmishes." The Archangel sighed. "Poor Ethan. His initiation into the immortal world was a lot to take in such a short period of time."

"To say the least," Kaden murmured.

"Yes, I understand you had a similar experience before you became an Immortal yourself." Jerahmeel sobered. "Unfortunately, this will be different for both of you. The demons searching for The Key are unlike any breed that you've already encountered. They are nothing to be trifled with, I can assure you."

Kaden scowled. "Worse than the Erinyes that Dory disposed of with the Dragon's Breath venom in her system? Or those heinous child-like acolytes that Deidre sicced on us during the battle on the Tor?"

Dory couldn't help the shudder that went through her at the mention of the Erinyes and that terrible day on the beach near Hilton Head.

"In many ways worse, yes," Jerahmeel said. "Which is why both the bounty hunter and the skinwalker are crucial for the mission ahead."

"Speaking of that," Dory began, "what exactly *is* the mission?" She wasn't sure how much information they were allowed to know, but if they were going to be thrown into 'the mix' with more demons, and those demons were worse than any they'd seen before, she wanted to know as much as possible.

The Archangel was quiet for a moment, and Dory wasn't entirely certain he was going to answer. Then he gave a very human-like shrug. "The Key is a very important entity, as she has the ability to mend time—to change the past, which, of course, changes the future. I'm certain that Morianna has explained some of the background, yes?"

Dory nodded. "She said that The Key has been used when a world-ending event has happened or is about to happen, that the...entity has been used to basically do a reset, to change time."

"That is correct."

Kaden frowned. "Then what event has happened or is about to happen that activated—for lack of a better word—The Key, this Charge of Angels?"

Jerahmeel nodded. "Excellent question, Kaden. Unfortunately, the answer is a bit complicated and not quite as straightforward as I'm certain you would like it to be. Again, as it always is when demons are part of the equation. You see, a particularly naughty demon and her horde have joined forces with one of your kind. They are looking to change history, and as I said, change the future."

Dory gaped at him. "An Immortal is working with these demons to wreak havoc on this world?"

"Sounds like shades of Deidre looking for more power and control," Ian murmured under his breath.

"I would agree, Ian," Jerahmeel said. "And yes, Isadora. An Immortal named Dorian Smyth is working with a demon named Verrine to change a few crucial events in the past in order to create a different here and now. And as Ian says, to gain control over this fallen world and the power that would accompany that control. This cannot be tolerated. The Almighty has a very specific plan for this world which He alone will exercise in His own time. Hence, The Key."

"So, the 'entity' or Key resides in a human being, and you know who that human being is, correct?" Kaden asked.

"Correct," Jerahmeel echoed.

"Well, then what do you need us for?" Kaden put up a hand. "Look, no offense, but you're an Archangel. Can't you just snatch The Key up and whisk her away to a safe haven where these evil players can't get to her? I mean, for that matter, can't God, the Supreme Being, or the Almighty—whatever name you want to use—simply remove her from the equation?"

Dory thought back to their earlier conversation with Morianna and the Ancient's answer to Dory's similar question.

Are you asking me to explain the plans and choices of a Supreme Being, Isadora? Or are you just questioning said Supreme Being's plans and choices?

Dory cleared her throat. "I think what Kaden means is what can we possibly do? We mean no disrespect but...what's the plan here?"

Jerahmeel stood and crossed to the sliding glass door, gazed out for a moment before speaking. "I have been with the entity known as The Key for centuries on this fallen world and beyond. I've guided and protected it in its many forms over those centuries and other worlds, as it has been reborn over and over again as needed. Kinna McComish is the human vessel containing the entity."

"So, she's The Key?" Dory asked.

Jerahmeel looked over his shoulder at her. "Precisely. She is The Key for this time and place."

"And she has no idea what she is or how important she is to this world?"

"Kinna has grown up knowing she was somehow different,

yet never understanding how or why. She's had visions and prophetic dreams most of her life and learned very quickly that telling her family or friends about these visions, what she was seeing in them, was a poor choice."

"No one believed her," Ian said quietly.

"Quite so, Ian. Though there was one individual but they had no control over the situation with Kinna." Jerahmeel turned back to gaze out at the backyard. "But more than disbelief, the adults in her life—her human parents—through no fault of their own, did their best to make things worse rather than better."

Kaden frowned. "Let me guess. They took her to doctors, therapists, ran tests, and generally made her feel as if she was crazy. And she was just a child."

The Archangel sighed. "Yes. That and more. So, Kinna has spent most of her adult life trying to block the power emanating from within her very soul, which, of course, is impossible." Jerahmeel turned away from the slider and retook his seat at the table next to Dory. "For the last six months or so, she's been seeing one of your kind for a potion of sorts to block her dreams and visions. However, those dreams and visions have returned over the last month, and she's had several new prophetic dreams."

Dory's eyes went wide. "Like a dream about Seattle destroyed and burning?"

Jerahmeel turned to her, sympathy evident in his stunning amethyst eyes. "You have been experiencing bits and pieces of Kinna's dreams for several weeks, and yes, you saw Kinna in the dream about Seattle burning."

"So, it seems like this Kinna's dreams are escalating just like Dory's have been," Kaden said. "Is that why you've come to us? Because of Dory's connection to Kinna's dreams?"

"Partially," Jerahmeel replied. "But the dreams themselves

are not the danger. It's *what* Kinna dreams, or should I say, *when*. During her dreams, she often travels."

"Travels?" Ian looked confused. "You mean, like astral projection?"

Jerahmeel shook his head slowly. "It's actually much more than that, Ian. When Kinna dreams, often she is traveling in time."

"Time traveling?" Kaden exclaimed. "Are you serious?"

"Very. The entity that lives inside Kinna is actually a Time Mender. The dreams she's been having about cities burning and destroyed are possible future outcomes, yet Kinna is actually in the future as it's happening." Jerahmeel's look was grim. "If she were to go back in time, she could change history."

"Change history. In her dreams?" Kaden blew out a breath. "This is getting worse by the minute."

"Yes, now you see why it is imperative that Kinna is protected from those who are looking for her. And that starts with finding her and helping her to understand who and what she is." Jerahmeel glanced at Dory. "And that is where you and your team come in."

Dory blinked up at him. "You want us to explain all of this to her? I'm not sure that's a good idea. I mean, why would she listen to us? I'm not sure I understand it enough to explain it to anyone. And if you've been with this entity for an eternity, wouldn't it be best for you to explain it to her?"

The Archangel's smile was gentle and had a bit of a calming effect. "You will do just fine. The Immortal that's been giving Kinna the potion to block her powers will act as an intermediary for the initial meeting. Her name is Sorcha Doyle, and she will be contacting you soon." He turned to Kaden. "In the meantime, you need to make those calls, get your team back together. Do your research, make a plan. Dorian Smyth is not the patient type, and the fact that he's working with Verrine will make it worse."

"Worse how?" Kaden asked.

Jerahmeel sighed again. "Verrine is a fallen angel who was once in the Order of Thrones. She is now a demon of impatience. Dorian Smyth may think he's in charge and working with her, but he is not. Verrine can be very persuasive, and I can guarantee that she has a plan of her own. They've not found Kinna yet, but they are closing in, may have pinpointed her already. They cannot be allowed to gain control of The Key. There are a few others who are trying to run interference, slow their progress, but bringing Kinna into the fold—so to speak—and getting her up to speed about what is coming for her is imperative."

Ian slowly raised a hand.

"Yes, Ian?"

"Again, no disrespect, but I still don't quite understand why you don't just sweep the lass up yourself."

Jerahmeel stood then and placed a hand on the old tracker's shoulder. "I'm sorry, Ian. As I said earlier, there are certain things I can't share, at least, not at this time. This can be a very tricky situation." The Archangel swept his gaze around the table. "Gather your team, do some research, and wait for Sorcha's call. It won't be long."

With that, the Archangel simply disappeared without fanfare.

Silence reigned in the kitchen for several moments as the three looked back and forth at each other.

Then Kaden spoke up. "Well, that was fun."

"That was bizarre," Dory countered. "I don't even know what to think about it all. I mean, where the hell do we start? I still feel like I've been given a slip of paper and told to follow the directions on it, but there's nothing written there, you know?"

"I am with ya, Isadora," Ian agreed. "I feel we've been hired for a job without knowing what we're supposed to do."

"Unfortunately, I think you're both right," Kaden said. "So, I suppose we just start, like Jerahmeel said. We get the rest of the team here and get the research going, make a plan. We get as prepared as we can be before this Sorcha Doyle calls. I'm hoping since she's 'one of our kind', as Jerahmeel said, that the initial meet doesn't go sideways. Regardless, it doesn't sound like we have much leeway, and I'd rather not let down an Archangel. Know what I mean?"

"Indeed, I do, my friend," Ian agreed with a nod.

"All right, then," Dory said. "Let's get to it."

Sorcha Doyle was just putting the finishing touches on a potion for a client to be delivered the following morning when she had a tingling at the back of her neck. Turning slowly, she nearly jumped out of her skin.

"Jesus, Mary, and Joseph!"

It wasn't every day you found that a celestial being had parked himself in a club chair next to your fireplace. Unfortunately, it seemed to happen to Sorcha more often than she liked.

"Good evening, Sorcha Doyle."

"For the love of...What is wrong with you, Jerahmeel? You just about scared the life out of me."

"Jerahmeel? My, my, how formal we are this evening. You used to simply call me Jerahm." The Archangel smiled and crossed his long legs. "I'm sorry if I startled you, dear Sorcha."

"Ha! No, you're not." Sorcha rolled her eyes at the Archangel. "I think you enjoy messing with us puny Immortals."

"Now, that's not true. I care for all humans. And though you've been blessed with immortality, you *are* still human, correct?"

"Whatever." Sorcha sighed. "You know, you can't just pop

into someone's private space without notice whenever you feel like it."

Jerahmeel laughed out loud, a deep, mesmerizing sound that washed over her like warm molasses. "Evidently, you can when you're an Archangel."

She took a deep breath and let it out slowly. "That's not what I meant, and you know it." Crossing her arms, she frowned at him. "It's rude and invasive, Jerahm. It's thoughtless to just...oh, never mind. I don't know why I'm wasting my breath. What do you want?"

She watched the Archangel gracefully rise and begin to make his way around her workspace, examining a bottle here, a canister there. He looked like a normal human male, she mused...well, an incredibly attractive human male. Tall and rugged, handsome in that 'bad boy' kind of way. *With an added touch of the ethereal,* Sorcha thought to herself. And heaven help her, he always *smelled* so damned good. *Like what she imagined Heaven would smell like*, she thought, and almost laughed out loud at her own joke.

Shaking her head, Sorcha struggled to focus. This wasn't a social call, it never was. Though it appeared as if there was no real purpose to his visit, she knew better. Angels never did anything without purpose...especially Archangels. He wanted something from her—yet again—but she would obviously have to wait him out. He would tell her in his own sweet time. That was another thing about angels. They couldn't, or wouldn't, be hurried. She was, however, surprised when he spoke up softly.

"What do I want?" The look he gave her was almost wistful. "Isn't it possible that I'm just checking in to see how you are?"

"I suppose it's possible." She watched him carefully. "But previous experience tells me it's not probable."

He grinned at that, and she felt the full wattage of his angelic charisma.

"So cynical, Sorcha, really. Times have changed. You Immortals are skeptical of everything these days."

"Trust me when I say that there's a plethora of reasons for that. It's also a trait we share with our mortal brethren."

"Perhaps I only want to offer you my assistance with whatever you're working on." He lifted a business card from the holder on a side table. "*The Wiccan Way.* A catchy name, but you're an Immortal not a witch or sorceress."

"Mmm, that's true," she said, then tilted her head and pursed her lips. "But as you say, times have changed. There was a time when the old Immortals like Merlin, Morianna, and Morgan le Fay, all the Ancients on the Immortal Council were treated like—"

"Gods?" The Archangel's eyes glittered dangerously for a moment.

Sorcha swallowed hard but nodded. "Perhaps. But the masses knew no better, and the Ancients have enormous power. If not given from God, then who? People came to them for help, Jerahm, and they did good work, healed afflictions, nurtured crops, and protected kings." She stopped and nodded. "Sure, there were those who abused their powers, coveted more. Morianna's cousin, Darius, was a perfect example. But most just wanted to make people's lives better, to be needed and be of use. Unfortunately, all of that is gone. Immortals live only in the shadows now."

"You don't," he murmured. "You still care for humanity."

"Yes, but do you know what happens when I tell a human—a mortal human—that I'm an Immortal, that I'm over two and a half centuries old?"

He smiled congenially, as if indulging a child. "Enlighten me."

"Best case scenario? That *skepticism* you were talking about is usually followed by ridicule and contempt. You're labeled as some kind of loon. Worse case? Maybe incarceration in a mental facility, drugs, shock therapy. But I guess that's not so bad considering that a hundred years ago or so it would have been burning at the stake or drowning in a pit, maybe even dismemberment."

He gave her a sad look. "There have been terrible times for the human race over the centuries."

"I would say that's an understatement, but these days are different. Now, when I tell that same mortal that I'm a white witch or that I'm a practicing Wiccan, they ask me for help. They're willing to pull out their wallets and pay me quite handsomely to ease their pain, improve their love life, or just their life in general." She shrugged. "I do what I can."

The angel continued to peruse Sorcha's worktable with interest. "First do no harm?" he asked quietly.

"Exactly. That's how I live my life these days. You know, most Immortals have special powers, and each has a different gift, but it doesn't hold a candle to that of an angel—let alone an Archangel. The dynamics between Immortals and angels is very similar to that of Immortals and ordinary humans. It's just reversed. But at one time or another, many of us have dealt with those of your kind who have fallen. It never ends well."

Jerahmeel held out his hand then and the look in his beautiful amethyst eyes was kind and full of love. "You have nothing to fear from me, child...ever," he whispered. "But I do require your assistance."

"Of course, you do," Sorcha replied with a resigned chuckle. *And here we go...*

"You've had a client recently that I'm interested in," he said, almost casually, but she got the impression that it was more than interest.

"Uh-huh. A client." She narrowed her eyes at him. "I'm listening."

"There is something I require of you in connection with this human."

She shook her head and sighed. "You know, your timing really kind of sucks. I've got a boatload of things on my list and not a lot of time to spare."

He went very still at that, and he tilted his head, his gaze becoming just a shade glacial. "I'm sorry. Is my visit an imposition?"

Putting up both hands in surrender, Sorcha sighed. "Look, don't get all *I am Archangel, hear me roar*. When have I ever refused to help when you've asked—especially when it comes to your precious humans?"

A hint of a smile played around his lips. "Of which, I do believe we've established, you are one."

She gave him a bland look.

"Sorcha, this human holds some importance. And time is of the essence for me as well."

She shook her head. "So, define 'importance'. Like important for the distant future? Important for tomorrow morning? The fate of the world? Important how?" When he continued to stare at her with the stillness of a sphinx, she scrubbed her hands over her face. "Okay, okay. Who is this client of mine who holds such importance?"

"Her human name is Kinna McComish."

Sorcha's mouth dropped open. "Oh...my...God!"

"Careful, Sorcha," he murmured and waggled his finger at her.

"Kinna? You're here for Kinna?" Ignoring his warning, she ran a hand through her thick ebony hair and sank down into the club chair he'd vacated. "Man, I knew there was something about her, something I couldn't quite put my finger on. She's got a very strong psychic river flowing through her."

"Among other things, yes."

"I got a quick glimpse of what's inside her on the first day we met. She took my hand before I could avoid it and *pow*! It was like a kaleidoscope in my head. Anyway, she came to me for a potion to block her visions and nightmares."

"I am aware of that as well. That is one of the reasons I'm here. You cannot give her any more of your potion. That must cease."

"I assume that you're also aware that she wants nothing to do with her abilities. It's why she came to me in the first place. She wanted it all to stop." Sorcha leaned forward. "I tried to talk her out of a potion, told her she should embrace her inner power, but she was adamant."

When the Archangel's gaze became shuttered, it came to her in a flash. "You know, I've been hearing chatter lately. Talk about finding an important artifact, something referred to as a key. I've heard there are people looking for it. One older Immortal specifically, who's leading the charge. He's a fairly nasty, power-hungry Immortal named Dorian Smyth. Does she have something to do with finding this key?"

Jerahmeel went back to perusing her worktable, and she waved away her question when it was obvious he wasn't going to tell her much more. Typical angel, sparse on the details. "Okay. I get it. No questions. Well, just one. What do you need from me? Other than no more potions for Kinna, which is going to be awkward since she made an appointment with me for Monday."

The grin he sent her was a thousand watts. "For now, simply an introduction."

"An introduction? For whom?" Sorcha smirked. "I'm assuming it's not for you, because, you know, Archangel and all."

Jerahmeel laughed out loud again. "You are most amusing, Sorcha Doyle. But you are quite correct. I need no introductions." He narrowed those beautiful amethyst eyes then. "You spoke of several Ancients earlier—Merlin, Morianna."

"Yes."

"Do you know them?"

Sorcha frowned. "I know *of* them but have never met them. They're part of the Immortal Council, but then, you would know that, too. You would also know that we do travel in very different circles, as they're *Ancients*." She paused. "Why? You want me to introduce them to Kinna?"

"Well, I assume Morianna will be leading this Immortal excursion that I require, but it's actually the Chosen One and her merry band that I want Kinna to meet."

For a second time in a matter of minutes, Sorcha's mouth dropped open. "The *Chosen One*? Are you kidding me? As in Isadora Winthrop?"

"Mmm, yes, the very same."

"Oh, my Go—"

"Ah, ah, ah." Jerahmeel shook his finger at her again. "You really must learn to curb your blasphemies. That tendency will not help you in the afterlife. That is, should the afterlife ever come for you, being Immortal and all."

"What does the Chosen One have to do with—Wait a minute." Sorcha jumped up and began to pace as thoughts started to swirl in her mind. "Wait just one damn minute." She stopped pacing and pointed a finger at the Archangel. "You said 'her *human name* is Kinna McComish'. Are you telling me that Kinna is...not actually human?"

"The Ancient, Morianna, will be in touch. I would like for you to make contact with the Chosen One and her group as soon as possible. Please accommodate them as best you can. You will be rewarded for your assistance—for the use of your 'spare time'."

Sorcha pressed her fingers to her eyes in frustration. "How am I supposed to contact them? And I don't need to be rewarded. I'm happy to help." But when she dropped her hands and looked, she was standing alone, talking to no one. "Nice visiting with you, Jerahm," she said to the room, and then went back to her potions, only to find a small card with the Chosen One's cell number written on the back laying on the table next to her supplies.

DORIAN SMYTH TOOK a sip of Scotch and stared out of the floor-to-ceiling windows of his penthouse at the magnificent view of the Portland night lights below. He'd spent a lot of time, energy, and attention to detail—as well as the blood and tears of count-less others—building his empire.

Power. The acquisition of more was a craving in his bones and something he'd gladly crush anyone in his way to achieve. And this latest plan would be his pathway to ultimate power. So much so that he'd been willing to join forces with a fallen angel and her demonic minions to make certain that it succeeded. Now, he was beginning to wonder if that had been such a wise decision after all.

"Tell me again why you think this human is connected to the key we seek," he demanded with a glance over his shoulder at the beautiful woman—demon underling, he reminded himself —seated casually on the plush sofa sipping a cocktail.

Dr. Victoria Newcomb said nothing but smiled seductively over the rim of her martini glass.

"What?" he asked impatiently, turning to study her.

She licked her lips and seemed to relish the pause. Finally, she took a breath and blew it out bit by bit as if its taste was something to be savored. "It's just that you say the word 'human' like it leaves a bad taste in your mouth, as if it's something to be pitied or disparaged, yet under your immortal veneer beats the heart of a human, isn't that so?"

He gave her a stony look. "Your point?"

She shook her head slowly. "Oh, no point, darling. I just find your expression of derision for your own kind amusing, that's all."

"My own kind?" Dorian frowned. "I may be human, but we Immortals are vastly different from ordinary humans."

"Really? And why is that?" She tilted her head and studied him. "I mean, in what way? Is it because you happen to have been made immortal at some point, or that you've been given a few powerful gifts? Do you think that makes you better than her, or any mortal human, for that matter? I wonder what plans you have for them once this scheme of yours is finished."

Dorian swirled the last of his Scotch and gave her a mean smile. "I would say that's above your pay grade, *darling*, and really none of your concern. And my thoughts about mortal humans have no relevance to this conversation. Now, answer my question. Why did you think she was connected to the key?"

"I have my reasons." Victoria took a sip of her martini and gave him a pissy look.

To which Dorian merely raised an eyebrow. "And those reasons would be?"

Victoria sighed but ultimately relented. "When we'd finally gotten rid of that fool, Addison, I spent a few weeks researching and analyzing a few of his patients who had been tagged as potential connections. Regression therapy and hypnosis for those who would consent, that kind of thing."

"Was this human you've settled on one of them?"

"Kinna had no interest in regression therapy or hypnosis. I think there had been some of that early on in her life."

Dorian crossed to the bar, threw back the last of his Scotch, and set the glass on the counter. This demon was working his last nerve. Turning to her, he gave her a hard stare. "None of this tells me why you've fixated on this specific human."

Victoria put up a hand. "Patience, darling. I'm getting to it. You see, she popped when I started to do more in-depth research on the handful of those I'd chosen. And so, it was mostly because of Addison's notes and records that I began to give Kinna McComish a closer look."

"And what did you find?"

"Well, it seemed that from the moment she was old enough to realize her parents, A: didn't believe anything she was saying, and B: were freaked out by her stories, Addison was the only one she felt safe enough to talk to. She confided in him about all her little secrets. The visions and dreams, the voices she'd heard from early on, even the fact that she'd seen her parents' death in a vision just days before it happened." Victoria made a disgusted face and got up to make herself another martini. "Unfortunately, her stupid, close-minded parents tried everything imaginable to block her abilities—which are considerable, I might add—from the time she was quite young. Bearing in mind all they put her through, as an adult she holds a fairly dim view of her gifts as you might imagine."

"You'd told me a few weeks ago that you were making progress in that area with the one you'd chosen."

"And I thought I was, but I came to realize that she was never really comfortable enough with me to transfer the trust she'd had in Addison to me. She began to give me platitudes when I pushed, and then outright lies toward the end." She shook her head and went back to the sofa and sat down with her fresh cocktail. "I tried to talk her out of blocking her abilities when she began to make noises in that direction. See, she just wanted the visions and nightmares to stop. She told me she'd think about it before making a final decision, but that was a lie, too. By that time, she'd already gone to see one of your kind—one who professes to be a witch—for a potion, and she'd been taking it for a couple months."

Dorian poured himself another two fingers of Scotch from the cut glass decanter, and then sat down in a club chair opposite her. He picked up his cigar from the elegant blown glass ashtray on the coffee table and re-lit it. "If she wasn't confiding in you, Victoria, how do you know that?"

"As I said, I started testing several potentials just after we'd gotten rid of Addison."

"Testing how?" Dorian asked with a frown.

She chewed thoughtfully on the olive from her martini. "I started throwing out subliminal questions and statements with several of them."

"And this Kinna responded?"

Victoria shook her head. "No. Not at first, but I kept trying because I just had this feeling about her after reading some of Addison's notes. Anyway, the last time I saw her something had changed, there was something quite different about her. So, I tried again. When she outright lied to me about not having any visions or dreams, I told her subliminally that it was probably because of the potion she'd gotten from the Immortal."

"And she responded this time?"

"Oh, yes. She literally blanched and the blood drained from her face. I'm telling you, I thought she was going to throw up her lunch right there on the office floor." The demon laughed out loud. "She even asked me what I'd said. Of course, I pretended not to know what she was talking about. But in that last session, just my physical presence seemed to make her ill. So, I knew she was sensing that I wasn't human. And then there was also the fact that my receptionist was meddling."

"I beg your pardon?"

"Tess was actually Addison's receptionist. She told me she would stay on for a few months, just for the transition."

"So, how do you know she was interfering? And in what way?"

Victoria's sly smile was back. "I have excellent hearing, darling. I overheard bits and pieces, enough to begin to suspect her assistance was less than supportive. After Kinna left that day, I went into session with my next patient. Tess was gone when we came out, and I haven't seen her since. But I felt there was something off about her from the start. She was always pleasant, and I can't prove it, but I don't think she's entirely human, either."

"Immortal? Or something else?"

"I'm not sure. It felt old, but not exactly like an Immortal. I could never put my finger on just what it was, but there was something different, I might even say magical, about her."

Dorian chewed on the end of his cigar and thought for a moment. Taking a pull and blowing out a stream of blue-gray smoke, he narrowed his eyes. "Getting back to this Kinna McComish. If you thought she was so special and perhaps the one we were looking for, then how in the hell did you let her slip away like that?" he growled angrily.

"Please," she murmured, and shrugging, waved away his irritation. "Look, don't pop a vein, okay? I know where she lives, and I've had a couple of Skuppar demons following her for weeks now. She can run but she can't hide." Crossing her legs, she smiled at him. "So not to worry, darling. She's the one. She'll eventually lead us right to this key we're all looking for, I'm certain of it. And if she doesn't, like I said, I know where to find her. We scoop her up and extract the information we need by any means we like."

Dorian rolled his cigar between his fingers and then tapped it over the ashtray. "I'm not a patient man, Victoria. And I'm certainly not willing to wait for eventualities. So, you scamper on back to your mistress and tell her you have until mid-week to get me the answers I'm looking for. I want the location of that key."

The demon's gaze hardened, and her smile became brittle.

"Verrine won't like an ultimatum, Dorian. You're playing with napalm. I would tread very carefully if I were you."

"Verrine and I have an understanding, so I don't need your pathetic warnings. Now, go."

She set her martini glass down on the coffee table with an unpleasant click and flounced from the room. When he heard the front door slam, he glanced out over the city and smiled. Once he had the key, whatever that was, things were going to change...and he would rule with an iron fist once they did.

"Dude, this situation is out of control," Ethan Walker groused as he took a bite of his toast. His dark brown eyes clearly conveyed his irritation. "Come on, seriously."

Ethan had arrived the night before with Lucy Devereux, and the group had waited until Sunday morning to discuss plans for the upcoming mission. They were just finishing breakfast, and Kaden was filling in the new arrivals. He knew Ethan was gonna bitch, especially when he learned that Tanner Sweetwater would be joining them again and would be arriving the following day, but there was no help for it. Kaden's former partner would just have to deal.

"So, let me get this straight," Ethan began as he sat back with his coffee. "Last time, there was the Immortal thing and getting up to speed with little time and under pressure. That was fun. Add to that, there was the demon thing that almost got you killed with Dragon's Breath, the poison that Dory barely beat, I might add. Oh, and of course, the shapeshifter thing that Sweetwater's got going on—"

"And my Halfling thing," Lucy chimed in with a grin. "Don't

forget that, babe. I mean, I am the daughter of an Immortal Ancient and a regular old human."

"You bet, darlin'. You know I'd never leave you out," Ethan said with a wink before turning back to Kaden. "And now we've got demons *and* angels? Really?"

"And you find that surprising...why exactly?" Dory asked. "Doesn't it follow that if there are demons in the world around us, there would be angels as well?"

"I know it seems crazy," Kaden added. "But then again, crazy is sort of relative for all of us these days."

"Man, I hear that, brother." Ethan shook his head. "I guess it shouldn't surprise me, especially with what we were up against on the Tor. I mean, those Erinyes on the beach were bad, right? But those incredibly horrific acolytes with their snake tongues and black inhuman eyes that Deidre—the heinous Ancient bitch—had with her on the Tor? Terrifying." He shook his head again. "However, after Lucy shared her ability with me back then, the capability to see past the subterfuge that demons and such—"

"Glamours, sweetie," Lucy corrected. "Demons and non-humans use glamours to hide in plain sight among us."

"Right. Glamours. Anyway, I gotta tell ya, I have seen some shit in the last few years that I can't *even* explain. So, you're right. I shouldn't be surprised. And it is comforting, in a way, to know that there are angels out there as well. But come on. What the hell's next?" He put up a hand. "Nope. Don't answer that. I'm pretty sure that I don't want to know."

"Ah, but this Jerahmeel is an Archangel, right?" Lucy asked, turning to Dory. "That's a bit different."

Dory nodded. "Yes. Definitely different."

"I bet it was a kick in the pants, though, meeting him that way, face-to-face." Lucy laughed out loud.

"Yeah, well, we'll see how gleeful you are after you meet him face-to-face, girlie," Ian murmured. "*I'd* say a bit terrifying in a quiet, pleasant sort of way."

Lucy jabbed a finger in the old tracker's direction. "Oooh, don't tease me, Ian. That's really intriguing."

Ian rolled his eyes and glanced at Dory. "Although, I think the Chosen One here had a much different experience with the Archangel than Kaden or I had."

Dory bristled. "What the hell is that supposed to mean?"

"Oh, you know, just that you had a goggly-eyed look on your face most of the time he was here. And it seemed to me like you couldn't quit smiling every time you looked at him."

Dory's face turned a lovely shade of red. "That's just ridiculous. Besides, you're one to talk. You could hardly put two words together while he was here, so no throwing stones, old man. He just...made me feel so warm and...happy."

"And I suppose the fact that he's tall, dark, and pretty didn't hurt much, either?"

At the grin on Ian's face, Dory's brows drew together in a frown, before a reluctant smile spread across her face. "Oh, sod off, you old fart. It was a freaky situation and the first time any of us have met, let alone spoken to an Archangel, so back the hell off."

"Okay, okay, let's none of us go throwing stones," Kaden admonished, wading into the fray with a grin of his own. "I think it's clear that the three of us had a bit of a time adjusting to Jerahmeel's first visit. I know I did. An Archangel suddenly appearing in your kitchen, eating your cookies, and just as casual as you please? Well, not something you can really prepare yourself for, am I right?"

"Aye," Ian grumbled. "To say that I was unprepared would be a dire understatement. That's true. Although, as you said, I don't know how a person could prepare for that kind of situation before hand, not knowin' what to expect and all."

Ethan zeroed in on the tracker. "So, what was he like, Ian? This angel?"

"Archangel, sweetie," Lucy said, patting him on the shoulder.

"Yeah, yeah, so what was this *Archangel* like?"

Ian narrowed his eyes. "We just told you. Were you not listening, ya idiot? One look stole the words from your brain and the spit dried up in your mouth. And that was with himself sittin' right there at the table with a smile on his face."

Dory burst out laughing. "Oh, for the love of God, Ian. It wasn't that bad."

"Oh, I don't know," Kaden replied. "I get what Ian's saying. There was a moment that my spit did a little evaporating."

"Aye. When you asked him if he was really an Archangel," Ian said with a snicker. "You paled just a smidge at his tone when he asked you if you needed proof."

"Okay, yeah," Dory said, giggling along with Ian. "That did feel a bit dicey. Jerahmeel asked the question pleasantly enough but it did have a kind of scary undertone."

Ethan's mouth dropped open. "K, dude, what did you say when he asked that?"

Ian hooked a thumb in Kaden's direction and answered Ethan's question before Kaden could open his mouth. "Boy-o here threw up his hands in surrender. 'I'm good' he says, that he was just checkin'. I thought he was gonna wet himself."

"To be honest, for a second, I thought I might, too." Kaden grinned, and then sobered a bit. "I don't know how either of you two felt, but I couldn't get over the power radiating off of him. It was hard to miss. It was like the air in the kitchen ramped up with high-octane energy or something."

Ian nodded, the grin slipping from his face. "I'm there with ya, Kaden. His whole presence was intimidating yet oddly mesmerizing."

"I agree on all counts," Dory added. "But then again, Jerahmeel is an Archangel, so like you said, it was hard to prepare for the impact of his presence."

"Oh, man!" Lucy exclaimed. "I would have *loved* to have been here for that."

"Oh, don't you worry yourself," Ian murmured with a nod. "You'll be gettin' your chance."

Ethan got up to refill his coffee cup. "Okay, so let's get down to it. What did he tell you, and what are we supposed to be doing?" He came back and sat down. "Please tell me that there's some kind of game plan."

Kaden rubbed his jaw and wasn't quite sure where to start. "Well, he was a little cryptic and pretty slim on the pertinent information. There were also some things he said he couldn't share yet. And as for a game plan? Well, that's a bit sketchy, too."

Kaden and Dory spent the next twenty minutes bringing Ethan and Lucy up to speed. However, when they got into the specifics about demons and the part about adding Tanner into the mix, Ethan put up a hand.

"Okay, I have to say, I don't know why we have to have demons again this time around." He made a pained face. "I mean, once was plenty good for me."

Dory shook her head, clearly amused at Kaden's former partner's cranky attitude. "Ethan, after all you've seen, you do realize that we have no control over that, don't you?"

Ethan grinned back at her. "Well, sure, but I just want to go on the record as being totally against having to deal with any kind of demons again. And on top of that, the Archangel actually said that you needed to bring wolf boy on board, too? Seems like overkill on the annoying entities, if you ask me."

"Preaching to the choir, buddy," Kaden murmured. "I'm not all that happy about having Mr. I-play-by-my-own-rules on the team, either. But trust me, I was *not* going to argue with an Archangel."

"It's because of the more dangerous demons we're certain to encounter before it's all said and done that Jerahmeel felt Tanner needed to be part of the team again," Dory explained. "Tanner has a pretty incredible knowledge of demonology that we're going to need."

"She's right, Ethan," Lucy added. "And on top of that, his information network is stellar, which will come in handy, I can assure you. So, I'm afraid that you two will just have to work out your issues for the duration."

Ethan sighed. "Whatever. So, if wolf boy is coming back, does that mean Mackintosh will be joining us as well?"

Kaden nodded. "It does. Jerahmeel was very clear that both would be needed, so we contacted them, and Tanner will be here sometime tomorrow. Wyatt was in Scotland finishing up a few things, and like you, wasn't all that jazzed about facing a more dangerous group of demons. He gave me some pretty good pushback, but when he heard that an Archangel was driving this train, he caved. He said he'll be here as soon as he can get clear."

"I just can't believe that an Immortal is working with demons in this scheme," Lucy said, then narrowed her eyes. "Although, considering that Deidre had those demonic acolytes of hers doing her dirty work to raise my...uh...that abomination, Darius, as well as the Erinyes that attacked us both on the beach and later on the Tor, I suppose I shouldn't be all that shocked."

"I know," Dory replied. "Jerahmeel said that this Verrine is a fallen angel and is very dangerous. He also indicated that Dorian Smyth may think they are working together but they're really not. He said Verrine is devious and will have her own plan of how to screw up this world by changing history, and thereby changing the future. Who knows what the hell that will look like."

"Well, isn't that just a horrible thought?" Ethan muttered.

"You can say that again," Lucy agreed. "I like my world just as it is, thank you very much." She turned to Dory. "So, the Archangel wants us to find this Key and protect her?"

Dory shook her head. "Not exactly. Jerahmeel knows who and where she is. But the woman, this Kinna McComish, has no idea of the power that she has inside of her or what her purpose actually is for this world. Jerahmeel is going to have Sorcha Doyle set up a meet with Kinna, and we're supposed to explain it all to her...somehow."

"So, who is Sorcha Doyle?" Ethan asked. "And what is her roll in this weirdness?"

"Evidently, Sorcha is an Immortal who's been helping Kinna stifle her visions and dreams with some kind of potion," Dory replied. "She's living under the guise of being a white witch. Anyway, from what Jerahmeel said, the visions and such are now bleeding through, which is how they knew that the entity inside her was waking. Though it sounds like they either don't know why, or just aren't saying."

"Uh-huh." Ethan looked skeptical. "So, to be clear, there's a bad Immortal working with a fallen angel and looking to dominate the world by changing history. And then there's a good Immortal, living as a witch, who's already helping The Key. Do I have that right?"

Dory and Kaden exchanged looks, and then Kaden chuckled. "Yeah, that's about it, buddy."

"All right." Ethan paused a moment, and then frowned. "So, why can't this good Immortal explain it all to this Kinna? Why do we have to do it? I mean, if Sorcha Doyle already has a relationship with her, I don't get why she can't do the deed."

"We asked the Archangel about that. You know, like, why us?" Ian chimed in. "But he was very evasive about that as well."

Ethan stared at Ian for a moment before giving a brief nod. "Okay, then. So, what's the sketchy plan? And how do we flesh it out and prop it up?"

Dory got up and cleared some space on the table then pulled out her notebook. "I made some notes just after Jerahmeel disappeared, while Kaden and Ian were making calls. I have some thoughts."

"Way to be on top of it, Chosen One," Ethan crowed. "At least somebody's working the case. What's up with you, K? Where are your notes?"

"Bite me, Walker," Kaden retorted. "Now, shut up and listen."

Ethan grinned again and put up his hands in surrender, then made a sweeping motion toward Dory. "By all means, proceed, Oh, Chosen One."

Dory laughed but soon got down to business. "All right, I've made a list of things we need to cover before we get the call from Sorcha Doyle. First, we need to do some research on this fallen angel Verrine. Since, evidently, she's very dangerous and may be stringing Dorian Smyth along, orchestrating things from behind the scenes."

"I can do that," Lucy said. "I know someone in Rome that will be able to give us that information, or at least, as much as there is." When Ethan turned to her with a quizzical look, she smirked. "What? Tanner isn't the only one with some stellar contacts."

"Okay, so Lucy will take that task." Dory ran her finger down the page in her notebook. "Next, we need to find out more about both Dorian Smyth and Sorcha Doyle. It will be good to know who we're up against, as well as who we will be working with."

"I could do that," Ethan volunteered, but Ian shook his head.

"No, boy-o, that'll be me," Ian murmured. "Don't forget, these are Immortals and not folks you can get info on by simply running them through a police database."

Kaden nodded. "He's right, Ethan. They probably have a whole crafted background that would give you a lot of false information, anyway."

Ian continued, "I know a couple of Sentinels from the old days that may be able to give us some good intel on both of them. After that, I can reach out to Merlin. He's pretty much the top of the food chain and usually knows the down and dirty on just about everything and everyone Immortal-wise."

"Then what do you want me to tackle?" Ethan asked.

Dory tapped her pen against her lip for a moment. "Well, you could actually put your police database to use by doing a rundown on Kinna McComish herself. Who she is, who her people are, where she comes from, what she's been doing, etcetera."

"Good deal. I'm on it."

"What are we going to be doing?" Kaden asked.

"We're going to start compiling everything we get, so that when Tanner and Wyatt get here, we'll have a clear outline down on paper, maybe adjust it with whatever they can give us, and then hammer down that sketchy plan." Dory paused and looked around the table. "We don't know how soon Jerahmeel will be talking to Sorcha Doyle, or how she will respond to his directive, but I want to know what we're getting into from all angles, and before we get a call from her. We may not have any choice in this mission, but if we're gonna do this, we're going to be as prepared as possible and go into it with our eyes wide open."

"Okay, people," Kaden said, getting up from the table. "Let's move like we've got somewhere to be."

They had a lot to do, Kaden thought. He could only hope that they could get it together before they found themselves in a situation they couldn't control. He had no idea how much—or little—time they had to prepare, but he had a terrible feeling that it wasn't gonna be enough.

10

"Okay, *please* tell me that you're not going back to that place," Kari exclaimed as Olivia handed her a glass of wine and then poured another for Kinna.

They'd come back to Olivia's condo in Portland's Pearl District Sunday night after a lovely dinner at their favorite Italian restaurant—something they did several times a month—where Kinna had just explained the strange occurrence which had taken place at her final therapy session on Friday.

"Seriously," Kari continued. "Whether what this Tess person said is true or not, the whole episode just seems really creepy and wrong. And, I'm sorry, speaking to you telepathically? The both of them?" Kari gave an exaggerated shiver. "I don't even have words for that."

"Creepy and wrong—that's exactly what *I* said!" Olivia replied, gesturing toward Kinna with her own wine glass. "I *told* you on Friday at lunch that there was something wrong with that woman, didn't I? I'm not kidding, Victoria Newcomb is wrong on so very many levels. And this Tess doesn't seem to be much better."

"Yeah, yeah." Kinna waved away Olivia's comment. "To

answer your question, Kari...hell no, I'm not going back there. I'd already decided to discontinue therapy before this last appointment, but after being weirded out by the whole thing? Well, I don't think I could get past what happened even if I wanted to continue with Dr. Newcomb. So, no, I'm not going back anytime soon."

"Hallelujah!" Olivia shouted, and then grinned when Kinna rolled her eyes. "I'm just saying. I worried about you seeing that horrible woman, so no matter how it came about, I'm glad you're not going back."

"So, what did the receptionist have to say when you called her?" Kari asked. "What was her story? Did she explain?"

"No. That's another odd thing." Kinna shook her head. "I've tried calling Tess several times since my appointment at the number she gave me, but it always goes straight to voicemail. I've left message after message, but she hasn't returned any of my calls. So, I still have no idea what it was all about."

Kari frowned. "That's a bit suspect, isn't it? I mean, if the situation was so dire that she'd put the fear of God into you like that and couldn't talk about it at the office, you'd think she'd be anxious to explain as soon as possible. At the very least, you'd think she'd return your phone messages."

"Well, I don't know why you'd want to contact her at all." Olivia poked a finger at Kinna. "The whole story sounds fishy to me. I say, be done with anything having to do with Victoria Newcomb, and good riddance."

"Way to be supportive, Liv," Kari said sarcastically.

"Oh, please. Look, I'm supportive of the fact that Kinna's done with that pathetic excuse for a therapist. That's what I'm supportive of."

"But aren't you at least curious?" Kinna asked.

"About what?"

"About what?" Kinna gawked at her. "Are you kidding me? Have you not been listening to anything I've said?"

Olivia put up a hand. "Okay, okay, don't unravel. I said the whole thing was creepy and wrong, didn't I?"

"You also said that you'd done some digging into Dr. Newcomb and think she's dangerous. I don't want to be looking over my shoulder and wondering what the hell Tess was talking about from here to eternity. I'm telling you, she seemed genuinely frightened for me. Freaked me out, I can tell you, whether I believe what she was saying or not. *She* obviously believed it."

"And if she's not answering her phone now, what if something happened to her because she warned Kinna?" Kari suggested.

"For the love of God, do you *hear* yourselves?" It was Olivia's turn to roll her eyes. "Take a breath, you two. This is not some kind of conspiracy. You both are beginning to sound like poorly written pulp fiction."

"But—"

"Listen, do I think Victoria Newcomb is dangerous? Hell yes! You're correct, Kinna, I did look into her background. And though what I found was more circumstantial than anything, there *were* some very disturbing inconsistencies as well. Meaning, I think she may be the worst therapist ever. Totally unqualified. But I never meant that she was dangerous in a *physical* way. Besides—and no offense, Kinna—like you said, if Newcomb was gonna target someone for whatever reason, why on earth would it be you?"

Kinna frowned into her wine glass. "I don't know. It's just all so bizarre and a shade alarming. I'd really like to find out what it all means, if for no other reason than to set my mind at ease."

Kari gave Olivia a considering look. "So, what about the voices Kinna heard? She's had crazy-wild abilities in the psychic area since she was little. You can't deny that whether you believe in it or not." She glanced at Kinna. "You're sure of what you heard, right?"

"Absolutely. Tess's thoughts were loud and clear, and like I said, she admitted as much later. As for Dr. Newcomb, it was definitely her voice in my head, though whether they were actually her thoughts or not, I can't say. It's never really happened to me like this before. I mean, I've heard voices in the past, but where they came from, I couldn't tell you. They were just random voices telling me about things that were going to happen. Tess was pretty wigged when I told her that I'd also heard the doctor's voice in my head."

"So, what if this all has to do with your gift?" Kari continued. "Maybe this shadowy group the doctor belongs to wants to use you in some way." She picked up her wine glass but set it back down as she warmed to her idea. "Tess said that they were looking for something valuable, right? Maybe they think you can help them find it, like maybe in one of your visions or dreams."

Olivia laughed out loud. "So, let me get this straight. Now you're saying that some shadow operation wants to use Kinna's abilities to find...what? Treasure? Are you kidding me with this?"

Kari narrowed her eyes. "Don't be an ass, Liv. This is some seriously weird shit, and you know it."

"Olivia, how do you explain the fact that I never told the doctor that I was taking the potion Sorcha Doyle gave me to block my visions and nightmares, yet she seemed to know, was clearly thinking it?"

"But honey, you just said that though it was Newcomb's voice you heard, you couldn't be sure they were really her thoughts." Olivia blew out a breath. "Look, I'm not trying to be difficult. I'm not," she insisted when Kari gave her a skeptical look. "I'm just playing devil's advocate here."

"Or spouting annoying attorney-speak," Kari muttered. "Just admit it. You've always had a smidgen of doubt when it came to Kinna's abilities."

Olivia glared in Kari's direction. "I have not. Don't be insulting."

"Come on, Olivia. You question everything."

"Well, of course I do. I mean, it's just that..." Olivia looked back and forth between Kari and Kinna before sighing. "Okay, I guess you have a fair point, but it's not that I don't believe what Kinna's experienced, I just..."

Kari tilted her head and smiled. "Require irrefutable proof, counselor?"

Kinna laughed out loud at the look on Olivia's face. "It's okay, Liv. Really. I don't hold it against you. There are things that I've seen in visions that have materialized, that I can prove happened, but I've had other visions where there's no way for me to know if they've occurred or not. Hell, half the time *I'm* not sure what's real. Sometimes I think I'm just slowly losing my mind for all to see."

"Okay, now that's just bullshit, and you know it. You are as sane as anyone I know," Olivia groused.

"Ha! That's not saying much, pal," Kari put in. "We both know some pretty crazy-ass people."

"Unfortunately, that's very true." Olivia grinned, and then shook her head. "Look, all I'm saying here is let's not get carried away with unsubstantiated theories just yet, okay? Let's just try to focus on what we know...irrefutably."

"That's precisely why we need to talk to Tess." Kari sighed and finished off her wine.

Olivia narrowed her eyes. "And who's 'we', Miss Thing?"

"I repeat, don't be an ass. Listen, I think we should go down there."

"And *I* repeat, who's we? I can't go into Newcomb's practice.

I've met her a few times, remember? And I probably wasn't the nicest person she's ever met as I didn't like her from the moment I met her."

"Shocking," Kari retorted with a grin.

"God, you're so funny! But trust me, she *will* remember me. And Kinna can't go back there, either. For God's sake, she just got away from that place. That wouldn't look suspicious or anything."

Kari shrugged. "Okay. So, we go down there, and you two can wait in the car. I'll go in and see if Tess is there."

Kinna considered the idea for a moment. "What if she's not there? What would you say?"

"Why, I'm looking for Dr. Addison, of course." Kari put on an insincere smile. "Oh, he's retired and no longer here? Well, gee, that's a shame, but thanks for your help. Sorry to have bothered you."

"And if she is there?" Olivia asked. "What then?"

"Duh. I ask her what the hell...obviously."

Olivia and Kinna looked at each other, and then both burst into laughter.

"Well, alright then," Olivia said a moment later. "Sounds like we're taking a road trip. Is tomorrow soon enough for you two conspiracy theorists for this covert operation?"

It was late by the time Kinna got back to the estate in Helvetia, and the conversation she'd had with her friends was still running around in her head. She'd tried the number Tess had given her again from Olivia's condo, but like before, it had gone straight to voicemail. The argument Olivia had made about the burden of proof still bothered her. Case in point, she really had no way of proving that the phone number was actually Tess's cell phone because the voicemail had an automated recording. She couldn't even point to the sticky note the receptionist had given her as proof because she seemed to have misplaced it.

It was frustrating, but what was worse, she'd only been half-kidding when she'd told Olivia that she sometimes thought she was slowly losing her mind.

They'd decided to meet at Java Jive the next day at noon and head over to Dr. Newcomb's office from there, so she figured she was going to need a good night's sleep. Though it was close to midnight, Kinna took a long, hot shower to try and wash away the dark thoughts and lull herself into a state of relaxation. Since Sorcha had called to say that she'd have to reschedule their Monday appointment, Kinna took the last of the potion Sorcha had already given her and finally climbed into bed just after one o'clock. She began to drift almost as soon as she closed her eyes.

"Are you ready for this, Kinna?" Olivia asked.

"Ready for what?" Kinna opened her eyes and saw that they were sitting in the parking lot of Dr. Newcomb's practice. And it was dark, with the only illumination coming from the few lights in the parking lot. "When did we get here? We were supposed to come during office hours." She turned then and found she was alone in the vehicle. "Liv?"

She was dreaming. That much she was aware of. But even knowing it, Kinna could feel her anxiety level begin to climb when she looked through the windshield and saw Olivia and Kari standing on the sidewalk in front of the doctor's office. Olivia turned slowly and motioned for her to join them.

No, Liv, I don't want to, Kinna thought. This wasn't the plan. But like the stupid heroine in a horror flick who hears a noise in the basement, then grabs a flashlight and heads down the creaky staircase to check it out, Kinna climbed out of the vehicle and started across the parking lot. Her anxiety quickly escalated into fear and her heart began to pound in her chest, but she was unsure just what it was that she was suddenly so afraid of. Her friends seemed miles away, and the distance between her and them was like slogging through waist-deep water, but after a time she finally stepped up onto the sidewalk between them.

"The door's locked, and there doesn't seem to be anyone here," Kari whispered.

"Well, that stands to reason, doesn't it? We were supposed to come during the day. It is long past office hours," Kinna replied inanely.

"But I swear I heard noises coming from inside. Can you see anything in there?"

Taking a ragged breath and tamping down the dread she felt, Kinna cupped her eyes as she peered through the side window into the office lobby. At first, she couldn't really make out anything. It was just as dark inside the lobby as it was where they stood. But after a few moments, her eyes adjusted and things began to take shape. Kinna could vaguely distinguish the dark outline of furniture—lobby chairs and tables—and toward the back of the room she could just make out the reception desk. While she strained to see more clearly, an eerie glow began to seep out from under the office door at the rear of the lobby, and as she continued to watch, the office door slowly started to open.

Abruptly backing away from the window, Kinna had a very bad feeling and was suddenly unwilling to see any more or get any closer to whatever was happening inside in the darkness. "I don't think this is such a good idea, you guys. I think we should go," she whispered.

"But you wanted to know what was happening here, remember?" Olivia asked.

"I know, but something about this feels...very wrong."

"I would say that's probably an understatement, Kinna McComish," a deep baritone voice said near her left ear, causing her to just about jump out of her skin.

Turning, she gasped. Her friends had vanished—as they some-

times did in dreamscapes—and standing next to her was the man from her apocalyptic nightmare. "You again!"

He was wearing much the same thing as the first time she'd conjured him: jeans, boots, and the long black duster over a shockingly white shirt. His amethyst eyes twinkled in the meager light, and when he smiled, his teeth seemed so brilliant as to glow in the darkness surrounding them.

"There is nothing good here, Child of Light. You are sensible to be wary."

"Yes. I am *wary, but I don't understand why. What am I doing here? What's inside there?"*

He reached out and slipped a strand of loose hair behind her ear in an almost parental fashion. "Evil lives here, child," *he murmured.* "Can't you feel it?"

A shiver made its way down Kinna's spine as she glanced fleetingly at the office window. "It made me nauseous before. I came away feeling ill for a time."

He nodded. "You were right to pull away when you did, but you waited much too long. It won't be that easy now."

"What are you talking about? What won't be easy?" *It felt like a bitter cold was oozing from her very bones, and she trembled with it. What did this all mean? And did she really want to know?*

"Sticking your head in the sand will serve no purpose, Kinna," *he said, as if reading her mind.* "As I told you before, it has begun, and it won't be long before you're found. We must prepare, child. Soon."

She shook her head and tried to back away but seemed to be rooted to the spot where she stood. "Who will find me? What does that even mean?"

"Soon all will be revealed. Until then..." *Reaching out, he lightly touched her forehead.*

"Wait!" Kinna jack-knifed straight up in bed, her nightshirt soaked through, pulse racing, and breath heaving as if she'd just run a marathon. "Sweet Jesus!" she gasped as she rubbed her forehead where she could still feel his touch. "Can't I just sleep through one fucking night without being frightened out of my mind?"

Glancing at the digital clock on the night stand, she squeezed her eyes shut briefly when she saw the time. Four a.m. With a sigh, she climbed out of bed and stumbled into the bathroom and did something she hadn't done in a very long time. She poured a glass of water and took two tablets of a prescription sleep aid. With any luck, it would at least allow her a few hours of decent sleep, preferably without the added nightmares.

Studying herself in the mirror, the hollow look in her eyes, the dark circles underneath them—and the faint golden smudge in the middle of her forehead—she shook her head. "What the hell is happening to me? And what's begun?"

Fortunately, the sleep aid seemed to do the trick. Kinna had dropped off and slept straight through until ten o'clock that morning, though as she pulled up in front of Java Jive two hours later, she felt a bit worse for wear. At least she hadn't been plagued by any other nightmares that she could remember.

She came in through the back entrance and went directly to Kari's office where she found both of her friends waiting for her.

"Dear God!" Olivia exclaimed when she walked in. "What the hell happened to you? You look exhausted."

"Gee thanks, Liv. It just so happens that I *am* exhausted."

"Oh, sweetie," Kari murmured. "Didn't sleep well?"

Kinna plopped down into the extra chair and rubbed her eyes. "You could say that. Had a doozy of a nightmare about our little mission today, only we were executing it late at night."

"Oooh, very covert," Olivia said, wiggling her eyebrows.

"Very unsettling, to say the least, and no fun at all. Had a real horror flick feel to it. Woke up drenched at four this morning."

"Crap. I'm sorry, Kinna," Kari replied, concern coloring her tone. "Did you get any decent sleep after that?"

Kinna sighed. "Slept from about four-thirty until ten. After I got up and took a couple sleeping pills, that is. And you *know* how much I like to do that."

"You know, we can wait and do this another time if you're not feeling up to it."

"No. I just want to get through it and be done."

"So, did this nightmare of yours give any clues as to what to watch for?" Olivia asked. "Or if your receptionist friend is there?"

"Olivia." Kari gave the woman a warning look.

"What?"

"Don't be a shit."

"How is that being a shit?" Olivia crossed her arms. "Kinna's dreams and nightmares are sometimes prophetic, aren't they? I just thought she might have seen something, and maybe we wouldn't have to even go."

Kinna chuckled and shook her head. "No such luck this time, Liv. It was more like, 'ignore that noise coming from the basement. No, no, don't go down there, you idiot!' I kid you not, I seriously considered just staying up the rest of the night. Anyway, didn't see anything..."

"Kinna?" Kari leaned forward. "What is it?"

Thinking back, Kinna frowned. "Well, there was one thing."

"And that would be?" Olivia prompted after a moment.

"The guy from Thursday evening's apocalyptic nightmare made an appearance in this one too."

"You mean that gorgeous hunk you imagined reappeared last night?" Olivia asked. "Interesting. What did he have to say this time? Anything useful?"

"We were outside the office, which was locked and dark. Like I said, it was evening in my dream. I was looking through the window into the office, trying to see if anyone was inside, and he was just there. He said, 'Evil lives here, Child of Light. Can't you feel it?'"

"Oh yes, very nice," Olivia sneered. "Why is it that the prettiest ones are always no help at all?"

"Speaking of no help at all." Kari gave Olivia a pointed look before turning to Kinna. "So, what did he mean with the 'Child of Light' bit?"

"I have no idea. He called me that the first time as well. Anyway, he said I was right to stop seeing Dr. Newcomb."

Olivia crossed her legs and nodded. "All right. I'll give him points for that."

"But he said that I'd done it too late," Kinna continued. "That it wouldn't be easy now."

Kari put up a hand. "Wait—what wouldn't be easy now?"

Kinna shook her head. "He didn't say. But right before I woke up, he told me that it wouldn't be long before they found me."

"Yeah, nothing cryptic about that," Olivia muttered. "The prosecution rests."

"That's it. I say let's go and get this recon mission over with. Maybe Tess can clear it all up for us." Kari stood up and grabbed her purse. "Olivia, you're driving."

"Fine. I'm parked out front. But I want another latte for the road."

They headed down the hall toward the front counter and, as Olivia stepped around to order, Kinna and Kari started for the door. As they did, Kinna scanned the room. The coffeehouse was fairly full at twelve-thirty, and as they reached the door, her scan caught a familiar face.

And she felt the blood drain from her own.

"Kinna?" Kari asked. "Are you okay? You've gone white as a sheet."

She swallowed hard and leaned toward her friend. "Kari, do you know that man in the corner? The one reading a book?"

Kari followed her gaze to find the man she was talking about, and then smiled. "Oh, yeah. I don't know his name, but he's the new coffeehouse hunk I told you about. Why?"

Before Kinna could find her voice, the man glanced up and their eyes met and held. Her breath backed up in her lungs, and she felt the power of his gaze from across the room. Grabbing Kari's shirt sleeve, she pulled her friend out the door.

"Hey! Kinna, what's going on? What's the matter?"

She ignored Kari's outburst and continued toward Olivia's car.

"You two do know you guys can't get into the car without me, right?" Olivia called as she followed them out into the front parking lot.

Kari finally tugged free of Kinna's grasp and pulled her around to face them. "Kinna, what's happened? Talk to us?"

Taking a deep breath, Kinna blew it out slowly and tried to quiet her unease. "That man in there? The girls' new coffee-house hunk? He's the guy from my dreams."

11

Tanner Sweetwater arrived late Monday afternoon. The man had come roaring up the winding gravel road, spewing dirt and rocks as he rounded the point, turned onto the short lane, and then into Kaden's driveway.

Kaden had just come back from a walk in the woods with Henry and watched Sweetwater climb out of the sleek, jet-black BMW. Tanner hadn't changed much since the last time Kaden had seen him, just a few years older. Now, in his late thirties, the shapeshifter was tall with deeply tanned skin and long, ebony hair worn in a braid down his back. And then there were the startling pearlescent-gray eyes—unique wolf's eyes—which always weirded Kaden out just a bit.

He smiled to himself. The one thing that was exactly the same was Tanner's appearance. The man was a study all in one color; black jeans, tight black t-shirt, black motorcycle boots, and an expensive-looking black leather bomber jacket that had seen as much mileage as the boots on his feet. And, of course, the rings on every finger and both thumbs, each with a different ancient symbol etched into its surface.

"Hey, Tanner." Kaden greeted him. "Glad you could make it. You have any trouble finding the place?"

Tanner grinned. "No, man. The GPS brought me right to your doorstep." He stuck out his hand. "Good to see you, Warrior."

Kaden shook his hand. *Guess our history is just that, history*, he thought. It looked as if Tanner held no grudges, so he wouldn't either. They'd lived through a pretty brutal couple of weeks together the last time they'd met, so that was something they had in common. Just the same, this time around, Kaden would be making sure the man was clear on what was expected from everyone on the team. And that started with complete honesty. No more secrets, no matter how small.

"Nice looking ride," Kaden said. "Yours or a rental?"

"Oh no, she's mine. I don't do rentals. I drove up from Santa Barbara, and in mid to late October, you never really know how the weather's going to change from northern California into Oregon. Or when that change will suddenly happen, for that matter. Especially, along the coast. Anyway, I usually leave the bike in the garage for the winter."

"You drove up from Santa Barbara straight through?"

"Oh, hell no. I drove up as far as Eureka on Sunday. Had to meet a guy about a thing," Tanner said with a grin. "Left Eureka this morning around eight. It was a pretty decent drive up 101."

Kaden gestured to the Beamer. "In that beauty, I guess it would be."

"That it was. Really fabulous in spots." Tanner looked down at the dog sitting next to Kaden. "And who is this big guy?"

"This would be Henry," Kaden replied. "My big lug."

"He's a good looking Rott. Hey, buddy." Tanner put out his hand for Henry to sniff.

Henry gave a cross between a growl and a whine before taking a few steps back.

"Geez, Henry. Don't be such a jerk," Kaden admonished.

Tanner laughed, unoffended. "No worries. Looks like he can sense my inner wolf. But we'll get past it. It may just take some time for him to get used to me."

Though Tanner seemed to leave their issues in the past, Kaden wasn't really ready to discuss Tanner's wolf side just yet. So, he thought it best to step out of the way and let Ethan and Tanner work through their issues first.

"Well, we'd better head inside," he said. "Ethan and Lucy got in Saturday night. We've already started with the research, and we'll bring you up to speed. You may be able to do some fleshing out with some of the data, especially on the demonology end of things."

"Good deal. Let me just grab my duffel from the rig."

The rest of the team was crowded around the kitchen table studying something that Lucy had received from her contact in Rome when Kaden and Tanner came into the room with Henry following close behind but still a little wary of Tanner.

"Look who Henry and I found in the driveway," Kaden said as Tanner dropped his duffel bag in the corner and came over to the table.

"Hey, Lucy," Tanner said, giving her a quick hug before turning to Ethan. "Mascot—I mean...Ethan." He grinned, and to everyone's surprise, stuck out his hand. "How's it goin', dude?"

Ethan sighed and, with a reluctant smile, shook his head and clasped the man's hand. "Wolf boy—I mean...Tanner," he answered in kind. "Not bad. How's it goin' with you?"

Tanner laughed. "Oh, you know. Another day, another weird-ass mission, right?" He turned to Dory and Ian. "And the Chosen One with my buddy, Ian. Looks like the gang's all here."

"Not quite, boy-o," Ian replied. "We've got one more on the way."

"Oh, yeah? Who's that?"

Dory tilted her head and narrowed her eyes. "Really? Who do you think it is, Tanner? Who's missing from this picture?"

Tanner looked around the room at the faces looking back at him. "Okay. I suppose the mercenary will be joining us as well?"

"Got it in one, dude," Ethan said with a smirk.

Tanner hooked his thumbs in his pockets and studied the floor for a moment before looking up with a nod. "That's probably a wise choice considering what we may be up against. From the little info I've gotten, I guess we can use all the help we can get."

"Who are you and what have you done with Tanner Sweetwater?" Lucy asked with a sober look.

After a brief pause, they all broke into laughter.

Even Tanner joined in. "Yeah, yeah. I get it. I was kind of a dick the last time around. I just wasn't used to working with a team. I've always been more comfortable working alone. That's not an excuse. It just is what it is. I guess you could say that I got a little clarity on the whole thing in the months after the Tor."

"And trust me when I say, I'm sure we will all be grateful for that clarity," Dory said with a chuckle. "Now, please do yourself and all of us a favor and try to hold on to it."

Tanner nodded. "Yes, ma'am. I can't promise that I won't backslide or act like a dick off and on, but I will do my best."

Kaden smiled. "That's all we can ask for. Well, that and honesty, transparency, etcetera."

"Dude, I have no more secrets to share. But if one comes up, I'll blurt it out immediately." Tanner looked over the paperwork on the table. "So, you want to bring me up to speed on what we're doing and where we're at? I mean, I got a visit from Morianna right after you called. She gave me the basics but not a ton of details, per her usual."

It took about twenty minutes to fill him in. Turned out that Tanner actually knew quite a bit about the situation, so Kaden figured Morianna had given him more details than he had let on. But the man had revealed Morianna's visit right up front, hadn't held anything back that Kaden could see, so he was willing to let it slide for now. However, Dory had questions.

"You don't seem surprised by the whole Archangel deal, Tanner," Dory said. "Is that just because Morianna told you about Jerahmeel? Or something more?"

"Are you asking me if I knew that angels existed? Or if I've ever had an encounter with one?"

"Either." Dory paused for a moment. "Or both, I guess. Just seems to me that with your knowledge and experience with demons, you may have had some encounters with the other side of that coin. And you definitely don't seem surprised by our visit from Jerahmeel."

Tanner pulled off his jacket, hanging it over the back of the chair next to Ian at the table, and then leaned down on the chair. "It's not exactly a stretch to come to that conclusion. I have heard stories among my people and beyond—known others who've told of encounters with angelic beings—but I've never seen one myself nor had any interaction with one. Having said that, my thoughts have always been that if there were demons in this world—of which there are plenty in all shapes and sizes, believe me—then why wouldn't there be angels here as well?" He pulled out the chair and sat down. "You know, my culture has stories and legends of hundreds of entities; spirits both evil and benevolent. Morianna did mention this Jerahmeel to me, but like I said, I'm not keeping anything to myself. I've never met or even seen an angel. That I know of, that is." He grinned, and then motioned to the paperwork on the table. "So, what's all this about?"

"I made some inquiries to a friend in Rome," Lucy replied. "I just got these documents via email from her."

"Who'd you talk to in Rome?"

Lucy grinned. "Celestina Notaro."

Tanner nodded. "Nice. So, what did you ask her for, and what did she give you?"

"It's some information on Verrine."

"Ah, a fallen angel?" Tanner asked. "Intriguing."

"You got it."

Ethan frowned. "Wait. I thought this Verrine was a demon. Like, of impatience or something."

Kaden nodded. "She is now, but Jerahmeel said that she's a fallen angel from the Order of Thrones."

"Yeah, in the beginning she was an angel of the First Sphere." Tanner narrowed his eyes in thought. "Order of Thrones sounds right."

"So, what's the difference between fallen angels and demons?" Ethan asked.

"Well, the term fallen angel doesn't really appear in the old texts. These are angels who've sinned or tempted humans to sin," Lucy explained. "They've 'fallen' from God's grace for one reason or another and have been expelled from heavenly realms. That's where the term comes from."

"But the difference is fairly simple from everything that I've read," Tanner added. "Fallen angels—for lack of a better term—can actually manifest corporally. Meaning, they can appear in full physical form, interact with this realm spiritually or physically. Demons are spirit and need to *inhabit* a physical body in order to interact with us."

Ian nodded. "Like that Sepivi demon we encountered in Texas that was hiding inside Hester Mayfield and attacked Kaden."

"Yeah, and those gruesome acolytes that Deidre had with her on the Tor." Ethan gave an exaggerated shudder. "Really creepy. They were once children, right?"

"Correct," Tanner said. "At some point, they were possessed

by Reiver demons. See, some demons, like the Sepivi, can be expelled once they've inhabited a body, and in most cases, either destroyed or returned to their own realm. As long as they are removed within a certain amount of time, the body they've inhabited can recover. But with Reivers, once they've taken over, whoever or whatever they inhabit is lost forever. The body deteriorates into what we saw and dealt with on the Tor."

"That's just wrong on so many levels," Ethan muttered.

"Agreed," Ian chimed in.

"So, what did your contact have to say about this Verrine?" Kaden asked. "Jerahmeel indicated that she was very dangerous and probably had her own plan. I got the feeling that Dorian Smyth doesn't know what he's dealing with in her."

"Dorian Smyth?" Tanner sat up. "The Immortal living in Portland? He's a real piece of work, too. Narcissistic, power hungry, ruthless." He shook his head. "He's the leader of sorts of an Immortal group in the West Hills. I'm not surprised he's part of this, but if he thinks he's working with Verrine, he's more of an idiot than I thought. Jerahmeel is correct. She's dangerous, but only because of how manipulative she is."

"Tanner's right," Lucy agreed. "From what Celestina says, Verrine is an influence peddler. She is the demon of impatience, so she uses her influence to manipulate humans to get what she wants. If she's somehow found out about Kinna and what the entity inside her can do, that could be really bad news."

"Absolutely," Tanner said. "If, as Jerahmeel told you, Kinna is a Time Mender, then I really hate to think about what kind of apocalyptic bullshit Verrine and her ilk could perpetrate on this world should she get her hands on Kinna."

"Yeah, that was pretty much what Jerahmeel had to say." Dory sat down at the table and thumbed through her notes. "He stressed that Dorian Smyth wasn't a patient man, and that if he and Verrine hadn't found Kinna yet, it won't take them long. He indicated that they were already closing in on her identity." She looked up and blew out a breath. "Sorcha Doyle will be getting in touch soon, so we've got to be prepared. We need to gather and digest as much intel as we can before we get the call, so we're not caught with our knickers around our ankles."

Tanner scrubbed his hands over his face, the rings on his fingers and thumbs winking in the overhead light. "For fuck's sake, it's just raining Immortals, isn't it? You guys do know that like Dorian Smyth, Sorcha Doyle is also one of you, right?"

"Yes, Tanner," Dory replied. "Jerahmeel told us that. It seems that she's living in Portland as well, under the guise of being a white witch."

"Ha." Tanner shook his head. "White witch. First do no harm."

"Anyway, it seems that she has a relationship with Kinna, has been helping her stifle the visions and dreams with potions to suppress them. But those visions and dreams are now beginning to seep through."

"Wow, this is getting better and better." Tanner looked around the table.

"Ian spoke to Merlin earlier about both Dorian Smyth and Sorcha Doyle. Merlin said pretty much the same thing about Smyth."

"Aye." Ian nodded. "Merlin said that Smyth is just over 500 years old, but that his immortality was a mistake made by an Ancient back in the day when the rules about such things were vague and 'flexible'." He added air quotes with his fingers for the latter part. "Merlin's distaste was evident. However, it was apparent that he felt the opposite way about Sorcha Doyle, said that she was a pretty straight shooter. She's been immortal for a couple centuries and has learned to keep her head down. These days, she spends her time helping those in need."

Dory smiled at Tanner. "So, yes, it seems first do no harm. I know you meant it in a disparaging way, but it sounds like she really does try to live by that adage."

Tanner shrugged. "To each their own, I guess. So, what's next? What else needs researching?"

"I spoke to one of my guys, and we did a run on Kinna McComish," Ethan answered, pulling out his own notebook. "Sounds like she had a rough time of it growing up. She was an only child. Then her parents were killed in a car crash when she was seventeen, so she went to live with her paternal grandfather, one Brenden McComish."

"Fuck me!" Tanner exclaimed. "*The* Brenden McComish? McComish Industries?"

"One and the same," Ethan confirmed. "There was no mention of anyone on the maternal side. It looks like he took guardianship of her just after her parents died. She must have felt comfortable with him because she continued to live with him after she turned eighteen."

Tanner whistled through his teeth. "The guy is loaded, has his fingers into a lot of different things."

"Yeah, well, the guy passed away about four years ago." Ethan put up a finger. "And wait for it...left the whole shebang to his granddaughter. Lock, stock, and barrel, as they say."

"Wow. So, rough childhood and now set for life."

Ethan frowned. "Well, sure, if you don't count being plagued with visions and prophetic dreams that you don't understand, losing your parents at seventeen, and then losing the only other adult in your life that grounds you. If you call that set for life, then yeah, she's set." He shook his head and gave Tanner a disappointed look. "You did say that you would probably backslide or act like a dick from time to time, right?"

Tanner put up his hands in surrender. "Okay, okay, don't blow a gasket. It just took me by surprise, is all. I mean, I've read articles about Brenden McComish. He was an entrepreneurial legend."

"In any event, Kinna sits on the boards of several of the companies he left her. She also started a hugely Popular coffee-house in Tanasbourne called Java Jive in his honor. Guess a good cup of joe was Brenden's drink of choice." Ethan flipped through his notes. "Anyway, that seems to be her baby and where she's focused most of the time. Hired one Kari Burke, a childhood friend, to manage the establishment. It looks like Kinna's surrounded herself there with solid friends."

Dory nodded. "That would make total sense with all she's dealt with over the years. There's no telling what she went through growing up, or how her parents handled the prophetic visions and dreams she most certainly had even as a child. After they die on her, she bonds with the only other adult she can trust. Then he's gone and who else is there?"

"Good point. Anyway, Brenden McComish built himself a sprawling English manor out in Helvetia a few decades ago, and left that to Kinna as well. That's where she continues to live today."

"Why wouldn't she?" Lucy asked. "I mean, it's probably the one place now that she feels safe, secure. And it undoubtedly holds precious memories of her grandfather."

"Okay," Kaden said. "Anything else, Ethan? Or is that it for Kinna?"

"That's about it. Like Sorcha Doyle, Kinna seems to keep her head down as well. Kind of flies under the radar, does her own thing. Nothing much else to dig up."

"I'd still like to know a bit more about the peripheral players, but this is a good start," Kaden replied. "Now, we just wait for Sorcha Doyle's call."

As if saying it out loud was a catalyst, Dory's cell phone suddenly blared heavy metal rock.

"What the hell is that?" Tanner asked.

"My ringtone. I do love heavy metal," Dory said as she picked up her phone and answered, putting the call on speaker. "Hello?"

"Is this Isadora Winthrop?" the female voice on the other end asked.

"It is."

"My name is Sorcha Doyle. I understand that you've been expecting my call."

"Yes, Sorcha. We have indeed."

Kaden shook his head. *And so it begins*, he thought.

K inna slept late on Tuesday. The previous afternoon had shaken her up pretty good after seeing the man from her dreams literally in the flesh at Java Jive. When he'd looked up from his book and their eyes had connected, she'd been stunned by the power of his gaze. For one brief moment, it had taken her breath away, but what had freaked her out the most was how oddly familiar it had been at the same time—and that familiarity went well beyond her dreams of him. At least, that was how it had felt in that instant. Like, *I have known you for an eternity*. But, of course, that was impossible. She was positive she'd never met him or even seen him before. She definitely would have remembered.

She'd had experiences with déjà vu in past visions and dreams—places, inanimate objects, and yes, random people that she'd known or had met, but she'd never come face-to-face with a complete stranger from those visions. Maybe they'd met in a previous life, because try as she might, she'd been unable to get the sensation of *knowing* him out of her head since that moment when their eyes had met.

After what the man had shown her in her dreams Sunday

night, and then seeing him in the coffeehouse like that the next afternoon, Kinna had been reluctant to follow through with the trip to Dr. Newcomb's office as she and her friends had discussed—even if that plan only had her waiting in the car with Olivia. Those eerie offices in the dark from her dreams, something moving in the inky black shadows at the back of the lobby just out of sight, the feeling of dread that had filled her. It had all followed her into the light of day on Monday, and she hadn't been certain she could handle getting anywhere near those offices.

Kari and Olivia had spent fifteen minutes with her in Java Jive's parking lot trying to talk her down off the ledge, giving her alternate explanations that would explain why the 'coffeehouse hunk' might have been visiting her with dire prophesies in her dreams. All the while, Kinna kept her gaze glued to the front door of the coffeehouse, certain that the man would follow them out to the parking lot at any moment. But he hadn't. And in the end, they'd gone anyway, with Kinna and Olivia waiting in the car in Dr. Newcomb's parking lot while Kari went in to look for Tess, just as they'd planned. However, that plan turned out to be a bust, as Dr. Newcomb had a new receptionist at the desk.

"What did you say when you got in there?" Olivia had asked Kari as she'd driven them back to her condo.

Kari had beamed. "Easy-peasy, pal. Some preppy guy was sitting at the desk. Gave me the once over and then asked if I had an appointment with Dr. Newcomb. I used my best dumb-blonde routine, asking who Dr. Newcomb was and where Dr. Addison had gone. Then I went in for the kill. You know, fluttered my eyelashes a bit."

"You're a brunette," Olivia had reminded her, stating the obvious.

"It's a figure of speech, counselor. Geez, Liv, do you always have to be so literal?"

"I'm an attorney, so yes."

Kari had rolled her eyes at the back of Olivia's head, making Kinna snicker and causing Oliva to glance in the rearview mirror, narrow her eyes, and say, "I saw that."

"You know I love you, Livvy." Kari grinned, then turned sideways in the back seat. "But back to my story. Preppy guy didn't know anything about Dr. Addison. Said he'd only been working there for a few days and didn't know who'd been there before Newcomb. I thanked him and left. Like I said, easy-peasy, lemon squeezy. In and out."

So, after everything was said and done, their excursion hadn't revealed anything they didn't already know, and Tess's whereabouts remained a mystery. Kinna felt her frustration rise again as she dressed in yoga pants and matching top then fed the cat and worked on her second cup of coffee while trying to plan out her day. The silver lining of it all seemed to be that between the shakeup of having her scary dream man come to life in her coffeehouse, and the letdown of learning nothing of Tess's fate at Dr. Newcomb's office, oddly, Kinna had slept through the night like a newborn baby. For the first time in a very long time, if she'd dreamed, she wasn't aware of it.

She was just rinsing her coffee cup and putting it into the dishwasher, trying to choose between doing a few loads of laundry or putting it off a while longer to do some shopping in Hillsboro, when her cell phone rang. When she picked it up and turned it over, she froze. For a second, she stared at the very number she'd been calling off and on since Thursday in the digital readout.

After a moment of surprise, she answered.

"Tess?"

"Oh, geez, Kinna. Thank the gods. Are you okay?"

"I'm fine, Tess. Where have you been? I've been calling and

calling. I was starting to get worried. We even went by the office yesterday to see if you were there."

"What? You went to Newcomb's office? Kinna, I told you never to go back there. Did anyone see you?"

Kinna could hear the panic in Tess's voice and wondered, for the umpteenth time, what the hell was going on with the woman. "I didn't go in, Tess. I went with two of my girlfriends. One of them went in to see if you were there while I waited in the car with the other one. There was some preppy guy sitting at the desk, and my friend was in and out in a few minutes."

"Okay. Good. That's good. So, your friend didn't ask for me?"

"No. She asked for Dr. Addison, but the guy didn't know who that was. Tess, what's going on? You sound scared."

There was a pause, and Kinna could almost feel the woman's hesitation through the phone. "I am scared," Tess finally replied. "And you should be, too."

"Yeah, so you've said, but I still don't know exactly why."

"Can you meet me now? I'll explain everything that I know."

"Tess, this is crazy."

"Kinna, please. I'm worried for you."

"For me? I don't understand. Why are you worried for me? I told you at the office, I'm nobody, remember? I mean, you say there's this malicious group searching for something rare and valuable, and that Dr. Newcomb belongs to this group. You tell me they're zeroed in on me, but I have nothing anyone would consider rare or valuable."

Tess sighed on the other end of the phone. "Kinna, just meet me, and I'll explain. We can meet anywhere you'd like. But it would be best if it was somewhere bright...with lots of people."

Kinna thought for a moment. This whole thing was getting weirder and scarier, if Tess was to be believed. Of course, the woman was sounding more and more like a loon, but on the other hand, if Kinna didn't meet with her, she would always wonder what this craziness had been about, regardless of what did or didn't happen.

She made a quick decision. "Do you know a little bistro in the Pearl called Martine's?"

"No, but I can find it."

"I'll meet you there in forty-five minutes." Kinna paused. "And, Tess, if you no-show on me—"

"Don't worry, I won't," Tess told her. "See you in forty-five minutes. And Kinna, watch your back."

Then the call ended, leaving Kinna with more questions than answers and an uneasy feeling in the pit of her stomach. *Well, I wanted to find out what the woman had been talking about,* she mused, *I guess this is my chance.* With chaotic thoughts buzzing around in her head, she went upstairs to change out of her yoga pants and into some street clothes.

KINNA GOT to Martine's with ten minutes to spare but didn't see Tess anywhere. Taking a table along the back wall with a clear view of the door, she sat down to wait. When the waiter came over, she explained that she was waiting for someone and ordered a glass of iced tea for something to do with her hands. She'd almost ordered a glass of wine, thinking it might steady her a bit, but in the end, thought it best to keep a clear head, especially if this meeting with Tess went sideways.

True to her word, Tess arrived right on time a few minutes later. Kinna watched her walk into the bistro and then look back over her shoulder toward the street as if half expecting to see someone follow her into the restaurant. When she finally turned toward the room, her anxious gaze bounced around until she spotted Kinna waving.

As Tess make her way across the room, Kinna couldn't help but notice the way she kept looking back toward the door. Had someone actually been following her, or was it just some sort of paranoid delusion? The way their last two conversations had gone, Kinna thought delusions wouldn't be a stretch.

This whole situation had taken on a really weird vibe and was more than a little confusing. Tess had always been so pleasant and personable for all of Kinna's appointments with Dr. Addison, and then over the last few months, with Dr. Newcomb. That was until the last few weeks and then with Kinna's final appointment on Thursday. There'd been no reason to suspect that the woman might be troubled or that she had a tenuous grip on reality, but then, she didn't really know Tess other than as the office receptionist.

"Did you have any trouble finding the place?" Kinna asked as Tess sat down on the banquette next to her with her back to the wall instead of taking a seat on the opposite side of the table.

Tess shook her head and made one last scan of the room before turning frightened eyes to Kinna. "Look, I'm sorry for all this cloak and dagger stuff, but I didn't know what else to do. I've been followed several times since leaving Newcomb's office right after you did on Thursday. I knew I couldn't be there when that evil thing got done with her last patient and came out of her office," she said, then murmured under her breath, "I didn't want to end up like Dr. Addison."

Kinna frowned. "Evil thing? Are you talking about Dr. Newcomb?" She lowered her voice. "And what do you mean, 'end up like Dr. Addison'?"

"Look, I told you on Thursday, Newcomb isn't what she seems. Gods, I need something stronger than iced tea." Tess gave her a strained smile and signaled the waiter. "Five o'clock some-where, right?"

"Come on, I know that's what you said about Dr. Newcomb in the office, that she 'wasn't from here', but you never really explained what you meant. Who is she, Tess? And where is she from, if not from here?"

"Like I said, she's evil. And don't look at me like that. I know you felt it, too. You heard her voice in your head, and you were chalk white and a little green around the gills when you came out of her office on Thursday. Don't bother to deny it."

Kinna thought back to those last few minutes in the office when Dr. Newcomb's mere touch had not only made her sick to her stomach, but also had panic rising in her chest. She remembered clearly how she couldn't get away from the place fast enough, and the thought of going back there had felt terrifying. No, she couldn't deny what she'd heard and experienced, but it suddenly seemed like she was tumbling down a rabbit hole and would find something horrific—and yes, evil—waiting at the bottom in the dark.

"Okay." Kinna acknowledged slowly. "You're right about all of that, but I heard your voice in my head as well, remember? And it still doesn't explain what you meant about Dr. Newcomb, does it?"

"Got me there." Tess laughed. "No. I guess it really doesn't explain anything, though you won't like what I have to say."

"Tess, what is it?"

They had to pause their conversation as the waiter interrupted them to take Tess's order.

"I'll just have an Irish coffee, please. And heavy on the Irish, if you know what I mean."

The waiter smiled and nodded. "Double shot of Irish. Got it."

Tess pinned Kinna with a look the minute the waiter walked away. "Like I said, you're not going to like this, but what I meant about Newcomb is that I'm pretty sure she's...not human."

Kinna stared at the woman for a good ten seconds, trying to process what she thought she'd heard and working to find her voice. "Come again? Did you say not human?" she finally asked before putting a hand to her mouth to keep the hysteria she felt from pouring out.

"Kinna, this isn't easy for me to say, let alone for you to comprehend, but what I'm telling you is true. Though I can't put my finger on exactly what Newcomb is, there is something really wrong with her. And yes, whatever it is, it's evil." Tess ran a hand through her shoulder-length, auburn hair and grimaced. "Look, I know how that sounds. You think I'm out of my mind. I get it. And I can't really blame you. It is pretty hard to wrap your mind around."

"I-I don't know what to think, Tess." But as Kinna studied the serious look on Tess's face, the sharpness in her terrified, bright-green eyes, she was thinking exactly that.

She actually believes what she's saying.

Kinna shook her head. "Why would you say that about Dr. Newcomb? And better still, how would you even know if she wasn't human?"

"I could sense it from the moment I met her because of my bloodline. The same bloodline that allowed me to talk to you without speaking aloud," Tess replied, and then leaned in a bit closer. "The same bloodline that allows me to hide behind a visual façade or disappear and reappear at will. See, I'm not what you think, either." Tess paused and tilted her head. "But then again, neither are you."

The rabbit hole is morphing and getting deeper, Kinna thought as the hysteria threated again. "Okay, seriously, you've lost me."

Tess sighed. "Kinna, I'm of fae descent."

"Fae descent? What does that mean," Kinna asked hesitantly.

"It means that I'm not exactly human. I have faerie lineage, faerie blood of my ancestors running through my veins."

"So...now you want me to believe that you're what? A faerie?"

Kinna tried to hide her surprise at the woman's confession but couldn't keep from staring at Tess with her mouth open.

At that moment, the waiter returned with Tess's drink. "Let me know when you two are ready to order," he said absently, seeming not to notice the weird vibe at the table or Kinna's dumbfounded look.

Tess took a couple swallows of her coffee, and then winced. "Now, that's a double shot—at least. Good boy." Tess cleared her throat and put up a hand before Kinna could speak. "Look, again, I know how this all sounds, but, Kinna, that's how I know that Newcomb isn't human, that she's some kind of really nasty being. Like I said, I'm not sure what she is, but I do know that much."

"Wait. You said that I wasn't what I seem, either. Do you think I'm not human?" Kinna closed her eyes for a moment. "Geez, I can't believe I even said that out loud." She opened her eyes, and shook her head. "Or that I'm entertaining any of this."

"Kinna—"

"And what about Dr. Addison? You said earlier that you didn't want to end up like him. Is he human?"

Tess sighed. "Yes, Dr. Addison was a kind, gentle *human* man who happened to be in the wrong place. He didn't deserve what they did to him."

"What who did to him? And you said *was* a kind man. What happened to him, Tess? I thought he retired."

Tess smirked and gave Kinna a cynical look. "No, you didn't, not deep down. You aren't that gullible. I know that you've wondered about Dr. Addison's disappearance from the start. That was something else I could sense. But if you want me to think that's the case, then let me be clear, Dr. Addison didn't suddenly retire, Kinna. He was made to disappear."

"I-I beg your pardon? What are you saying?"

"I'm saying that one day he was there in his office on a

Friday, seeing patients as usual. The following Monday, he was gone, and Newcomb was there in his place with some ridiculous story about how he'd suddenly decided to retire...over the damned weekend. She said that he'd asked her to take over for him, that he would fax over the transfer documents and then contact his patients to let them know."

"Via email, you mean," Kinna whispered.

Tess nodded. "Exactly. An email from the good doctor's account? Who's going to question that, right? Needless to say, I never saw any transfer documents for the practice, either, as if that's how it's done in the first place. But there was no one to complain or to question the whole thing, and the ones who did? Well, they were just given referrals to other therapists. Clean and tidy."

Kinna felt like the she was losing touch with reality, and her conversation with Olivia from Thursday's lunch before her final appointment with Newcomb filled her head.

That was the most sudden and suspicious retirement in the history of therapy, Kinna.

And to announce it to his patient list via email? Are you kidding me? Who does that? Then encourage all those patients to transfer to Slick Vicky—without actual proof that it was him doing the encouraging, I might add. Then to just disappear...literally overnight? You do know that no one has seen or heard from him since, right?

Kinna shook her head. "This is all just too much. I mean, it doesn't make any sense at all. Why do any of this?"

Tess drank down half of the Irish coffee in her mug, then wiped her mouth with her napkin. "I told you. She and some of the weirdos in her group are looking for something. Something they think you can help them find." She put up a hand. "And don't ask me what that is, because I don't know. I could never find out. All I could dig up was that they thought one of Dr. Addison's patients was the key to finding what they're looking for. They had whittled it down to about five or six patients until Newcomb found something in one of Dr. Addison's files. It was your file, Kinna. From that minute on, she turned her focus to you. Do you remember anything specific that she asked you in those last few sessions that might give us a clue?"

Kinna shook her head. "No, there wasn't..."

"Kinna? What is it?"

"Well, over the last month, month and a half, Dr. Newcomb had become really interested in my dreams and visions. They were so frequent back when I was seeing Dr. Addison in the beginning. I used to talk to him about them in almost every session."

Tess leaned in. "What did you tell Newcomb, Kinna?"

"Hardly anything. By the time she started asking me about them, I was already taking a...tonic that I got from..."

"From whom?"

Kinna sighed. The fact that she was taking a potion from a white witch didn't sound any more ridiculous than the things Tess had just told her in the last ten minutes. She shrugged. "I was taking a potion from a friend of a friend who's a witch. You have to understand, I'd tried everything I could over the years to make the visions and weird—sometimes terrifying—dreams stop. The potion I got from Sorcha did the trick, so I had nothing to tell Dr. Newcomb."

"Wait. That wouldn't be Sorcha Doyle, would it?"

Kinna blinked and nodded. "Do you know her?"

"I do, but that's a story for another day. One baby step at a time."

"What does that mean?" Kinna asked with narrowed eyes.

"Like I said, not everyone or everything is what it seems, and we can talk about Sorcha later, but she's not the problem. Back to Newcomb. When you told her you were no longer having visions, I bet she kept pushing, didn't she?" Tess asked with a sly look.

"Yes. She did." Kinna ran a hand over her face. "And by the time I came in for that last session with her, I was starting to have the visions again. You'd told me not to tell her anything of importance, so I denied it when she asked. Though, I'm pretty sure she didn't believe me." She looked over at Tess and felt the panic begin to spread. "Remember when I came out of her office and said that I'd heard her voice in my head?"

"Yeah."

"Well, at the point I heard her voice, I'd just told her that I wasn't having any visions or dreams of any kind. And what she said in my head was, 'Or maybe it's because of the witch's potion you've been taking. Did you really think you could hide it from me?'"

"Oh, Kinna. That's not good."

"Ya think?" Hysterical laughter bubbled out of Kinna before she could stop it, and she slapped her hand over her mouth.

"Oh, no," Tess whispered, her gaze riveted on the street-side window next to the door. "We have to go."

"What?" Kinna followed the woman's gaze and saw a couple standing outside the bistro. The woman looked over her shoulder into the restaurant in a studied way, and Kinna felt Tess's anxiety rise next to her. "Who are they, Tess?"

"No one we want to deal with, and I can't emphasize that strongly enough. We need to go. Now."

"How? They're right outside next to the door."

Tess threw back the last of her Irish coffee and tossed a twenty dollar bill down on the table. "Kinna, I can get us out of here unseen, but you're going to have to trust me. Which after this conversation, is a tall order, I'm aware. Think you can do that?"

"Yes, but—"

Before she could say anything else, Tess flicked her hand toward the waiter clearing a table on the other side of the bistro, and the tray he'd been loading crashed to the floor with a racket. Everyone in the place looked in that direction.

"Take a deep breath...and hold on," Tess murmured, taking Kinna's hand.

In the next moment, Kinna felt the strangest pull in her belly and the sensation of flying as the bistro disappeared from her sight.

13

Tuesday morning had arrived with the same blue skies, more frost on the ground, and the requisite cool snap in the air. They'd had the same weather for almost two weeks straight, but Dory could feel the change coming. Soon there would be rain, then ice, then possibly snow. She was okay with the cold, the ice, the snow. It was much the same as it was in the UK, though she hadn't lived in her homeland for almost a decade now. What she didn't look forward to was the sideways rain, which was typical for the coastal regions both here and in the north of England during the winter season.

She had set the meeting with Sorcha Doyle for Wednesday afternoon, and the team had spent most of their time this morning from breakfast to the lunch hour haggling over their plan. Though they couldn't really predict the outcome of the meeting, they'd all finally agreed on the few points that Dory now had down on paper and could expand on beforehand.

First and foremost, they were going to need as much information about Kinna McComish as possible from Doyle's point of view. Since the Immortal had been working with Kinna for some time, she would have a clearer picture of the woman's thoughts and emotions. The team had put together a basic file, but it was pretty sparse and devoid of any of the woman's personality traits, which was a problem in Dory's view. What Sorcha Doyle had seen, heard, and discussed with Kinna—her perceptions of the woman that carried the entity within her— would be crucial data to have before actually meeting with Kinna in person in the coming days. Dory was still concerned about how to approach the woman, so every minute detail Doyle could provide would be critical.

As she finished rinsing her coffee cup, Dory stared out of the kitchen window above the sink, trying to imagine how Kinna would react to a team of strangers converging on her with an unbelievable story of who and what they were—strangers with an even more outrageous story of who *she* was and what she actually carried within her.

Dory could still remember her shock and disbelief when Morianna had appeared in her bed chamber over three centuries ago to explain that she'd been made immortal, that her life would never be the same. Hearing that the fate of the world had been placed upon her shoulders had been a daunting, unimaginable realization, and it had taken her years to get past the denial and come to grips with it whether she wanted to or not. Now, she was making plans to have much the same discussion with a total stranger.

How the hell am I supposed to start that conversation?

However, when an Archangel requested your assistance there was no way that you refused. And after the initial shock, the team seemed to embrace the challenge which baffled the hell out of Dory. Of course, they didn't have the entire weight of the situation on their shoulders, either. Their perspective was quite different. She could only hope that she would find a way to pull it all off, to make Kinna McComish understand and accept what she would be told. And for that, Dory was certain that the way in was going to be on an emotional level. Which was why she felt Doyle's observations could provide that opening.

"What's going on in that beautiful head of yours, darlin'? I could almost hear you thinking from the other room," Kaden said, bringing her thoughts back to the present as he slipped his arms around her waist from behind.

Dory chuckled and leaned back into his embrace. "Oh, you know. This and that. Mostly, just obsessing over how I'm gonna handle Kinna McComish when we finally do meet."

He turned her around to face him, searching her countenance with concern in his eyes. "You worried about it?"

"Worried? No. Only slightly terrified." Dory grinned and then blew out a breath. "Seriously, worrying about it would just be a waste of time and energy, don't you think? I mean, it is what it is. All we can do is see what insights Sorcha Doyle can give us tomorrow. Then, we put one foot in front of the other and keep moving forward, right?"

Kaden frowned. "You know that you aren't alone in this, Dory. The whole team will be right there with you."

She sighed and shook her head. "I know that, love. It's just that—"

"That you're always the tip of the spear?" he asked, pulling her to him.

Dory grimaced. "I guess you could put it that way. Any time we're called up for anything, it mostly rests on my shoulders to make sure everything works. Sometimes being the Chosen One is overwhelming and comes with a good dose of exhaustion. That's all." She shrugged. "Don't get me wrong, I couldn't do any of this without you and the rest of the team."

Kaden cocked his head. "Yeah? Well, correct me if I'm wrong, but didn't you do it all by yourself for a few centuries before we even met?"

She chuckled. "I suppose that's fair, though there wasn't as much outside drama with crazies trying to destroy the world back then like there has been in recent years. In the beginning, I was just fighting to stay alive and had no idea why Darius was trying to kill me every time he was let out of his stasis prison." She gave him an apologetic look. "I'm sorry. I guess I'm just tired and whiny this afternoon."

"Hey, you're entitled. No need to apologize, love. You're a strong woman, Dory, but you don't have to be every minute of every day. And this whole situation? It's a lot...and would be for anyone."

"Yeah, well, I probably should have said that I wouldn't *want* to do this without you and the rest of the team." She lifted a hand to his cheek. "I don't say it enough, but I love you, Kaden Crenshaw. I waited so long, and I'm just so grateful to have you with me. But then again, you are—for better or worse—my Chosen Warrior. So, you're kind of stuck with me and all my centuries-worth of baggage."

Kaden turned his face and placed a warm kiss to her palm, then took her hand and pressed it to his heart. "For better or worse...and for always, darlin'."

"In any case, whatever understanding Sorcha Doyle can share with us about Kinna McComish will give me a better idea of how to go about the meeting with her, how to explain in the most appropriate way to make her understand how her life is about to change forever."

"Of course, you can look to your own experience with that as well, right?"

Dory shook her head. "Another time, another era. My story is very different. But yes, there are some elements that I can absolutely understand. The shock, the denial. I had a myriad of emotions, but I'm not sure they would compare to the here and now. What she has inside of her? I can't even comprehend."

"You may not comprehend the entity inside Kinna, but

remember, we still don't know what you're capable of as the Chosen One, what power lies within you. Not even the Immortal Council knows that." When she started to speak, he put up a hand. "However, I'm well aware that this is more apples and oranges here and not quite the same thing, so we'll set that aside for now. But, Dory, part of your power is that you've actually seen quite a few of Kinna's dreams and visions. You know the destruction that she's seen, the consequences of what's at stake. Who better to speak to her on that basic level?"

"I wish I had your confidence," Dory said with a smile. "My centuries of going it on my own, keeping my distance for not only my safety but for the protection of others? Well, it's left my people skills a bit wanting. You know?"

Kaden didn't laugh along with her as she'd hoped but leaned right down into her face with a pointed look. "Your people skills are just fine, pal. But speaking of dreams and visions, what was last night's escapade about?"

He always seemed to see right through to her core. There was a time, before he'd become immortal, when she'd shut him out in an effort to protect him from what was coming for her. It had worked pretty well for the moment until Morianna had stuck her nose into things. The Ancient had shown him just what Dory was trying to do, convincing him that his place was by her side, no matter how she was trying to push him away. Nowadays, Dory could rarely hide anything from him. He seemed to see everything, and sometimes more clearly than she could.

"More nightmares?" he prompted when she didn't respond.

With a sigh, she shook her head again. "Not exactly. Although, there was a creepy element to a few of the snippets."

Kaden tugged on her hand and led her over to the kitchen table where they both sat down. They were alone in the house for the moment. The team had been working all morning, so they were taking a much-needed break. Ian had gone into town with Ethan and Lucy, and Tanner had muttered something about 'going out' to make some calls. Whatever that meant. Why he had to go out to do that was an interesting puzzle that she'd think about later.

"Okay. Spill it," Kaden began. "So, no Dragon's Breath veining? No death and destruction?"

She shook her head. "Not for the last week or so. Just a bit of creepiness."

"Okay." He frowned. "Define creepiness."

Dory let her mind drift back to the scenes she'd witnessed in sleep. At least, what she could remember of them. It was a little unnerving that she was remembering more and more of her dreams—Kinna's dreams—over the last week or so.

"Well, most of the dreams up to this point have been like watching from a distance, but night before last it changed up and was different. It was like I was seeing the scene through Kinna's eyes instead of watching the scene from afar. There was a coffeehouse—I'm assuming the coffeehouse she owns—and she was leaving with two other women. Just before she gets to the door, she sees Jerahmeel in the corner reading a book. When he looks up...man, it was so powerful, and I could literally feel the panic flood her system."

Dory looked over at Kaden, and she could sense the fear of what followed in the dream as it began to rise up in her chest. "In the next moment, she was standing outside of an office of some sort looking in the windows. It was late at night, and of course, the office was closed, but that's where the creepiness comes in. Looking through the window, I could see an eerie glow under a door at the very back of the darkened lobby. I don't know how to explain it, but it was more than just a light under a door. Anyway, then the door starts to slowly swing open. You know, like in all those scary horror flicks? And I'm thinking,

'Run! Get the hell out of there.' But it was like Kinna was rooted to the spot, so I was, too. Then there was the panic again, but this time it was bordering on sheer terror, like there was a part of her that knew what was behind that door, and she really didn't want to wait for it to materialize but had no choice."

When Dory took a moment for a deep breath, trying to push the residual fear from her chest, Kaden took her hand. "It's okay, babe. Just breathe. What happened next? Get it all out."

Dory nodded. Just having her hand in his, that warmth and connection, helped her move through the panic she felt, even at the retelling of the dream. She took another deep breath and let it out slowly. "The next thing I knew, Jerahmeel was there next to me—to Kinna."

"What did he say?"

"He said, '*You're right to be wary. Evil lives here, child. Can't you feel it?*' It was so weird, Kaden, because I *could* feel it right down to my toes. And because that feeling was so strong, I know that it was exactly what Kinna was feeling as well. There was more to the dream, but I can't remember all of it now."

Kaden got up and went into the kitchen, bringing her back a glass of cool water from a pitcher in the refrigerator. He sat down next to her again and handed it to her. Dory came close to draining half the glass before she even took a breath.

"You said that dream was the night before last, so Sunday night. What was going on last night? You weren't as active as Sunday night, but you were mumbling off and on, though I couldn't understand much of what you were saying." Kaden smoothed back a few wayward strands of her hair that had escaped from the braid down her back. "About the only thing I heard clearly was you calling someone Tess, and then there was something about a Dr. Newcomb."

Dory took another sip of the cool water and nodded. "Yes, I —Kinna was meeting with someone in a restaurant. The whole thing seemed clandestine and anxiety-ridden, but at least, creepiness-free. I don't remember much of it other than the Tess person talking about this Newcomb character, saying that he or she wasn't human. Whatever that means."

"Well, we've learned to work with shapeshifters and Halflings. We've been attacked and fought demons and winged monsters. And now we have angels. What else could there be?"

"Geez, Kaden. Don't even say that out loud." She gave him a wide-eyed look. "The universe is a very snarky thing, so don't tempt it to put something else ugly and dangerous in our path, okay? We barely made it through the whole Dragon's Breath saga with our lives. And I'm still not certain that I've gotten beyond it yet."

"Alright, alright. I'm just sayin'," Kaden replied, then pointed a finger at her. "But I'm gonna go ahead and stick with the notion that you are until we have proof that you're not." He tilted his head then as if considering another idea. "You know, I'm actually waiting for the real werewolves, and not just Tanner's shifting deal...or maybe the vampires I accused you of being in the beginning. Or maybe we'll get really lucky and there'll be elves or faeries."

Dory snorted. "Yeah, you bet."

"Don't scoff, buddy. You don't know. Just remember, we didn't know about the demons or skin-walkers like Tanner until we suddenly were faced with them. We had no idea about angels, either, until Jerahmeel showed up on Thursday in this very kitchen."

She grinned and shook her head. Dear Lord, but she loved this man. How she'd existed for over three centuries without him was completely incomprehensible to her. "Tell you what, my love. If it gives you that much pleasure, I hope there's that and more out there just waiting for us to uncover."

Laughing out loud, Kaden leaned in and, taking her face in

his hands, looked deep into her eyes. "I really don't care what's out there, babe. As long as we're together, we're invincible."

"Well, since we're both immortal now, it looks like we'll be together for a really long time. So, I hope you're right."

He closed the distance between them and brushed his lips over hers, and Dory felt her pulse jump just as it always did at his touch.

"Kaden, I'm sorry that these dreams have been so constant and disturbing," she murmured against his lips. "I could sleep in the spare room for a while so you can get a good night's sleep if you want."

He pulled back then, and the look in his whiskey-colored eyes was pretty clear. "Try it," was all he said. And then he was kissing her...and her thoughts scattered like confetti.

It never ceased to amaze and stagger her how one touch, one kiss from this man could light a fire inside her within seconds. Her breath backed up into her chest, and she moved from her chair to his lap, straddling him and spearing her hands into his thick, sandy-blond hair. She hadn't realized how much she needed this. Closer, she really needed to be closer to him, preferably skin-to-skin.

His hands moved like lightning underneath her shirt and up over her back, as he picked up the pace and his mouth did wonderful things down the line of her neck. Finding a sensitive spot along her collarbone, he exploited it without mercy, and her blood began to pound, her skin to heat.

"Oh, yes," she sighed tilting her head to give him better access. "Right there."

She felt the soft rumble of his chuckle against the line of her neck as he began his ascent back up to her lips. "Not right here?" he murmured as his teeth tugged at her earlobe, shooting delightful tremors up her spine.

"Mmm, yes. That's quite good as well," she replied with a gasp.

His fingers found the hem of her top, pulling it up and over her head as she tried to work the buttons of his flannel shirt with hands gone suddenly clumsy and trembling. After a moment, Kaden took pity on her and shrugged out of his shirt, giving her free access to hard muscle and warm skin. She traced her fingers across the expanse of his chest, slipping down over his rock-hard abdomen, and feeling his body react, his muscles rippling at her touch. He hissed in a breath when she replaced her fingers with her mouth and tongue.

Before she could get much farther, Kaden leaned forward with a growl and stood, carrying her with him.

"What are you doing?" she gasped, wrapping her legs around him and pressing her breasts flat against his bare chest, her arms around his neck.

"Taking you upstairs to bed," he said, his big hands cupping the curves of her ass. "I am in no mood to be interrupted in the middle of having my way with you here in the kitchen. The team will be back soon enough, and I'm gonna need some time and privacy for what I have in mind."

"Is that so?" Dory murmured, nipping at his ear. "And just what are you thinking?"

Kaden stopped in the hallway and pressed her against the wall. "I guess you're just going to have to wait and see, pal."

Their eyes caught and held, fire reflecting fire, before he took her mouth again, his tongue dancing with hers in a smoldering kiss so hot that it left her gasping and craving more, so much more. He ground his hips against hers in a sensuous rhythm that had desire spreading its heat. He ravaged her mouth, nipping and licking at her lips, giving her more, but it wasn't enough. Never enough.

"I want you," she begged, slipping her hand between them and mindlessly fumbling for the button on his jeans.

"I know."

But then he was stumbling with her down the hallway, pausing only to touch here, taste there, driving her closer and closer to the heat, the white-hot hunger threatening to devour her in one greedy bite.

In the midst of their frenzy, her bra disappeared, and she almost whimpered with the intense pleasure when he pressed her against the wall again to bury his face at her breasts. Her heart was pounding wildly in her ears, and she couldn't breathe as he continued to use his mouth on her, trailing fire.

"Kaden, please," she pleaded, her voice raspy with desire.

"I know," he murmured, the sensation of his breath against her bare skin driving her mad.

"I mean it!"

Then he was moving again, staggering with her toward the staircase. The stairs didn't seem to be much of an obstacle for him even as she continued to use her teeth and tongue along his jawline and down his neck. In fits and starts, they finally gained the second floor, and he carried her into the master bedroom, dropping down onto the lake-of-a-bed they shared, covering her with his weight. In a renewed fever, they rolled across the surface of the bed, clothes being stripped away, tasting and touching exposed flesh. There was the sound of ripping material as they fought the last barriers until they were finally skin to skin.

Dory marveled as she always did at his strength, at his hard, ripped frame, and she wallowed in it. His hands raced over her, drawing out the pleasure and torturing her with sensation after sensation. His lips blazed a path to her breasts, teasing the nipples to hardened peaks with his tongue, before trailing more fire down the length of her body, and she cried out when he found her core and feasted.

"I want you inside me...now," she gasped.

"In a minute. I'm busy," he growled, his mouth continuing to assault her senses, driving her toward that first peak. "My God, I love the taste of you."

A moment later, with the hunger again burning out of control, she bowed up into him as the first orgasm ripped through her in an explosion of light and fury, leaving her breathless and shaken.

But Kaden wasn't finished. Sliding up her body, he slipped a hand between them, and then his fingers into her, into all that wet heat. His gaze was golden fire as he stared down at her.

"Go up again," he demanded in a voice gone deep and hoarse. "I want to watch your eyes go blind with the heat."

"Please," was all she could get out as the craving rose again with savage speed, and she struggled to breathe around the building pressure. Her vision blurred, and she screamed his name as the second climax burst through her without mercy.

Even before she had time to think, to settle, he stunned her as he replaced his fingers with the hard length of him, driving into her over and over again at a frantic pace until the unrelenting need was lashing them both. Dory held on, matching his thrusts as the incredible yearning continued to build, as they were trapped on the knife's edge of desire. Then, in the next moment, she was gasping and flooded with pleasure as they crashed over the edge together.

There was silence for several moments, with the only sound in the room, their erratic breathing. Kaden tried to roll off of her, but Dory wrapped her legs around him. "No. Please. Not yet. Give me a minute."

Kaden leaned down, placing a kiss on her forehead, his breath rasping in and out. "You can have as much time as you like, love. But if we stay this way, I can't guarantee that I'll be ready to let you up in a minute."

Dory closed her eyes and smiled. "That's some bold talk, mister." Then, mere moments later, her eyes flew open when she felt him grow hard again inside her. "Really?"

He grinned down at her. "Hey, I warned you."

"That you did," she replied as she pulled him down for a heated kiss, and then rolled with him across the bed. Straddling him, she sat up and ran her fingers over his abdomen, watched the muscles ripple and twitch. "Then I guess there's nothing to be done but to get this itch out of our systems."

As she began to move, Kaden slid his hands up her torso and covered her breasts. "Darlin'," he ground out. "I'm fairly certain that this 'itch' will never be out of our systems, but by all means, I'm game to try. As many times as you want."

14

K aden and Dory had just come downstairs and were retrieving their discarded clothing—evidence of their forty-five minute 'break'—when they heard a car door close. Dory had found her bra in the hallway, but grabbed both her discarded top and Kaden's flannel shirt from the kitchen where they'd been dropped, and quickly headed for the laundry room. Re-joining Kaden in the kitchen moments later, she gave him a puzzled look when the doorbell sounded.

With a shrug, he headed to the front door with her right behind him. The doorbell rang again just as Kaden pulled open the front door.

"Well, looks like we have the right house after all," Wyatt Mackintosh said as he turned to the petite woman standing next to him on the porch. "Should have known you'd have the directions locked down."

"Vee?" Dory blurted in surprise as she shoved past Kaden and grabbed her Sentinel up into a bear hug.

"Ugh! You don't have to squeeze me to death," Velma Reed complained with a laugh. "I don't need broken ribs for you to heal, Isadora."

Dory pulled back, and the look on her face mirrored the surprise that Kaden felt at seeing Velma show up with Wyatt Mackintosh, though they were both aware that the relationship between the two had changed significantly.

"What are you doing here, Vee?" Dory asked, giving her Sentinel the once over. "I just talked to you on the phone yesterday morning."

Velma shook her head and gave Dory a sardonic look. "I know that I usually make the travel arrangements for you, but you do realize that one can fly from the UK to the west coast of the US in about ten hours, right? We left London early this morning and got into Seattle around noon."

Dory rolled her eyes. "Okay, that's not what I meant, and you know it."

Kaden laughed and squeezed in between the two to give Velma a hug of his own. "Good to see you, Vee. It's been way too long since we've seen you face to face." Turning, he stuck out his hand to the mercenary. "Wyatt. Welcome to craziness 2.0."

Wyatt shook Kaden's hand and smirked. "Thanks. No offense, but I would rather be somewhere else instead of in the thick of another Immortal situation." Velma hissed and elbowed the mercenary in the ribs. "Having said that," he added, rubbing his ribcage. "I'm always glad to assist the Chosen pair whenever needed."

"As long as Morianna leaves your organs on the inside of your body where they belong, right?" Velma asked sweetly. A reminder of the last time Wyatt had been allowed to 'assist' in an Immortal situation.

"Indeed, *Mo Leannan*," Wyatt replied with a grin.

"And I told you not to call me that. I'm not your lover."

"Ah, but you are my sweetheart."

Velma bristled. "Oh, for the love of—"

"How about we all go inside so we can be comfortable for

the sniping and awkward conversation to come," Kaden inter-rupted, putting up a hand.

"Yes. Thank you, Kaden," Velma said, giving Wyatt a stern look that he answered with rumbling laughter.

Kaden swept his hand toward the door. "After you, darlin'."

Dory took hold of Velma's arm and ushered her into the house while Kaden shook his head and grinned at Wyatt.

"Don't I know it," Wyatt said, seeming to know exactly what Kaden was thinking. "Who would've thought, right?"

"I didn't say a word, buddy."

Wyatt smirked. "Didn't have to," he grumbled as he entered the house.

Kaden followed him in then led the way to the kitchen where the women were already seated at the table.

"Now, where's that sweet, loveable mutt of yours, Kaden?" Velma asked. "I was looking forward to actually meeting Henry face-to-face instead of over a computer screen."

"Sent him off to camp for a week or two. With the timetable and probable progression of plans with this new craziness we've been thrown into, we felt it was best all-around to send him out to my buddy's farm. Ernie will take good care of him, and he won't be under foot here if we need to move quickly at any point. Once this is over, I'll go get him so you can have that meet."

"So, why are you here, Vee?" Dory asked.

"You mean, instead of sitting at home at the townhouse waiting for your call and missing out on all the action?"

Kaden sat down next to Wyatt opposite the women. "As I recall, Vee, you weren't so fond of the action when you went with me to the Tor that first time, when Dory met Darius for that final battle."

Velma sighed. "I suppose that's fair. That was pretty scary, and not just because of Darius, though that was terrifying enough. I mean, you did die at the end of that battle, Kaden. But the Tor itself was more than eerie that day, and I was definitely not ready for fieldwork. However, this is a very different situation. I mean, come on, *angels*? Really?"

"Well, I'm not sure this situation is any less frightening. And Jerahmeel is an Archangel...and quite formidable," Kaden replied.

"Define formidable," Wyatt requested with a pointed side glance.

Kaden turned and answered the man in a droll tone. "Ever been so terrified that the spit dries up in your mouth and you think you may wet yourself at any moment?"

Wyatt let loose a shout of laughter. "I have indeed, and fairly recently. That Ancient bitch Deidre gave me several of those moments in a relatively short period of time."

"Yeah, well, I can guarantee that Deidre's bullshit doesn't hold a candle to one cool, steely look from an Archangel. Trust me."

Wyatt nodded gravely. "Enough said."

"It wasn't that bad," Dory scoffed. "At least, not as bad as you and Ian made it out to be."

Kaden narrowed his eyes. "Uh-huh. And we've already established that you had a very different experience, haven't we?"

Dory's face pinkened, and Velma looked from her to Kaden with a quizzical look. "What's that supposed to mean?"

"Well, I think the Chosen One here was a bit smitten with our Archangel."

"That's so not true," Dory sputtered. "Jerahmeel just has an... overpowering presence. That's all."

Kaden gave her a doubtful look and shook his head. "Please. You weren't the recipient of one of his silent but lethal stares. You sat there with a sloppy grin on your face almost the entire time he was here in this kitchen."

"I did not." Dory's answer was half-hearted. "He just...oh, never mind." She turned to Velma. "There was an undercurrent of power that was definitely intimidating, I will give Kaden that. But then again, what would you expect from an Archangel?" She reached over and took Velma's hand, deftly changing the subject. "I do confess, though, it will be quite handy having you here instead of half a world away. I have a feeling we're going to need your skills more than ever, before it's all said and done."

Kaden turned to Wyatt. "Did you get any kind of briefing for this, other than our call?"

"Some." Wyatt nodded. "I got a short visit from the Ancient, which is always a joy." He wrinkled his nose. "Morianna filled in some of the blanks but not all, then disappeared as quickly as she arrived. I think I'd like to hear your version of it because I'm of a mind that I wasn't given the full picture."

Kaden and Dory spent the next thirty minutes filling in Wyatt and Velma on all that they'd been told, pausing here and there to answer pointed questions.

"So, let me get this straight," Wyatt began when they got to the end of the information that they'd compiled. "This Key carries an entity that can correct time, so to speak? Can actually change the past, thereby changing the future?"

Kaden nodded. "Sounds like it's been done off and on over a millennium. Evidently, this entity is always around but not always required. In which case, it usually stays dormant, which is weird, in my opinion. There have been centuries where it hasn't been needed at all, yet it's here just in case. The way we heard it, Kinna McComish is the host that carries the entity at this point in time, therefore, she's the current Key."

"And this entity actually lives or exists in a human being?" Velma asked with a disgusted look and a shake of her head. "That's just irresponsible and doesn't give me much comfort...at all. We humans tend to be so very unreliable, in my experience.

Why would any kind of supreme being put something that powerful into a human?"

Dory snickered at the look on the Sentinel's face. "After living over three hundred years on this planet, I would tend to agree with you, Vee. But far be it for me to question anything a supreme being does or doesn't do."

"So, what or who activated this Key, then? And why now?" Velma asked.

"Excellent questions, Vee," Kaden replied with a wink. "Which I also asked, but got no definitive answers."

"That is, other than the theme that there were some things that couldn't be shared, at least not yet," Dory added.

Velma huffed out a breath. "Well, that's just ridiculous."

"Okay, but getting back to the players in all of this," Wyatt began. "So, we've got this Key—who doesn't know she's The Key —who could potentially save or destroy humanity. We've got more evil-ass Immortals in the mix, one who's working with a fallen angel and a demon horde, for God's sake. And they're looking to find and use the entity this Kinna McComish carries inside her for who knows what. Plus, I'm gonna go ahead and climb way out on a very short limb and assume that time is running short to head off calamity. Which will probably end in a battle with more demons and/or heinous monsters that our merry band of do-gooders will have to wage. That about it so far?"

Kaden grinned and nodded. "Why, yes. I think you've got the gist of it...so far."

Wyatt stared at him for a moment and then shook his head. "Again, I don't fancy this whole scenario, but all right, then. However, let me just add another log or two onto this lovely bonfire you've got burnin' here."

Kaden frowned. "Okay. And what would that be?"

"Well, two things. First, I had a conversation with a mate of mine before Velma and I got on a plane. Don't know how he got this information, but although Dorian Smyth doesn't know that Kinna McComish is The Key, he does know who she is, and in a twist of irony, thinks she knows where to find The Key. He's known for a few days. My mate also said that Smyth isn't known to be the patient type, and that if he hasn't already, he'll try to scoop her up as soon as possible to get the information he needs. Which, of course, would be disastrous, since she *is* The Key."

"Yeah, that's not good news. And Jerahmeel also mentioned Smyth's lack of patience." Kaden ran a hand through his hair. "And the other thing?"

"Dorian Smyth isn't the only one looking."

Kaden exchanged a look with Dory. "That's not good, either. Who else is looking?"

Wyatt shook his head. "That's the sticky wicket, mate. My chum didn't have names, but he did say that he'd had a conversation with one or two of his buddies who'd been approached by a couple of 'sketchy' types who seemed a bit off and were asking questions. They said they were lookin' to hire some outside help in running down 'an entity'. Like I said, my friend didn't have names as his buddies didn't get a proper introduction before telling said sketchy gits to sod off."

"Okay. Good to know." Kaden gave Dory a look. "Could be more players on the field. Or could just be this Verrine sending around underlings to try to find The Key before Smyth does. Then she could just kick him to the curb and do whatever she has planned. Jerahmeel did say that if Smyth thought he was working with Verrine, he was wrong, that the fallen angel would have her own strategy. In any case, we'll need to keep an eye out for that along with the rest."

"So, anything else you want to tell us?" Wyatt asked. "Anything you've left out?"

"Well, I suppose that I should tell you that Jerahmeel called you and Tanner out by name."

Wyatt went perfectly still, and his eyes went wide. "Beg pardon?"

"Yeah, the Archangel knows your name, son. So, don't think there was any way you were gonna be able to skate on this mission in the first place." Kaden grinned as he leaned back in his chair. It was a bit of a giggle to see Wyatt so rattled. "Evidently, we're going to be encountering more demons during this little spree, and Jerahmeel was of the mind that you and Tanner would be assets in that area."

"Oh, goodie." Wyatt paled a bit and hung his head briefly. When he looked up again, he smirked at Kaden. "I imagine Ethan was pretty pleased to hear about the probability of more demons."

Kaden nodded and laughed out loud, jabbing a finger in the man's direction. "That's exactly what I said. And no, as you will undoubtedly not be surprised to hear, he was so not pleased."

"Speaking of Ethan, I thought he and the Halfling were already here."

"Oh, they are. So's Ian. We'd been working on research and the plan going forward all morning, so they went into town for a break. They've been gone for a while. Should be back any time now."

"Oh, and Wyatt, in full disclosure, Tanner is also here." Dory gave the mercenary a sympathetic look.

Had it been up to Tanner, the team would have left Wyatt to die on the beach at Hilton Head after their battle with the Erinyes. The mercenary had been at death's door, and Kaden, using his newly acquired healing skills, had shored the man up just enough to get him back to the house in Savannah where Morianna could finish the job.

Since Wyatt had started out working for Deidre in killing

Immortals, once healed, Morianna had made certain that Wyatt would play nice with the team, issuing a clear promise of an ugly death for betrayal. But if it hadn't been for Wyatt, Kaden was certain that the team wouldn't have survived Deidre's trap. Both Kaden and Dory had come to trust the man, but Tanner was another story. Kaden wasn't exactly sure how the two would deal with past aggression, but then again, Tanner seemed to have found a new path, so they would just have to wait and see.

On the heels of that thought, Kaden heard a commotion from the front door. From the sounds of it, Ethan, Lucy, and Ian were back. But when the group came into the kitchen, Tanner was with them as well.

"Hey, Wyatt. Good to see you, man. About time you got here." Ethan grinned and clapped the mercenary on the back. "I thought you may miss all the fun, my friend. And have you heard? There's gonna be more demons, and from the sound of it, worse by far."

Wyatt grinned. "Yeah. Kaden and Dory have just filled us in. Should be a good time, especially with the 'more demons' part of it, right?"

Ethan grunted and then rounded the table, pulling Velma out of her chair. "And the beautiful Velma," he said, giving her a hug. Leaning back, he shook his head. "What on earth were you thinking coming over here?"

Velma grinned. "I don't know, I may have finally gone round the bend, for sure."

"I'm gonna need me a bit of a scrunch also, lassie," Ian said as he grabbed Velma up into his embrace, and indeed, gave her a hug. "So good to see you again."

"You, too, Ian." Velma looked over at Lucy. "Well, get over here, girl, and give me a proper scrunch as well."

Lucy complied, but then all eyes turned to the last of the group still standing in the doorway looking at Wyatt.

"Good to see you again, too, Tanner," Velma said with her arm still around Lucy.

Wyatt looked up as Tanner crossed to the table with a shuttered look on his face. Kaden held his breath.

"Skinwalker," Wyatt acknowledged.

"Mercenary," Tanner replied as a slow smile eased across his face. Holding out his hand, his smile became a grin. "No hard feelings? What's in the past, is in the past?"

Wyatt stared at the man's hand for a moment, and Kaden wasn't sure how the scenario would play out. But then the mercenary shook his head and took Tanner's outstretched hand. "Yeah, yeah. Doesn't mean that I don't think you can be a wanker, but past is past. I'm pretty sure we've stepped into it this time, and we're gonna have a bit more to worry about than past bad behavior, right?"

"Ha! Absolutely."

Kaden exchanged another look with Dory and inwardly breathed a sigh of relief. All they needed was infighting and more 'bad behavior' before this situation could be neutralized to royally screw up everything.

"Well, now that that's handled, let's get everyone settled with the sleeping arrangements, and then we need to sit down and go over tomorrow's meeting," Kaden said. "This is going to be a pretty crucial first step with our contact before approaching Kinna McComish, so we want to make sure everyone's on the same page before we head over the hill to meet with her."

"Meeting?" Wyatt asked. "What meeting is this?"

"Oh, geez," Dory muttered. "I'm sorry, Wyatt. We kind of got off track with the rest of it, but we have a meeting with an Immortal who's been living as a white witch here in the area—dispensing potions and the like. She's been working with Kinna McComish for some time. We're all meeting with Sorcha Doyle tomorrow to get a clearer picture of McComish from her observations."

The mercenary went very still, and frowned. "I'm sorry, did you say Sorcha Doyle?" he asked in a hesitant tone.

Dory glanced at Kaden and then back at Wyatt. "I did. Why? Do you know her?"

Wyatt blew out a breath and his gaze flew to Velma. "I do...or did. Haven't seen her in over a decade," he added in haste.

"Okay," Dory said slowly. "And?"

He ran a hand over his face. "Well, we hooked up for a while, but like I said, it was a long time ago."

"Why do I feel like there's something more to this story?" Ethan asked, giving Wyatt a cheeky grin.

"Not helpful, Ethan," Dory scolded, and then addressed Wyatt. "And, of course, I'm not really interested in your prior hook-ups, Wyatt. However, to Ethan's point, what aren't you saying? Can we trust this woman? Or is there something else we need to know before the meeting tomorrow?"

The mercenary scratched his bearded chin and heaved a sigh. "The Sorcha Doyle I knew ten years ago was solid. I'd trust her with my life, and did on a few occasions, so you have no worries there. Though a lot can change in ten years."

"Then what?" Kaden asked. "Because it's obvious that there's something more."

Wyatt gave Kaden a sheepish look. "Well, mate, the something more would be that I just don't know how she'll react to me being on the team, seeing my ugly face again after all this time. I mean, there wasn't a nasty split or anything like that. It's just that..."

"Oh, awesome! An uncomfortable situation to enjoy that has nothing to do with me," Tanner said with a snicker.

Wyatt gave the man a nod in agreement, but then shifted his gaze to Velma again.

The Sentinel had been listening to the conversation with a studied look but held Wyatt's gaze and said nothing.

Dory cleared her throat. "Okay, then. If there's nothing else of consequence, back to sleeping arrangements. Vee, Wyatt, all the beds are full, but we can figure something out. Ethan and Lucy have the bedroom upstairs. Ian's been sleeping in the office down here. It has a Murphy bed, full size. The living room sofa pulls out into a full, and Tanner has been sleeping there, but we can also shuffle around a bit, if need be," Dory said, throwing a cautious look toward her Sentinel.

"I can bunk with Tanner in the living room," Ian said, and looked to Tanner, who nodded.

"That means you can take the Murphy bed, Vee," Dory added. "We can also make do with air mattresses and sleeping bags. Won't be the best but everyone will have a decent place to sleep."

Velma didn't acknowledge right away but continued to gaze at the mercenary with an unreadable look. Then she stood and followed Dory around the table. Grabbing one of the lapels of Wyatt's leather jacket, she urged him out of the chair. "Don't look so apprehensive, Isadora, we won't be needing the sleeping bags," she said without taking her eyes from Wyatt. "The mercenary and I will be just fine on the pull-down in the office." Her lips twitched with the beginning of a smile. "What's in the past, is in the past, right? Come on, sugar. Let's go get the bags."

Wyatt's eyebrows shot up. "Right behind you, *Mo Leannan*."

"And I told you not to call me that," she replied over her shoulder.

He gave the rest of the group a thousand-watt grin as he followed Velma out of the room to the whistles and catcalls of the others.

Dory rolled her eyes and glanced at Kaden. "Saints help us."

"Indeed, love," Kaden replied with a burst of laughter. "Indeed."

～

"WHAT IN THE hell do you mean you lost them?" Dorian Smyth shouted at the couple standing at attention in his living room. Verrine stood at the floor-to-ceiling windows overlooking the river with her back to them, and Victoria sat leisurely sipping yet another martini on the sofa.

The woman looked at the man standing next to her, then back at Dorian. "You know that we've been looking for the Archer woman off and on since she disappeared from Dr. Newcomb's office that day, but every time we'd get a bead on her, she always seemed to give us the slip. I mean, we'd see her going into a shop or restaurant, but she'd be gone when we went in after her."

"Which is exactly what happened again today," the man added.

"Tess Archer should have been dealt with weeks ago, before she even had a chance to run. I don't know what is so hard about finding one receptionist when you were given her home address and phone number from the office files," Victoria muttered with a glare for both of them. "I mean, seriously, are you idiots?"

Dorian shot her an annoyed look. "Thank you, but I don't need comments from the demon gallery, Victoria."

"Look, Buford put a tracker on McComish's car a week ago," the man continued. "And he called today to say that she'd headed into the city, that he thought she was meeting with Archer. And we actually picked up Archer's trail again this morning and followed her around Portland for a couple of friggin' hours. We'd lose her then catch up to her again."

The woman nodded. "Then we finally caught up to her and

followed her at a distance to a restaurant in the Pearl. But it was so weird. When we went into the bistro, neither of them were there."

"Pathetic," Victoria said quietly, before downing the rest of her martini.

The man shot a finger at her. "And you can just fuck right off. We've done everything possible to get a hold of these women. If you wouldn't have run both of them off in the first place, we wouldn't be in this predicament, now would we?"

Victoria threw out a hand, curling her fingers, and the man began to gasp for air. His fingers flew to his throat as if trying to pry open his airways.

"Do not ever address me in that manner again. I'm not the problem here. Your incompetence is—"

"Victoria, let him go...*now*!" Dorian barked. "This is not your place. I said *let him go*!"

"Victoria?" Though she never turned from the window, Verrine's soft voice seemed to whisper throughout the room. "Be a good girl, and do as you're told."

That was all that it took to have the invisible pressure at the man's throat released. He nearly collapsed where he stood, gasping for air, his face a mottled shade of red.

Dorian glared at Victoria, a tic working his jawline, before turning back to the couple in front of him. "The two of you stay available and wait for my call. Now, get out of my sight, both of you."

The couple scurried from the room and, after Dorian heard the front door close, he turned on Victoria. "And you as well. Get your shit and get out."

"But—"

Dorian put up a hand. "I don't want to hear it. Don't come back here until you can keep yourself under control, and at least, *try* to act like a normal human."

Victoria set her empty martini glass down on the glass coffee table with a snap, grabbed her purse, and stomped out of the room.

Silence reigned for several moments as Dorian worked to let go of his anger. Victoria hadn't done anything that he hadn't wanted to do himself, but there had to be rules and a chain of command. And he was at the top of that chain.

"Darling." Verrine glanced over her shoulder at him, and her soft voice caressed his mind. "You really can't let underlings get you so wound up. This is a minor setback, yes?"

Dorian cleared his throat. "Yes. I'll make a call tomorrow. We'll scoop up the McComish woman in the next day or two. And once she tells us where it is, we'll have The Key soon after."

Verrine gave him a sly smile as she sauntered toward him. "Of course. Soon we'll all have everything we want."

15

I sadora Winthrop. *The friggin' Chosen One.*

Sorcha wasn't exactly sure how one prepared for a meeting with a legend, which Winthrop most certainly was to the vast majority of the Immortal world. She had no idea what this meeting was supposed to involve, thanks to Jerahm's lack of details, which was typical. She shook her head at herself in the mirror as she braided her hair. Morianna, Ancient Immortal and High Priestess of Avalon would be in touch, he'd said. The instructions of 'Contact them as soon as possible' and 'Accommodate them as best you can' were not any kind of help at all. But then, that was an Archangel for you. Riddles, sketchy suggestions, and vague directions.

The exalted Morianna had dropped by—well, had appeared and disappeared—as Jerahm had indicated she would. However, the Ancient hadn't been much help in the details department, either, other than reiterating the contact information for Winthrop that Jerahm had already given her. For some reason, Sorcha found that pretty hysterical. An Ancient, probably a thousand years old or better, rattling off a cell phone number to a child in Immortal terms. However, it was the brief highlight of a short, fairly daunting visit.

Sorcha had been so incredibly intimidated by the Ancient that she'd barely asked a handful of questions. But then, seriously, no matter how prepared you were, what did one even say to an Ancient Immortal who just appeared in your workroom unannounced? An Immortal who had seen and lived through unimaginable situations and landscapes, fought in wars listed only in history books, and more that probably weren't listed anywhere at all. Though Sorcha had known Jerahm for many years, assisted him in a handful of instances, seeing Morianna in person, actually speaking to her, was mind-blowing on a different level.

So, with very little information to go on, Sorcha had called to set up the meeting with Winthrop and her crew which had been almost as overwhelming. It was also a bit of a surprise, because no matter what she'd anticipated, Winthrop sounded like a normal, rational human being over the phone. But Sorcha wouldn't be lulled into expecting too much. She'd met her share of Immortals who were just plain assholes. So, she'd hold off judgment until the woman walked through her front door.

Sorcha had done some research since Jerahm's visit, and while she herself had crossed the 260 year mark just over a month ago, Winthrop had only about a hundred years on her from what she could learn. Yet Isadora Winthrop was the Chosen One of Prophesy, the one destined to defeat Darius, Morianna's evil cousin. Darius, an Ancient as old as Morianna. And at slightly over 300 years old, Winthrop had done just that —bested an Ancient exactly as the Prophesy had foretold.

Of course, most of what Sorcha could dig up was just vague word of mouth and pieces of ancient tomes. She didn't actually know anyone who'd met the Chosen One, or had even seen her, for that matter. So, it made this meeting all the more worrisome.

To find out that the Chosen One and her Warrior were living less than a hundred miles from Sorcha's home had been another revelation.

And here she was, having to do what? Hold a meeting with Winthrop and her crew to discuss Kinna McComish? A meeting that was to start—she checked her watch—in about ten minutes. And after that meeting, was she just supposed to introduce them to Kinna? And what else? Jerahm had only said that she was to contact the Chosen One and give her whatever assistance she needed, which again, was no help at all.

But why Kinna? Her mind just kept circling back to that one thought.

Sorcha had several Immortal gifts outside of healing and imbuing potions, protection spells and combat acumen. She was also an Intuit, sensing the emotions and feelings of others by touch. But the gift that had brought Jerahm into her life was her ability to access the visions and dreams of others. As she'd told the Archangel, she'd gotten a flash of something incredible the very first time she and Kinna had met when the woman had taken her hand. It was just a quick jumble of images, but she'd known instantly that the woman had an extremely powerful psychic current running through her.

But then there was also the scuttlebutt she'd heard about The Key. She had no idea what this Key was or what its purpose would be, but from the Archangel's reaction, or pointed lack thereof, Kinna was somehow connected to the search for it. Was it because of that strong psychic stream the woman had at her core? Or was there something else?

Then there was the comment Jerahm had made that Sorcha had almost missed.

Her human name is Kinna McComish...

Human name? What had the Archangel meant by that?

When she'd asked, he'd deftly changed the subject, signaling that the topic was not up for discussion.

Sorcha had a myriad of questions rolling around in her head while she did her best to straighten the house in her last few minutes before her Immortal guests would be arriving. She supposed it wouldn't do for her not to put her best foot forward when one of the most famous Immortals of her world would be stopping by for a meeting. But the mindless task did nothing to sort the continuous swirl of questions and possibilities.

Of course, she wasn't at all certain the Chosen One would give her any more answers than Jerahm or Morianna had done. However, if Isadora Winthrop wanted her help, she would have to give her something in return. She'd already made up her mind.

With the sound of her doorbell a few minutes later, it seemed like she was about to find out what answers the Chosen One would or would not share. She sighed and tried to calm herself as she headed to the front door to find out.

WHILE THEY WAITED for Sorcha Doyle to answer the door, Dory glanced around, taking in the green fields surrounding the property and the huge garden just visible from the wrap-around porch of Doyle's lovely, old farmhouse. The flower beds were neatly edged and looked to be well tended and ready for winter. And though at the end of the fall season there wasn't much in the way of blooms, Dory could easily identify a few perennial herbs growing here and there which seemed to be thriving. She thought it was a perfect place for an Immortal masquerading as a white witch to live.

On the heels of that thought, the front door swung open to reveal a tall, curvy woman with pale skin, ice-blue eyes, and an ebony braid hanging over her left shoulder that, no doubt, would fall halfway down her back. She was dressed in jeans and a gauzy, brightly-colored top in blues and yellows. She was definitely a spot of color for the gray background of the house and end of the fall season. Dory judged the woman to be in her mid-thirties, but if this was Sorcha Doyle, their research had indicated that she'd just turned 260 years old.

"Sorcha Doyle?" Dory asked.

With a nod, the woman let out a breath. "You would be the Chosen One? Isadora Winthrop?"

"That would be me," Dory replied. "But please, call me Dory. Isadora was from another lifetime. Long ago and far away, as they say."

"Well, best come in out of the cold." Sorcha held the door wide in invitation.

"Sorry to invade your space this way and on such short notice," Dory said as she led the entire team into the foyer. "I know there are quite a few of us."

"Eight to be exact," Kaden added.

"No worries." Sorcha studied him for a moment. "Are you the Chosen Warrior, then?"

Kaden grinned. "I am that."

The woman shook her head. "I don't know exactly what I expected, but I don't think either of you are that."

Dory laughed. "Yeah. We've heard that before."

"Well, why don't we just go into—" the woman began but stopped speaking abruptly as she scanned the group, and her gaze came to rest on Wyatt. "It...can't...be. Wyatt? Wyatt Mackintosh?" she asked in a whisper with a stunned look to match. "I-Is that really you?"

"Hey, Sorcha. Been a while, yes?"

"It's...ah...yes. It has."

"Like Dory said, sorry to turn up like this." Wyatt gave her a careful look then rambled on. "I only just found out last evening that it was you we were coming to see but wasn't really sure it would actually be you, you know? I mean, what are the odds, right? Last time I saw you was—"

"Edinburgh. Ten years ago, or better." Sorcha blinked then and looked around at the faces watching her closely and seemed to get hold of herself. "Yes, well, please come in, all of you. We'll see if we can get settled in the parlor. I'm not sure we'll all fit comfortably, but if not, we can move into the dining room. The table is huge, and it seats ten. In any case, we can at least make the introductions first and then get down to the business of why you're here."

With that, she started down the long hallway before turning to the left and entering a room halfway down the corridor. Tanner, Ian, Lucy, and Ethan followed.

Dory looked over at Wyatt, who'd watched Sorcha's receding back with a shuttered look. Velma leaned in and whispered, "Are you okay?"

With a brief shake of his head as if to clear his thoughts, he gave her a quick smile. "I'm fine, love. Just quite a shock, you know? A blast from the past, so to speak."

"Yep. And more than a few memories to boot?"

"A few," he agreed as they followed the rest of the group into the parlor with Dory and Kaden bringing up the rear.

Once there, they went around the room with introductions, and then Sorcha decided that the dining room table would indeed be a better fit, so they all moved into the dining room together.

It was obvious that the woman had anticipated a group and a possible move into the dining room, as there was a tray of tumblers in the center of the table. As everyone was getting seated, Sorcha went through the swinging door at the end of the room and returned a few moments later with two good-sized pitchers—one, she said was strawberry lemonade, and the other, unsweetened tea.

"If anyone would like coffee or hot tea instead, I can have it made in a jiffy."

Dory shook her head. "Please don't go to any trouble, Sorcha. This is lovely. Thank you."

"All right. Then I guess we should get down to it," Sorcha said as she sat at the kitchen end of the table with Dory on her right and Kaden on her left. "Although, to be honest, I'm not exactly sure what *it* is? Jerahm didn't give me much to go on other than I needed to set up this meeting, and that you were looking for some information about Kinna McComish. And the Ancient wasn't any more forthcoming than the Archangel was."

"Trust me when I say, we are well aware of how tight-lipped Morianna can be. Like getting blood from a stone, right?" Dory asked.

Sorcha smiled at that, but it was brief before the frown settled in. "I'm just not certain what this is all about. I mean, I have some idea but only because of my Immortal gifts. Jerahm may not have actually said anything, but his silence spoke volumes."

"Your Immortal gifts?" Lucy asked. "What do you mean? Are you talking about Immortal powers and abilities?"

Sorcha looked down at her hands, turning her intricate gold thumb ring around and around, as if collecting her thoughts. When she looked up, her eyes swept the table at the faces awaiting her answer. "I get feelings and emotions, you see. Sometimes flashes of thoughts or images. By touch."

"Oh, my gosh. You're an Intuit?" Lucy asked with wide eyes. "That's very rare in Immortals."

Sorcha nodded. "It is. I can also access the visions and dreams of others. That's what brought Jerahm into my life."

"If you don't mind me asking, how long have you known

Jerahmeel, Sorcha?" Kaden began. "That you call him by a shortened name tells me that you've probably known him for quite a while."

"Aye," Ian added with an apprehensive look. "I can't even imagine calling an Archangel by a nickname. Seems like folly to me."

Sorcha's smile this time was full blown and stayed in place. "Jerahm's not so bad, Ian."

"That's what I said." Dory narrowed her eyes and pointed a finger at Kaden.

"Yeah, right," Kaden retorted with a bland look. "I think we've already covered your situation, haven't we?"

Dory opened her mouth to respond but then thought better of it. She didn't want to get caught up in that whole conversation again.

"He's actually kind of a teddy bear," Sorcha continued. "I mean, an incredibly handsome, incredibly powerful—and sometimes incredibly formidable—teddy bear. So, I can see how you might be a touch apprehensive."

"A touch?" Ian muttered. "'Tis a tad more than that, lassie. And I think calling Jerahmeel *formidable* is quite the understatement."

"In any case, you are correct, Kaden," Sorcha said with humor lacing her tone. "I've known Jerahm for a long time because of my rarer gifts. As you know, the more common abilities, those that most Immortals acquire early like the capacity to heal, to imbue objects with emotions or power, protection skills, usually manifest within the Immortal's first ten to fifteen years. Though, sometimes sooner, and other times later—each Immortal is different. My abilities manifested quite early, literally within the first four years of my immortality."

"Really? Which ones?" Dory asked. Healing was always the

first ability any new Immortal acquired followed by the capability to protect oneself using the elements.

"All of them."

Sorcha's answer hung in the air like an inexplicable object, and Dory stared at the woman in stunned silence for a moment, then two. "*All* of them?" she finally blurted out. "Are you serious?"

"Quite." Sorcha nodded. "And that's how I met Jerahm, because of my special gifts."

"The Archangel of visions and dreams," Dory murmured.

"Among other things, yes." Sorcha replied.

"Amazing," Lucy all but whispered.

"Indeed," Ian agreed.

But Sorcha leaned toward Dory with a pointed look. "What I have inside me is a wonderment, for certain. However, I've read all I can about you. No one seems to have a clue as to what power you hold within you. Jerahm asked me to assist you in any way that you need, and I am willing to do just that, but I'm going to need a few things in return."

Dory frowned. Well, this was an unexpected development. What on earth could the woman want?

"What things, Sorcha?" Dory finally asked.

The woman leaned back in her chair, and her gaze moved around the table from one person to another until she came back to Dory. "First, tell me what you need from me."

"Is this some kind of negotiation?" Kaden asked.

"If you like," Sorcha replied. "This is about Kinna McComish, yes?"

"Yes," Dory said with a nod.

"Well, you and I have been given unbelievable gifts, and I don't know what it is that lives inside that woman, but Kinna is special. That I do know. I've seen glimpses of it that I can't even put into words." Sorcha glanced at Kaden. "So, you can call this whatever you like, but Kinna is an innocent who has been plagued by something she doesn't understand for as long as she can remember. I need to know what you're looking for, what it will mean to her, before we can move forward."

Dory looked at Kaden and then shrugged. "He didn't say we couldn't tell her anything."

"He didn't. Your call."

Turning back to Sorcha, Dory nodded. "Deal. What do you want to know?"

Sorcha poured herself a glass of the lemonade from the pitcher and then sat back again with narrowed eyes. "Why do you want to meet with her? For what purpose? I've heard chatter about those looking for some kind of key. Is Kinna connected to that? If so, how? Jerahm indicated that she was special, but that's all he would say—other than time was an issue. Of course, I'd sensed the special part already, but I don't really know what it means."

Dory cleared her throat. "Sorcha, Kinna has something amazing, something incredibly rare and old as time itself inside of her. Like, one of a kind. She's not connected to The Key. She *is* The Key. The entity inside of her is a Time Mender."

Sorcha paled, and her eyes took on a distant look. "Oh," she whispered in a long, drawn-out breath, as if seeing something in the air that none of the rest of them could. "Of course, I see it now."

"What do you see?" Lucy asked.

The woman shook her head as if trying to free herself from the vision in her mind, and then looked directly at Wyatt for a beat before turning her focus on Lucy. "The first time Kinna came to me, she took hold of my hand before I could avoid it. As I said, I'm an Intuit by touch, so I try not to invade anyone's privacy. I'm pretty careful about it. I can block it if I'm prepared, but I was caught off guard." She lifted a hand in a pleading gesture. "She was just so hopeful that I would have something to block out the visions and nightmares that were getting increasingly worse...and much more frightening and vivid than ever before." She waved her hand in the air and then dropped it into her lap. "Anyway, it was only for a moment, but it was like an explosion of images and sounds that filled my head for an instant. Like I said before, I couldn't put into words what I experienced."

"Have you encountered a Time Mender before?" Ethan asked. "The Archangel said that there was only one per generation, in case of disaster."

Sorcha shook her head. "No, I've never met a Time Mender, but I have read a few ancient tomes that speak of it, though they don't say much in the way of importance or clarity. It seems to be a great secret. Do you know what it entails?"

Kaden nodded. "It's a great secret for a reason, believe me. The entity is meant to be a failsafe of sorts in the case of a world-ending event. From what we've learned, it has been used a handful of times over the centuries. Seems the Supreme Being has a specific plan for this world, and the entity is there to make sure we don't fuck it up before the Supreme's plan is executed." He grinned. "At least, that's my take on the whole thing."

"That would track, I suppose, and as good a take as any." Sorcha looked thoughtful for a moment, and then frowned. "But why now? I mean, I'm guessing that Kinna's visions and nightmares are a sign that the entity within her is stirring, but why? What event has started the process?"

Dory shook her head. "That's unclear as well, or at least information that we weren't given. However, as you said, there are others looking for The Key, others that have no business even getting near it."

"Yes," Sorcha agreed. "There is an Immortal in Portland that I've specifically heard is looking. And he is a real piece of work."

"Dorian Smyth?" Wyatt asked with a flare of heat in his eyes.

Sorcha was obviously surprised but nodded. "You've heard it too?"

Kaden sighed. "There's a lot more to that story, and it gets nothing but worse. We think that the 'nothing but worse' part is why the entity is waking. It's preparing to possibly mend time to avert whatever these idiots are planning."

"Which is why we're here," Dory added. "We need to know as much as we can about Kinna McComish because Jerahmeel wants us to meet with her and explain this whole mess to her in a way she'll understand, if that's even possible. Then, get her to a safe place out of reach and protect her while we neutralize the threat."

"I see." Sorcha stared at Dory for several beats before nodding. "All right. I'll tell you everything I can about Kinna, give you all the details you'll need." She leaned forward and tapped the table. "But here's my price. I want in. Your team just grew to nine."

D ory and Kaden did their best to discourage Sorcha's request to join the team, arguing that they didn't want to put anyone else at risk, but she'd been adamant. And after thirty minutes of arguing—much to Dory's chagrin— Wyatt had joined in, saying that Sorcha's rare gifts would come in as handy as any that the rest of the team could provide, and maybe more so. Kaden had pointed out that Jerahmeel had said nothing about her joining the team. Sorcha had then countered that her impression was that the Archangel probably had it in mind when he'd sought her out in the first place. After another twenty minutes of haggling and pleading, Dory had finally thrown up her hands when Sorcha continued to be unmoved and several others around the table were beginning to make noises of consent.

So, after all was said and done, at just before one o'clock on Friday, the team was back at Sorcha's farmhouse for the meeting with Kinna McComish. Sorcha had arranged for the meeting on the pretext of providing Kinna with another supply of the potion she had requested. At the wary look on Kinna's face as she entered Sorcha's workroom to find eight strangers looking back at her, Dory figured they were not off to a great start. However, Sorcha seemed undeterred and took control of the situation, much to Dory's great relief.

"Kinna, I'm going to apologize right off the bat for getting you here under false pretenses," Sorcha began. "But you know me. You know I've tried to help you with your visions and dreams. I also hope that you know I would never do anything to put you in harm's way or to compromise our friendship."

"Okay," Kinna said slowly, looking around the room at the rest of the team. "What's this all about? And who are these people?"

"Well, honey, come over here and have a seat next to me, and let me introduce you to everyone. This is Dory Winthrop," Sorcha said, gesturing to Dory. "She and I have a very important story to tell you, a story that may seem extraordinary, even impossible to believe, but every word of it is true."

Kinna dropped down in the armchair next to Sorcha's and shook her head with a wry smile. "You have no idea what the last couple weeks of my life have been like. I've already heard some very hard to believe stories, but hey, knock yourselves out. I'm all ears."

Sorcha's eyebrows rose in surprise, and her returned smile was hesitant. "While I'm interested to hear about that, I think we'll hold off on my curiosity for now. I can't believe that whatever you've heard is harder to accept than what we have to tell you, but we'll see how it goes. Anyway, I guess I'll start," she said, addressing Dory. "If that's okay with you."

"Oh, please do. I've had this conversation too many times over the centuries, and never with a stellar outcome." Dory gave a go-ahead gesture with a hand. "So, please...be my guest." She was so looking forward to hearing how Sorcha would address the immortality issue.

"Over the centuries?" Kinna asked. "What does that mean?"

Sorcha turned back to Kinna. "We'll get to that in a moment, but for starters, in the beginning before you came to me for help, you were told that I was a white witch who dealt in potions and such, yes?"

Kinna nodded. "I got your name from Olivia De Santis, a friend of mine. She said you *professed* to be a white witch. But I'll tell you right now, she's an attorney and doesn't actually believe in anything without factual proof." Kinna grinned. "However, I don't care what you are, because your potions have worked quite well up to this point. That's all I really cared about."

"Yes, it's the 'up to this point' part of that sentence that we'll also need to address, but first things first. As you have probably guessed by now, I'm not really a witch, though I am very accomplished in alchemy and the magical sciences of cleansing and healing. You see...I'm actually 260 years old. I'm what's known as an Immortal as are several of us in this room."

Sorcha paused, obviously waiting for a response—any response—from Kinna. The woman's gaze, devoid of any emotion, went around the room, pausing on each person, before coming back to Sorcha. With a frown, Sorcha searched Kinna's face. "And as bizarre as what I just told you sounds, you don't seem surprised by the revelation at all."

"Again, I've had a very strange couple of weeks. This isn't the most bizarre thing that I've been told recently." Kinna tilted her head and narrowed her eyes. "But why don't we start by you explaining what you mean by Immortal, what that entails. I mean, 260 years old? That does seem...extraordinary. But are you actually human, or something else?"

Kaden let out a sudden burst of laughter. "I had the same thoughts the first time I saw Dory die and come back to life within moments. At the time, I actually called her a vampire."

Dory sighed. "Yes, and are you ever going to stop telling people that story? It's getting really old."

"Probably not." Kaden winked at Kinna. "She really hates it when I repeat the story of how I found out that she was an Immortal."

Kinna grinned at Kaden, then turned curious eyes to Dory. "So, you're an Immortal, too?"

"Yes. I'm an Immortal."

Wyatt barked out a laugh. "Don't let her fool you, Kinna. She's *the* Immortal."

"Wyatt..." Dory cautioned quietly, but he didn't seem to heed her warning.

"What?" he replied with a raised eyebrow. "You're the Chosen One, and Kaden is your Chosen Warrior. You're both named so by ancient Prophesy. You're the Immortal savior, for lack of a better term. Whether you like it or not, you and Kaden are in this world to safeguard humanity. It's part of the story, Isadora. And holding back the part of your story that makes you uncomfortable will do nothing but fuel distrust."

Dory stared at the mercenary for a moment. He wasn't wrong. She'd never been comfortable with her story, her destiny, as she and Morianna had recently discussed. It was something she was going to have to deal with sooner or later, as it was something she couldn't change. And she had to admit, ignoring it was no longer an option.

"Okay. Point taken." Turning to Kinna, Dory began to fill in the blanks. "To your first question, yes, I am human."

"All Immortals are human, Kinna," Sorcha added. "We've just been given immortality along with other gifts from a higher being at some point."

"Uh-huh," Kinna murmured. "A higher being? Do you mean God?"

"You can call it what you like, lassie," Ian answered, jumping into the discussion. "God, the Holy Trinity, Great Spirit, Kali,

Allah, the Creator, Anima Mundi, the Divine One. Every culture has a name for the Supreme Being."

Wyatt chuckled. "Yeah, that puzzle's been around since the beginning of time."

Ian nodded. "True. Though being a good Catholic boy, my choice is always God, from whom all blessings flow, as the Bible says."

"I'm with ya, old man," Wyatt returned.

"So, which of you are Immortals, besides you three?" Kinna asked, gesturing to Sorcha, Dory, and Kaden.

Ian slowly lifted a finger, while Ethan nudged a reluctant Lucy.

"I'm an Immortal but have only been so for a handful of years," Ian admitted.

"Yeah, but a heartbeat longer than me," Kaden added with a grin for the old Scot.

Kinna pointed at Lucy. "And you? You look like you have something to say, though maybe aren't real happy about it."

Lucy shot a brief glance at Dory before clearing her throat. "It's not that I'm unhappy to talk about it, it's just that I'm something different. While I am human, I'm actually not Immortal. I'm what's known in the Immortal world as a Halfling. My mother was mortal, but my...sire was an Ancient like Merlin and Morianna. So, I'm not immortal per se, but very close to it."

"Merlin?" Kinna's brows drew together. "Are you talking about the Merlin from the Arthurian legend?"

"Oh, sorry, yes," Dory replied. "It's actually not a legend, though Merlin is an Immortal Ancient and not a sorcerer. He's the head of the Immortal High Council." With a sigh, Dory rubbed her forehead where she could feel a headache beginning to form. "Kinna, there are a lot of moving parts to the Immortal story, believe me. It's not the easiest thing to explain...to anyone."

Kinna sat in silence for a few minutes, and Dory could almost see the wheels turning in the woman's head as she processed what she'd been told so far. This seemed to be going a whole lot better than Dory had hoped, but the woman's next question doused those feelings of hope like a bucket of ice-cold water.

"So, exactly what does all of this have to do with me?" Kinna asked, pinning Dory with a hard stare. "I mean, why are you telling me all of this? I'm nobody, just a normal human being."

Dory knew exactly what Kinna was feeling. Hadn't she felt the same way off and on over the last three centuries? And hadn't she just told Morianna that she didn't feel special.

Actually, it's just the opposite. I often feel like a fraud and think that perhaps the Prophesy has made a horrible mistake.

Wasn't that the equivalent to Kinna's 'I'm nobody'?

Pushing the thoughts aside, Dory leaned forward, shaking her head and giving Kinna a sympathetic look. "Fortunately for humanity, you aren't *nobody*, Kinna. You are so much more than simply a normal human being. You carry a rare and valuable entity inside of you. The Key is a precaution, a safety measure for this world. And it is as old as time itself."

"And that's why my potion is no longer working to block your visions and dreams. Why I can no longer give it to you in any form," Sorcha added. "Remember in the beginning? How I urged your to embrace your visions?"

Kinna nodded, eyes wide. "I didn't understand them, and sometimes they were almost overwhelming. I wanted them to stop."

"Well, as it turns out, those visions are part of the incredible gift inside of you. The Key, that safety measure, is waking because there is something terrible coming, something you were specifically made to protect the world from."

Kinna slowly shook her head, her gaze unfocused, as if

seeing something none of those in the room could. "Was this what she was trying to tell me?" she whispered. "Trying to make me see?"

"Who was trying to tell you, Kinna?" Sorcha asked gently.

The woman blinked a few times and then re-focused on Sorcha. "Tess Archer. She was the receptionist at my therapist's office. I'd known her for several years, but...this week I found out that I really didn't know her at all."

"What do you mean?" Dory asked.

Kinna related the way Tess had spoken to her without words during that last appointment with Dr. Newcomb, how she'd been afraid for Kinna without a clear reason why, that she somehow knew that Dr. Newcomb was evil and wasn't human at all. The entire story poured out of the woman, including the failed attempt on Monday to find Tess for more information. Kinna ended her story with the revelation that Tess was of fae descent, explaining the way they'd eluded the couple on the street outside the bistro where she and Tess had met.

"Tess and Dr. Newcomb," Kaden said quietly with a significant look for Dory. "Those were the two names you repeated while you were dreaming Monday night."

"Yes. At least that makes sense now," Dory replied.

"Wait—fae descent? What the...?" Ethan shook his head. "Are you talking about faeries?"

"Yes, Ethan. There is quite a robust fae community in the Portland area," Sorcha replied. "I know a few of them."

Kaden burst into laughter and pointed a finger in Dory's direction. "What did I tell you, pal? Elves or faeries. Most excellent," he crowed.

"Would you two just shut the hell up and let Kinna speak?" Dory admonished. "You're both acting like goofy children who aren't all that right in the head." Turning to Kinna, she urged her on with an apologetic look. "Ignore them, Kinna. Please continue."

Kinna sighed. "Well, Tess just kept saying that there were people looking for something valuable, and that they were zeroed in on me because they thought I could help them find this thing."

Kaden nodded. "Tess was right to be worried. There are people looking for something valuable. You are that something, Kinna. Although, thankfully, we don't think that the people looking know that yet."

"Where is this faerie, this Tess person now?" Ethan asked. "You said she basically teleported you both from the bistro to an alley a few blocks away. Did she accompany you to your car? Or did you go your separate ways?"

"We split up at that point. Tess thought it would be better because she'd been followed off and on, and she didn't want to put me in harm's way. So, I walked back to where my car was parked, and she headed home in the opposite direction. That was the last time that I saw her." Kinna rubbed her temples, then turned to Sorcha. "This is all just so crazy. I guess you get the prize for the most impossible story to believe."

"Trust me," Sorcha replied. "That gives me absolutely no joy."

"One question, though."

"Only one?" Ethan grinned. At Dory's glare, the grin faded slightly. "Come on, just a bit of levity. Don't you think we need a little after all of this?"

Dory shook her head and then turned to Kinna. "What's your question?"

"Well, there are actually two." Kinna looked at Dory, then pointed at Kaden. "First, you said Tess and Dr. Newcomb were the two names she repeated while she was dreaming Monday night. How is that possible. And second, how did you know to look for me? Or even that I'm this Key, for that matter. You say there are others looking for it, but you don't think they know that it's me yet. How did *you* know? Or how did you come to think that."

Dory exchanged looks with Kaden, and then taking a deep breath, blew it out slowly. "I've been seeing your dreams...well, nightmares for weeks now, Kinna. I actually saw you a few nights ago in—"

"Seattle." With a surprised look, Kinna finished the sentence Dory had started. "I remember you now. Seattle was on fire, destroyed. You were there at one point." Kinna frowned, and her eyes took on that faraway look again. "So was...he," she ended in a whisper.

Dory nodded. "Yes. You're talking about Jerahmeel. I didn't see him, but I know now that he was also there. He's been in several of your dreams. Like the one Sunday night."

Kinna's eyes widened again. "You were there, too? I didn't see you then."

"That's because I was seeing the nightmare from your point of view. It was pretty creepy, but Jerahmeel was there as well, telling you that *You're right to be wary. Evil lives here, child.* And *Can't you feel it?.* It was frightening in a horror flick kind of way."

The woman nodded. "It was. So, who is this Jerahmeel? I've actually seen him in real life, which has never happened like that before. He's been frequenting the coffeehouse. I saw him on—"

"Monday afternoon?" Dory finished for her.

"Yes!" Kinna jabbed a finger at Dory. "You saw him too? I thought you said you saw my dreams. That was during the day... in reality."

"I know, I can't explain it but I saw it in a dream Monday night."

Kinna shook her head. "I was out of Sorcha's potion so I took an over-the-counter sleep aid. I don't remember dreaming at all on Monday night."

"I don't know how, but I saw you leaving the coffeehouse with another woman."

"That was Kari Burke, Java Jive's manager. She's one of my oldest friends. My other friend, Olivia, was getting a coffee for the road. Like I said, that was when we were going to see if we could find Tess, since I hadn't been able to reach her. She'd said she would explain the cryptic things that she'd told me at my last visit with Dr. Newcomb."

"And then Jerahmeel was just there in the coffeehouse." Dory remembered Kinna's initial shock at seeing him. "I could literally feel your panic when you saw him there, when your eyes met...but there was something else. It was brief but very powerful."

Dory could see it in Kinna's eyes, that something else. She definitely knew what Dory was asking her about. "What was it, Kinna?"

The woman took a deep breath, and her hand trembled slightly as she tucked a strand of hair behind her ear. "I didn't want to think about it, about that feeling, that first thought I had when our eyes met. Yes, I could feel his power, but what scared me the most was how familiar it felt, and not just because I'd already seen him in my dreams. But for a split second...well, I remember thinking, '*I have known you for an eternity*'. It's something he said to me in that apocalyptic nightmare about Seattle. He said he'd been with me for centuries."

Dory shook her head. "But you don't have to fear him, Kinna. He's here to protect and guide you, and yes, like he's done for centuries with the entity that you carry inside you."

Kinna frowned. "But how is that even possible? It can't be, yet when I saw him in the coffeehouse and he looked up at me, I had the weirdest feeling of recognition...of rightness."

"There is a reason for that, sweetie. And it makes perfect sense when you know who and what Jerahmeel is," Sorcha said. "See, Jerahmeel is an Archangel, Kinna."

The woman's mouth dropped open. "I beg your pardon? Did you say angel?"

Sorcha shook her head. "No. I said Archangel, which is very different."

"I-I...don't...," Kinna began, but stopped and simply shook her head.

"I know this entire thing is really overwhelming, but I've known Jerahmeel for a very long time," Sorcha continued. "Of course, not as long as the entity within you has, but a good stretch in human terms. Which is why I know you have nothing to fear from him. Jerahmeel's very name means 'Mercy of God', and his specialty is interpretation of clairvoyance and spiritual visions, which is why he is also known as the 'Angel of Visions and Dreams' and the 'Angel of Hope'. He is here to protect you, has been for over a millennium."

Suddenly, Kinna stood up. "I can't hear anymore right now. I-I need some time to process this."

"Kinna, there isn't a lot of time." Dory put out a hand. "There are people looking for you. They may not know that you carry the entity inside you, which they want, but as Tess told you, they think that you can lead them to it, which is frighteningly true. Don't you think it would be better to come with us, to let us watch over you, to let Jerahmeel protect you until the danger is neutralized?"

Kinna's eyes narrowed. "Are you telling me that I can't leave?"

Dory put up both hands in surrender. "Absolutely not. We aren't here to cause you harm, Kinna. Or prevent you from leaving, for that matter. It's just not safe for you, and it's only going to get worse. Please. Let us help you."

Kinna picked up her bag and slipped it over her shoulder. "I can take care of myself. And like I said, I need to think about everything you've told me. It's just too much right now."

When Dory started to argue, Sorcha put up a finger in her direction. "You're right, Kinna. It's a lot. And we just want to make sure that you are safe. So, how about this. You take a day or two to think, and then give me a call. If I don't hear from you in that time, I'll reach out to check on you. Deal?"

The woman ran a shaky hand through her hair and then nodded. "Deal."

"Okay. And if at any time you feel unsafe or afraid, you can call me. Day or night." Sorcha smiled. "Come on, I'll walk you to your car."

As she watched the women exit the room, Dory exchanged looks with Kaden. "So, that went better than I'd expected, but what are we supposed to do now? Especially if she doesn't want our help."

Kaden shook his head. "Not a clue. The Archangel only asked us to meet with Kinna and explain, which we've done."

"I guess if he wants us to do more, he'll let us know," Ian added quietly.

Dory glanced out the window at the fields beyond. "In the meantime, Sorcha's got her number and can check on her. But I gotta say, I don't like the idea of just waiting and hoping that Kinna can stay clear of Smyth and his ilk for a couple days. We need to at least get someone in place to keep an eye on her... discreetly."

"I know a couple ex-Sentinels here on the coast that I can call," Tanner offered. "Make sure she's covered until we can bring her into the fold."

"The Archangel didn't say anything about that." Ian frowned. "Seems to me he would be handling that, don't you think?"

"I think having eyes on McComish is a good idea whether the Archangel asked for it or not," Kaden replied.

"Yes. I agree," Dory said. "Give the ex-Sentinels a call, Tanner. We need to have them in place as soon as possible. I don't mind a bit of overkill when it comes to security. Especially with a Time Mender."

But Dory couldn't help feeling like they were all sitting on a hefty explosive device. And the timer was counting down.

KINNA'S MIND was a whirl of questions and emotions as she drove back toward Java Jive. Her afternoon, like the last week and a half, had deteriorated into something resembling science fiction or borderline horror. Faeries, Immortals, and now angels. *Huh-uh,* she thought. *Archangels.* And all because of the damn visions and dreams that she'd had most of her life? It was ludicrous.

But was it really? A voice in her head whispered. Didn't some, if not most, of what she'd been told make perfect sense when looking at the course of her life, the inconceivable twists and turns?

Though her parents were disturbed by their only daughter's tales of the things she saw at night in her dreams, in the visions she had in the light of day, her grandfather had always said that she should embrace every part of herself. He'd never been afraid of her visions as her parents had been. He'd even been comforting and understanding when, at seventeen and guilt-ridden, she'd confessed to have seen her parents death by car crash in the weeks before it happened.

"It's not your fault, Kinna. But just know that you're special in more ways than you can fathom, my precious girl," he'd said at the time.

If he only knew.

After a moment of thought, Kinna began to remember other bits of conversations she'd had with him.

You have no idea what you're capable of.

You are a gift from God, sweetness.

You will do great things someday, Kinna.

If only your parents could've seen with better eyes.

Surely, this couldn't have been what he meant. Could it?

She had to put it all out of her head for a while, come back to it after she'd gotten some distance. Even now, as she turned into the parking lot at Java Jive and drove around to the back of the building to park in her spot, she was wondering if it had all been real or just another hallucination.

She probably would've seen the man walking toward her sooner had her mind not been still churning with the craziness of the meeting at Sorcha's. She leaned in to grab her bag, and when she closed the car door and turned, he was just...there.

"Miss McComish, I'm so glad I caught you," the man said, his odd, hazel eyes full of worry. "We need to talk to you immediately. We have something very important to tell you."

Kinna studied him for a moment. Dull, brown hair, white, long-sleeved, button-down shirt with a dark brown jacket, jeans, and oxfords on his feet. He looked normal enough, but that didn't necessarily mean that he was, did it?

Stop it, Kinna, she thought. *You can't see crazy in every face, no matter what you've just heard.*

She tilted her head and frowned. "I'm sorry. Do I know you?"

The man hesitated. "Well, no, not me, but my employer really needs to talk to you. He sent me to get you. If you could just come with me—"

"Exactly what's this about Mr....?"

"Jonah. My name is Jonah. And Mr. Smyth has important business to discuss with you."

Mr. Smyth? As in Dorian Smyth? The attorney that Olivia spoke so scathingly of?

Kinna sighed. "Look, Jonah, I'm sorry but I don't have time for this right now."

"But you have to come," he continued. "It's a matter of great concern, especially for your safety. There are people looking for you."

"Uh-huh. What people?"

"See, that's what Mr. Smyth wants to discuss with you," Jonah said, taking her arm and trying to pull her around the car toward the side lot. "You really need to come with me now."

"Hey!" she shouted, jerking free of his grasp. "Don't grab me like that. And I told you, I don't have time for this right now."

This time when he turned to her, there was an angry fire in those odd hazel eyes. The tiny flecks of gold looked almost molten. He grabbed her with both hands and shoved her back against the trunk of her car.

"I said you need to come with me, so you will come...one way or another."

Before she could respond, a deep, rumbling laughter drew the attention of them both.

The coffeehouse hunk—Jerahmeel, she reminded herself—was leaning against the back of Kari's Honda, shaking his head with mirth.

"Really? Jonah, is it?" The Archangel narrowed his eyes. "I don't think the lady wishes to go anywhere with you."

An unnatural hissing sound came from the man as he took a step back.

Jerahmeel pushed off of the Honda and took two slow steps toward them. "Yes, you know who I am," he said quietly. "And I know where you come from, demon. So, I would go. Go now. While you still can."

"This is no business of yours," Jonah screeched, then turned to Kinna. "He is not to be trusted. He will tell you lies."

"Ah, it's ironic you should speak of lies. Shall we show Kinna where the lies are kept?" Jerahmeel asked in that same quiet voice now laced with amusement. "Shall I show her what hides under your façade?"

"No!"

With a fan of one hand, Jerahmeel wiped away the glamour that hid the demon's hideous features. Kinna gasped as the demon shrieked and clawed hands made to cover what had been exposed.

"You will pay for this," it cried as it continued to back away.

"No. I will not. But you will. Tell your mistress that I am here. That is, if she doesn't already know. Now, go. Before I change my mind."

As the demon scrambled away, Kinna saw her chance to escape. She wasn't ready for this. She had to get away and think. Turning, she jumped into her car and fired up the engine. She let out a shriek of her own when she looked out the side window to find Jerahmeel standing there, staring down at her.

You can't ignore your destiny forever, Child of Light...nor can you avoid me for long.

She heard his words with crystal clarity in her head, which only added to the whole freaky situation. Without a second thought, Kinna put the car in reverse and backed out. The last thing she saw as she was driving away was Jerahmeel standing where she'd left him with arms crossed, shaking his head.

Dorian heaved the crystal paperweight in his hand across the room, shattering the elegant, blown glass vase on the fireplace mantel and putting a fist-sized dent in the wall behind it. Colorful shards of glass flew in all directions with the force, and the paperweight broke into several pieces as well.

"Dorian, you have got to calm down. You know there's nothing to be done about it," Verrine murmured in a honeyed voice. "So, take a breath, my sweet. We'll find our way through this. We cannot be deterred, nor can we let the actions of others dictate our path forward."

She watched the Immortal carefully and sensed his blood pressure slowly beginning to drop, his heaving breath to ease. Going to him, she ran a light hand over his shoulder. "You must trust me, love. Remember, we're already closer than we were yesterday."

Dorian took a deep breath and let it out slowly. "I don't know how you can be so calm, Verrine," he muttered. "This worthless creature should be destroyed. Painfully, in my opinion." Dorian nodded to the anxious demon kneeling before them on the carpet in the middle of the living room, his voice carrying his anger. "The piece of shit had one job. One! It was sent on a simple catch and retrieve mission and couldn't even handle one scrawny, mortal female. And what's worse, it waited almost a day and a half to tell us, costing us precious time that we could have recouped had we known earlier of its failure. It's infuriating."

Verrine eyed the demon with pity. "Mmm, yes, it is disappointing. But then again, this is just a lowly Tracker demon, aren't you, Jonah? It is a shame, though," she told the demon. "I went through a lot of trouble to find you a very nice, very fit human body to inhabit. So young, so firm and virile." Her tone became stern as her own anger flared briefly. "However, Dorian is correct. That you couldn't get the job done is really quite unacceptable."

"I told you," Jonah cried, his eyes wildly going back and forth between her and Dorian. "It wasn't my fault. She refused to come with me. I tried."

Dorian grabbed Jonah by the throat. "Excuses!" he shouted.

Verrine could feel his blood pressure escalating again. "Dorian...Darling, let the poor thing go, and let me handle this."

After several beats, the Immortal literally threw the demon to the carpet. With a growl, he turned on his heel, went to the bar, and poured himself a drink.

Verrine hunched down in front of the gagging, red-faced Jonah.

"You say it wasn't your fault, Jonah, so what happened? Why were you unable to secure the human? You know that she is integral to our success, do you not? She can help us in our quest for The Key." Verrine took a breath and pouted. "How could you have let us down this way?"

"It really wasn't my fault, mistress," Jonah whispered in a conspiratorial tone with a quick glance in Dorian's direction. "I was taking her, I really was. She was resisting but I would have prevailed, but...then *he* was there."

Verrine frowned at his meaningful look. "He? Explain, please."

Jonah nodded. "He stripped away my glamour and ordered me to go, said to tell you that he was here if you didn't already know." The demon narrowed his eyes. "You know who I mean, right? It was Jerah—"

Before the demon could say the Archangel's name out loud, Verrine waved a hand in front of his face and rose. She listened to the death throes of the young human's body without a backward glance as the Tracker demon that had occupied it was ejected, returned to the realm from which it came.

Dorian turned from the bar with a frown just as the body fell lifelessly to the carpet, face first. "What the hell, Verrine? You tell me to let it go, and then you snuff it out before we can get any more details? What are you playing at?"

She sauntered over to him with a sensual look and took the glass of Scotch from his hand. Taking a deep swallow, she smiled up at him serenely. "We'd gotten all we were going to get from it. Kinna McComish obviously outwitted the sad thing, and then got into her car and drove away before it could figure out what to do and how to respond. That's simply all that happened. He had no more vital information to give us." Verrine took another sip of Scotch and then gestured with the glass. "Besides, demons always lie, darling. Don't you know that? They mix their lies with just a bit of truth. That's the challenge and the fun of it, don't you think? To sift out the truth from the lies?"

With a shake of his head, Dorian grinned down at her. "You are a ruthless one, aren't you? We are such a pair, you and I. Perfectly matched."

Verrine smiled back at him over the rim of the glass. "Do you think?"

"I do," he replied in a husky, suggestive tone.

As he reached out for her, she slipped out of range and wandered to the floor-to-ceiling windows that overlooked the river. "I've been thinking, Dorian," she said with a sigh. "It may be time for you to take control of the situation."

"What do you mean?" he asked with a testy attitude as he stepped up next to her. "We're doing everything we can. If it wasn't for the incompetence of these creatures you've brought with you from God knows where, we probably would have had the McComish bitch by now—maybe even The Key. We'd be well on our way to changing the timeline and creating a whole new world for ourselves. What more do you think I should be doing?"

Turning, she held his gaze, reaching out with her mind, wielding her influential will with her seductive voice. "Ah, but don't you see? That's just what I'm talking about, darling. Don't you think you should go ahead and have this Kinna McComish picked up yourself?" She handed his glass of Scotch back to him. "I mean, really, why are we using inferior demons? Creatures, I might add, which need human bodies to inhabit to function on this plane. That process is no easy feat, I can assure you. However, you have a plethora of Immortals and Immortal wannabes at your disposal who are willing and more than capable of scooping her up and bringing her to you tomorrow."

Dorian nodded, a docile look coming over his face, a touch of adoration entering his eyes. That look always filled Verrine with pleasure. Humans, Immortal or not, were so very easy to control, and it gave her such joy.

She ran the back of her hand over his cheek. "All I'm saying is that we should step up our game with the tools at our disposal. Right?"

"Yes, Of course. That is an excellent idea, love," he murmured. "I will see to it the first thing—"

The conversation was interrupted by a commotion in the foyer. In the next moment, three of Dorian's men entered the room dragging an unconscious female between them followed by Victoria Newcomb. The men deposited the unconscious female on the carpet next to the young man's dead body and stood back.

"Well, well, well, what do we have here?" Verrine asked, rubbing her hands together in her excitement.

"Yes. What the hell is this?" Dorian asked with irritation.

"This is Tess Archer. She's my previous receptionist," Victoria replied. "Well, Dr. Addison's receptionist. She was nothing but trouble from the moment we got rid of the fine doctor and I took over his practice. She was also a serious pain in the ass to get a hold of, I'll tell you that much. We actually had to make several attempts, which took a hellava lot more time than I'd liked. However, come to find out, there was a reason for that."

"Oh? Do tell." Verrine raised a perfectly arched eyebrow.

"Well, as it turns out, our little Tessie here is fae." Victoria giggled. "We had to sneak up on her and then dose her on the spot with a little concoction of my own design. It's particularly effective on elves, faeries, shapeshifters, and the like. Although, elves and faeries can sometimes be the most slippery with the whole disappearing ability and all, but damn if this one wasn't especially so." She frowned. "I'm just annoyed that I never could put my finger on something that should have been a no-brainer and completely obvious."

"Yes, but you bested her in the end, didn't you? Excellent," Verrine purred. "Really fine work, Victoria. I'm very impressed."

"Are we done with the preening show and tell?" Dorian asked in a bored tone. "Can we move on, please.?"

"Hey, you've had your people trying to get a hold of this one for weeks," Victoria snapped. "These two thugs may be your minions, but *I* delivered the goods, so don't be a sore loser, Dorian. Pouting is for weaklings, you arrogant ass."

"Why, you fucking little demon cun—"

"Now, now. No bickering children." Verrine stifled a yawn and then gave Dorian a simpering look. "And no naughty language, my love. You know how that upsets me." She patted his cheek again as if he really was a child. "Remember, as good leaders, we should always give praise where praise is due, don't you think?"

At Dorian's glare, Verrine turned and pointed at the two men who were waiting off to one side after depositing the unconscious female onto the rug. "You two strap our little faerie friend to a chair and move her closer to the fireplace. We're going to need to have a long conversation with Miss Tess when she awakens."

"And then get rid of this other body on your way out," Dorian added then frowned at Verrine. "And what do you mean, when she awakens? I say, let's give her a rude awakening right now, and get this damn party started. I want to know where this Key is without any further delays. And if we can get the information out of this one, we may not have to worry about picking up the McComish woman at all, which will save time and energy."

Verrine laughed out loud. "Yes, darling. You may be right. However, let's not get ahead of ourselves. Why don't you go make us all some drinks—just to rev up our interrogation juices. You know, get the perfect vibe going? Then we'll wake the faerie and see what's what."

Verrine waited until Dorian had gone to the bar to get the drinks started before turning to Victoria and speaking with her mind-to-mind. *We need to, as he just said, get this party started immediately because I've just found out that Jerahmeel is here. He was the reason that the Tracker demon couldn't bring in the McComish woman.*

Victoria's eyes grew big at that news. *That's not good. Jerah-meel could ruin everything.* Her gaze slid to Dorian's back at the bar on the other side of the room. *Does he know?*

Verrine shook her head slightly. *I sent the Tracker demon on its way the minute it told me that Jerahmeel was here. Dorian wasn't within earshot. He still thinks we're right on track with no one the wiser.*

What a putz he is. Victoria glanced in the Immortal's direction again before turning back to Verrine with a frown. *Look, I got Tess here like you asked, but I don't know why we're wasting time with her instead of just picking up McComish now. I mean, we know where the woman lives, and this faerie isn't going to tell us anything we don't already know. McComish is the one we need to be concentrating on, I'm telling you.*

That is probably true. However, this step will do one thing for us. Interrogating the fae will keep Dorian occupied and on task even if we don't acquire any new information. I was just giving him a little nudge right before you brought her in about picking up the McComish woman. Verrine smiled. *I have a feeling, since Jerahmeel is here and interrupted the planned abduction, that she's where we'll find the information we seek.*

And when we have that information? What about him? Victoria nodded in Dorian's direction as the Immortal turned from the bar with a tray of drinks and started toward them.

Verrine shot Victoria a hard look. *That is none of your concern. I will handle the Immortal,* she finished, then sent a brilliant smile to Dorian as he came to her first, like a child looking for praise.

"The champagne cocktail is obviously for you, love. Your favorite," he murmured, ignoring Victoria completely.

Verrine reached out and took the champagne flute from the tray. "Thank you, my sweet. This will whet my appetite for interrogation perfectly." She took a slow sip and then glanced at Victoria. "I'm assuming you have a way to wake the fae from her drugged sleep without having to worry about her immediately disappearing on us. Yes?"

"I do," Victoria responded, taking the martini glass Dorian offered from the tray. "The concoction I came up with suppresses the ability to use certain powers—the ability to disappear being one of them. She'll be groggy if I wake her before the mixture has left her system, but she won't be able to elude us in that way. We should have sufficient time to grill her."

"Excellent." Verrine gestured to the unconscious Tess. "Then, why don't you wake her up, and we'll get on with the interrogation? No time like the present."

A SENSE OF DRIFTING, confusion, something cold under her nose. Taking in a deep breath, an explosion of pain shot through her skull and coughing wracked her body as if she'd breathed in a mouthful of horseradish. After a moment, the sensation subsided and, shaking her head in an effort to clear the ringing in her ears, Tess tried to blink open eyes that felt heavy and coated in glue.

"Ah, yes, there she is," a sultry voice murmured somewhere to her right. "She's coming around. Tess? Can you hear me?"

"Come on, faerie. Open your eyes," another voice—a very familiar one—crooned.

She should know who that voice belonged to, should be able to put a face to it, but her head was so full of fog making her thoughts a jumble.

"Really, Tess," that familiar voice said. "Is this how you want to go out? As a weakling faerie who couldn't even open her eyes to look at her captors?"

Newcomb! The answer came to Tess in a flash of clarity. The afternoon of running, eluding, and ultimately being dosed with...something. Then blackness. It all came rushing back to her in that moment, but it was all mixed up. She fought to open her eyes and finally succeeded, only to find the blurry, distorted face of Victoria Newcomb leaning in.

"That's better," Victoria said. "How do you feel?"

"How to you think I feel, you demon fuck?" Tess replied in a voice rusty to her own ears.

Victoria grinned evilly. "So, you've finally snapped to it, have you? I know you've been wondering about my origins for some time—what I am? It's funny. I've been doing the same thing with you since I took over at the clinic. I knew you were somehow different, not quite human, but I could never quite put my finger on it. Fae. Go figure. I'm quite disappointed in myself, as it should have been obvious. But then, we don't always see what's right in front of us, do we?"

"What did you do to me?" Tess shook her head again as the room made a lazy circle. The fog was beginning to clear a bit, but she was still groggy, her thought process sluggish.

Victoria chuckled. "It's just a little potion I came up with a few years ago. It won't cause any long-lasting damage, but it does suppress all those pesky abilities like disappearing, just so you know. However, I'm afraid you've got bigger fish to fry than my potion." Victoria looked confused for a moment, then glanced over her shoulder at the man standing back. "And what exactly does that phrase even mean? Do you know? I've been living in this body for several years now and these random phrases from this human's memories still continue to pop up from time to time. And most of them just don't make any sense to me."

"Oh, for Christ's sake," he muttered. "Get on with it, already."

"You're such a downer, Dorian," Victoria sniped. "I mean, where is the trust building, the clarifications, the simple fun of taunting the victim?"

"Alright, alright, enough, both of you," the first voice Tess had heard spoke up. "We'll get nowhere with bickering."

Then Newcomb stepped back, and a different woman altogether hunched down in front of Tess. This woman was beautiful, almost ethereal. Yet, there was something really off here as well, and Tess felt like that something was just out of reach. If she could just clear her head, she was sure she would know what was wrong with the picture.

"Tess, my name is Verrine. I'm sorry that bringing you here like this had to be so...unpleasant, but we really need some information from you. It's very important, and we're running short on time," the woman said. "So, we're going to ask you some questions, and if you can answer them for us, this can all be over quickly. If not...well...then this is going to be a very drawn out, painful process. Do you understand?"

Tess frowned at the woman. "Are you a demon, too?"

The woman smiled, almost kindly, then shook her head. "I'm...something very different. But you shouldn't worry about that now. What you really need to concentrate on is answering our questions. Are you listening to me?"

"Sure, but I don't know what you think I can tell you?" Tess licked her dry lips and shook her head. "Can I get some water?"

"Of course." Verrine turned to the man. "Dorian, would you get Tess a cup of water, please?"

The man frowned. "Water? Really? Are we gonna feed her dinner as well?"

"Dorian, don't be difficult. What is this small gesture going to hurt? Please?"

"Fine," Dorian grumbled and walked away shaking his head.

"I'm sorry about that," Verrine apologized. "Dorian is very impatient for some answers. So, here's the first question. We're looking for The Key. It's very valuable, and we need it for our plans going forward, so what can you tell us about its location?"

"I don't know anything about a key," Tess replied, still trying to bring her thoughts into some kind of order. Everything was still sort of swirling in her mind.

"Come on, Tess," Victoria complained. "I know you were aware that we were looking for something valuable, so don't try to pretend otherwise."

Tess nodded as Dorian came back with a cup of water and handed it to Verrine. "That's true. I knew you were looking for something, but I didn't know what it was. Still don't."

Verrine held the cup to Tess's lips so that she could take a sip. Her mouth was so dry, probably from whatever she'd been dosed with. If she could get a bit more water into her body, maybe it would help clear her mind and give her a better chance of finding a way out of this situation. Because she was pretty sure that if she didn't find a way, she wouldn't live to see another sunrise.

"Let's try something else," Verrine murmured. "Tell us what you know about Kinna McComish."

Tess's heart began to pound at the mention of Kinna's name, but she kept a confused look on her face. This was why they'd drugged her, had brought her here. They wanted information about Kinna, just like she'd told Kinna in the first place. She had to direct them away from the woman.

"Kinna McComish? She's a patient at the clinic."

Victoria scoffed. "What did you tell her last week? You made her another appointment, but then you disappeared. I think there was something else you told her. Isn't that right? Did you tell her that we were looking at her? That we were watching her closely?"

"Does Kinna know where The Key is?" Verrine asked quietly. Then she leaned down, and Tess heard the woman's voice in her head. *Is Kinna The Key? Is that what you're hiding?*

"I don't know what that is. What key are you talking about?" Tess said out loud in a frantic voice.

Think! She had to think.

Verrine sighed and stood up. "That's very disappointing, Tess. I had hoped that we could have a friendly conversation."

"Really?" Tess replied. She wiggled her fingers where the tingly feeling told her that her abilities were waking up. If she could just hang on, she might get out of this place alive. "So, let me get this straight. You thought that drugging me, abducting me, and torturing me was going to lead to a friendly conversation? In what world?"

"Yes, I see now that's not possible." She turned to Dorian. "She's all yours, darling. Maybe you can get our answers from her your way."

Dorian smiled, and hunkered down in front of Tess. "This is going to be unpleasant, little faerie. And I can guarantee it is not going to end well for you."

It took another two hours, a lot of pain and loss of hope, but with her last breath, Tess finally came to the realization that Dorian had been correct.

It didn't end well for her.

M id-afternoon on Sunday, and for the third time in
less than a week, Dory, Kaden, and the rest of the
team again headed over the hill to Sorcha Doyle's
place. Kinna McComish had said she'd needed time to process
what she'd been told at their Friday afternoon meeting, and that
she'd be in contact within a day or two. However, when Dory
had spoken to Sorcha earlier that morning, the Immortal had
said that she'd tried calling Kinna several times, and so far, there
had been no response to any of the messages left.

It was a definite concern.

Dory was trying not to read too much into it, but the situation was tenuous and time was short. If Dorian Smyth and
Verrine, the fallen angel he was working with, hadn't figured out
that Kinna was The Key—the entity that they were searching for
—they soon would. And then all bets were off. There was no
telling what they might do, and Kinna would be in grave danger
as would they all.

Kinna had listened to everything Dory had told her on
Friday, seemingly with an open mind, but she'd become increasingly overwhelmed. That didn't surprise Dory in the least. It was

a feeling that she herself knew all too well. Although, in Dory's case, there had been no one to explain the details of how her life would change, what it meant to be the Chosen One, or who may be out to do her harm in the future. She supposed that was one of the reasons that she'd fought so long against accepting her destiny. There had been no playbook, no guiding light to show her the way forward. And definitely no guardian angel.

Archangel, she corrected herself.

Kinna, on the other hand—though in somewhat of the same predicament—now had a group of very capable allies that could walk her though a very dicey situation, help her to come to grips with her purpose. If only she would let them, trust them enough to do so. Knowing who to trust had been a huge part of what Dory had struggled with for the first two centuries of her immortality. Even with her Sentinel Velma—and Velma's ancestors who had come before her at the end of that first century—it had taken work to embrace that trust, to let down her guard and welcome them in.

She'd gotten so used to being on her own, running, protecting herself. Finally letting go of that isolation, and yes, the constant fear of getting too close to anyone, was something that had been a long time coming for her. It was something she continued to work on to this day.

But then along came Kaden Crenshaw.

After three hundred plus years of a near solitary existence, the Chosen Warrior had entered her life at a point where she'd been ready to give up, to succumb to a true and final death, had expected it, even prayed for it. She'd continued to go through the motions of survival, but she could now admit to herself that in her own mind she'd been at her end.

But then her heart had disregarded her better judgment, and she'd fallen for Kaden. Hard. It had terrified her, and in that panicked freefall, she'd tried desperately to push him away with just as much force as she could muster. She could accept her own death, having already made the decision, but she could never sacrifice him, condemn him to the same fate. However, she hadn't counted on his steely will, his determination...and finally, the depth of his love for her.

And thank God for it, she thought.

Kaden had saved her, completed her.

In the end, when he'd died a mortal death because of her, she'd been unable to let him go. Now he was hers for an eternity. Together they were the first two links in a chain that had become a trusted team. She'd learned so very much about herself in the last few years, and most of the substantial realizations she'd come to had been because of Kaden. He never pushed, never lectured—well, maybe sometimes when even she could admit that it was needed—but he constantly enabled her in every way to make good decisions, to be all that she could be.

She still stumbled...a lot. But Kaden was always there to right her. It humbled her how he'd taken control of his own immortality, learned what he could, continued to push his boundaries and move forward. While she, on the other hand, had...how had Morianna put it? Oh, yeah...had continued to waste time and act like a petulant child made to do something she didn't want to do. Looking at the Immortal portion of her life as a whole, she supposed that analogy was fair. She hadn't wanted to be the Chosen One in the first place, to live forever, to watch friends and family wither and die. Why on earth an ancient, nebulous Prophesy would choose her—out of all the possible choices out there—as the world's savior was still pretty inconceivable to her even now.

"So, what's going on in that head of yours?" Kaden asked, interrupting her self-examination.

She turned to him and studied his profile. He hadn't even

taken his eyes off the road, yet again, somehow seemed to know something was troubling her. "What do you mean?"

"Please. You're thinkin' real loud, darlin'. And I gotta say, it feels kinda painful."

"So, what? Now you can hear me thinking? Is this some new Immortal power you've added to your collection?"

Kaden snorted. "I don't need any special powers to know that you're working something over in your head with a great big hammer."

She sighed. "Just going over some old issues, trying to make some sense of a few things."

"You want to tell me about it sometime soon? Or is this something else you'd rather keep to yourself?"

"Don't be a jerk. I said I was sorry before. I wasn't keeping secrets intentionally," she muttered, but couldn't stop the grin that began to spread. What had she just been thinking? He never pushed?

"Uh-huh," Kaden grunted with a roll of his eyes.

"You know what I mean, smart-ass. And yes, I would love to tell you all about it, but not just yet, and definitely not here in a van-full of ears." She hooked a thumb over her shoulder, indicating the rest of the team in the back of the van. "Besides, I'm not quite finished hammering yet."

Kaden chuckled. "Okay, okay. Just let me know when you're ready."

"You'll be the first to hear." She looked out of the side window at the gray, overcast day. The dark green of the forested land was thinning as they descended the other side of the mountain toward Sorcha Doyle's place in the rural outskirts of the metro area.

And suddenly she felt it, like a slow injection of some kind of hateful poison. Something was coming, something not so good.

It poured over her, through her like a thick, suffocating liquid freshly soured. It appeared quickly, then faded a bit to hover in the background of her senses, but she couldn't quite get the taste of it out of her throat or a handle on what it meant. But something was up, and it wasn't far off. She could only hope that it didn't involve Kinna, but she wasn't putting money on that just yet. If Smyth and his bunch had figured out that Kinna was the prize they were seeking, then all hell might be just about to explode all over them.

"Did you just feel that?" Kaden asked as if reading her mind. "Something's..."

"Coming," she finished for him. "Yes, I was just thinking that. You felt it too?"

He nodded. "Oh, hell yeah, like something...ugly and thick, something not right in the air all of a sudden. Felt like it coated the back of my throat. And it seemed just a bit too close for comfort. Know what I mean?"

"Agreed. I really want to get to Doyle's and find out where Kinna is, if she's safe. Because whatever it is..."

"It's really not good," he finished for her this time. "Yeah, I got that much."

Before they could get any farther in the discussion, Lucy leaned forward in between the seats and tapped Dory on the shoulder.

"Hey, y'all. I don't want to come across as a Nervous Nellie here, but did you two just feel something weird?" she asked quietly, taking care not to alert the others.

"You mean like something coming that isn't quite right?" Dory replied under her breath. "Maybe something decidedly unpleasant on the wind?"

Lucy shook her head. "What I felt was a whole lot worse than unpleasant. More like something ripping through the fabric of the atmosphere, you know?" She paused for a moment.

"Do you guys remember that feeling on the beach at Hilton Head?"

"I've been trying to forget it for several years now," Kaden murmured. "But yeah, we both felt it, too. Any ideas of what it could be?"

"I don't know, but it's not good...and not far away."

Dory nodded. "My thoughts exactly. Pass the word toward the back. Keep your eyes peeled and your ears wide open. I'd really like to at least get to Sorcha's without any trouble, and then we'll see what's what."

"Will do," Lucy replied. "I'll also talk to Wyatt, see what he thinks. He's known Sorcha for a long time, knows her abilities. Maybe she felt it too and can explain what it means."

Dory nodded. "I guess we'll see when we get there. And Lucy, tell Tanner to reach out to the Sentinels keeping an eye on Kinna. Get a report on her status."

"You bet."

Thirty minutes later, Kaden was exiting the highway onto a rural county road, and then in another ten, they were bumping along Sorcha's long, rutted driveway. They all piled out of the van the minute Kaden parked the rig and shut it down.

Evidently, Dory and Lucy were not alone in thinking about that beach in South Carolina where they'd all just about lost their lives, where the Dragon's Breath in Dory's system had ultimately saved them from the heinous Erinyes that had attacked them in search of Lucy's blood. Every member of the team seemed to be scouring the overcast sky for any anomaly.

Lucy's parallel of something ripping through the fabric of the atmosphere rang true to Dory, which was just what it felt like on that beach back then. A murky, gray line on the horizon, as if someone had unzipped the sky with monsters just pouring through the opening like a greasy, putrid stain. This had the same feel, for sure, but seeing nothing out of the ordinary, one by one, they all turned toward the farmhouse where Sorcha stepped out onto the porch just as Dory and Kaden climbed the steps.

"I see you've felt it, too," Sorcha said before Dory could even open her mouth in greeting.

"What? The creepiness in the air? The bad taste in my mouth?" Dory nodded. "Yeah, kinda hard to miss, right? It hit us just as we were coming down this side of the mountain. We were wondering if you'd felt it here. Wyatt seemed to think that it was likely you would have."

Sorcha looked past Dory to where the mercenary was bringing up the rear with Velma. "Yes, you're right. It was hard to miss," she murmured. "Y'all better come in. We definitely need to talk."

Dory glanced at Kaden, who raised an eyebrow before they both followed Sorcha into the house.

"So, do you know what's happening or about to happen, Sorcha?" Lucy asked when they all settled in around the big dining room table as they'd done before. "I mean, we were just talking about how it had almost the same feel as it did on the beach at Hilton Head right before the horizon split open and hundreds of those flying monsters came screaming at us."

"And if you know what this is, please tell me it doesn't have anything to do with Kinna McComish," Dory added. "That's all we need right now."

Sorcha shook her head. "Not sure. I don't think it's to do with Kinna, at least not directly, but I do have some thoughts that are a bit concerning."

"Speaking of Kinna, have you reached her yet?" Tanner asked. "I got a hold of Conner and Sanchez, the Sentinels keeping an eye on her. They say she's fine, but it seems odd that she's gone silent."

"Yes, I finally go through to her. We spoke on the phone about an hour ago."

"And?" Dory prodded. By the look on the woman's face, she was almost afraid to hear the result of that conversation. "Your demeanor doesn't exactly inspire confidence in a positive outcome, Sorcha."

The Immortal frowned. "It's not that it wasn't positive. It's just that she was vague and non-committal on meeting again. It seems that she's taking some time to get her 'hands dirty' at Java Jive, said she's been neglecting the business and wanted to spend some time and effort there. Although, I sensed that she actually believed what she was saying and conveyed it honesty, I'm not sure that I completely buy what she was selling. However, the good news is that she'll be surrounded by people who care about her, so that's a plus."

"I guess you could call it that," Dory said with skepticism. "But it doesn't give me much comfort, even with our Sentinels standing watch when she's at home."

"Yeah, her being surrounded by friends during the day is all well and good," Ethan added. "But what about going to and from the coffeehouse? And is somebody going to be with her at home or every other damned minute of her day? Seems like gaping holes in a non-existent security protocol to me. And those Sentinels can't be everywhere at once."

"You're the law enforcement officer, Ethan. So, I guess you'd know. But yes, we'll need to keep an eye on her," Sorcha agreed then looked in Dory's direction. "I'm glad that you took steps to get some security in place. I'm not sure she's taking this whole thing as seriously as we thought, or as she should, for that matter. And I told her so...as gently as I could."

"We may not have a lot of time for 'gently', lass," Ian suggested. "We've been running on borrowed time with this whole mess from the get-go, in my humble opinion. And this feeling or premonition or whatever it is that we've felt tells me that what little time we may have is nearly gone."

"I do agree with you there, Ian. Time is definitely one of the problems." Sorcha's gaze swept the faces around the table, coming to rest on Dory. "And not just for Kinna."

"That sounds a bit dark," Kaden said with a puzzled look. "What do you mean, Sorcha?"

"I told you I had some apprehensive thoughts regarding this 'feeling' of something bad coming. Though I don't think it's about Kinna directly, I do think it's related. However, it felt more ominous to me...and somehow connected in other ways. I'm not sure if that make any sense or not?"

"Unfortunately, yes. It does," Dory replied. "I felt a strong connection the minute it happened...and it felt almost personal. At least, that was my first thought when the thick, ugly sensation shot through me. As Lucy said, it felt similar to the feeling we all had just before the beach attack that we barely lived through."

Sorcha nodded. "I thought so. And as well it should. I think it has to do with you, Dory."

"Me?" Dory blanched. "Why would you say that?"

Sorcha folded her hands on the table and gave Dory an intense look. "Because of another phone conversation I had earlier today not too long after we spoke on the phone this morning. I got a call from an acquaintance of mine—a fae acquaintance—who had some worrying questions and troubling information to pass on. First, she told me that a friend of hers, another faerie, had been found by some boaters floating face down in the Willamette river early this morning." She paused as if deciding how to go on. "The name of the dead faerie was Tess Archer."

Dory felt the blood drain from her face. "The faerie Kinna had told us about during the meeting on Friday. The Tess that I dreamed about."

"Yes. Evidently, she was killed sometime late last night or in the wee hours before dawn."

"Oh, my gosh!" Lucy exclaimed. "What happened? Did your friend know?"

Sorcha shook her head. "Not exactly, but she did say that there was evidence of torture. She said Tess had obviously been bound and beaten horribly, along with a few other details that I won't repeat, but that was all she knew for sure."

"That's terrible. The poor soul," Velma murmured and then frowned. "But that doesn't explain why you think this feeling you've all experienced has something to do with Dory. I mean, sad to say, but it seems to speak more to the connection with Kinna than with Dory, right?"

"That's where the other, more disturbing, piece of information she gave me comes in." Sorcha took a breath and let it out slowly. "She point blank asked me about the Chosen One."

"What the fuck?" Kaden shot a glance to Dory.

Sorcha nodded. "Yeah, she said she'd heard—from more than one source—that there were Immortals looking for something very valuable, something they were willing to kill over, and that the Chosen One was involved."

"How the hell did that get around?" Kaden asked angrily. "You said more than one source. That means someone has been talking, giving out information about our operation." His gaze scanned the table. "That hole will need to be choked off at the source."

Dory laid a calming hand on Kaden's arm. "We'll handle that, love. But first things first." She turned back to Sorcha. "Was that it? Or is there more?"

"Oh, there's more," Sorcha said in a sour tone. "She also wanted to know if it was true that you were part of the plan these Immortals had to find this valuable thing. Because it was her belief that Tess was killed for something she knew about what these Immortals were looking for. She indicated that she thought they may have been responsible for Tess's death." Sorcha bit her lip and then continued, "The last thing she told me was that she'd heard that these Immortals were working with a fallen angel...and that there were demons involved as well."

"Where the hell would she get that kind of information?" Wyatt asked heatedly. "None of this makes any sense."

"Except it does." Dory glanced at Kaden. "It's all connected, right? And it does seem to circle back to me, doesn't it?"

"Dory—"

"No, Kaden, it's true. I mean, obviously there's a leak somewhere that needs to be dealt with, but the other thing I've kept coming back to over and over again for quite a while now is..."

"The Dragon's Breath." He finished for her.

She nodded. "It would make sense. If the Dragon's Breath did bond with my system, changed me on a molecular level as Morianna theorized, and if what's coming is demonic in origin like the Erinyes, then we can only hope that it's still waiting somewhere inside me. Pray that I can access it when the time comes." She looked into his furious eyes and tried to give him a smile but knew it fell short. "Look, I'm not all that thrilled about it, either. Trust me. But as long as I'm not burning up from the inside out like before, I'm not opposed to having a bit of it inside me to use as a very powerful weapon, you know?"

Kaden took her hand and lifted her palm to his lips. "I gotta say, the possibility of that nasty black shit lingering in your system, doesn't exactly thrill me, either, but we'll get through this one way or another, love. I believe that. We just need some time to figure something out, find the best course of action. Maybe we can somehow test the theory."

She started to respond, but in the next instant, the terrible sensation she'd felt on the mountain seemed to rise up from nowhere. It swirled through her with a vengeance, momentarily robbing her breath and filling her with dread.

And then, they all looked toward the dining room windows as the sky quickly began to darken beyond, and the wind outside picked up and howled, rattling the panes.

Looking into Kaden's eyes, Dory swallowed hard. "I'd love to test the theory, but I don't think we have any time left," she said with resignation. "Whatever it is, it's here now."

A s everyone scrambled from the table in unison, getting as far as possible from the windows and whatever was out there in the quickly brewing maelstrom, time seemed to shift into slow motion. Panic flooded Dory's system, and her brain screamed to *do something!* But for one drawn out moment, she felt short-circuited and couldn't get the rest of her body to comply. It was like trying to run full out in neck-deep water. Then in the next instant, like a movie on pause suddenly resuming at top speed, everything surged forward into real time with a cacophony of sound and a flurry of activity.

"What the actual fuck?" Ethan shouted over the din of the escalating wind. He looked at his watch. "It's only three-thirty in the afternoon, and suddenly it's twilight out there? Seriously? And where the hell did the hurricane-force winds come from?"

"I know it's been a few years, mate, but do you not remember Hilton Head? Correct me if I'm wrong, but you were there, right?" Wyatt shouted back as he pulled his katana from the sheath on his back. "And please tell me you're carrying a weapon of some sort because if what's out there is anything like the Erinyes attack, we've another shit-show in the making."

Dory watched Ethan pull one side of his jacket aside and remove his Glock from his shoulder harness. "I've only got this with one full magazine. The rest of my ammo is in the van, which at this point, seems really inconvenient. And trust me, bro, I have a very clear memory of Hilton Head. The horror of *that* shit-show ain't never gonna fade."

Spurred into motion, Dory grabbed Velma by the arm, pulling the Sentinel down and shoving her under the dining room table. The thought of harm coming to her friend because she herself hadn't been prepared for the worst, filled Dory with icy fear. "Stay here, Vee. Keep your head down. I have no idea what we're gonna be up against, but I'm damn sure that this is going to get ugly. And I mean, really ugly."

At least Velma seemed somewhat prepared for a bit of trouble, as she dug a small pistol out of her handbag. "I'll be fine, Isadora. Don't worry about me. Just go!"

"Don't do anything rash," Dory told her. "And don't use that thing unless you've no other choice. Conserve your ammo for as long as you can."

"Please. Wyatt and I have been training for months. Trust me, this may be just a pea shooter, but I've got this. I can take care of myself."

At Velma's thumbs up, Dory was skeptical but rose and surveyed the dining room. The windows were holding against the pounding winds, but she was certain that out there in the darkness, the wind was the least of their worries. She sure as hell didn't want whatever was out there to find its way inside with them. Wyatt and Ethan were armed for now, and Tanner could shift into wolf form within seconds, but most of the team's weapon supply and backup ammo was in the van. And that could be a really dicey situation depending on what was between them and the van.

"Babe, Sorcha's got a whole store of weapons here in the

house," Kaden said, coming up beside her. "Mostly medieval stuff like we used on the Tor and at Hilton Head, and according to her, it hasn't been used in a few decades, but it's better than nothing at all. And depending on what's on its way, it may be more effective than modern weapons anyway. She and Ian went to retrieve what they can. Lucy went with them, and Tanner followed them into the hallway. I think he was looking for a place to shift."

"That's good. I don't know how much time we'll have before we get an up-close-and-personal look at whatever's out there gnashing its teeth in the wind and the dark." Dory shook her head. "We should have been better prepared, Kaden, should have brought some of the weapons in with us from the van. We stood there like fools searching the sky for the danger we knew was there somewhere, but when it wasn't immediately found, we just wandered into the house like we had good sense."

Kaden nodded. "Yeah, not the brightest of moves, for sure."

"Wyatt's okay. He's got his katana. And Ethan has his precious Glock, but no extra ammo. Geez, Kaden, we knew something was coming. Getting caught like this with our asses hanging out is the height of stupidity."

"Agreed. A rookie move, but there's nothing we can do about it," Kaden said. "So, let's just concentrate on how we can prepare now and get it done quickly."

On the heels of that thought, Sorcha and Ian appeared, arms loaded with weaponry that they then dumped onto the dining room table. Ian immediately grabbed a couple of the battle axes twirling them in each hand as if testing their weight.

"Think I'll take a quick look around," he yelled. "We don't want a nasty surprise at our backs when we least expect it. And who knows where that surprise will break through."

"I'll go with you, old man," Ethan said, ready with Glock in hand.

With a grim smile and a nod, Ian led the way, and together they headed toward the living room.

Sorcha had both a beautifully crafted sword and an embellished battle axe of her own. Dory caught her eye and the other Immortal grinned. "My own personal finery," she yelled over the wind that seemed to fill the room around them. "Haven't used them in years. There was no need. But I have to say, they feel pretty good in my hands, even after all this time."

"You are terrifying, you know that?" Dory laughed in spite of herself and the ominous situation they found themselves in, before turning to Kaden and nodding toward the table. "Grab whatever works for you, love. And get comfortable with it in a hurry."

"Just so you know," Sorcha added, walking backward toward the hallway. "All these armaments were spelled in the past. Don't know how the spells have held up, but it may be a plus, if needed."

"Good to know," Kaden acknowledged, studying the spiked ball of a morning star before discarding it for a flange mace in one hand and a double-sided battle axe in the other. He looked up and grinned. "Yeah, I think these two will do some damage."

Dory shook her head. "Look, Vee's under the table with her pistol, but we need to keep an eye on her."

"I'm going to be fine, Isadora," Velma hollered from under the table. "Just throw me down something sharp, spelled, and pointy to go with my pea shooter. Then get on with it, Chosen One."

Kaden laughed out loud, an almost normal sound over the wind, considering the chaos churning around them. He picked up the morning star that he'd just discarded and hunkered down, handing the weapon to Velma. When he stood, he gave Dory a wink. "I'm pretty sure she'll hold her own, pal."

"From your mouth to God's ears."

"Oh, she'll do better than hold her own. That I can tell you," Wyatt shouted from Dory's left, before squatting down to fist bump with Velma. "Remember, just like we practiced, *Mo Leannan*. No hesitation, no mercy."

"No hesitation, no mercy, my sweet," the Sentinel repeated.

Dory blinked in fascination. What the hell had happened to her bookish Sentinel?

Turning away from the scene and taking a deep breath to center herself, Dory gave the room one last scan to make sure everyone was as ready as they could be. Lucy was standing in the hallway just outside the dining room and was adding a couple of long knives to the sheaths in a scarred vest she'd found somewhere. She'd also appropriated a katana much like Wyatt's. So, it looked as if everyone had armed themselves in one way or another. It wasn't ideal, especially since none of them had the protection of body armor like they'd had in South Carolina, but it would have to do. They had no other choice.

Holding her hands in front of her about eight inches apart, Dory began to generate heat, and a bright, white-gold electrical energy instantly flared to life, snapping and crackling between her palms. Yes, she could still produce her formidable and innate form of power but she still couldn't feel anything resembling the Dragon's Breath that she'd been able to wield on that beach at Hilton Head or on the Tor during that final battle.

Maybe she'd been wrong. Maybe her nightmares of the inky veining spreading up her arms, covering her chest and neck, the solid blackness filling her eyes, were all just that—nightmares. If that was the case, they were all in really big trouble. None of them would have lived through the Erinyes's attack without it. At least inside the house they had some semblance of cover and weren't as vulnerable as they'd been on the beach, but if this ended up being as bad or worse, they were pretty much screwed.

Just as she turned, following Kaden toward the hallway, the

large window along the back wall of the dining room suddenly shattered, blowing in from the force of the screaming wind. She spun around in time to see what followed that wind. And like the Erinyes they'd encountered before, it was an abomination.

Flying, four-foot monsters with wingspans of close to twice that came pouring through the opening one after another, their unearthly shrieks like something out of a horror film. With leathery, mottled skin and wings of a sickly gray, short muscular arms and legs with what looked to be at least five-inch lethal talons on every digit at the end of each limb.

And the smell.

Dear God, it was horrific, like a dead carcass that had been putrefying in the sun for days. Dory's stomach lurched, and she had to swallow hard and breathe through her mouth to keep from retching. But it was their ugly, demonic faces with huge, gaping maws, jam-packed with four-inch, razor-sharp teeth that held her attention.

Until the sound of gun shots were heard from somewhere in the house, indicating that the dining room was not the only area under siege.

At her left, Kaden swung first with the flange mace, knocking the closest creature to the dining room floor, and then literally chopping its head from its body with the double-sided axe before taking out another one with a back swing. He continued to hack his way toward the opposite end of the room, disappearing through the swinging door into the kitchen where Dory caught a brief glimpse of more of the heinous creatures. To her right, Wyatt was deftly holding his own with his katana in an almost-graceful killing routine. Slicing and spinning, and then slicing again.

White-gold, electric energy arced and snapped from Dory's fingertips as she raised her hands and wielded a lethal blast in a broad stroke. The creatures it caught in its path literally disintegrated into ash on contact. But as fast as the winged abominations were dispatched, others continued to take their places, coming through the ruined window at an alarming rate.

At one point, Ian, already covered in ichor, blood, and some other nasty-looking fluids that Dory didn't *even* want to think about, appeared at her side to pick up some of the slack, wielding his battle axes as if they were a part of him.

"They broke through the bay window in the living room," he yelled. "But Lucy's holding her own. Ethan is out of ammo but he's pounding away with some kind of spiky, medieval mallet. Tanner's in wolf form and disappeared toward the back of the house."

Dory nodded, and then took a few more of the horde down with a sizzling blast of lightning-hot energy. "That your blood, old man?" she asked, eyeing the bloody slice through his shirt at the shoulder.

"Got caught by one of the bastards before I could dodge. Hurt like a bitch, but I got lucky and it's not too deep. Hopefully, there's no poison to be had from their talons." Before she could reply, the Scot's eyes went wide, and he hefted one of his battle axes. "Get down!" he shouted, and swung the axe the moment she did, cleaving one of the monsters in half at mid-torso as it dove at them, soaking Dory in a layer of putrid gore.

Ian grinned as she stood up. "Sorry about that. That one was a sneaky bastard."

Dory grimaced at the horrific smell of the liquid she was now covered in. She was pretty sure she was going to throw up what little was in her stomach before this was all over. "No worries. I love being covered in rotting goo."

Generating another round of sizzling energy, she sprayed the fresh batch of abominations coming through the window but was concerned to see more appear behind them. She wondered just how many of the horrific beasts were out there in the dark or if it was going to be an endless supply. "What about Sorcha, Ian?"

"That lass is battle-ready, I can tell you. She wields those weapons of her like it's second nature," the old Scot said as he sliced the head off of one creature to his left and then buried the other axe he held into another's chest as it descended on them from the ceiling. He turned to Dory with a grin. "Watchin' her, you'd think that this was an everyday event."

"Figures," Dory shouted just as another shriek split the air. Turning, she was horrified to see one of the creatures had crawled halfway under the dining room table.

Velma! Dory thought.

Then there were more gunshots...much closer this time.

"No! Vee!" Dory screamed as Wyatt charged toward the nasty thing and sliced the creature in two from behind. Dropping to one knee, he flung the pieces of the abomination's body away in a desperate attempt to get to Velma. Dory wielded her electrical energy to cover him, praying for her friend but fearing the worst.

Without notice, a creature suddenly flew in from the hallway behind them, and before Dory could scream a warning at Ian, it knocked the old Scot to the floor. To his credit, he rolled quickly and swung one of his battle axes at the heinous thing but it grabbed the axe with its talons, jerking it from Ian's grasp. Without missing a beat, he rolled to his feet and sliced the nasty thing in half with his other axe.

A blinding rage exploded in Dory's head. They were barely holding their own and she'd be damned if she'd stand by and watch her team, her friends, die in this way. In a furious haze, she continued to take down the abominations swirling around her one after another.

Then time slowed again, and along with it, she felt a new sensation rise. A distinctly familiar sensation. Heat was not just snapping from her fingertips now but seemed to be building deep inside her chest and radiating out of her pores as well. Along with the unbearable heat was a pressure that felt as if it would burst through her body at any moment. And by the look on Ian's face as he turned to her, she knew in that instant that what she was feeling was the Dragon's Breath inside her. It had finally reared its head.

"Everyone get down!" Ian yelled before diving under the table with Wyatt.

Dory hoped that those in the other parts of the house had heard his shout but couldn't worry about that in the moment. It hadn't taken long, but she was burning from the inside out as the terrible heat and pressure continued to grow within her, and like before, she wasn't certain she could contain or control it. But as a cluster of the flying monsters closed in on her, she raised her arms as if welcoming them in, and instinctively throwing her head back, the inky black poison spewed from her throat as it had on that South Carolina beach. It soared like a guided missile of fluid, annihilating every one of the horrible fiends in the dining room as well as in the kitchen beyond.

But it didn't end there. The inky, poisonous stream continued to flow like it had a mind of its own. Or maybe it was her own mind directing it, but it flooded the hallway and beyond. And Dory could almost see it in her mind's eye, spreading throughout the house, destroying every abomination it came across.

Then, as quickly as it started...it was over. The terrible heat and pressure slowly began to diminish and, breathing hard as if she'd just ran a marathon, Dory dropped to her knees trying to catch her breath and get her wild heartbeat under control.

The wind subsided as if it had never been, and the darkness cleared to the overcast gray of the day outside. The stillness was almost eerie compared to the cacophony of sound from only moments before.

Desperate to know if Velma was alright, Dory tried unsuccessfully a couple of times to get up, but found that she was too wobbly to stand on her own. Then a steadying hand took hold of her arm and helped her to her feet.

Ethan smiled down at her. "So, since you're radiating heat again and look like you've been through a grinder, I'm gonna go ahead and assume that you and the Dragon's Breath saved our asses again this time around. Am I right?"

"That you are, boy-o," Ian said as he climbed out from beneath the dining table. "Her eyes were as black as coal with it. I dove for cover right quick, I can tell ya."

"Vee?" Dory asked, fear for her friend filling her voice. "Is she—"

"She's fine," Ian said, holding up a hand. "Or, at least, she will be. She took a pretty good swipe to her mid-section with the bastard's talons, which evidently, made her quite angry. So, our girl stabbed the nasty with the morning star, and then gave it a couple slugs from the pea shooter for good measure. Of course, the mercenary cut the thing in half directly after, so all's well. Our Vee may need a bit of healing, but nothing life-threatening, Isadora."

Dory relaxed for the moment, but when Wyatt helped Velma out from underneath the table, she panicked all over again. The front of Velma's shirt was covered in blood with several evenly spaced slashes in the fabric.

"Ian, clear off the table," Dory demanded. "Wyatt, lay her on the table so I can heal her. Now."

"Stop fussing, Isadora," Velma said. "It's not as bad as it looks."

"Then it won't take long to fix, will it?" Dory replied with a raised eyebrow.

As Ian began to clear the glass and debris from the table, Sorcha and Lucy came in from the hallway, followed by Tanner who was just buttoning up his shirt and replacing the rings on his fingers.

"Now that was intense," Lucy told Dory. "I saw that black wave coming and dived behind the sofa like my ass was on fire."

"Yes, and I'm thankful that she pulled me down behind the sofa with her," Sorcha added. "I had no idea what that black liquid flowing toward us was, but it became pretty clear when those heinous monsters started crashing and burning. Had to squeeze my eyes shut before the heat could burn them out of their sockets."

Ian nodded. "Kaden huddled us all together behind Isadora on the beach that first time. It was a harrowing experience, as the heat was quite intense, but none of us had seen how the Chosen One had looked with it. I got a pretty good glimpse today. 'Tis an alarming sight, her eyes being completely filled with blackness, and all."

"Yeah, you should feel it from the inside," Dory said, in a weak voice. She was gradually feeling more like herself and getting her breath back when she looked around the room and realized the Warrior wasn't with them. "Speaking of Kaden. Where is he?"

"Last I saw, he was hacking his way into the kitchen," Wyatt replied.

"Kaden!" Dory yelled and broke into a run toward the swinging door at the other end of the room with Ethan right behind her. They burst into the kitchen and stopped dead in their tracks. The room was littered with smoldering piles where the beasts had been struck down by the Dragon's Breath. Kaden was nowhere to be found, but his flange mace was laying amongst the steaming remains.

"*Kaden!*" Dory screamed again, filled with terror.

No answer came, and to add to her terror, a trail of blood ran from the center of the room and his discarded weapon to the back door, which was standing wide open.

No, no, no, Dory thought as she and Ethan raced across the room and out into the side yard where, to her astonishment and relief, her Chosen Warrior was limping toward them holding a battle axe in his left hand. She ran to meet him, searching his ashen face and body for injuries. What she saw gave her pause. The right leg of his jeans was saturated with blood, as was his right boot.

"Kaden, love, are you okay?" she asked when she reached him.

"K, you're looking a little pale," Ethan added. "Where's the blood coming from, bro? And how much have you lost?"

Kaden seemed a bit dazed and shook his head as if to clear it. "Wasn't sure I was going to make it out of there. So many of them in the small space. Missed the one that hit me from behind."

He stumbled then and would've gone down if Ethan hadn't caught him.

"Okay, okay, come on, K," Ethan said, taking the battle axe from Kaden and handing it to Dory, then wrapping his arm around Kaden's waist. "Just hang onto me, buddy. Let's get you into the house and see what's what. Dory will fix you right up."

"Kaden, look at me," Dory said, lifting his head and checking his vision. With a nod, she took his other side, and they did an odd sort of three-person stagger toward the house.

Once they got Kaden inside, Sorcha led the way to a spare room with a double bed where Ethan got him situated. After a brief scan, Dory breathed a sigh of relief. Though his leg injury was severe, and he seemed to have lost a whole lot more blood than she would've liked, it only took about twenty minutes to reverse the damage and heal him.

When he started to rise, she put a hand on his chest. "Huh-uh. You stay right there for another ten or fifteen minutes."

Kaden frowned. "Dory, you've healed me. There's no need."

"*I* need it," she told him. "Rationally, I know that I've healed you, but my heart isn't there yet, love. Please. Humor me."

With a brief nod, he lay back. "Ten or fifteen minutes is all your poor heart's gonna get, pal."

"Thank you," she replied with a smile. "I'll be back in a bit. I just have to see to Vee. She's in need of some healing as well."

However, Velma had been correct when she'd said that her wounds looked worse than they were which the Sentinel reiterated several times in the ten minutes it took to heal the gashes the creature had inflicted.

With Velma healed and Kaden's fifteen minutes in the recuperation box complete, the team surveyed Sorcha's poor, abused farmhouse. The damage to the structure itself was fairly minimal, with the worse of it limited to a handful of windows where the wind and beasts had broken into the dwelling. They set about temporarily boarding up the broken windows, and then, while the rest of the team got to the job of cleaning away the remnants of the disintegrating bodies and the mess that had been caused by the attack, Dory stepped outside to get some air and take a moment to herself. She walked across the side yard to the garden area and then to the fence at the pasture beyond.

While she was glad that the Dragon's Breath had saved them...again, she was conflicted. Her nightmares had seemed to be spot on. Though there had been no veining, no outward evidence of its existence inside her, Morianna had been correct when she'd wondered if the poison had bonded with Dory's system, if the Chosen One would be able to use the Dragon's Breath as a weapon. That it was obviously still inside her, had become part of her, and that she could possibly generate more of it when needed was what Dory was having a hard time accepting.

"You and your team had a rough afternoon," a deep voice said to her left.

She turned to find Jerahmeel leaning against the fence and studying her. "My fault. I should have seen it coming," she told him.

He tilted his head in that way he had, a half-smile playing around his perfectly carved lips. "Really? I suppose you and your team could have been better prepared, but how was this your fault, Isadora?"

Looking up into his beautiful and caring amethyst eyes, she suddenly had an urge to weep. Did she even deserve to be in the presence of an Archangel with what she had sleeping inside her? Was she worthy? Hadn't she always wondered if being selected as Chosen One was a mistake?

"Ah," he murmured as if he'd figured out a difficult puzzle... or had read her thoughts. "The Dragon's Breath. It worries you."

Tears welled and spilled down her cheeks. Her throat snapped shut, and she could only nod.

He looked out over the pasture beyond as he spoke. "You've had a hard time over the centuries with accepting that the Prophesy chose you. That out of all souls out there, it couldn't be you, as you are not worthy."

She choked back a sob but nodded again. It felt as if he was looking right into her heart, her very soul. And perhaps he was.

Jerahmeel turned with compassion in his gaze. "But it did choose you, Isadora."

She swiped at the tears that continued to flow. "But why? I don't understand. I don't *feel* worthy."

"So, are you saying that the Almighty has made a mistake?" The question was asked in a quiet tone, yet there was humor in his eyes.

"I-I…no, it's just…"

The Archangel reached out and placed a hand on her chest, and she felt a calm pour through her all the way to her toes. "Know that you are just who and what you need to be, child. You have so much waiting inside you, have been given unimaginable gifts that you have yet to discover. That you also have demon poison inside you isn't a curse. It doesn't make you unworthy of God's love or His trust. He chose you, Isadora. Before you even were, He chose you." He brushed a few loose strands of hair back from her face. "Never doubt that. Unfortunately, only you can come to terms with your destiny and own it. Until you find a way to do so, your struggles will continue." With a smile he asked her one more question. "Why do you think it is that I tasked you with this mission?"

A cross between a sob and a laugh bubbled up and out of her. Dory shook her head. "Because Kinna is facing the same dilemma?"

Jerahmeel chuckled and framed her face with his hands. "There is so much more to it than that, but see? Deep down, you know and understand exactly how this will all play out…for both of you. And I have all the faith in Heaven and on Earth that you will prevail in all that you do once you find *your* faith and acceptance." Straightening, he gave her one last smile. "Now, there is much to do, so go. And be worthy, Chosen One."

With that, the Archangel disappeared.

"I'm sorry, but that's just about the most ludicrous story I've ever heard." Olivia turned sideways on her bar stool and crossed her long legs. "Please tell me that you didn't buy the crap this Tess character was pushing."

Kinna sighed. She, Kari, and Olivia were sitting at the bar in Olivia's condo where they were enjoying a glass or two of wine after their regular Sunday night dinner in the Pearl. Kinna was trying—obviously, without a great deal of success—to explain to her friends what her last week had been like. She hadn't gotten very far.

Unfortunately, her explanation had started with her Tuesday afternoon meeting at Martine's with Tess Archer. Even she had to admit that Olivia did have a point. Unless you had a very open mind and a vivid imagination to go with it, the story that the woman had told her was pretty ludicrous on the surface. That is, until you got to the end of the meeting. which they'd yet to do. That was where ludicrous tipped right on over into freaky. She wondered how Olivia would react when she got to that part of the story, let alone to Friday's events.

"Again, you're just a great big bundle of support, aren't you, Liv?" Kari shook her head with a sour look.

Olivia scoffed. "Support for what? A story about faeries and vague, unsupported conspiracy theories? About humans that aren't really human but something else?"

"Would you just let Kinna finish before you climb up onto your prosecutor's soap box and start shooting everything down?" Kari argued.

"Oh, so you're buying all of this, are you?"

"I don't know. I haven't heard it all yet, now have I? You keep interrupting with your lawyerly bullshit after every third sentence that comes out of Kinna's mouth."

Olivia waved away Kari's objections. "Come on, I'll be the first one to admit that there's something really wrong with Victoria Newcomb, and I've told Kinna that on several occasions. Look, I am thrilled to the bone that Kinna's no longer seeing that quack, but to suggest that Newcomb's not of this world?" Olivia emphasized this last part of her tirade with air quotes, presumably to highlight the 'ludicrous crap' she was talking about. "We're supposed to believe that Victoria Newcomb is some kind of alien? Really?"

The back and forth between her two friends was like watching a very uncomfortable tennis match, and Kinna hated the fact that she'd brought this subject up at all. *But as the saying goes, in for a penny,* she thought. "Okay, Liv, Tess never said anything about Dr. Newcomb being an alien," she corrected.

"Right. Just that she wasn't human," Olivia replied with a smirk. "And this coming from a professed *faerie*?"

"For the love of God, Olivia," Kari snapped. "You're obviously having trouble with keeping an open mind, let alone keeping your mouth shut. However, you're not in a courtroom here, and there's no need to hammer Kinna as if she was under oath."

"Enough!" Kinna set down her glass and looked back and

forth between Olivia and Kari. She was trying not to take Olivia's reactions personally, but it was damned hard. She supposed that she really couldn't blame her, as the story was pretty hard to swallow. However, she was starting to feel like a fool for telling either of her friends anything at all.

"Look, I love you both, and trust me, I thought long and hard about whether to even mention any of the weird stuff that happened to me this week." Kinna shook her head. "I mean, the meeting with Tess on Tuesday was only the tip of the iceberg. And yes, she told me some things that had me thinking perhaps she was dealing with some mental issues at first."

"At first?" Olivia sputtered. "What do you mean, at first?"

"Olivia! Shut it and let her speak," Kari demanded. "You heard her. There's more."

Olivia picked up her wine glass and drained the contents. "I'm definitely gonna need more vino for this." She slipped off her bar stool and went directly to the wine fridge. "But don't stop and wait for me," she called over her shoulder. "I'm listening."

"Hard to tell," Kari muttered under her breath.

"And I have excellent hearing, Burke," Olivia replied from the other side of the kitchen.

Kari rolled her eyes, and then grinned at Kinna. "You heard the counselor. The floor is yours, my friend."

Kinna continued filling them in on the rest of the conversation she'd had with Tess, but when she got to the part about how they'd given the slip to the couple that had been following the woman, she hesitated. How did she tell them that Tess had... made them disappear? Even the thought was cringe-worthy.

"So, how did you get out of Martine's without the couple seeing you both? I mean, since they were on the sidewalk right outside," Kari asked, as if reading Kinna's mind. "Did you take a run through the kitchen like in the movies?"

Kinna took a breath and answered on a sigh. "Not exactly."

"Well?" Olivia prompted as she came back with another bottle of wine and refilled her glass. She sat the new bottle on the counter and then got comfortable again on her stool. "The witness needs to answer the question."

Kari huffed and shook her head at Olivia, who grinned over the top of her wine glass.

"Um...well...so...Tess took my hand..."

Kari frowned when Kinna hesitated. "Uh-huh. She took your hand. And?"

Just rip off the bandage, Kinna thought, *but do it quick.* "She took my hand and said, 'take a deep breath and hold on'. And then we just disappeared. We reappeared in, like, seconds, in an alley a few blocks away," she blurted then picked up her wine glass and took several large gulps.

Olivia, with her own glass halfway to her lips, paused. "I beg your pardon?"

Kinna wiped her mouth with the back of her hand. "Believe me, I know how this sounds. It was *so* weird. And I have no words to convey exactly how weird it was, but as crazy and unbelievable as it sounds, it happened. I was there and lived through it."

Olivia carefully set her glass down on the bar. "Kinna—"

"No, Liv," Kinna began before Olivia could finish her thought. "I know what you're gonna say, but it was not a hallucination, not some dream that I had. It was real. I don't know how, or even how to explain it, but it did happen."

"Kinna, I don't think that's what Olivia was going to say," Kari began, but she was visibly as stunned as Olivia at Kinna's admission.

"Of course, it was, Kari. And I'd bet money that you were thinking along those lines as well which is why I almost didn't bring any of this up at all."

"I wasn't thinking that," Kari countered, but her cautious tone and the look on her face said otherwise.

"Well, I was," Olivia confirmed as she picked up her glass and sucked down more wine.

Kinna couldn't help herself. She laughed at the look on both of her friends' faces, faces that said they both thought perhaps she'd lost a step or five. But with a sigh, she shook her head and put up a hand. "You know what? You're both right. It's too bizarre and does make me sound like a loon. So, we should probably just drop it. I plainly did not think this through long and hard enough."

"Oh, no you don't," Olivia retorted, leaning in. "You can't just toss something like that out there and then not tell us the rest."

"Why not?" Kinna countered. "You clearly don't believe what I'm telling you now, think that I've lost it, so how will it help for me to continue with the rest of my wild tale?"

It was the first time in recent memory that Kinna had actually seen her friend almost speechless. "I...well, you just...can't."

"Good cross, Counselor," Kari said in a sarcastic tone, then laughed at Olivia's loss of words. "Look, Kinna, sweetie, whether Olivia believes you or not, *I* want to know the rest of it," she said as she pushed her empty wine glass aside. "This is starting to sound like one of those epic fantasy novels. You know, the plucky heroine finds herself swept up into a strange world of magic and intrigue. Man, I love those stories."

"Oh, do shut up," Olivia grumbled with a disgusted look.

Kari flipped Olivia off, and then turned back to Kinna. "So, you said Tess made you disappear? My first question would be, how so? And the second would be, what was that like?"

"Well, again, I'm not really sure how she did it, so I have no answer for that, but it felt a bit like being on one of those humongous roller coasters. Like the feeling you get in your stomach when you crest the top of a really steep part and then just freefall down the other side."

"Wow. And then you just ended up in an alley blocks away?" Kari asked in surprise.

"Yes. That's exactly what happened. It was so fast. I literally blinked, and we were there. It was...*surreal* is the only word I can think of that fits how it felt. I know it does sound ludicrous, but I'm telling you, it really did happen. I'm still trying to wrap my mind around it even now."

Olivia set her glass down on the counter and emitted a low growl. "Okay, enough about disappearing and roller coasters. I'm waiting for the rest of your story. You said this was the tip of the iceberg, and that there's more. So, what more?"

Kinna shook her head. "If you didn't like the part about faeries, non-humans, and disappearing on a whim, you're definitely not going to like the rest of my week."

"Look, regardless of whether *either* of us believe what you're telling us, we're your friends," Olivia said.

"Your best friends," Kari corrected.

"Right." Olivia nodded and jabbed a finger in Kari's direction. "We're her *best* friends." Giving Kinna a saccharine smile, she continued, "And we'll stand by you through thick and thin, looney tunes or not, no matter what. Just tell us the rest, Kinna."

Now that she'd started this whole conversation, Kinna wasn't sure it was such a good idea to continue, but she really needed to tell someone, get it all out before her head exploded. And who better to tell than her best friends, whether they'd believe it all or not. "Yeah, well, then buckle up, girls. Because like I said, the meeting with Tess on Tuesday was just the beginning, and it only gets weirder from there. It continued down the rabbit hole with my visit out to Sorcha Doyle's on Friday afternoon..."

KINNA GOT to Java Jive on Tuesday afternoon just before one o'clock, intent on assisting wherever they needed her for the afternoon rush as she'd done over the last three days. She'd been leery to come back to the coffeehouse after the sketchy encounter in the parking lot on Friday, but in the end, she'd refused to let it keep her from the business that she'd started in her grandfather's memory. She may have inherited Brenden McComish's entire empire, but Java Jive was precious to her. It was hers and hers alone, and she'd never let anyone or anything, no matter how bizarre, take that from her.

She'd worked alongside her employees on Saturday, Sunday, and Monday. That there had been no other such incidents like the creepiness in the parking lot on Friday was a relief. However, she hadn't seen Jerahmeel since Friday, either, which should have made her happy, but oddly, did nothing but give her anxiety. It was like waiting for the other shoe to drop.

The after-dinner conversation with Olivia and Kari on Sunday evening had not started out well. It had been a bit of a shit-show trying to explain what she could of the recent unbelievable occurrences in her life over the last week. From the meeting with Tess a week ago Tuesday through the meeting with Sorcha and the rest of the 'Immortal' group on Friday, it had been a lot to swallow for her two best friends. Olivia was obviously having trouble believing much of her story, and Kari had remained on the fence, but they'd both peppered her with questions just the same. For most of which, she'd had few answers to give.

She wasn't sure why, but she'd left out the part about being accosted by the man in the parking lot after the meeting at Sorcha's as well as Jerahmeel's timely intervention. Maybe because it seemed like overkill. But then again, after faeries and Immortals, how much more surreal could it have been to add in a possible demon or Archangel aspect? Regardless, by the end of the evening, both women seemed to, if not fully believe, at least accept that *she* believed what she'd told them.

However, the meeting at Sorcha's on Friday was what weighed heavily on Kinna's mind. When she'd left Sorcha's house that afternoon, she'd vowed to contact the woman in two days' time after some thought about what she'd been told. But then she'd put it off. And then put it off some more. Long enough for Sorcha to reach out to check on her when she hadn't heard back.

Truth be told, after the conversation with Olivia and Kari on Sunday night, Kinna had started to doubt herself, to think that perhaps Olivia may have been right to insinuate that she'd dreamed the scenarios. After all, she'd had prophetic dreams and visions all of her life. The fact that her friends were checking in with her more frequently than usual didn't help, either. Neither Olivia nor Kari were stellar at hiding their concerns. But even though she'd had other nightmares, dreams, and visions in her past, Kinna couldn't get herself to write these recent events off that easily...because they'd happened in real time.

Then Sorcha had called, and everything Kinna had experienced became solid in her mind all over again. She'd put the woman off once more, explaining that she'd been neglecting Java Jive and needed to spend some time rectifying that. It wasn't a lie, per se, but wasn't completely true, either. The bottom line was that she just wasn't sure whether to move forward, pursue what she'd been told. She was conflicted, wanting to know more, to understand, but then filled with apprehension of what *more* she would find, and what it would mean to her world, her reality.

"Here you are," Kari said from the doorway, interrupting Kinna's thoughts. "I was wondering where you'd gotten off to.

Thought maybe you'd gotten bored and went home, but I see that you're just hiding out."

Kinna slipped another box of napkins onto the nearest shelf and sighed. "I'm not bored, Kari. And I'm certainly not hiding out. I was just doing some stock room organization."

"Uh-huh." Kari narrowed her eyes and gave Kinna a look full of speculation with the ever-present touch of concern. "And the air in here, laden with heavy thoughts, has nothing to do with you?"

Kinna straightened and set a box of coffee cups on a nearby stool, then gave her friend a skeptical look. "I know what you and Olivia are doing."

"Oh? And what's that?"

"Checking up on me constantly because you both think I've lost my mind."

Kari rolled her eyes in a very Kari fashion. "That's ridiculous. You're as sane as me or Olivia...although, I'm not so sure that's a compliment."

"Seriously, you guys don't have to worry about me. Yes, some strange stuff has happened recently, but I'm not seeing things or hearing voices." Kinna grinned. "Well, I do have visions from time to time, and I have heard voices recently, so that's not entirely true, but these last happenings were not hallucinations or visions."

"Okay, okay. I'm sorry we've made you feel that way." Kari put up her hands in surrender. "We just care about you, Kin. I hope you know that both Olivia and I are here for you for anything that you need. Even if it's just to talk...or to leave you alone," she finished with a grin.

"I know, and I do appreciate it, but right now—"

"It's the latter," Kari said with a nod. "Understood. Then I'll let you get back to your organizing. I've got a few purchase orders to get done. If you need me, I'll be in the office."

"Thanks, Kari."

Kinna watched her friend go and stood for a moment looking around the room. She supposed she'd spent enough time organizing—and rehashing the strange occurrences in her life. She wasn't going to get any answers to her questions or have any epiphanies cleaning up the stock room. Hefting the box of coffee cups, Kinna left the room and her dilemma behind, heading out to restock the front counter.

Ah, I wondered when you were going to grace us with your presence.

The words—so clearly spoken in an amused tone inside her head—startled Kinna as she walked out into the storefront from the back room. Scanning the coffeehouse, she found Jerahmeel seated at his usual table in the far corner of the room. Though he didn't even look up, there was a barely perceptible smile playing about his lips as he turned the page of the book he appeared to be reading.

"You! What are you doing here?" she demanded out loud before she could catch herself.

"You...talking to me?" Charlie asked in a hesitant tone, looking over at her from the espresso machine at the counter where he was steaming a small pitcher of milk.

"Uh, no. Sorry, Charlie. Just mumbling to myself. Never mind."

Kinna narrowed her eyes in Jerahmeel's direction and silently addressed the supposed Archangel. *Get out of my head and quit stalking me.*

Oh, Kinna, as I've told you before, you can't avoid your destiny. Or me, for that matter. He looked up from his book then, pinning her with his mesmerizing gaze. *There are others who are coming for you, others who seek to use your gift for their own nefarious plans—plans that will end quite poorly for this world of yours. The sooner you stop acting like a sullen child, the easier this will be. I'm simply here to guide and protect you.*

Guide and protect me from what? And who are these 'others' you keep yammering on about? What proof do you have of all this? They said that you're an angel—

Make no mistake. I am an Archangel, *child. There is a difference.* Though he continued to smile, a stern look came into his eyes as he very deliberately closed his book and placed it on the table.

Kinna felt a chill run down her back, and she suddenly had a sense of the danger he'd been talking about.

But if you require proof, I will be happy to oblige...

As she watched him put a finger to his pursed lips in a *shhh* gesture, Kinna's mouth dropped open as everything in the room around them went not only silent but completely still. It was as if time itself had stopped. In looking around the room, Kinna was shocked to see patrons with coffee cups halfway to their lips, Charlie frozen at the espresso machine—the steam the machine generated a solid, unmoving fog in the air, a gentleman at the counter holding a five-dollar bill out to Sissy for payment. Everything and everyone in the room was as motionless as a painting in a gallery.

"What the...?" Was she somehow hallucinating? In broad daylight?

You know you are not, Jerahmeel silently answered the question in her head.

"How are you doing this?" she asked in a whisper.

He rose from his seat and came toward her then, weaving around a customer who was motionless in the act of donning her jacket. "As I told you before, I am an Archangel and with that comes unimaginable power, but just think of me as your guardian for now. I've watched over your reincarnations through several centuries—in this world and others. I've been by your side, given you guidance when your gift was needed. I know that you feel that connection even now, though perhaps you don't understand why. However, this is something you cannot ignore, Kinna. It is your destiny, your purpose."

"What is?" she whispered again.

When she blinked, Jerahmeel was suddenly standing next to her behind the counter. He held out his hand. "Come. Let me show you."

"I-I'm afraid."

His smile was warm, comforting. "You have nothing to fear from me, Child of Light. Ever."

Kinna reached out but then hesitated. "What about them?" she asked, taking a last look around the room, its inhabitants so still, so motionless.

"We won't be long. They will go back to their day without harm. Trust me, Kinna."

With a deep breath, she placed her hand in his. And when she blinked, they'd left the coffeehouse behind and were standing on the top of a ringed hill on a lovely summer's day. She took a deep breath to make sure the vista was real. The air was warm—fresh and sweet with the scent of clover and the wildflowers that dotted each wide ring below. A short distance away, she could make out a quaint village with old brick buildings, houses with thatched roofs, all surrounded by pastures, some with sheep and other livestock. It all seemed somehow familiar but how could that be?

"Where are we?" she asked Jerahmeel, who was watching her closely.

"This is the heart of Avalon, the Isle of Glass, the birthplace of that which lives within you. Can you feel it?"

Kinna closed her eyes and instinctively lifted her hands, could actually feel the pulse of this place in the air around her. She nodded. "There's a heartbeat here, as if this place is alive."

"It is alive in a way. There is power here. The Chosen One was also reborn in this very spot centuries ago."

Kinna opened her eyes. "The Winthrop woman that I met on Friday? She said she was an Immortal."

Jerahmeel looked out over the rolling hills in the distance. "Isadora is that and more, as are you. You both have incredible power that lives within you. And though you are both connected through this place, you have different fates, different purposes." He turned his gaze on her. "Would you like me to show you your purpose?"

Mesmerized, she nodded.

He stepped around behind her and placed his hands on her shoulders, then leaned down and spoke softly in her ear. "As Isadora is the Chosen One, an Immortal savior reborn into this world to protect humanity, your purpose, while different, is connected."

"She told me that I was a precaution, a safety measure for this world, though she didn't explain the how or why of it."

"That is true. You are a Time Mender, Kinna. The Key, the entity you carry, was placed in this world as a safeguard. It gives you the ability to not only correct atrocities, possible world-ending events, but more importantly, remove them from the timeline."

"Are you talking about time travel? Is that what you meant in Seattle? I mean, during my dream of Seattle burning I remember you saying something like that."

In this moment, this is the future.

"Yes. When you dream, you are often traveling in time. So, what you saw in the dream of Seattle burning was actually the future—or one possible outcome of the future."

"And that's how this entity inside of me removes these terrible events? It actually mends time?"

"It does, and has over the centuries. The Key is not always

needed. In fact, surprisingly, even with man's penchant for destruction, it has been a rare occasion. You are the host of The Key for this period in time." His breath was soft and warm at her ear as he spoke. "Let me show you."

With that, the lovely vista was gone, replaced by travel. It was like flying, only instead of flying through the air, they were soaring through time. Hundreds of years of the planet's history flashed across her vision like images on a movie screen. Growth, war, rebirth. The human progression, the historic events that had shaped the world, changed the world, then reshaped it again. The process was endless, escalating as humanity grew, learned, evolved. And the horrors that sometimes went with that evolution were also displayed prominently.

It seemed like they traveled through the fabric of time for hours, but as quickly as the show began, it was over. Kinna squeezed her eyes shut and took a deep breath. When she opened them again, she was standing on the ringed hill in the same spot with the same lovely view.

She glanced to her right, and found Jerahmeel standing next to her looking out at that same view. "It's daunting," she murmured. "The unfolding of time, of history."

He nodded. "It can be, yes."

"But it also felt full of hope. What came before emphasizes the possibilities of what humanity could accomplish, how it can move forward."

He turned then, and she felt the full force of his angelic power in his gaze. "There is a plan for this fallen world, Kinna. The Father's plan is perfect, and both you and Isadora have important roles to play. You are the guardrails, and are both needed now." He took her by the shoulders and his voice conveyed his concern for her. "You must contact Isadora, let her and her team keep you safe until you are needed."

She nodded. "All right."

He lifted a hand and touched a finger to her forehead, and she felt something stir and shift deep inside her. An odd sense of awakening seemed to fill her entire being like an old, cherished memory once forgotten now recaptured.

"What was that?" she whispered in wonder.

"The vital part of your being stretching its legs, preparing."

"Preparing for what?"

Jerahmeel's smile was gentle. "Close your eyes, Child of Light. Your time is near."

When she did, she felt first his lips upon her forehead, and then heard the sound of voices, breathed in the warm, comforting scent of coffee. And she smiled as well.

"Are you okay, boss?"

Kinna opened her eyes to find that she was standing exactly where she'd been before she'd placed her hand in Jerahmeel's and he had taken her away. Charlie was still steaming milk at the espresso machine but was staring at her as if he wasn't certain that she was quite right.

It took her a moment to realize that nothing here had changed, though it felt like she'd been gone for hours. She scanned the room, but the Archangel was no longer at his table, nowhere to be seen.

"Kinna?" Charlie asked again, this time with more concern in his tone. "What's wrong?"

With a shake of her head, she found her voice. "Nothing, Charlie. Everything's fine. I was just having a moment."

"One of those mindfulness meditation deals?" he asked with a grin. "My sister does that all the time."

"Mindful meditation? Yes, something like that."

Something like that, but a whole lot more, she thought. And wondered at the more to come.

21

The invitation for Sorcha to come home with the team in the aftermath of the attack on Sunday had gone unaccepted. She'd thanked them for the thought, but in the end, chose to stay in her own home. By the time they had put her house partially in order, at least as best they could, and then drove back over the hill to the coast that evening, the entire team had been, in Dory's words, knackered.

Kaden had to wait until early Tuesday evening to address the information leak that had come to light just before the attack at Sorcha's place. That there'd even been a need to dig down to find out how their security had been breached was infuriating and had been a thorn in his ass for the better part of two days, making him cranky and sharp. And while there were justifiable reasons for the delay—time to recover from the attack, along with cleanup and generally helping Sorcha set her home to rights—there was another more maddening reason for his concerns.

Tanner Sweetwater had skipped out just as soon as Kaden had pulled the van into the driveway, saying only that an important issue had come to his attention and he would return as soon as he could. They'd not seen him again until just about forty-five minutes ago, at which time he'd been annoyingly vague on what that issue was, how he'd suddenly heard of it, or why it was of such immediate importance.

At this point, Kaden was not of a mind to wait any longer for a come-to-Jesus meeting with the entire group. He intended to make it very clear to every member of the team that trust and security were of the utmost importance, especially with the shifter since there was also something else that had been nagging him since the attack.

Tanner's location during the battle.

Everyone else had been accounted for but him. During the clash with the Erinyes on the beach in South Carolina, the bulk of the team had found out that Tanner was a skinwalker when he'd shifted into wolf form not long after the attack had begun. He'd gone up the beach and spent most of that fray battling the abominations on his own, which had always stuck in Kaden's craw. Sunday night had been a similar situation, with Tanner shifting and then disappearing almost as soon as the first of the winged monsters came through the dining room window.

Tanner had made it clear back in South Carolina that he preferred working on his own, but he'd appeared to adjust to the team's rules right up front this time around. However, at Sorcha's on Sunday, Ian was the only one who seemed to know which way the shifter had gone when the battle got underway. No one else had seen him until it was all said and done. With the security breach foremost in his mind, Kaden needed to find out where Tanner had been and why he was backsliding on his vow to be open, honest, and transparent...and not act like a dick, for that matter.

As the team got comfortable around the dining room table, Kaden stood at one end next to Dory's chair and scanned their faces. He hated to admit it, but he was all but certain that someone sitting at the table had been responsible for the breach. The leaked information could only have come from someone in this room. He wanted to know who had blabbed and how that had happened. Had it been an accident? Or if the breach was intentional, he intended to find out why the team had been betrayed in this manner.

Though he didn't want to leap to conclusions, there were really only a couple out of the eight members here that he was looking at closely. He'd been partners with Ethan for years in L.A., and Kaden knew in his gut that there was no way his old partner would betray him let alone the team. To his mind, that probably left Lucy out of the mix as well, but he couldn't make that call for certain as there had been some earlier transparency issues on her part. Ian was in the clear. The old Scot was as solid as they came, and he couldn't see Velma in a schemed betrayal, as she'd been with Dory through thick and thin for a whole lotta years.

That left only two: Wyatt and Tanner. And with this latest bullshit, Kaden was leaning heavily in the shifter's direction.

"Okay, now that we're all here," he began with a pointed look toward Tanner. "Let's get this meeting underway. I have some questions. Questions that need answers before we can move forward in any way as a team."

"This is about the breach, right?" Ethan asked.

"Affirmative." Kaden swept the table with another steely look. "The information that Sorcha was given by her fae friend was pretty specific. And I want to know if anyone at this table knows how that happened. If so, this would be the time to step up and explain."

"You making accusations, mate?" Wyatt asked, anger flaring in his eyes. "You think one of us is responsible? Betrayed the team?"

"It had crossed my mind, yes. Like I said, the information

was very specific and especially so about the Chosen One."
Kaden leaned down on the table and gave the mercenary a hard
stare. "And no, I'm not making accusations, *mate*. I'm fucking
asking straight out. Because if I find out—"

"Whoa, whoa, whoa, let's just take it down a notch or two
before this all gets out of hand. Okay?" Tanner put up a hand.
"I'm pretty sure that I'm responsible for the leak."

All eyes turned to the skinwalker.

"Oh, Tanner," Lucy said quietly. "What have you done?"

"Yeah, what the hell, dude?" Ethan added.

"I put a little too much trust in someone, Luce," he said, but
his eyes never left Kaden's as he spoke. "I was making calls when
I first got here, remember? Doing some research, like we all
were. I know now that I said a bit too much in one of those
calls."

"Ya think?" Wyatt asked with a grimace.

"That's not like you, Tanner," Lucy murmured.

The man's smile was self-deprecating. "No. Not usually, Luce.
I got sloppy, I guess." He nodded at Kaden. "When Sorcha told
us about the issue before the attack, it was like a slap in the face
because I started going over some of those early conversations in
my mind. And one stood out for me. That's what the last two
days have been about. Clean up."

"Was it just the one, Tanner?" Dory asked quietly. "Because
Sorcha did say her fae associate told her that she'd heard it from
several sources."

Tanner nodded. "Just the one. But, Dory, that could have
been enough. The ripple effect, you know? I can't say how it
trickled down or to whom, but that's how this probably got started." The man looked around at the faces staring back at him.
"And I've addressed the issue with the original source. I'm confident that this kind of thing is never going to happen again with

him, mostly because he's no longer on the trusted contact list. And his removal was a bit...painful for him."

"Aye, that's all well and good, but the damage is now done, isn't it?" Ian murmured.

Tanner took a deep breath, blew it out slowly, then nodded and addressed Kaden. "Come on, this was not intentional, okay? Sloppy, careless? Absolutely. But I promise you, I never would have knowingly or deliberately compromised the team. I meant what I said the day I arrived. I may not be used to working with a team, may backslide from time to time, but I'm all in with this mission." When Kaden just continued to stare at him, the man put up his hands again. "Look, I handled the situation the best way I knew how, and as soon as I could. I also admitted my mistake the minute we sat down here to discuss it."

"Yes, but you didn't tell any of us where you were going on Sunday night or why," Lucy pointed out. "You knew or at least suspected then, and yet you went off on your own to 'handle the situation'. That doesn't inspire much trust, my friend."

"Yeah, I can see that now. I miscalculated." He shrugged. "Old habits, I guess. All I can do at this point is apologize. I can't change what I did."

Kaden straightened and crossed his arms. "Okay, well, Dory and I will discuss that later, but there is another issue I want cleared up before then."

"Okay," Tanner said slowly. "And what's that?"

"Your whereabouts during the attack."

The shifter frowned. "What do you mean? I was in wolf form, you know that. I was fighting those bastards like everyone else?"

"What I know is that everyone's whereabouts are confirmed but yours. Ian said he'd seen you in wolf form heading toward the back of the house, that's true. However, no one saw you after that."

"Not until after I'd used the Dragon's Breath and the attack was over," Dory said. "I saw you come in then."

Tanner shook his head, and shock crossed his face. "Look, I don't know where you think I went or what you're accusing me of doing, but you're wrong. Yes, I went to the back of the house where I immediately sensed that those abominations had broken through a bedroom window. I don't know how it was going up front, but they were relentless back there, and pouring in almost as fast as I could handle them. I got sliced up pretty good, but as you know, it doesn't take long for me to heal. So, I have no proof of that, only my word."

"Sure, but how do we know—" Kaden began, but Dory stopped him with a hand on his arm.

"Tanner, we want to be able to move forward, to trust that we're all on the same team. But you do see our concerns, don't you?" She leaned forward. "We had these same kinds of issues the last time around, specifically in Savannah. And I do want to believe you when you say that you're all in, but we need to have absolute trust in each other. All of us."

Tanner started to speak and then paused and nodded. "I get it. Considering how our last go round went, I suppose I would have concerns as well. If you want, I'll pack up and hit the road. No hard feelings. But, I didn't do any of this on purpose. The leak was a stupid mistake. That's all. And I was right there in the mix for battling those winged bastards on Sunday." He shrugged again, but this time the look in his eyes said that he was not as indifferent to the options as he sounded.

Kaden looked down at Dory. "What's the verdict, boss?"

Dory sighed and shook her head, before looking back at the shifter. "All right, Tanner. Let's put this behind us for now. We've got some work to do, and we'll need all hands on deck to get it done. But please don't make me change my mind."

Tanner leaned back in his chair, and Kaden literally watched the tension drain from the man's shoulders. "Understood."

"Okay, next topic. Dory heard from Morianna earlier who said that Jerahmeel has persuaded Kinna McComish to accept our protection. So, that's a win. She's supposed to contact us tomorrow. The security team was beefed up a bit and is still in place. They'll stay that way until we tell them different. I want to be ready with a plan going forward. We'll probably need to go back over the hill and pick her up, bring her here."

"Yes, and that means that we'll need to do some reshuffling of sleeping arrangements again as we're full up," Dory added, and Kaden watched her rub her eyes at the mention of sleeping.

The tension over the leak discussion had held on through the rest of the meeting hovering in the background like unfinished business. They spent another hour debating how they were going to handle the coverage for Kinna McComish once they brought her into the fold since they weren't certain how long it was going to take to neutralize the threat or how Jerahmeel planned to end it. Then they worked on a plan to move forward, hammering out a few more security precautions that needed to be put into place before this next phase was set in motion. The strategy was fairly fluid, and when they were finished, everyone seemed to be clear on the part each would play within the plan as it stood.

Kaden watched Dory yawn for the umpteenth time and finally called it. "I think that's plenty for now. Everyone needs to get a good night's sleep. I'm anticipating an early start in the morning if we need to head back over the hill."

As everyone drifted off to their own areas to get settled, Kaden pulled Dory into his arms and kissed the top of her head. "You still look kinda whipped, love. It's been a couple of days since the attack. Any indication that the Dragon's Breath is lingering? You seem like you're still struggling a bit."

She sighed as she laid her head on his shoulder. "No, my temperature's back to normal. I'm still a little fatigued, but like before, I don't really even feel the Dragon's Breath. It's like it was never there...again. But does that mean it's really gone? Or has it just retreated to wherever it's been hiding all this time?"

"Don't have that answer, babe. But we should head upstairs, and you should definitely try to get some rest."

He took her hand and led her up to the bedroom. As he sat down on the bed and pulled off his boots, he looked over his shoulder to where she'd sunk down in the reading chair in the alcove near the window. The Dragon's Breath may have retreated a couple days ago, but her fatigue and the smudges under her eyes said that she'd yet to fully recover from the wielding of it.

"So, we keep Tanner on the team, but do we trust him? I know what my answer would be, but what are you thinking?"

She leaned her head back against the chair, and her eyes slipped shut. "That I'm probably thinking the same thing you are. We keep him on the team, but keep a close eye on him. No, I don't trust him." She opened tired eyes and removed the band from her plaited hair, began unraveling the length with her fingers. "How can we, when he continues to evade and conceal? I get that there was a very short window to discuss anything after Sorcha revealed what she'd heard. We were suddenly in the thick of it. But if he would've just told us about his part in the leak on the drive home before running off to handle it himself, then I would probably feel differently."

"Agreed. It's the concealment, the hiding pertinent information like he did before that is really hard for me to get past."

He got up, set his boots next to the closet, and then came to her. Taking her hands, he pulled her out of the chair. "You need to sleep, love. Let's get you undressed and under the covers."

A seductive smile spread across her face. "Mmm, undressed

and under the covers? I like the sound of that, but I can think of something much more pleasurable than sleep that we can do in that situation."

"Is that so?" he asked as he began to unbutton her shirt. "Do tell. I'm all ears."

She backed him up to the bed, and then gave him a shove, following him down to straddle his hips before stripping off her blouse and bra. "It'll be easier if I just show you."

"Ah, my dark angel. We're just agreeing on all sorts of things tonight, aren't we?" He skimmed his hands up her ribs to cup those lovely breasts that she'd revealed for him before sitting up and pulling her to him. "You know what they say about great minds?"

She tugged his t-shirt up and off, then wrapped herself around him, skin to skin.

"No. What do they say?" she asked, her lips a whisper away, her hips slowly grinding against his.

Desire, white-hot, rose so quickly that it nearly took his breath, as it always did with her.

"Something about thinking alike, but it's really not important now," he murmured as his lips took hers in a heart-pounding kiss full of urgency and need.

They rolled over the bed as the heat between them grew, and then lost themselves in each other.

KINNA WOKE up on Wednesday morning, a bit groggy and with her lanky Russian Blue stretched across her stomach. The lazy feline complained in a terse tone when Kinna dislodged herself and slid from beneath the covers.

"Yeah, yeah, I know," she said on a yawn. "You think it's all about you, except that I'm sorry to tell you, it's really not. I am in serious need of coffee, princess. Then I need a hot shower. So, suck it up."

She threw on a robe and started for the door, before turning back to the cat. "Okay, look, I'm going down for that cup of Joe now, and I'll get you your morning pâté if you come with me now. Otherwise, you'll have to wait until I'm out of the shower and dressed. Your choice."

Heading downstairs, she heard the soft thump as the feline jumped down off the bed. Even before she got to the bottom of the stairs, the little freeloader raced past her and was in the kitchen sitting next to her empty dish when Kinna came into the room.

"You are a very sad case, girlfriend. And so predictable." She poured some half and half into a cup, dropped a coffee pod into the machine, and got the important morning liquid rolling before pulling the cat food basket out of the cupboard. "So, what's it to be this morning? Catfish and tuna, salmon, or turkey?"

The cat eyed the basket, and then meowed pitifully.

Kinna sighed as the scent of brewing coffee filled her nostrils. "Catfish and tuna it is."

Grabbing the empty dish from the floor and putting it in the dishwasher, she pulled a clean dish from the cabinet and opened the fresh can, spooning a healthy amount of the pâté onto it. The feline pounced on the food the minute Kinna set the dish down in front of her.

"Oh, for the love of—don't bolt it down like an alley cat. Geez, you act like you haven't eaten in days, which we both know is so not true." Shaking her head, Kinna grabbed her coffee cup and headed up for her shower, murmuring, "So unladylike," under her breath as she left the kitchen.

She spent a good thirty minutes in the shower, the first ten of which was just standing under the hot spray and thinking about what the day would hold. Tuesday had been the weirdest of the weird with a visit from an Archangel and a journey that had upended Kinna's whole image of her life.

A Time Mender. Who would've thought that all of the visions, prophetic dreams, and general mayhem of her youth would point to something so wild. The images Jerahmeel had shown her, the things that he'd explained had finally made some sense of her history. It also connected up with some of the things her grandfather had told her. Had he known? Brenden McComish had always been supportive of her strange abilities, much more so than her own parents ever had.

You have no idea what you're capable of.

You are a gift from God, sweetness.

Yes, she thought. *You knew, didn't you, Pops? I think you just ran out of time. We both did.*

But today, she would do something about that. She would contact Dory Winthrop as she'd promised Jerahmeel she would. She would let Winthrop's team protect her until her gift was needed and the Archangel could make her world safe for her again.

Dragging herself out of her warm, shower cocoon, Kinna dressed in jeans, a gray hip-length sweater, and boots. She pulled down her largest duffel and packed it with enough clothes for several days. She wasn't sure how long she'd be gone, but couldn't imagine that it would be more than a week or two. And she figured that Winthrop had a washing machine, if it came to that.

Next she called the Immortal, and together they made plans. Dory said that the team would head over from the coast and pick her up as soon as they could get there. It sounded like they'd been ready and just awaiting her to contact them.

After that, Kinna made one more call. To Kari.

"Hey, Kin," Kari greeted her when she answered the phone. "Are you coming in today?"

"No, Kari. That's actually why I'm calling. I have to go out of town for the next week or so, and I was wondering if you'd take cat duty until I get back. Or you could house-sit if you'd like."

"What's up? More board meetings?"

"Uh, this is something else. You can get me on my cell, if you need me." Kinna hated that she couldn't really explain where she was going or why. "And if you don't have time, Kari, it's okay. My little furball should be just fine for a few days plus she can go out whenever she wants through the cat door. But I'll probably be gone longer than usual, so I'd feel better if I knew someone was looking after her in my absence."

Kari sighed on the other end of the phone. "Of course I'll take cat duty, Kinna. Don't be stupid. But...is everything okay?"

Kinna could hear the concern in her friend's voice and knew exactly what her friend was probably thinking. "It will be. Just a bit of cleanup for something important, but I'll be fine. I'll explain everything when I get back. And like I said, you can always get me on my cell phone if something comes up."

"No worries. I'll take care of your little freeloader. But call me if you need me."

"I will," Kinna replied, knowing that she probably couldn't even if she wanted to.

As if reading Kinna's thoughts, Kari sighed again. "I mean it, Kinna. If you need...anything you call me. Promise?"

"Promise."

Guilt reared its ugly head as Kinna hung up the phone. She didn't know how this next week would go, but she sure as hell didn't want to put her friend in any danger. And danger was definitely lurking nearby from what she'd been told.

Just as she was going up to grab the packed duffel and set everything that she would be taking with her in the foyer in preparation for the team's arrival, the doorbell rang. She couldn't imagine that Winthrop's team was already here. It had only been forty-five minutes since she'd spoken with her, and it would take at least an hour for them to get to the house. But maybe they'd been in route when Kinna had called Dory's cell.

"That was fast," she began as she opened the front door.

But what she found waiting for her wasn't Dory or her team. She saw the syringe too late, wasn't fast enough to elude the muscular men on the front steps as they grabbed her, held her. It all happened so fast.

And then everything went black.

22

"Well, you were right, Verrine." Dorian's tone was ecstatic, his excitement pouring off him as he came into the living room from his office up the hall.

"Of course I was right," Verrine replied absently without looking up from the trite fashion magazine she was skimming.

Humans had the strangest obsession with clothing, she thought. Really all things material. Anything to make their pitiful lives seem better. It was tragic but left so many interesting opportunities wide open for those like herself who dealt in influence and chaos.

"Refresh my memory, darling. I'm right about so many things that it's hard to keep track. Which subject are we talking about?"

"About the McComish woman. I should have had her picked up a week ago when we talked about it. We may have had The Key in our hands by now."

Verrine sighed and pushed the contempt she felt for him away. "Yes, Dorian. This is not news. I do remember having that discussion, and on several occasions, as I recall. I have to say, I am growing tired of waiting. You did promise me so you really should get to it." She looked up then, and pinned him with a narrowed glance. "So, why are you smiling at me like you've just won a lottery or the keys to heaven's gate?"

"Because we may just have," he replied, rubbing his hands together with glee. "Won the lottery, that is. I received a phone call a bit ago from one of my lieutenants who had some great news for us."

When he waited a beat with a ridiculous grin on his face and didn't seem inclined to add further detail anytime soon, Verrine realized that he was waiting for her to beg him for more information. She had to further restrain herself from throttling the man. Dorian was another thing in this boring world that she was tiring of very quickly. *Her* good news was that she could remedy that situation as soon as she had The Key in her possession. And remedy it she would—with prejudice. In the meantime...

"And?" she prompted in a syrupy tone. "What is this great news you have for us? Enlighten me."

"Well, it seems that the squad I sent just picked up the woman and are in route here as we speak."

Verrine tossed the magazine aside as her smile grew. "Really?" she cooed. *Why the hell didn't you say so in the first place*, she thought. "Tell me more. How? Where? How soon will she be here? Details, darling. Details."

Dorian went directly to the bar and poured himself a Scotch. "I had them go out to her house today. They took her on her front porch about twenty minutes ago. Garrison said that there were a couple of pathetic humans obviously keeping an eye on her that they had to deal. He also indicated that with the way she answered the door it seemed as if she was expecting someone else, so they subdued her quickly and got out of there fast so as not to meet up with any further compli-cations."

"Subdued?" Verrine frowned. If the McComish woman had been damaged before she got the chance to...She took a deep breath to calm herself. "Subdued how? She wasn't harmed, was she?"

Dorian turned with a grin. "No, no, just a quick poke with a knock-out drug. She'll be fine. Like Archer, we'll wake her up, extract the whereabouts of The Key, then be done with her and dispose of her body like we did with the faerie."

Well, we'll be done, that's for sure, she thought, *but not quite in the way you think. However, the disposal part will be my pleasure.* Giving him a sultry smile, she wandered toward him. "That's brilliant, my sweet. However, you will let me interrogate her, won't you? I mean, after we get her awake and clear on where she is and what we want?"

"Of course, my love," the Immortal murmured with a dreamy smile. "Whatever you want. You can have as much time with her as you wish."

Verrine watched Dorian's eyes glaze over at her interrogation suggestion and the ever-so-slight mental push she'd given him. She would let this imbecile have the first few minutes with McComish, but as soon as she was certain of her suspicions, she would take over...in more ways than one. Then she would implement her own plan. And that had nothing whatsoever to do with Dorian Smyth.

She'd already come to the conclusion that McComish may actually *be* The Key. The terror that had flared in Tess Archer's eyes when she'd silently asked her that question during the final interrogation session with the faerie had nearly said it all. Oh, Archer had deflected, hadn't actually said so, but the look on her face for that split second? Well, it was exactly what Verrine had been waiting for.

"Excellent." Verrine patted Dorian's cheek and gave him another slight mental push. "You'll get me a cocktail now, won't you?"

"Yes, yes, I'll see to it immediately."

She turned and went back to the sofa, sinking down and crossing her legs. The cashmere pants and sweater she wore were whisper-soft and fit her corporeal body like a glove. Glancing at the magazine she'd tossed aside, she supposed she could understand how the obsession with fashions could happen. After all, she did look exceptional.

She watched Dorian as he mixed her cocktail, and when he brought it to her and sat down next to her on the sofa, she took a first sip, enjoying the bite of the concoction. Yes, there were some delightful things that this fallen world had to offer. "Very tasty, darling. Now, tell me, how soon is our guest going to arrive?"

"Garrison called after they were already in route. She lives out in Helvetia, which is only thirty minutes or so in light traffic. Unfortunately, light traffic is getting to be harder to find these days, so we'll see. However, it shouldn't be long. Probably less than an hour's time." He looked thoughtful as he savored his Scotch. "I've instructed them to bring her up in the freight elevator in a laundry cart, so even if they're spotted, she won't be."

"Ooh, good thinking. Looks like you have it all under control then." *And perhaps we'll have another use for the laundry cart afterward*, she thought and then smiled brightly at him.

Thirty-five minutes later, Dorian's domestic let the squad with the laundry cart into the penthouse condo.

Verrine looked down at the unconscious woman curled up under the blanket in the cart and smiled. Yes, her wait was almost over, and then she'd have her way with this world. And that fool Jerahmeel would be shit out of luck.

THE TEAM HAD MADE good time from the coast, even with stopping to pick up Sorcha. Kaden made the turn through the gates of the McComish property and started up the long driveway lined with alder trees and flanked by wide open fields. He couldn't get over his surprise and awe of the place, and they hadn't even gotten to the massive English-style manor yet, the top of which could be seen over the trees in the near distance at the crest of the slight incline. The driveway itself was paved, no gravel or pot holes here. Kaden knew it would have cost a pretty penny to put down that much concrete, even back in the day when the sprawling mansion was built.

When they rounded the last curve and the manor came fully into view, the majesty of the place became more apparent. Brenden McComish had built a stunning masterpiece and had left it to his granddaughter along with his entire empire. As a building contractor himself, Kaden couldn't wait to get an eyeball on the inside of this monster and hopefully score a full tour once they were done with this whole situation and their lives went back to normal.

As they got to the top of the rise, the wide concrete driveway became brick and circled around a large, stone fountain in front of the manor itself. He parked at the portico with its wide stone steps and then sat for a moment just enjoying the beauty of the place.

"Man, Brenden McComish really had a builder's eye for property, placement, structure…" he trailed off when words failed him.

"And this isn't the only mansion the guy built, either," Tanner said from the back. "If he left his entire empire to Kinna, then she's got several more of these beasts around the world."

"Well, let's go in then, and see what the beast looks like on the inside," Dory said. "Maybe she'll give us a quick tour before we get back on the road."

They all piled out of the van, and this time the team was prepared for anything as they climbed those stone steps. Everyone was armed in one way or another. Kaden wanted to make certain they wouldn't get caught as unprepared as they had been on Sunday at Sorcha's place. They'd been incredibly lucky that day. However, they couldn't count on that luck holding every time. As he led the pack up the steps toward the huge, oak double doors, he stopped short when he realized that one of said doors was standing slightly ajar.

"Yeah, this doesn't look good," he muttered as he pulled his Glock from its shoulder holster. He heard the whisper-sound behind him of Wyatt's katana sliding out of its sheath and knew that everyone else was now on guard. Gingerly, he pushed the door open farther. "Hello? Kinna? It's Kaden Crenshaw."

When there was no answer, Kaden stepped over the threshold with his weapon at high ready. He wasn't taking any chances, but as they all entered the foyer, the silence was deafening.

"Kinna," Dory called into the quiet. "It's Dory Winthrop. We're here to pick you up."

Still no answer.

"Oh, no. Kaden?" Dory turned to him with dread in her eyes. "Where's the security detail?"

He shook his head. "We don't know anything for sure, so let's not panic. We'll split up and search this place from top to bottom."

"She could've changed her mind and took off," Tanner began, then shrugged when Lucy gave him the stink-eye. "What? It happens." He shook his head and pulled out his phone. "Conner or Sanchez would have sent a text or called if something went sideways, but I'll give Conner a call. In the meantime,

I'm gonna go check the garage for her car while you guys get started in here."

As Tanner left the house in search of Kinna's car, Kaden turned to the group. "Ethan, you and Lucy on this level, west side. Wyatt, you and Vee take the east side. Ian, Dory, Sorcha, and I will take the second floor. Down and dirty, people, but be careful and thorough. If she's not here, we need to know where she's gone and if it was voluntary or forced. And stay sharp."

Everyone moved with a purpose, and as Kaden's group got to the landing at the top of the sweeping staircase, they split up with Ian and Sorcha taking the west wing, and he and Dory taking the east side. They cleared rooms as they went, looking for any obvious or not-so-obvious clues...plus any signs of foul play.

"Geez, how many bedrooms does this behemoth have?" Dory asked as they'd cleared the fourth bedroom in the east wing and were just coming up on what Kaden was pretty sure would be the master. "I mean, seriously. How much space does one man or one woman need?"

"From a structural perspective, I have to say, that so far, this is the coolest," Kaden said as they approached the last set of double doors. "But yeah, I get your point. I'm thinking this will be the master, so it could be Kinna's space now."

He eased open the doors and entered the sitting area of an enormous master suite. On a quick sweep they found a full bath with glassed-in shower and jet tub, a generous sleeping area with a king-size bed, and a massive walk-in closet with separate dressing area.

"Sweet, precious, Jesus," Dory all but whispered. "This is... well, words fail me."

"Yeah, I'm with ya on that."

"Oh, Kaden. Look." Dory walked to the king-size bed in the sleeping area where they found a packed duffel bag, insulated jacket with a hood, and a smaller backpack neatly lined up as if ready to go.

And nestled among the pillows, was a beautiful, velvet-gray cat watching them with big eyes. "Well, hello there, sweet thing. Where has you're human gotten off to?" Dory sighed. "If only you could tell us." Unzipping the duffel, Dory shook her head. "She was all packed. No way she changed her mind and took off like Tanner suggested."

"With the damp towel in the bathroom and the packed duffel? No. Not likely." Kaden scanned the room more closely. "I'm gonna say that Tanner will probably find her car in the garage as well. No, she didn't run, which means that she was taken. And I'd say within the last hour. Probably right after you talked to her on the phone."

"But by whom? And where the hell is the security detail? How are we gonna find her, Kaden?"

"I don't know, babe. Let's head back down and see if they found any meaningful clues downstairs."

On their way back, they met Ian and Sorcha at the head of the stairs where Ian just shook his head. Nothing found in their search, either. When they got downstairs everyone else was congregated in the kitchen. And there was more disturbing news.

"K, there's no signs of a struggle, but we did find Kinna's purse here on the counter, and her cell phone was right there next to it." Ethan shook his head. "And there's more bad news. Tanner says he found her car parked in that gigantic five-car garage with several others on the west side of the manor...along with the bodies of both Sentinels. So she didn't go anywhere. At least, not on her own...or voluntarily."

"Oh no." Dory squeezed her eyes shut briefly. "More death that could have been avoided if we'd taken steps sooner," she said with sorrow in her voice.

Tanner shook his head. "Okay, it sucks, yes, but it's not your fault, Dory, so don't take it on. Conner and Sanchez knew what the stakes were going in. They'd both been Sentinels for a very long time. I know for a fact that they'd both seen horrible things in the past, been involved in dicey situations before. They knew what they were doing and were good at it."

"Knowing all that doesn't make it any better, Tanner," Lucy murmured. "But you're right, whoever did this is at fault. We did everything we could to protect Kinna."

"Perhaps you're right, but that doesn't matter now, does it?" Dory asked with a sigh. "Regardless, we were thinking that Kinna may have been abducted after what we found upstairs. There was a packed duffel, jacket, and backpack sitting on the bed in the master. They were ready to go." She shook her head. "It all had to have happened between the time I spoke with her on the phone and when we arrived."

"Well, from the look of things, whatever happened didn't take place in the house," Ethan replied. "This place is spotless. I mean, there was nothing to find in the areas we searched."

"None on our side of the manor, either," Wyatt acknowledged.

Ethan met Kaden's gaze. "If I were to guess, I'd say whoever grabbed her took out the Sentinels first and stashed the bodies in the garage, then grabbed her right at the front door."

"Yeah, that would be my take as well," Wyatt agreed. "Knock on the door, she opens it, grab her, subdue her, throw her in the back of a vehicle and blow before anyone's the wiser."

"That would track," Kaden murmured. "There's a camera out there on the portico, so I would imagine there are quite a few more around the property. If we can access the security feed, we may be able to see exactly what happened. Maybe catch a break with a license plate or something. Or maybe facial recognition."

"Good idea," Ian said. "Hopefully, the security cams aren't some kind of an app on her cell, as that's pass coded."

Ethan blew out a breath. "Doubtful. Remember, she wasn't the original occupant of the manor, and she didn't build the place."

"Good point. Anyone come across an electronics center during the search?" Kaden asked.

"Brenden McComish would've had a state-of-the-art system installed," Tanner said. "We can only hope that Kinna knows where it is, how it works, and uses it consistently."

"I know exactly where the security set-up is," Velma chimed in.

"You do?" Ethan asked with raised eyebrows.

"It's got its own room off the utility at the back of the house." She paused when everyone just stared at her. "What?" she asked in a snippy tone. "Hello? Security is one of my things, remember?"

Wyatt beamed with approval. "That's my girl."

"Alrighty, then. Let's get to it, sister," Ethan said with a grin.

KINNA DRIFTED toward consciousness ever so slowly with a blasting headache, and her mouth was desert-dry. She wanted to open her eyes, willed herself to, but her eyelids felt as if they were coated in cement, so she let herself float a bit longer. What the hell had happened to her? She was groggy, and her thoughts were all jumbled together in a way that made absolutely no sense to her, even as she tried to rearrange them in her head. She remembered feeding the cat, taking a shower, and then after that, talking first to Kari and then to Dory Winthrop on the phone. She'd packed...Someone at the door. A few thoughts sprang out from the jumble. Yes, men at the door...a syringe... darkness.

"Come, come, now, Kinna. Open your eyes," a deep voice said in her ear, and she tried to jerk away from it only to find that she couldn't move.

Prying her eyes open, she found that she was sitting upright in a chair. "What the hell?" The words came out rusty, and she cleared her throat as she looked around. "Where am I? And why am I strapped to this chair?"

Her vision was a bit bleary, but as clarity returned, she realized that she was in a large living room with a handsome man looking to be in his late forties or early fifties and a woman with white-white hair and skin to match. The woman wore little makeup and had an almost ethereal look to her. But those eyes. Crystalline blue, nearly see-through eyes that were both mesmerizing and somewhat frightening at the same time.

"Kinna?" The man snapped his fingers in front of her face to regain her attention. "You are going to want to focus, my dear. We have some important questions to ask you, and we will need prompt, honest answers."

"Who are you people?" Kinna asked. She struggled to think through the haze and shook her head in an attempt to clear it which only made it worse. Panic began to set in. Obviously, she'd been abducted before Dory and her team could arrive to pick her up. But why? Were these the people that she'd been warned about? "Where am I, and what do you want?"

"My name is Dorian Smyth. And what I want is for you to tell us the location of The Key." He leaned down and narrowed his eyes. "I'm aware that you know the location so don't bother to lie to me. You will tell me right now, if you know what's good for you."

The Key? So, these *were* the people looking for her, and they wanted to know her location. She still felt loopy from whatever they'd injected her with, and hysteria bubbled up and out of her. "You're looking for The Key?" she asked on a giggle. "Like, its actual location?"

In the next instant, her mirth died in her throat, and her head snapped back with the force of Smyth's backhand. "Do you think this is funny, you little pissant?" he asked in anger. "This is not a laughing matter. You will tell me where The Key is this instant, or I'll beat it out of you."

"Dorian, stop." The woman spoke quietly, but Kinna could see the immediate effect it had on Smyth, and when she turned, Kinna heard the woman's voice clearly in her head.

I'm here to help you, Kinna. This man is not. Are you The Key? If so, tell me. Let me help you.

With eyes watering from the stinging backhand, Kinna glared up at the man, then turned to the woman with a mutinous stare.

Please, Kinna. You can trust me.

How do I know that? You're here with him, aren't you? That doesn't inspire confidence or trust.

Unfortunately, you have no other choice. There is little time. Please, Kinna. Give me the word, and I will save you from him.

With her head now mostly clear, Kinna realized what the woman said was true. She didn't have much of a choice. Trusting the woman was a terrible gamble—and one she would probably regret sooner rather than later—but if it gave her some time to figure a way out of this, it was a gamble she would have to take.

She looked the woman in the eye and gave a brief nod.

You are The Key, then?

Yes. I am.

The smile that spread across the woman's face was almost as scary as those crystalline eyes, and Kinna had a sick feeling that she'd made a horrible mistake, but it was too late now.

The woman nodded. *Then I suggest you look away if you have a weak stomach.*

Before Kinna could ask her why, she watched in horror as the fingers on the woman's right hand grew into razor-sharp knives. In the next second, she took Smyth's arm with her left hand and turned him slightly toward her, shoving her weaponized hand into his chest and literally pulling out his still-beating heart.

And Kinna began to scream.

As it turned out, Velma was a whiz with the electronic security system. They all crowded around the Sentinel while she spent twenty minutes working her magic on the attached laptop and searching for a way into the system.

"Ah-ha! There you are, you bloody bastard," she crowed with a fist in the air as the screen changed to an options menu. "Now, let's see. It looks as if the system is set to re-write every forty-eight hours, so we should be fine there."

"Can you locate the feed from the front entry, Vee?" Kaden asked. "That's really the only thing we need."

Velma's fingers stilled on the keyboard, and she slowly turned her head, giving him a steely look over her shoulder. "Do you mean to insult me, then? Do you not see me looking for it, Kaden Crenshaw? Is that not what we're all doing here packed into this teeny-tiny room like sardines?"

Kaden put up his hands and struggled to keep a straight face. "Sorry, darlin'. I'm just a little anxious, that's all."

"As are we all," the Sentinel said, turning back to the screen with a pissy look on her face.

Dory had to work not to snicker, but she did give Kaden a wink of commiseration. She'd been on that end of Velma's annoyance herself many times over the years.

Watching Velma's fingers resume their rapid flight over the keyboard, coupled with her intermittent clicking of the mouse, Dory lost track of how many menus Velma buzzed through before they got another, 'Ah-ha!' moment from her and the screen changed to the team's van sitting out front where they'd left it.

"Okay, yes." Velma pointed at the time stamp at the top of the computer screen. "This is obviously the live feed, but this," she said, clicking another icon and gesturing toward the new page. "This is the recorded stuff. Let's just scan back through, shall we? We'll see who we find and what shenanigans were afoot."

The time stamp began running backward and the images on the screen started moving in reverse from the team's arrival. From that point back there was nothing on the recorded feed for forty minutes or so before, bingo! Another van—this one black and shiny with dark windows—appeared. Unfortunately, on the heels of that, the fate of the two Sentinels and the team's suspicion that Kinna had been abducted played out before their eyes.

"Damn. There are times that I hate being right," Ethan muttered. "Especially about something like this. I mean, looks like Conner and Sanchez tried to intervene, waded right in to confront the three guys about to go up the steps to the door but didn't count on the other two guys still in the van. The assholes overwhelmed them, then dragged them off, presumably to the garage where Tanner found them. Then, easy-peasey, took Kinna down on her own front porch. Bastards."

"Run it forward again, *Mo Leannan*," Wyatt requested. "Let's see if we can catch a view of the license plate, if it's got one."

"No need," Sorcha said quietly. "I know the one asshole with the syringe. Well, don't actually know him, but I know who he is. His name's Garrison." She turned to Kaden. "And he works for Dorian Smyth."

"Shite," Dory spat. This was so not what she'd hoped to find. If Smyth or Verrine had snapped to the fact that Kinna was The Key, they were all in big trouble. It was something they'd all worked to avoid. "Well, Jerahmeel did tell us that Smyth wasn't a patient sort."

"Aye, and all we can hope for now is that he's still in the dark about Kinna being a Time Mender, that he's just looking for information on The Key," Ian murmured. "Though I'm afraid with this development we may be well beyond that now."

"Agreed." Wyatt crossed his arms and looked over Velma's shoulder. "And by the look of this time stamp, they have almost an hour head start on us. They could be anywhere by now."

"Mmm, maybe not anywhere." Tanner stared at the van on the screen. "Smyth owns a penthouse condo in one of the high-rises in the Pearl. It's his main residence in the Portland area. Ten to one, that's where they've taken her."

Lucy frowned. "How would you know that?"

The shifter gave her a humorous look before shaking his head. "How would I know that? Really, Luce? It's like you don't even know me."

Lucy snorted. "Ha-ha. Very funny."

"I know because I did my research on all the players right after I got here. Some of them—like Smyth—I already knew about but brushed up on and did a deeper dive to get a clear picture of what we'd be dealing with." Tanner looked back at the screen. "But if he's taken her there, I hope someone in the group is good with passcodes. We'll need it to get into the building, let alone into his penthouse."

Wyatt grinned and rubbed his hands together with obvious

glee. "No worries there, mate. I'll wager that I can get us in, and right quick."

Dory sighed and shook her head. Of course the mercenary would have breaking and entering skills. Why wouldn't he? "Uh, I don't even want to know how you'll do that." She turned to Tanner. "But first, why do you think Smyth will take her to his residence? I mean, the chances of someone hearing or seeing something they shouldn't would be pretty high."

"Yeah, if it was me, I'd take her somewhere quiet and as secluded as possible," Ethan agreed. "I mean, you don't want your inquisitive neighbor poking his nose in while you're doing your nefarious deeds, now do you?"

"I suppose that's true." Tanner considered a moment. "But it is a place to start, right? Which, correct me if I'm wrong, is something we seem to be lacking as it stands."

"You do have a point," Dory said, then gestured to the image of Kinna's abduction still on the computer screen. "And if these guys are Smyth's underlings, then we start by paying Mr. Smyth a visit. We're already too far behind for my liking as it is, and if nothing else, we cross it off the list and move on. But if this asshole's got Kinna, we can't afford to give him any more time alone with her than he's already had." She narrowed her eyes at the screen, and her tone was stone cold when she added, "And if Kinna's been harmed in any way when we find her, I will end whoever's responsible."

There was a moment of silence after her comment, and Dory figured she may have shocked a few of the team members, but she was rock-solid on that point.

"Alrighty then," Ethan finally said into the silence. "I guess the Chosen One has spoken."

"I guess so," Kaden replied.

But Dory held up a hand. "However, before we can head out, we need to take care of Conner and Sanchez." She turned to

Tanner. "Can you handle that, Tanner? We can't leave them here. They need to be taken home. Arrangements need to be made."

"I'm on it. I'll take care of them," the shifter murmured.

"Okay, then let's hit it, people."

They all headed back out to the driveway, piled into the van, and were on their way into the city ten minutes later. Unfortunately, travel was slow going. The highway was down to three lanes with a two-vehicle accident blocking the fourth lane on the far right just past the 217 interchange. And though it had little to do with the inside lane they were using, with the looky-loos slowing traffic even more, they didn't pick up the pace until they'd finally inched their way past the crash. But even then, they were held to about half the speed limit, and it was still stop and go all the way to the I405 cutoff.

The longer they were delayed, the higher Dory's anxiety rose. She couldn't stop speculating about where they'd taken Kinna and what plans they had for her. With a Time Mender under their control, the possibilities were frightening...for everyone globally. She stewed about it all the way into the Pearl District where Tanner directed Kaden to the block that housed Smyth's high-rise.

"Take a right here and then go up a couple blocks. There's a public parking structure. I don't think it would be wise to park on the street right in front of the building. That is, if we could even find a vacant spot this time of day."

"Probably not," Kaden replied. He pulled the van into the overpark that the shifter had indicated and lucked into a spot on the first level close to the streetside door that would put them just a two and a half block stroll from Smyth's building. As they all got out of the vehicle, Kaden turned to Wyatt. "Okay, buddy. How are you gonna get us into the building?"

Wyatt grinned. "Watch and learn, Warrior. However, a

suggestion first. I think it would also be unwise for us all to go traipsing down there together. Eight sketchy sorts like this group piling through the door behind me as I crime my way into the building probably wouldn't go unnoticed. And if we're wanting to stay under the radar, perhaps we should pare it down a bit. I'd say maybe four of us, five at the most."

"That's a solid thought," Kaden said with a nod. He looked around at the group, then turned to Dory. "I say you, me, obviously Wyatt, Sorcha, and Tanner. What do you think?"

"Aw, K, come on," Ethan muttered.

Dory shook her head. "Sorry, Ethan, but I agree with Kaden. Tanner has the demonology background we may need. Sorcha has skills that none of us have which could be very helpful as well. Wyatt's our B and E guy. He gets us into the building. So, with Kaden and me, that's five. That's the entry team."

Ethan pouted for a few beats and then pointed a finger at Kaden. "Okay, fine. But next time we're criming, I want in, too. I'm a cop, remember? I never get to do this kind of shit."

Kaden chuckled. "You got it, buddy. The rest of you just hang here until I call for an assist or we come back. Hopefully, this won't take too long."

The five of them went streetside through the double doors and walked the two blocks to where Smyth's building was located, but as they crossed the street, Wyatt halted the group at the corner. He was scrolling through something on his cell phone and kept looking around as if checking directions. After a few minutes, he pointed down the street to the right. "Okay, we need to go this way. There should be a courtyard between buildings about mid-block that will lead us back to a side entrance for Smyth's building. That should give us the best cover and be the easiest entry point."

They headed that way and found that the bounty hunter's directions were spot on. Crossing through the courtyard, there was indeed a side entrance set back from the street and not all that noticeable. Dory went up the steps to the glass door with Wyatt indicating that the others should hang back in the court-yard until the mercenary could get them into the building.

As Wyatt took a generic-looking card out of his wallet to get to work on the swipe plate next to the door, it turned out that luck was on their side. Dory watched through the glass door as an older couple crossed the lobby toward them, and she put her hand on Wyatt's arm to get him to hold off.

The older gentleman opened the door, holding it wide for the woman with him.

"Good afternoon," Dory greeted them with a bright smile. "Looks like you're all bundled up good. It's quite chilly out here today. Guess winter really is just around the corner, right?"

The woman smiled back. "Oh yes, I think that's very true."

"I absolutely love your knit hat, by the way. Bet it keeps your ears nice and warm."

"It certainly does. But where's yours, dear? Aren't your ears cold?"

"Yes. Freezing." Taking advantage of the fact that the man was still holding the door open, Dory took Wyatt's hand and started into the lobby, pulling him along with her. "I forgot both my hat and my gloves when we left earlier. I won't forget again, I'll tell you that. Have a nice walk."

Dory waved over her shoulder as she and Wyatt kept walk-ing, and she didn't look back until they got to the elevator bank around the corner. Then she peeked back around to make certain the couple had cleared the building before hurrying back to the side door to let the others in.

"Well, that was pretty convenient," Kaden remarked as they headed for the elevators where Wyatt was waiting and holding one of the doors open for them. Studying the buttons on the panel as they crowded into the lift, Kaden selected the button marked PH before turning to Tanner. "Since you said penthouse, I'm assuming the top floor is where we're going, but do you know which penthouse is Smyth's?"

"I texted a buddy of mine while we were waiting in the courtyard. He said there should only be three units on sixteen, and he thought it was unit 1603," Tanner replied with a bit of hesitation.

"He *thought*?" Dory asked in disbelief. "Are you kidding me? We came all this way, lucked into the building, and you don't know for sure which unit is Smyth's?"

"My guy was pretty sure."

"Seriously, dude?" Kaden stared at the shifter before running a hand over his face with his obvious frustration.

"Okay, let's all calm down," Sorcha said. "I can probably figure it out by touch."

"By touch?" Dory asked. "What? Like touching the door?"

Sorcha nodded, then tilted her head. "Well, the door handle more specifically. They can usually be good for intuiting some relevant information. Especially if they've been used fairly recently."

"I thought you could only sense or feel things from touching people," Dory replied. "Like visions and thoughts."

"Well, that's mostly true, but I can pick up sensations, sometimes even visual images from inanimate objects. We'll check 1603 first. I should be able to tell if there's certain kinds of energy in or around the unit. You know, like otherworldly."

"Of course, we could just press the buzzer or knock. See who answers the door," Tanner added.

Dory shook her head as the elevator doors opened onto the sixteenth floor, the small lobby of which had huge glass windows overlooking the river beyond. "Well, let's get this over with before I can really dwell on how stupid this endeavor is."

She led the way around the corner and down the wide

hallway to 1603's door. She looked at Sorcha and made a sweeping motion. "It's all yours. Give me some good news."

Sorcha stepped over to the door, and closing her eyes, laid a hand gently on the handle. It only took a few moments to have her gasping and jerking her hand back as if she'd been burned.

"Sorcha, *auld charaid*, what is it?" Wyatt asked his old friend. "What did you see?"

The Immortal swallowed hard. "Nothing good," she whispered. "I would say that this is the place we're looking for...but there is death here."

"Open the door, Wyatt," Kaden instructed. "Now."

Watching the mercenary was pretty impressive, as it took him less than forty-five seconds to unlock the door and discover that the deadbolt had not been engaged at all. Again, Dory couldn't help but wonder where he'd learned the skill but figured it came in handy in his line of work.

"Nicely done," she murmured. "And in under a minute. I don't even want to know where you learned that skill, but I'm glad for it at the moment."

When she moved to open the door, Kaden blocked her way and shook his head. "Nope. I go in first, love. Warrior, remember?"

She smirked at him but stepped back and followed him in as he slowly opened the door and entered the foyer. The first thing she noticed was how incredibly quiet it was, unnaturally so. And Sorcha had been right.

It smelled of death.

Kaden motioned for Wyatt and Tanner to check down the hallway to the left, while he, Dory, and Sorcha moved toward the living area. And there was where they found the death Sorcha had sensed.

And not just one death but three.

Dorian Smyth's ruined body was sprawled on the white rug

in the living room surrounded by his own blood, and Dory could tell before they even got to his body that there was a gaping wound in his chest where his immortal heart had been. There were only a few ways that an Immortal could actually die, and having your heart removed was one of them. Dorian Smyth was gone for good.

Sorcha knelt down—careful to avoid the blood that had saturated the previously white carpet—and laid a hand on the deceased Immortal's forehead. She closed her eyes and took several deep breaths. Dory watched her eyes move rapidly back and forth behind her eyelids, and after a few minutes, she opened her eyes and there was anger burning in their depths.

"What is it?" Dory asked with trepidation. "Kinna?"

The Immortal shook her head. "I don't know about Kinna, but this was done by Verrine."

"Verrine?" Kaden asked. "The fallen angel did this to him?"

"He didn't even see it coming. Arrogant git. He thought they were partners, that they would somehow rule together when his plan came to fruition. Ignorance." Sorcha stood and backed away from the body. "Also, Tanner was correct. Dorian had Kinna brought here to interrogate her. He didn't know that she was The Key." Her gaze tracked around the room coming to rest on the chair by the fireplace. "They tied Kinna to that chair, and when she refused to answer Dorian's questions, he threatened to beat her. However, in that next moment, Verrine turned to him... and ripped out his heart. It was the last thing he saw before death, true death, took him."

"Okay, that's unsettling," Kaden said. "To say the very least."

"And there's more," Sorcha added with a nod. "This is where Tess Archer died as well. Right here in this room tied to a chair in much the same way. That was his plan for Kinna once she'd told them the location of The Key."

"Obviously, Verrine wasn't on board with that plan." Dory

looked around the room. "I'm gonna say that our fallen angel had figured out that Kinna is The Key. She didn't need Smyth anymore."

"Yeah, but where did she take Kinna?" Tanner asked as he and Wyatt came into the room.

"Exactly," Kaden replied. "And how do we track them?"

"Well, there's nothing down the hall in any of the bedrooms," Wyatt said. "One room looks to be Smyth's office. Maybe we could find some intel in there, but it will take some time. Precious time that Kinna may not have."

Before Dory could respond, there was a soft moan from the other side of the room near the wall of windows. Following the sound, they found that one of the bodies wasn't actually dead but close to it. She hunched down and took the man's hand, the man Sorcha had identified as Garrison from the security feed they'd watched at Kinna's earlier.

"Garrison, can you hear me?" Dory asked.

The man's lips moved as if he were speaking but no sound accompanied the movement.

"If you can hear me, squeeze my hand."

There it was, so slight but a squeeze nonetheless.

"You're going to die, Garrison. You know that, right? Can you tell me what happened to the woman you abducted?"

Again, the man's lips moved but without sound.

Dory looked up at Sorcha. "He's fading fast. I can heal him to a point, see if we can get him to talk but—"

"No. You can't," Sorcha interrupted Dory. "This was his choice. He was Smyth's guy. He won't give up anything willingly."

"And even if you heal him, he'll just be one more loose end in this carnage to explain," Wyatt agreed.

Dory was thinking the same thing but was glad that they were all on the same page. She looked at Sorcha. "Okay. Then can you see if you can get anything from him before he's gone?"

Sorcha nodded and took Dory's place next to the man. "Relax, Garrison," she began in a soothing tone. "Let me help you cross over. Just breathe and relax your mind." She closed her eyes and took a couple deep breaths as she had with Smyth. It took less than five minutes before Garrison expelled one long, final breath and Sorcha opened her eyes.

"So?" Dory asked. "Anything?"

Sorcha stood and nodded. "Yes, a great many things but most importantly, the location of the warehouse that Verrine is using. It's where she's taken Kinna."

"And you can find this warehouse?" Wyatt asked.

"I can."

"Okay, then," Kaden said. "Let's police our movements, anything you touched gets wiped. Then we go find Kinna."

Seattle was burning. No, not just Seattle, she realized. Like a slide show in her mind, Kinna watched in horror as city after burning city, devastated and in ruin, crossed her field of vision. What was this? Her mind struggled to remember how she'd come to be here. She instinctively knew that she was dreaming. It was like so many of the nightmares from her past, and she wondered if Jerahmeel was here waiting for her somewhere within the destruction she was witnessing.

"He's deceitful, you know..."

The voice was soft, compassionate...female.

"Who's deceitful?"

"The Archangel has been disingenuous with you, about your gifts, and about what sleeps inside you," the voice replied.

"Are you saying Jerahmeel lied to me? About my destiny?"

"Perhaps lie is a strong word, but an omission of truth amounts to the same thing, doesn't it?"

Kinna scanned this last cityscape with its burned-out buildings, scorched earth, smoldering fields and found no individual to go with the voice she heard. *"What omission of truth? Who are you? Where are you?"*

"My name is Verrine, and I'm right here...waiting for you to come back to your place in time. I saved you, remember? I'm a new friend who has come to help you. We will help each other to get what we each want."

Kinna frowned. Was this person waiting outside of her dream? In her own time? And how had she been saved? From what? Her mind was a jumble of thoughts, images. She couldn't discern what was real and what was from her nightmare. What did this 'new friend' think she wanted that she couldn't get for herself?

"Ah, that is the question, isn't it? Shall I tell you? Give you a few ideas, a few options?" the voice continued.

"I'm a failsafe for this world."

"Are you? How do you know that? Is that what the Archangel told you?"

"No. He showed me how it's been in the past, how the entity has corrected time to protect this world." Kinna gestured to the devastation around her. "With my gift, I can assure that this never happens to my world, that it won't ever be our future."

"I suppose that could be true, but how do you know what you're seeing is the future? Just because he said so? And what about your needs?"

"My needs? What do you mean?"

"Well, your family, for one thing. Were they not taken from you in death? Wouldn't you like to regain the time with them that was stolen from you? Or maybe you'd like to have your beloved grandfather back again for guidance and comfort."

Kinna shook her head. "My parents died, but they weren't stolen from me. An accident...it's the circle of life. It was the same with my Pops. He had lived a long, fruitful life, and it was his time. I mean, I miss them very much but our time in this world is limited to the Supreme Being's plan. We can't change what is."

"Oh, my sweet girl, but it's different for you. Don't you understand *that? You don't have to be bound by that plan. You're a Time Mender, Kinna McComish. The Father gave you that gift. You do realize that with the entity inside you, anything is possible, right? I'll wager that's the one tidbit that Jerahmeel withheld from you. And do you know why?"*

Kinna shook her head as that thought started to take root.

"They want to use you and your gift as they see fit for their purposes only. Yet, you were never given a choice, were you? They didn't ask you if this was what you wanted, did they? No, of course not."

"I was chosen like Dory. We're both guardrails for this world, safety nets."

"Ah, yes. The Immortal. She even carries the name The Chosen One. Yet even she has struggled with a destiny not of her choosing. A destiny that was thrust upon her when she was close to your age. Did she tell you that?"

"No, but..."

"Wake from your dreams, Time Mender. Come back to the present and let me guide you to a destiny of your own making. Just...breathe."

Kinna did then. And the breath she took was filled with an acrid odor that fairly scorched her nostrils, had her eyes watering. The destroyed city before her faded like the devastating nightmare it was, leaving nothing but blackness behind.

"That's it, Time Mender. Awaken and open your eyes," that same female voice demanded. "We have much to discuss, you and I."

Taking another deep breath to clear the pungent smell from her nose, Kinna blinked in the dim light, staring at the rafters high above her head. Where was she now? And how did she get here? Was this another dream?

"It is not," the voice told her. "This is the present."

Turning her head slightly, Kinna realized that she was laying on a cot in a cavernous space. And the voice belonged to the wraithlike woman sitting in the chair toward the end of the cot. The memories of being abducted, of this woman ripping out a man's heart before her very eyes came flooding back to Kinna in a dreadful torrent.

"You!" Kinna cried, shrinking back. "You murdered that man. You tore his heart out with...your fingers were knives."

The woman put up her hands—which now appeared completely normal—and a compassionate look crossed her pale face. "I'm sorry you had to see that, Kinna, but I needed to save you before Dorian had a chance to really hurt you. He was a terrible man who would have exploited your gift for his own desires. He would have ruined your world and then murdered you when he'd gotten what he wanted. I couldn't let him do that."

"Who are you? *What* are you?"

"My name is Verrine. And I was an angel, once upon a time."

"But you were with him, working with him."

Verrine shook her head. "I know it must have seemed that way, but I was only with him because I knew he was looking for the entity you carry. I was there to intervene when he found you before he could do any harm to you or this world."

Kinna sat up and surveyed her surroundings before putting her feet on the floor. "You said that you *were* an angel. You're not anymore? What are you now?"

"I'm something different. It's...complicated." Verrine tipped her head and gave Kinna a considering look. "Just think of me as a new friend who only wants to see you get your due, to help you make your own choices."

Standing, Kinna swayed a bit before nodding. "Okay. If that's true, then my choice would be to go home now. I appreciate you saving me from Dorian and all, but can you give me a ride?"

"Kinna." Verrine *tsked* before standing as well. Her voice was soft, enticing as she spoke. "Is that really what you want? Don't you want to go back and make those alterations to your past? You know that's all it would take to have your family back. Think of how just a few small changes could transform your here and now."

Kinna could literally feel the woman's words pushing at the outer edges of her mind, soothing, compelling. What if Verrine was right? What if she could have her parents back again? Her Pops? Would those few small changes make any difference in the wide-reaching scheme of things?

"You said that we could help each other get what we each wanted," she said. "What is it that you want?"

Verrine held out her hand. "Come. Let's sit for a while and discuss our options, shall we?"

"OKAY, TURN HERE," Sorcha said, eyes closed, pointing in the direction of the next street to the right as if seeing it in her mind. "The warehouse they're at is a couple blocks up on the left."

"And how do you know that?" Ethan asked in a confounded tone. "You've got your eyes closed."

The Immortal smiled. "I see clearly in my mind what Garrison saw on several occasions. You see, he was playing both sides of his situation. He'd been Dorian's guy from the start but what if Verrine wanted something else? What he didn't count on was that she'd brought all the help she needed with her and would leave no loose ends that she couldn't fully trust." Sorcha opened her eyes and looked at Ethan. "I'm pretty sure Verrine had a definite plan of her own from the start. All she needed Dorian for was a bit of direction and muscle. And, of course, a really lovely penthouse to spend her time in while she waited. Like Dory said, after finding Kinna, she didn't need Dorian Smyth or his goons anymore."

"So, you got all of that from those few minutes before Garrison died?" Ethan asked. "That's pretty amazing."

"You think so? I suppose it may seem that way from the outside looking in, but it's extremely draining. Feeling what others feel, seeing what they've seen. And it's especially so when they've passed over." She sighed and glanced out the window. "It's this next dilapidated warehouse on the left, Kaden. There's the loading dock, but there's also a side door up that driveway next to the building. That's where the entrance is that Garrison used on several occasions."

"Like back at the condo, it'll probably be best not to park right in front of the warehouse, Kaden," Wyatt suggested.

"Yep. Was just thinking the same thing." Kaden drove on past the warehouse and around the corner, found an open spot, and parked. "We walk from here, folks."

"V—" Dory began but Velma cut her off.

"Don't even go there, Isadora. I'm not cooling my heels in the van while you all risk your lives. I'm going in with you."

Dory sighed but didn't argue. Just one more thing for her to worry about.

Climbing out of the van, they each armed themselves with their various chosen weapons before Dory and Kaden led the team back toward the warehouse.

Dory had listened to Sorcha's explanation in the van and thought it was spot on—and though she didn't have Garrison's images and thoughts in her head, it was just what she herself had worked out since leaving the penthouse. She was pretty sure that Verrine was going to be the most dangerous part of this whole thing but had really no idea how to get around her or what that would involve. How did one defeat a fallen angel? What kind of powers would one still command? And where the hell was Jerahmeel when they needed him most?

Once they got to the warehouse, Kaden divided the team

into two groups. "I think it will be best for us to come at this from a couple different directions. Wyatt, Ethan, Lucy, Tanner, and I will head in directly through the loading docks. Dory, Sorcha, Ian, and Velma, you four slip in the side door that Sorcha saw through her connection with Garrison. Keep sharp. We don't know what we're gonna find once we're inside this place."

"Yes, and since a fallen angel-turned-demon is heading up this shit-show, there's probably going to be other nasties with her," Sorcha added.

"Bet on it, and who knows what that will entail," Dory agreed. "More demons are likely, but we could see human beings under her control or even rogue Immortals since they are so easily controlled. So, don't assume anything, and like Kaden said, look sharp and don't take any chances."

"Okay. Let's head out," Kaden said then pulled Dory to him and gave her a hard kiss. "Take care of my Chosen One. I'll see you on the other side."

With that, the two groups split up. Without looking back, Dory led hers down the driveway to the side entrance. She couldn't worry about Kaden and that part of the team. She had to stay focused and on task with an eye toward protecting those with her.

Cement steps led up to the steel door they were looking for, and she could only hope that it wasn't locked, because if it was, they'd have to find another way in quickly.

Ian stepped up in front of her before she could start up the steps. "Nope. I'll take point, Isadora."

Dory blew out a breath in frustration but gestured to the door. "Fine. Be my guest, old man."

Fortunately, the door opened easily when Ian tried it, and Dory followed him into the gloom with trepidation. They took the unlit corridor to the right heading toward the back of the warehouse. It was fairly apparent that there had been squatters living there at some point, the evidence of which was old and smelled of decay and mildew. The hallway took a sharp left at the end of the building and opened up onto the main area of the old warehouse about twenty feet later, but their view of the space was blocked by several tall stacks of dusty wooden pallets. However, they could hear voices from unseen sources echoing from farther inside the warehouse.

Dory slipped between two of the pallet stacks and peered around them to get a better view. What she saw across the open expanse was Kinna sitting at a small table with another woman —presumably Verrine—and looking to be in deep conversation. Around the perimeter of the open space, several men seemed to be standing guard or just awaiting orders.

Unfortunately, before she could decide how to proceed, there was a sudden disturbance with shouting coming from the direction of the loading docks. The chaos and commotion that ensued was punctuated by the sound of gunshots. Dory watched several of the men at her end of the warehouse run in that direction.

Seeing an opening that the distraction provided, she stepped out from behind the pallets with Ian beside her, and Sorcha and Velma bringing up the rear as they started for the table where Verrine and Kinna were sitting. Intent on getting to Kinna, Dory almost missed a sudden movement to her right, but the condescending voice that accompanied it stopped her cold.

"Well, well, well. What do we have here? The Chosen One and her pitiful gang of losers?"

Turning, Dory watched a tall, elegantly dressed woman followed by a handful of armed men walk toward them.

"And you would be?" Dory drawled in a bored tone. "I'm sorry, but we don't have much time for chitchat. As you can see, we're kinda busy here."

The woman's eyes flashed with her annoyance. "I'm Victoria Newcomb," she announced with self-importance.

Dory tilted her head and gave the woman an obvious once-over. "No. I don't believe so. Oh, you may be occupying the body of the poor, deceased *human* Victoria Newcomb, but you are definitely not her. So, what kind of pathetic demon are you? Because I'm assuming that's what you really are under Newcomb's finery. A sub-human thing of some sort?"

This time more than annoyance flared in Newcomb's eyes before she took a breath and sneered. "You think you're above everything, better than everyone else because you're the Chosen One, but you're not. And you're going to find that out very soon."

"Is that so?"

Newcomb's gaze swung from Dory to Ian and then to Sorcha, but stopped at Velma, and a pleased look crossed her face. "So, three Immortals and one lowly human. What's your name, sugar?" she asked Velma.

"Piss off, you manky toad. And don't call me sugar," Velma spat.

Dory's eruption of laughter was short-lived with Newcomb's next remark.

"Now, that's just rude." The woman shot out a hand in Velma's direction curling her fingers into a fist.

Velma immediately began to struggle, grabbing at her throat. She was obviously fighting for air and her eyes went wide.

However, before Dory could intervene, Ian stepped up. "Oh, no you didn't, you worthless cow. You don't mess with our Velma." In the next moment, he threw a hard punch in Newcomb's direction, and along with it, a burst of energy that Dory felt as it whipped past her. It tore open one side of the demon's face and quite literally knocked her off her four-inch pumps. She flew backward a good twenty feet, crash landing on the cement floor and tumbling to a stop where she ended up lying motionless.

Dory turned to the Scotsman with a stunned look. "Okay, that's new."

Ian grinned. "Just a little something I've been working on."

Throwing out some energy of her own, Dory gave the handful of armed men coming for them now the same treatment, making certain they were all down for the count before turning to Velma. "You okay?"

"I'm fine," Velma replied rubbing her throat, then she pointed toward the other side of the warehouse. "But look there. The others are fighting their way in and giving us some good cover. Let's go rescue Kinna and get this over with."

Following the Sentinel's direction, Dory saw Kaden and Ethan fighting back-to-back, and Wyatt and Lucy each holding their own and moving closer to the interior of the warehouse. Tanner was in wolf form and tearing into a couple of men on the far side of the building. They all seemed to be relatively unharmed and intact so she tried to put them out of her mind for the moment.

Without waiting any longer, she and her team started toward the table where Kinna was now sitting alone. Verrine had disappeared, which made Dory a bit wary, but her bigger concern was Kinna. The closer they got to the Time Mender, she realized that there was something terribly wrong. Kinna was sitting very still with her hands on the table and her eyes wide open. But her eyes...they were a milky white and almost opaque.

"Kinna?" Dory called softly. "Can you hear me?"

"Oh, you're far too late for that, Chosen One," Verrine said, stepping out from the gloom. "The Time Mender is going to rock your world. Well, maybe not rock it, but she is going to shake it up but good."

"What have you done to her?" Dory asked in a deathly quiet voice.

"Me? Why, I've done nothing at all. I simply pointed out that she had choices. She didn't have to comply with the wishes of a Supreme Being who would use her as a tool." The fallen angel's look was condescending. "In fact, you should know all about that. I don't believe you were ever given a choice, either. Were you?"

"You know nothing about me, demon. So don't pretend that you do," Dory replied quietly. "You're just another asshole looking to cause chaos and destruction."

"Really? I know more than you think." Verrine spread her arms wide. "Can you honestly tell me that you have always accepted the destiny that was shoved down your throat, *Chosen One*? Have you not struggled against that destiny for centuries? What I know is that you've never felt worthy, and you've wished for a true death as a way out more times than you can count."

Dory scoffed, though the truth in Verrine's word stung more than a bit and made her snappish. "Your point? Or do you even have one?"

"My point is that I can help you, Isadora, as I've helped the Time Mender. I can show you how to make your own destiny. Wouldn't you like that? Wouldn't that be better going forward than more of the centuries-old suffering you've endured, to be able to make decisions about your own life? To live your life on your own terms and no one else's? Aren't you tired of it all? Peace and quiet. Isn't that what you really want? What you crave?"

Verrine's words swirled through Dory's mind like an intoxicating tonic. Wasn't that true? Wasn't it what she'd yearned for over the years? Just a bit of peace and quiet. To not be the one to hold the fate of the world on her shoulders. It was exhausting.

"Dory! Don't listen to her."

Her vision began to blur and she heard someone calling her name as if from a great distance, but it seemed so far away and unimportant compared to the lovely vision beginning to form in her head.

"You see? I do know you better than you think, Isadora," Verrine was saying in a soothing, honeyed tone. "Yes, that peace and quiet, that's where you want to live, don't you? With Kaden? In a life where you don't have to wonder if you're worthy of what you have. A life with no responsibilities, no constant turmoil, no judgement. I can show you how, if you'll let me."

In her mind's eye, Dory *could* almost see it, what her life could be like without the continuous struggle of being the Chosen One, the ever-present threat of world-ending events where she was required to be the shield for all.

A life shared with Kaden filled with nothing but love and joy.

"Yes, you can see it, can't you?" Verrine murmured, nodding her head.

Dory felt dazed, dizzy with the promise of it all before realizing in that very moment what was actually happening to her.

With herculean effort, Dory shook her head and blinked away the gossamer images Verrine had spun in her mind. Rubbing her palms together and discreetly generating electric energy, she glowered at the fallen angel. "Like I said, you know nothing about me. So, get the fuck out of my head, bitch." With that, she flung the volatile energy at Verrine like a guided rocket where it hit its mark and exploded.

Unfortunately, the fallen angel had put up her arms at the last minute, shielding herself and blocking the bulk of the blast. Verrine shook her blackened arms and pinned Dory with an evil glare. "Do you really want to take me on, Immortal? You know that you're no match for me. I am an angel."

"You mean fallen angel, now a demon, don't you? So, I guess we'll see, right?"

In the next second, there was a rush of movement coming out of the shadows to the left of Verrine, and Tanner, in wolf form, leapt at her.

"Tanner, *stop!*" Dory shouted, but it was too late for the shifter.

Without a sideways glance, Verrine lifted a hand and caught the wolf by the throat in mid-air. There was a *yip* of pain before the demon shook Tanner and then hurled his limp body into the shadows.

And then there was silence.

"*No!*" Dory shouted. In anguish, she sent a torrent of golden fireballs at Verrine one after the other after the other and watched the fallen angel stagger backward.

Verrine regained her balance sooner than expected. She threw out a hand toward Dory and, with it, a shot of energy that Dory barely had time to block. Struggling to defend them all from the blast, she just about went to her knees before returning another volley of electric plasma with all the strength that she had in her. But the fallen angel held off most of the barrage and, in the aftermath, Dory realized that it wasn't going to be enough, not nearly enough.

"I told you that you were no match for me, Immortal," Verrine sneered as she brushed at the burnt spots on the sleeves of the sweater she wore. "You are about to find out that my wrath is a terrible thing to behold."

Before Dory could respond, the fallen angel snapped out a hand and grabbed her by the throat with an invisible force, lifting Dory several feet off the ground. With the other hand, Verrine took hold of Ian, Sorcha, and Velma as well. Panic flooded Dory's mind as she struggled to breathe, struggled to think, to fight back.

"All you had to do was give in and join me, to let it all go," Verrine told her. "You never wanted to be the Chosen One in the first place, could never accept your destiny. And now look at you."

Dory thrashed in Verrine's grip, prayed that the Dragon's Breath would come to life inside her, rescue them all as it had before. But she sensed nothing, felt nothing, and with terror rising, her hope began to fade.

"Looks like you've been right all these years, Isadora," Verrine murmured with a sly smile. "The Prophesy was obviously mistaken when it chose you, as I think you've known all along. I can sense the darkness in you as well. I'm surprised the Father has let you exist on this plane for over three centuries. You truly are unworthy of all that you've been given. And now, you'll finally get your most deep-seated wish. You will die, as will all of your team with you."

"No!" Dory ground out. "I won't let you destroy this world."

"You won't *let* me?" Verrine's laughter rang out in the cavernous space. "How will you stop me, protect this world? You can't even protect yourself."

Only you can come to terms with your destiny and own it.

You have so much waiting inside you, have been given unimaginable gifts that you have yet to discover.

I have all the faith in Heaven and on Earth that you will prevail in all that you do once you find your faith and acceptance.

Jerahmeel's words arose in Dory's mind like a beacon for that fading hope, strong and confident.

...find your faith and acceptance.

With that thought, Dory realized that she'd been moving toward both for some time. She stopped struggling and felt a strange sense of calm sweep through her, and with a smile for Verrine, she spread her arms out wide.

"W-what are you...doing?" the fallen angel asked in a

confused tone. "Do you not understand that you are about to die?"

"I'm fully accepting my destiny, Verrine. And I don't think I am about to die, but if I am, then I can accept that as part of my path," Dory murmured. "To that end, I'm reaching out in faith and forgiveness. Can't you feel it?"

"You...what are you...stop!"

Dory felt increasingly filled with light, brilliant and warm. This was different than anything she'd felt before. Not the burning heat of the Dragon's Breath but a comforting glow that was getting brighter and brighter. It was like being filled with sunlight from head to toe. And that incredible light was bursting out of her now, indeed, rushing toward the fallen angel.

"No!" Verrine shouted. "It can't be. Only He has that power."

It was so strange to feel the warmth, the light pouring out of her, to watch that same brilliant light driving into Verrine, lighting her up from the inside out.

"The Prophesy was handed down from the Supreme Being, Verrine. I was chosen before I even existed." Jerahmeel's words to her said it all. "You're right, there is darkness in me, but also light. So, yes, I *am* worthy. Worthy of His love and every gift He's given me. And I forgive you for the pain and suffering you've caused here."

The grip at Dory's throat began to slacken and she was slowly lowered to the cement floor, as were the others. However, the brilliant light did not fade away along with it but only continued to grow in intensity. She and the fallen angel seemed to be joined by it as it streamed from Dory and into Verrine.

And then the fallen angel began to keen.

"Stop. Please stop," she begged.

But Dory had no idea how to stop it even if she could. She watched in fascination as the light began to pulse under Verrine's skin getting brighter and brighter until it poured from her eyes and mouth like a living thing. Then, the fallen angel simply burst into a million glittering shards and disappeared completely.

And the brilliant light winked out.

For several moments, silence reigned. Then, a gentle hand took hold of Dory's arm.

Ian's face was full of compassion as he searched her eyes and held her close. "Are you all right, Isadora?"

"Yes, Ian. I actually...feel quite tranquil. Which is very strange after vanquishing a fallen angel." She looked around and saw that, with the exception of Tanner, the team all seemed to be still standing, and several of them were staring at her in wonder. Then Kaden was there, taking her into his arms.

"That was incredible. You lit up like a roman candle and saved our asses again, babe."

Pulling back, she shook her head. "I'm not so sure about that. We still need to help Kinna, and fast. I'm afraid she's going to do something terrible because of what Verrine may have put into her head." Turning to Sorcha, she motioned her over. "We need to do something right now. And I hope we're not too late."

"Agreed," Sorcha replied.

"Kaden, while we do this, please take care of Tanner. We can't leave him here. He needs to be taken home."

"Don't worry, darlin'. We'll take care of him. Now, go do what you need to do."

Dory and Sorcha both sat down on each side of the Time Mender and took her hands forming a linked chain.

"Are you ready for this, Chosen One?" Sorcha asked.

"I guess we'll see. This seems to be a day of firsts."

"You can do this. As we've just witnessed, like Kinna, you have so much inside of you that's unexplored. So much that you've yet to find."

"So I'm told. Do you think that between the two of us we can reach her before she makes a change that can't be undone?" Dory asked. "I've never done anything like this, Sorcha. I'm out of my depth here, so you'll have to take the lead."

Sorcha nodded. "I will. But once we find her, you're the one who will have to take that lead. It will be up to you to bring her back. Can you do that?"

Dory sighed. "No pressure, huh? Again...fate of the world stuff. Okay, how does this work?"

"It's fairly straight forward. You simply close your eyes and open yourself to her energy. Kind seeks out kind, Dory. You two are connected in a way that I'm not. You may find her before I do, if I find her at all."

With one last breath, Dory did as Sorcha instructed and felt her way along. Soon her mind began to drift and she could sense something in the distance. As it became clearer and clearer, she could see a calm, wide river flowing gently through an area of tall, thick trees.

And there on its tranquil banks two people sat side by side in the shade.

"Kinna?"

B renden McComish.

She'd found him. He wore a fishing hat with a handful of lures attached and held a pole in his hands. Kinna watch her grandfather for a moment as he cast his line into the river, made sure it was set, and then slipped the end of the rod into a holder he'd pushed into the moist earth along the shore.

When he'd finished, he turned to her with a grin. "Well, are you just going to stand there and stare at me, little girl? Or are you going to come over here and give me a hug?"

With a cry of joy, she ran to him then, unable to hold herself back. Throwing her arms around him, she squeezed him tight, reveled in the solid feel of him, drank in the spicy scent of his cologne. She'd been without him for so long and here he was just as she remembered. In that moment, she realized how she'd longed for him, the hole he'd left in her life with his passing.

"Careful now," he admonished. "You'll break my bones."

Pulling back, the tears brimmed and spilled over at the sight of his craggy face, emotion clogged her throat blocking all the words that filled her mind as they pushed to get out.

"Here now, what's this?" he asked as he ran the rough pad of his thumb over her cheek, wiping away her tears.

"Oh, Pops. I've missed you so much, been so lost without you."

"There, there. Come now, you are a strong capable young woman, and you've done just fine on your own. Besides, I'll always be here, watching over you. It's just the circle of life, darlin'."

Kinna shook her head. "But Pops, it doesn't have to be, not with what I have inside of me. You know what I'm talking about. I think you've always known."

Her grandfather slowly nodded. "That is true. I've known from the start what your parents denied. You're special. And I've always known why. You're a Time Mender, baby girl."

"Geez, Pops, if you knew that, why didn't you tell me. After all the visions, the prophetic dreams that I didn't understand, you were always there for me but never said a word about the gift I had or what it all meant. Why?"

"Why?" Sadness colored his eyes, and Brendon sighed as he pulled her down beside him onto the soft, grassy riverbank. "Pure selfishness, that's why. I told myself I was giving you time to mature so you could better understand what I was to tell you. But in fact, I selfishly wanted to have more time with you, to watch you grow into the fine young woman that you've become. Unfortunately, I was the one who ran short on that predetermined commodity in the end. That was my failing, and I'm sorry, sweetheart."

Kinna slipped her arm through his and shook her head. "But that's just it, Pops. It really doesn't matter. I've just been shown that I can fix it, that we can all be together again. You and me, momma and daddy. We can go back to the way it should have been and be a family again."

"Absolutely not." Her grandfather's word were stern, and he

turned to her so suddenly that she was taken aback by the anger that briefly flashed in his eyes. "Who filled your head with such twaddle? Who told you that you could use the gift you carry as you pleased? For your own desires? Surely not Jerahmeel."

"N-no. He showed me how the entity has protected the world in the past. He said that I was a failsafe. But don't you see? I was never given a choice in any of it."

Her grandfather sighed and his shoulders sagged a bit. The anger faded from his gaze and was replaced by compassion and understanding. "Kinna Marie, none of us have a choice, don't you know that? We are given life, and that life has an expiration date, but more importantly, a trajectory, a destiny. We each have our path. You cannot change that, even with the gift inside you."

"But why not? She said that I can, that I deserve to choose my own fate."

"Who told you that?"

"Her name is Verrine. She was also an angel at one time, and she knows, Pops. She knows how I've struggled, how much worse the visions and nightmares have gotten. Cities burning, so much destruction. I've tried so many things to make it all stop, but she made me see that I didn't have to follow someone else's plan, that I could design my own destiny. That I could have my family back. I miss you, Pops. So much that it sometimes feels like it will swallow me whole."

Brenden pursed his lips and studied her. When he finally spoke, it was with disappointment. "And what about all the other lives that would surely be impacted by your decision?"

Kinna blinked. "What other lives?"

"Well, everything is connected, Kinna. Say you use this incredible gift to change history by bringing back your parents or me. Do you realize how many lives you would change in ways you can't even fathom? Changing history has consequences, darlin'. You want to change your history, but in doing so, would change hundreds maybe thousands of lives in the process. Tell me, where would their choices be?"

"I never thought about that."

"Of course not. And what did this Verrine want from you? If she used to be an angel, what is she now? There is probably a very good reason that she is no longer an angel, so what did she want? Because if you do this, there will be a price to pay. And I can guarantee that it will be a harsh one."

"She didn't say what she wanted, just that we could help each other." Kinna scrubbed her hands over her face. "I'm so confused, Pops. I wish I had you with me to guide me. I have no family now, and I'm all alone."

Brenden put an arm around her and pulled her close. "Hogwash. You are not alone. There are people in your life that care deeply about you, Kinna. They may not be family by blood, but they are family all the same. Humanity is your family. You have an incredible destiny. You now must go back and live your life. Reach out and grab it with both hands."

"Kinna?" a voice called from behind them.

Kinna turned slightly and watched Dory walk toward them. "Hello, Dory. Come. Sit with us a while."

Crossing to the riverbank, Dory sat down next to Kinna. "Are you all right? We were so worried about you."

Kinna smiled. "It's been a very weird day in a string of very weird days. At least, I think it's only been a day. Time is a strange thing, you know?"

"I do." Dory looked at the older man sitting on the other side of Kinna. "Who is this with you?"

"Oh, gosh, sorry. This is my Pops."

"Brenden McComish, little lady," he told Dory. "And you must be the Chosen One."

Dory looked surprised but then nodded. "I-I am, yes."

"Kinna and I were just discussing her future," he said. "I told her that she must go back and live her life. She's always been special, you see. I knew it from the start. I was supposed to prepare her for her role as Time Mender but I ran out of time myself, so it was left to you, for which I am extremely grateful."

Kinna leaned her head on Brenden's shoulder. "You were always there for me, Pops. You understood me. We just both ran out of time, that's all."

He patted her hand and kissed the top of her head. "You have something inside you of huge importance, baby girl. And you must take great care to protect it with your life and to use it only when called upon. Which is why you absolutely cannot change a whit of time as that evil thing tried to get you to do. You hear me now?"

With a sigh, Kinna nodded then looked at Dory. "I suppose it's time for us to go back, isn't it?"

"It is," Dory murmured.

"Is she still there?"

"No. Verrine is gone for good."

Kinna took Dory's hand and asked the question hovering in her mind. "She said that you struggled with your destiny, too. That you didn't want to be the Chosen One, and like me, weren't given a choice, either. Is that true?"

Dory blew out a breath. "It is. I was chosen by a Prophesy long before I was even born, so no, I had no choice. And I did struggle. I do to this day, but it is my purpose. I'm only now just coming to grips with that, realizing what it all means in the vast scheme. A scheme that is greater than you or I." She squeezed Kinna's hand. "We can't change who or what we are, Kinna. Jerahmeel said something to me recently that has finally resonated."

"What was that?"

"Only you can come to terms with your destiny and own it. That holds true for you as well. You and I both can continue to struggle or we can grab hold of our destiny and move forward. I know what I've chosen. What about you?"

"Ha!" Brenden cackled. "That Archangel is quite the pip, isn't he. Well, baby girl? What's it gonna be?"

"I don't want to go, to leave you." Kinna leaned over and brushed a kiss on her grandfather's cheek. "But I suppose I just have to move forward, right?"

"Good girl."

"I will miss you terribly, Pops. And for a really long time."

Brenden stood then, pulling Kinna to her feet and then into his embrace. "I will always be with you, my sweet, sweet girl. And you're very lucky to have what you have inside you because I'll be waiting right here in your dreams any time you need me." With a final kiss, he set her away from him. "Now, go with Dory and own your destiny."

Dory held out her hand as Kinna turned from him, and together they walked away from the man and his river.

THIS PARTICULAR MONDAY looked much the same as it had for the last few weeks as Dory stepped out onto the deck and into the crisp, late fall morning with Henry close behind her. Perhaps the frost on the ground was a bit heavier, the temperature a few degrees cooler, but the sun was hovering on the horizon signaling a beautiful day awakening. Thursday would be Halloween, and then they would start the final descent into winter.

She stood for a moment watching Henry race around the backyard, just breathing in the brisk coastal air, her warm jacket pulled close and steam rising from the humongous cup of coffee she held. It was hard to believe that it had only been a little over two weeks since Morianna had appeared to tell them of the impending doom. It seemed now like closer to a month. Or longer. They'd won the war—for now—but as always, had lost too much in the battle. And for her, losing Tanner without even being able to say goodbye was almost too much to bear. Although, she wasn't certain of what his fate had actually been, as when Kaden and the team had went to collect his body, it was gone. Had Morianna intervened as she'd done with Ian years ago? Had the Archangel taken him? She supposed they may never know.

Shaking her head, she crossed to the set of weathered deck chairs and sat down to watch the sun's brilliant rise. Kaden had gone into town to meet with his crew and catch up on all things building/remodeling, so she had a few hours to herself to decompress and find a place for the emotions still running through her at warp speed and nipping at the back of her mind.

They'd had a time of it with Tanner during their association. He'd been a loner, confident, unapologetic. But he'd also been a great warrior in Dory's mind, fearless. Tanner had enhanced the team even as he'd annoyed and confounded. With his knowledge and network, he'd given the team an edge. The thought that she and Kaden had worried about his loyalty, struggled with trusting him, ate at her. Oh, he'd frustrated the hell out of her, for sure, but on top of it all, Dory had liked the shifter and would miss the wolf, his snarky comments, and his warrior spirit on any future endeavors. As with all of those who'd gone before, she would mourn him, and his absence would leave a hole. It was one of the reasons that she'd avoided close ties early on in her immortality. It had been too painful to watch those she'd cared about die.

She knew in her head that it was bollocks, but in her heart, she felt partially responsible for his death. What had Kaden said early on, that she was always the point of the spear? Every mission rested heavily on her shoulders. So, she couldn't help thinking that if she'd been more aware, moved just a bit faster, things might have been different. It broke her heart a little that in the end she couldn't save Tanner.

"Ah, now you know you can't save everyone, right?" a deep voice to her left said quietly. "At least, not for this world."

Dory turned to find Jerahmeel sitting in the deck chair next to her looking comfortable as you please.

"To coin a phrase," he continued. "The Almighty has a plan and path for all creatures great and small, Isadora. And that path is not always the one expected or embraced, but it is always perfect and what is required."

She gave a slight nod. "I'm aware. At least in my head."

"Mmm, yes, but the human heart is a different matter, is it not?"

"It is, indeed."

"So, what is it that you think you could have done differently?"

"I don't know. Moved faster, planned better." Dory watched the morning sun paint the trees in golden light and sighed. "Nothing really, I guess. I just have a hard time letting go of it."

"I see. So, feeling responsible? Or guilty that you didn't do more, be more?"

"Something like that." She glanced back at him. "I suppose... maybe a little of both."

"Such arrogance." Jerahmeel shook his head and stretched out his long legs, contemplated the sunrise as she had done. "I have found that human beings—especially immortal human beings—expect to be able to fix any situation, even those not of their own making. Unfortunately, this is an incredible misconception. Only the Creator has that power."

Dory frowned. "Yet you sent me and my team to fix this particular situation when He could have done it with a thought.

Why? I know it was more than just to assist Kinna, to help her to understand her destiny. You said as much before. So, why?"

A smile spread across the Archangel's face. "Why do you think? What have you learned through these last perilous days?" he asked. "Any revelations you'd like to share?"

She ran her hand over her face in frustration, then took a sip of her coffee before setting it down on the small table between them. "I don't know," she said with a bit of stubborn exasperation.

"Come, come, Isadora. That's an easy answer and beneath you. I would wager that you've had several revelations over these last couple of weeks. And yes, you are correct. He could have resolved the situation with a thought, but deep down you know exactly why you and your team were tasked with this mission." He turned then, and there was a challenge in his beautiful eyes. "Do you not?"

"All right, yes. I was questioning my purpose." Dory closed her eyes and nodded. When she opened them again, she could literally feel him watching her. "I've fought against my destiny for centuries because, yes, I've always felt unworthy as Chosen One, wanted to be anything but the end all be all. There were more times than I care to acknowledge that I just wanted it all to be over." She glanced at him then and mortification flooded her. "I'd fallen for Kaden after so many stark years and then selfishly made him an Immortal—even though I knew how he felt about it—because I just couldn't let him go. I love him beyond reason and have watched him embrace his immortality as I've never done. It shames me that I've been given this gift and have always thought of it as a curse, yet I've been jealous of how Kaden has adapted in such a short period of time."

Jerahmeel's voice was soft when he spoke. "Kaden has blind trust. It's always been about trust and faith, Isadora. Faith in the plan, even when you don't know the details of it. And yet trusting just the same."

Tears drenched her eyes, spilled over. She swiped at them and shook her head. "I've felt sorry for myself for hundreds of years because I had no one to show me the way. I let self-pity swamp me instead of forging my own path, actively accepting my destiny and doing whatever it took to grow and embrace my way forward. I've always worried that I was not as strong as I should be. Thought, how can I be trusted with such power when I don't know what I'm doing half the time?"

He reached out a hand, and the moment she placed her hand in his, the doubt, the fear all fell away.

"As I told you before, you are exactly who and what He needs you to be. You have more strength than you know, child, and have only just scratched the surface of what sleeps inside you. And I'm not talking about the Dragon's Breath now. You saw as much in that warehouse with the Radiant Light you experienced when you faced Verrine. And there is so much more awaiting discovery right there within you. You have no idea of your potential, of what you can become." His next words were infused with a touch of humor. "And how dare you question your God-given abilities."

A short laugh burst out of her, and she took a deep breath. "I get that now. Yes, these last couple of weeks have been a revelation in themselves. I see now that this wasn't entirely about Kinna and the impending doom, was it?"

He gave her hand a quick squeeze and then sat back in his chair. "As I said before, only you can come to terms with your destiny and own it, but perhaps you just needed a slight nudge."

She gave him a sideways look with raised eyebrows. "Or a firm shove?" Leaning forward, she rested her elbows on her knees and watched a pair of fat robins chase each other through the fir trees as Henry watched with avid concentration. "So, what happens now?"

"What do you mean?"

"Do we just go on as we have been? The Chosen One, her Warrior, and the rest of the team as needed?"

"Is that what you want?" He crossed a booted foot over his knee. "Are you content here, Isadora?"

"I've lived in many places over my time as an Immortal and am as content here as I've ever been. Kaden and I have a good life together, even with all the world-ending craziness from time to time. Oh, eventually we will have to relocate because of the no-aging thing, but that goes with being an Immortal. Why do you ask?"

"Oh, I was just wondering. What if, say, I had a proposition for you? Perhaps an offer of Ascension? Considering how you've struggled here on this plane for so long, how would you feel about that?"

Dory opened and closed her mouth several times as thoughts collided in her head, but she couldn't seem to find her words, felt the blood drain from her face. *Ascension*? Had she heard him correctly? She didn't know how to react, what to even say to that.

"Isadora? Are you unwell? You've lost a bit of color, child."

She shook her head slowly. "Are you actually offering me... Ascension?"

The Archangel tilted his head and gave her a considering look. "And what if I were? After all your struggles, all that you've learned, would you even be interested?"

She shoved up and out of her chair, paced to the end of the deck and stared out at the blue-blue morning sky, the dark evergreens spearing up into that sky. *Ascension*. She had little idea—other than another plane of existence—what Ascending even entailed. After being Chosen One, would there be another use for her in a different reality? Would another be selected to take her place here?

Then, the most important thought struck her. She turned and marched back to where Jerahmeel waited for her response, seemingly with the patience of Job. "Would I go alone, or would Kaden go with me?"

The Archangel sighed and gave her a sorrowful look. "Ascension would be for you alone," he said simply.

It was like a punch to the gut. It was true, she'd never wanted to be the Chosen One. She'd resisted, fought against it for most of her three centuries on this planet. And just when she'd finally come to terms with it, had accepted her destiny and was ready to fully embrace it, Jerahmeel was offering her something she'd prayed for all these years.

But she would have to leave Kaden behind to accept the offer.

Slowly, she began to shake her head. "I could never go without Kaden. He's my compass. My sun, my moon, my beating heart. Though I don't really know what Ascension would involve, I do know that I would be an empty vessel without him by my side. So, no. I'm sorry."

"Why are you sorry?" The humor was back in his gaze, his tone.

She frowned. "I-I don't know. I guess it's because..."

"Because you've finally accepted and embraced your calling?" he finished as a question. "Perhaps you've realized that this is what you were meant for, created for. And then maybe you're just a bit curious as well."

"Curious?" she whispered. "About what?"

The Archangel's smile was brilliant, and his amethyst eyes sparkled with his mirth. "Why, after what you've recently seen, about all that *more* inside of you, of course."

Dory plopped down into her chair and studied him with

narrowed eyes. "You knew that I would turn down Ascension, didn't you? Just like Morianna knew that I would save Kaden by absorbing the Dragon's Breath in Savannah. Was this written in the Prophesy as well?"

When his smile grew into a grin but he didn't reply, she shook her head. "Mind games. You two are stellar at them."

Jerahmeel laughed out loud at that, the sound of which turned her insides to goo and had her laughing along with him. "I prefer to think of it as teasing out potential."

Then another thought hit her, and she pointed her finger at him. "You know, you never told us how The Key was activated. Who activated it, and was it really needed? I mean, if it hadn't been triggered, Verrine, Victoria Newcomb, Dorian Smyth, none of them may ever have suspected Kinna of holding the entity inside her, right?"

The Archangel's humor slowly faded, and he seemed hesitant. "The Key...was activated in anticipation of need...for a coming crisis that has yet to unfold."

Dory sat up at that. "Has yet to unfold? What do you mean? Are you saying the world-ending event it was activated for is not what Verrine and Dorian Smyth were planning? That there's something worse coming?"

"Unfortunately, yes. What that event will look like or exactly when it will arrive, I cannot tell you at this time. However, it is imminent."

"Well, that's not what I'd hoped to hear." Dory ran a hand over her face. "You're telling me that something terrible is coming but it has nothing to do with the threat that we just averted?"

"Verrine had stumbled onto the notion of The Key quite by accident and already had her underlings searching for it before its activation." He sighed. "She knew *of* it but not exactly what she was looking for, hence Dorian Smyth's involvement. Yet, he was not the only pawn in her scheme."

"So, she was always the driving force behind Smyth's plans?"

Jerahmeel nodded. "Verrine was the Demon of Impatience, an influence peddler. She could make the most stalwart of men bend to her will and have them thinking that it was their own idea."

"Yeah, I got quite the nasty taste of that in the warehouse. It was pretty frightening how powerful it felt. So, that was how she was controlling Smyth?"

"Yes. She was hoping to have the entity change history so that she could take control of this fallen world, and she used him to that end. Of course, when she was certain that Kinna was The Key, he became obsolete."

"Was she the only fallen angel or demon who knew of The Key?" Dory asked, very much afraid of the answer. She really dreaded going through something worse in the near future than they had in the last few weeks. "I mean, if there were others who knew about The Key, couldn't they come for Kinna? Wouldn't she be vulnerable?"

Jerahmeel shook his head. "Verrine was a special case, and she didn't play well with others. When you destroyed her, that possibility was removed, and there are no others, angel or demon, with that information. So, you can rest easy for now. You and your team are the only ones who know that Kinna McComish is The Key."

"Well, that's something, I guess."

"Regrettably, the threat is still out there and the entity continues to be active in anticipation of it. The good news is that Kinna is now aware of her purpose, thanks in part, to you. She will live her life with a guardian close by to monitor her premonitions and dreams, to help her through them until the entity is needed for that coming threat. The guardian will keep her safe and on the path until needed."

"The guardian? You?"

He inclined his head. "I have been guardian to the entity for millennia and will continue to do so going forward."

With a nod, one last question circled her mind, yet she hesitated to ask it. Knew that it was not her place. But still...

"What is it, child? I see the query hovering in your eyes."

Dory took a deep breath and let it out slowly before turning to him. "It's about Tanner," she all but whispered. "It's just that Kaden said his body was missing when they went to get him. I-I need to know what..."

The Archangel shook his head and his eyes were full of compassion. "Isadora, you are feeling guilty about something that was out of your control from the start. Do not worry yourself over his fate. Everyone has their own path. You cannot change that fact."

He stood then, and Dory realized that was the only answer she was going to get from him regarding the shifter, yet it was really no answer at all. She sighed and watched as Henry noticed their unique visitor and came running. The Archangel bent down and gave the Rottweiler's head a rub.

"I would never leave without saying goodbye to you, my furry friend," Jerahmeel told him. The dog whined and gave a soft *woof*. "I will visit from time to time and always keep watch, but in the interim, I count on you to keep a close eye on them for me. Can you do that?"

Henry gave another *woof*, and with tongue lolling, sat down next to Dory's chair.

"Excellent," Jerahmeel replied. "Now, Chosen One, give the Warrior my best and take care of each other until we meet again."

Dory stood and didn't quite know what to do or say. "I will," she answered lamely.

He took her by the shoulders then and there was love in his gaze. "Close your eyes, Isadora Winthrop," he murmured softly.

When she did, she felt his lips at her forehead, and all of her worries melted away. But when she opened her eyes moments later, she was standing alone on the deck, a flush on her cheeks and the sun warming her face.

With a shake of her head, Dory turned to Henry. "Come on, buddy. Let's go see what we can scrounge up for your breakfast. Then we've got some planning to do when the Warrior gets home."

With another look out at the beauty of the morning, she turned toward the house and stopped short. There, standing just inside the open slider, arms crossed and leaning against the doorjamb, was Kaden.

As their eyes met and held, a half-smile tugged at his mouth. "Have a final angelic visit, did we?"

"We did," she replied and felt her own smile begin.

"Everything okay?"

She tipped her head and gave him a considering look just as the Archangel had with her before her smile spread into a grin. "I do believe everything is just right. For now."

Pushing away from the jamb, he held out a hand to her. "Excellent news."

She took his hand, but her smile dimmed just a bit. "But there is something coming, Kaden. Something more that we need to discuss."

Kaden narrowed his eyes then gave a nod. "Well, come on, then. I'll make us some breakfast and you can fill me in."

With a contented sigh, the Chosen One followed her Warrior into the house to work on the destiny that it had taken her so long to own.

And to prepare for what was coming...

ABOUT THE AUTHOR

A native of Oregon, Joni Sauer-Folger spent twenty-two years with an airline traveling and moving around the country before settling down near the beautiful Pacific Ocean with her three very spoiled cats. She writes Urban Fantasy and Paranormal Romance under the name J.G. Sauer, and Cozy Mysteries and Romantic Suspense under Joni Folger. When she's not spending quality time with the characters she creates, she enjoys gardening, crafting, and working in local theater.

For more information, visit:
www.jonisauerfolger.com

 X

ALSO BY J.G. SAUER

Written as Joni Folger

River Bend Vineyard Cozy Mystery series

Grapes of Death

Of Merlot and Murder

Performance of a Deadly Vintage

Enchanted Affairs Cozy Mystery series

Monkshood, Tea, & Murder

Written as J. G. Sauer

Immortal Series

Immortal Reckoning – Novella Prequel

Immortal Obsession

Immortal Savior

Immortal Ascending

Guardian Series:

Tarnished Guardian – Novella Prequel

Search for the Mystic Stone

Looking Glass Series:

New Years Through the Looking Glass

Madness Through the Looking Glass